At twenty-six years old, Polly has worked in investment banking and consultancy since graduating from Cambridge in 2002. Like many fellow engineers, Polly turned her back on the crankshafts and oil rags in search of the glitz of the city life – something she has yet to find. For more about Polly, go to her website, www.pollycourtney.com.

Polly Courtney

Golden Handcuffs

Matador
9 De Montfort Mews
Leicester LE1 7FW, UK
Tel: (+44) 116 255 9311 / 9312
Email: books@troubador.co.uk
Web: www.troubador.co.uk/matador

ISBN 10: 1-905886-34-9
ISBN 13: 978-1-905886-34-0

Typeset in 10pt Bembo by Troubador Publishing Ltd, Leicester, UK
Printed in the UK by The Cromwell Press Ltd, Trowbridge, Wilts, UK

Matador is an imprint of Troubador Publishing Ltd

*To everyone who housed me, fed me, employed me
and provided me with places to write in my post-banking days.
And of course, to everyone who never knew
they were providing inspiration…*

Golden Handcuffs

Polly started to write *Golden Handcuffs* in a taxi on the way home from work at 4a.m. It was dark, she was tired, and when she later retrieved the notes from amongst some screwed up spreadsheet print-offs, she wasn't even sure who'd written them. That, in a way, was the point of what later became her first novel.

1

THE SOUND of high heeled shoes echoed around the vast, white atrium. A young blonde was striding purposefully towards the reception desk.

"Hi," the girl said brightly. "My name's Abigail Turner. I'm here to interview."

That much is obvious, thought the receptionist, noting the innocent, brown eyes and the forced smile. Despite the aura of self-confidence she was trying to exude, there was something that gave her away. She was clearly petrified.

"Which department?"

"Corporate Finance."

"For the position of... secretary, yes?"

"No – *analyst,*" the girl replied, her expression suddenly hardening.

Ooh. So she was one of them. The receptionist nodded calmly. She'd come across girls like this before – hoity-toity twenty-somethings who thought they could hack it in the world of investment banking. She glanced disdainfully at the scowling blonde, who looked *exactly* like a secretary: skinny, attractive and well-dressed in a cheap sort of way, with exceptionally long legs. No, she thought. This girl wouldn't last five minutes as an analyst – not at Cray McKinley.

★ ★ ★

Abby snatched the temporary pass from the woman and turned abruptly on her heel. *Secretary, for God's sake.* She'd show them. She

1

wasn't spending four years at Cambridge learning thermodynamics and quantum mechanics to do dictations and answer the phone.

She pretended to fiddle with the pin on her pass as she studied the turnstiles up ahead. A young man barged through, slamming his pass down on the side as he rammed into the barrier. Abby took a deep breath and did the same, then instantly became disorientated. A pure, brilliant whiteness surrounded her, and she lost all sense of direction. It was impossible to tell where the walls ended and the ceiling began. She looked around, searching for some sort of reference point.

A set of lifts appeared from nowhere, along with a group of suited young men. As Abby approached, something struck her about the men: *they all looked exactly the same.* They were all in their mid-twenties with spiky hair and shiny, tanned skin, wearing immaculately ironed shirts. And they were all incredibly good-looking.

Abby stationed herself on the edge of the group, maintaining an air of indifference. Inside, she was panicking. She felt sure her nylon suit stood out as cheap, and her friend's pointy shoes were making her too tall.

The ride up to the twentieth floor was excruciating. The bankers didn't speak. They just stood, shoulder to shoulder, like a huddle of penguins with newspapers tucked under their wings. Occasionally one would clear his throat or surreptitiously check his hair in the mirrored wall, but as soon as Abby managed to catch his eye, he'd get back to staring at his feet. Had she not felt so nervous, Abby would have taken offence. None of the men had given her a second glance since she'd stepped into the lift. She exhaled shakily and wiped her sweaty palms on the sides of her trousers. There was a churning sensation in the pit of her stomach.

As the doors slid shut on the nineteenth floor, Abby looked across at the one remaining passenger – a tall, suave guy with dark hair. He was good-looking in an unconventional way: dusky skin and a shallow dent in the middle of his nose.

He looked up, suddenly. Abby held his gaze for a fraction of a second, then turned away, blushing. His eyes were incredible. Bottle-green, like the colour of the sea on an airbrushed postcard. The temporary swipe-card clipped to his jacket told Abby that his name was Mike. He was another applicant.

2

"Can I take your names, please?" said a high-pitched female voice.

Abby stepped out of the lift and stepped into what looked like an airport lounge —vast and airy, and dotted with brown leather armchairs, matching coffee tables and pots of identical ferns. But the most distracting feature was the wall straight ahead. It was made of tinted glass, and extended from floor to ceiling all the way across, revealing a vast, sepia image of the City of London. The Millennium Dome, Canary Wharf, Tower Bridge, St Paul's Cathedral, the OXO tower, the London Eye—

"Your *name*?"

The voice was coming from behind a clipboard, and sounded rather agitated this time.

"Abigail Turner," she replied hastily. The voice, it turned out, belonged to a tall, striking brunette – probably no older than Abby – with unfeasibly large breasts and a suspiciously healthy tan for the time of year.

"Great," the young woman said brusquely, drawing a tick on her clipboard in a very self-important manner and fixing a smile on her rubbery lips. "I'm Claudia. Just take a seat and make yourself at home." She motioned to the clusters of nervous-looking candidates who were perching on the uncomfortably low armchairs. "My colleague, Stephanie, will be along shortly. She'll call you for your interviews and numerical assessments."

Abby nodded politely. There was a frenzy of pouting, hair-flicking and eyelash-batting as Claudia moved on to the good-looking guy behind her. Abby headed for the pots of coffee.

"Uh-huh! Another female!" said a timid-looking girl who was concentrating very hard on pouring the milk into her cup. "Not many of us here today, are there?"

Abby's feeling of insecurity began to seep away. This gawky creature with her fuzzy hair and ill-fitting lilac suit was Abby's competition for the day.

"No," Abby smiled at the nervous wreck. "But I guess that's banking for you."

The girl tittered awkwardly.

"I'm Abby, by the way."

"Um, oh – Jackie Crump." The girl giggled again, not quite brave enough to reach out and shake Abby's hand.

Abby was feeling more and more confident by the second. There were only three girls in the room, as far as she could see, and it was likely that the firm would accept at least one. If the other girl was anything like this Jackie Crump, Abby was laughing all the way to her desk.

"You came all the way from *York,* did you?" a small, weasly fellow in a brown tweed suit was asking, staring in horror at the applicant in the armchair opposite. "Good God – that's practically *Scotland!* I'm glad I didn't have that far to come – I only came from *Oxford.*"

Abby pulled up a small leather foot-rest and sat down. They were obviously trying to out-university each other.

"I'm Abby," she announced, thrusting her hand at the tweed-clad rodent.

"Pleasure," he said patronisingly. "I'm Humphrey. Humphrey Dartington, like the crystal – ahahahahaha!"

Abby gave an obliging grunt and moved her hand round to the York undergraduate, who nervously introduced himself as Mark.

"Nice to meet you," he muttered, looking everywhere but into her eyes. He had the limpest grasp Abby had ever experienced; it was like shaking hands with a fish.

The dumpy young man to her right didn't notice her hand as it was waved in front of his nose, and after a few seconds, she gave up and put it away. He seemed to be engrossed in the book on his lap, which he was propping open with his elbows, his fingers stuffed in his ears.

The Revolution in Corporate Finance, Abby read in the top left corner of the page. Jesus Christ. The guy was revising for his interview.

Humphrey Dartington turned to Abby. "Did *you* have far to come today?"

"Oh – not really!" she replied breezily.

He looked annoyed. "I was just saying, luckily I only had to travel from *Oxford.* What about you?"

Abby shrugged. "Same distance, I guess – about an hour by train." She wasn't going to rise to the bait.

The young man nodded sullenly. "So... what do we all think of the proposed changes to the Listing Rules, eh?"

Abby raised her eyebrows questioningly. "I'm sorry?"

"You know – the FSA? The Listing Rules? The proposal to take account of treasury shares?"

Mark from York looked anxiously from Humphrey to Abby, then back again.

"Oh, I shouldn't think it'll happen," Abby said boldly. She had no idea what Humphrey was on about, but she had a feeling that neither did he.

"Wha-" Mark had turned quite pale.

"Do we know what time these interviews are due to start?" asked Abby, glancing around the table.

The guy on her right started flapping his elbows from side to side in an attempt to turn a page of The Revolution in Corporate Finance without unplugging his ears.

"They'll start at ten, I should imagine," Humphrey declared. "Always the way with these American banks – herd all the applicants into one room, then let them sit and stew for an hour before grilling them over a case study."

Mark looked horrified. "Case stud-"

"How d'you know?" asked Abby. She wasn't fazed. She'd met his type before. "Have you interviewed with other banks?"

"Oh no!" Humphrey laughed as if the very notion was absurd. "Contacts." He winked and tapped the side of his nose. "Contacts."

She smiled falsely. "Right."

"This is my first interview," ventured a sweet looking guy with lots of freckles whose badge proclaimed him to be Alan. "I haven't heard back from the others yet."

Mark from York smiled with relief. "Me neith-"

"Ah, you will," Humphrey assured them. "Give it a couple of weeks – they usually get back to the dead-certs first, then wait to see who accepts before trawling through all the borderline CVs. That's how they do it these days," he explained.

"Oh, is that so?" Abby asked loudly. The busty HR girl lowered her clipboard and glowered at her from across the room.

"Certainly is," Humphrey muttered, reaching down to the

coffee table and idly flicking through the Financial Times.

Abby exchanged a sly grin with the freckly Alan. Her tolerance level for pompous, tweed-wearing know-alls was fairly high after four years at Cambridge, but this Humphrey Dartington twat was really starting to bug her.

"ABBY TURNER?" called a female voice. Abby looked up to see another brunette – this one taller and slimmer than the first, with more realistically-sized breasts – standing by the lifts. "COULD YOU FOLLOW ME TO YOUR FIRST INTERVIEW?"

2

ROOM 20.02 WAS like a miniature version of the waiting room: thick pile carpets, silky cream wallpaper, unrealistically green pot plants and leather armchairs in chocolate brown. By the window was a large, polished mahogany table, behind which were two silhouettes.

Mike pressed the door shut behind him and marched purposefully towards the empty chair. He impulsively ran a hand through his short, dark hair and realised – with satisfaction – that one of his interviewers was a woman.

She was clearly of the no-nonsense variety, wearing immaculate makeup and a neat little suit. Her chestnut hair was cut in a severe-looking bob. As Mike approached, she slipped off her chair – which made virtually no difference to her height, he noticed – and thrust out a hand weighed down with a rock-like jewel.

"You must be Michael," she said authoritatively. "I'm Jennifer Armstrong. And this is Paul Fletcher."

Paul Fletcher was tall and muscular, possibly more stacked than Mike, with a strong jaw line and cropped blonde hair. He smiled warmly as they exchanged a bone-crushing handshake.

"Right," said Jennifer, hopping back onto her seat and tapping her pen impatiently on the table. "It says here you're applying to work in the Paris branch of Cray McKinley; is this correct?"

Mike smiled. He'd successfully predicted the first question. "Yes that's right – I've been studying French at Edinburgh for four years, and I'm keen to put my skills into practice. I figured Cray McKinley Paris would be a good place to do that."

Paul nodded encouragingly, then stopped, and pointed his finger at Mike. "Y'know things happen a little differently in the Paris office," he said, with a thick New York accent. "It's kinda small-scale over there; less glitzy – more low-key. Y'know that, dontcha?"

Mike hadn't known that. His mind drifted back to that impressive white atrium twenty floors below, and the slick young bankers he'd seen strutting through the doors. He wondered if he was making a terrible mistake. *Less glitzy. More low-key.* What was that supposed to mean? Was the office tucked away in a dingy basement of some graffiti-scrawled tower block in the outskirts of Paris? Would there be no glamorous receptionist? No in-house Starbucks? Mike pulled himself together. Now was not the time to be having doubts.

"Yeah – I heard that. But I figured that as a first-year analyst, I'd get a greater share of the responsibility if the deals and teams were smaller." Mike had always been good at bullshitting.

"Right," Paul nodded. "Yeah – I guess you're probably right."

The woman scowled at her colleague, then looked at Mike.

"Why did you apply to Cray McKinley?"

Mike paused for a suitable length of time. These questions were a piece of cake. "Well, I'm an ambitious person, and I always aim for the best–"

"Have you applied to other investment banks?" she interrupted.

"Well–"

"Be honest – don't lie."

"No," Mike lied.

"Slightly *over*-confident, wouldn't you say, applying to just one bank?"

"Well I did apply to a *couple* of others–"

"I see." She looked unimpressed. "Now tell me, Michael, is it the salary that appeals to you in this job?"

"Oh no – it's–"

"So you're not driven by money?"

"No."

"You want to be a banker," she said slowly, "but you're not driven by money. OK…"

"Oh, well I like *working* with financial–"

"Good. Now it says here you're the captain of the university

8

rugby team. Tell me, how do you see your team mates? Do you see them as equals? Or as subordinates?"

"Well, obviously I'm in *charge* of them—"

"So you're a leader, are you?"

"Yes, definitely."

"You like giving orders?"

"Well, yes."

"So you're not very good at *taking* orders, presumably?"

"Oh, I don't mind taking orders—"

"Hmm. Are you a sociable person, Michael?"

"Yes — very."

"You go out a lot?"

"Yes."

"Do you ever let your friends down?"

"Oh no — I never let people down. I do my utmost to—"

"So if you were put on an important transaction that meant working through the weekend, you'd still meet up with your friends on the Saturday night?"

"Oh, well if *that* was the case, I'd cancel my—"

"You'd let your friends down?"

"No. Yes—"

"You are aware of the long hours required of our analysts here, aren't you?"

"Oh yes." He nodded sagely. Everybody knew about the long hours.

"Good. And your rugby — do you intend to keep playing in London?"

"Well, I hope to play a little, obviously not as much as—"

"Do you have a girlfriend?"

"Er, n–no—"

"Good." Jennifer Armstrong clasped her little hands together, and looked meaningfully at her colleague. Mike took the opportunity to rearrange his features: shoulders back, head casually to one side, face calm and expressionless. He felt tense after the barrage of questions — some of them really quite obscure, he thought — and was becoming increasingly aware of his body language letting him down.

"So Michael…" Paul began, as if he didn't really know what to ask. "Tell me about a deal, y'know, a deal that caught your eye in the press recently."

Great. They were back on track. Mike put a hand up to his chin, and pretended he was thinking about the question for the first time in his life. "Hmm. Ooh – I was reading the other day about the Sentron IPO…" And he was off. Mike had done his homework. He knew just about every detail of the Sentron IPO that was in the public domain.

"Well," said Paul, leaning back in his chair at the end of Mike's enthusiastic overview. "Y'know what? I *worked* on that IPO, and I didn't know half that stuff!" He shook his head, chuckling to himself, until he caught the look in his colleague's eye. "Er, anyway. Right. So, have you ever worked in finance before?"

Mike recalled his pre-made response. This part was going to be tricky. "Oh yes." He nodded with conviction. "In fact, not only *worked*, but *traded*, as it happens. I've been dabbling in the markets for some time–"not strictly true, but he'd once inherited some shares – "and I like to keep an eye on what's-"

"You do understand the difference between Investment Banking and Equity Trading, don't you Michael?" Jennifer Armstrong cut in.

"Yes, absol–"

"You won't be 'dabbling in the markets' if you join Corporate Finance, you know."

"Oh I didn't mean–"

"In fact, perhaps you could define the role of Corporate Finance within the bank?"

"Well…" Mike scoured his memory for the definition he'd seen on the company website. "Corporate Finance is the area of finance involving decision-making by the management of corporations, for example take-over bids, public offerings and certain types of restructuring."

That was one of the benefits of being an arts student: the ability to rote-learn chunks of text. The woman raised her pencilled-on eyebrows and nodded reluctantly at Mike.

"So…" muttered Paul. He seemed to be finding the interview as stressful as Mike was. "Say… What's your greatest achievement in life?"

Straight from the Interviewer's Handbook, thought Mike. He had a number of pre-prepared answers up his sleeve. There was the time he'd saved his sister's life in the pool when he was eight... but that was a long time ago, and sounded rather pathetic now, coming from a twenty-two year old. There was the modelling he'd done for Marks and Spencer... but it wasn't really an *achievement*. And then there was the village fete he'd helped to organise last year... He looked at Paul.

"Running the New York Marathon."

Paul's eyes lit up. "Which year?" he cried excitably. "I ran it in 2003!"

"Oh really?! I did it the year after!" This was good; they were bonding.

Jennifer Armstrong looked cross. "How's your maths, Michael?"

"Well," Mike shrugged. "Obviously, I've been studying languages for the last-"

"What's thirteen percent of two hundred and fifty?"

Mike thought carefully. This was easy, he told himself. He'd always been good at maths.

"Thirty-two and a half."

She nodded curtly, and scribbled something on her notepad. Mike thought he saw Paul smile faintly. Yes – they were definitely bonding.

"OK," Jennifer Armstrong snapped, ripping off the sheet from her pad like a doctor issuing a prescription. "That'll be all. Paul, do you have any more questions?"

He let out a long 'phhhhhhh' noise and slowly shook his head.

"Good. Michael, do you have any for us?"

Mike had a selection of 'sensible questions' up his sleeve for moments exactly like this. "Well, I-"

Ms Armstrong suddenly jerked her head backwards, tapping her watch irritably.

"-think that just about covers everything," he concluded.

The tiny figure jumped down from her chair and held out her hand. Paul did the same, with considerably more ease.

"What position d'you play on the field, then?" he asked.

Mike looked up and smiled. "Number eight. You play?"

"I have done – more of a football man myself. *American* football to you I guess,"

"Oh! I once–"

"Excellent. Well, thank you for coming, Michael," the woman cut in. "I believe you're to make your way back to the reception area now."

Striding down the corridor, Mike let out an exhausted sigh. It was mid-afternoon, and he'd been under observation since nine o'clock that morning. He'd been put through two interviews, a numerical assessment, a psychometric test and a tiresome teambuilding exercise involving a shoebox, some string and a hard-boiled egg. He wondered what he'd have to do next. A corporate pantomime? A spelling test? A wheelbarrow race around the twentieth floor?

The tension in the lounge appeared to have slackened off a little since lunch. Mike meandered over to the tea-trolley, where two candidates were chatting, and a third one, a girl, was loitering awkwardly beside them, trying to join in.

"No, no! The answer is *definitely* six hundred and twenty million," declared the shorter young man – an Etonian, Mike presumed, judging by the brown tweed jacket and the accent.

"I'm not saying you're *wrong*," argued the taller one, a Geordie. "I'm just saying I dorn't think there *is* a right answer. The point is, they dorn't care *what* figure y'say; they just want to hear how y'get to it, dorn't they? To make sure you're good at reasoning, like."

"Oh dear – I think I messed that one up *completely!*" muttered the girl, pulling her mouth into a straight line.

The Etonian pressed his face up to Mike's. "Did *you* get asked the ice cream question?"

"Er, what?"

"How many ice creams d'you think are sold in the UK each year?"

Mike frowned.

"I mean, I *know* the answer's six hundred and twenty million – I've had that question before! I looked it up on the Internet!"

"Dear me," whispered the girl, "I was a long way off!"

The Geordie lad pulled an exasperated face.

12

"OK!" screeched a loud female voice.

Mike looked round to see the HR girl standing by the window, clapping her hands above her head, making her enormous tits bounce up and down.

"OK! Listen up! Those of you in Group A, you're done — you may leave. You'll be notified either way within the next three days. Everyone in Group A, you're free to go!"

Mike picked up his jacket and made for the lifts. It was the first good thing she'd said all day.

3

THERE WAS A honking noise as Abby squeezed on the brakes and continued to hurtle across the gravel, heading straight for the brick wall. Flinging her legs out wide and trailing her feet along the ground, she brought the bike to a wobbly halt. She slung a chain round its back wheel, dumped it in a hedge and ran onto the sidelines.

"What's the score?" she asked one of the spectators, a lanky fellow she didn't recognise – presumably a sub for the opposition.

"One all," he grunted, keeping his eyes on the game. "Two minutes left."

Abby squinted into the low winter sun, and saw the little white ball skim to the far side of the pitch. A Cambridge player with sandy blonde hair launched himself across the astroturf and hooked the ball with his stick. Abby smiled as Ben took command of the game, dribbling the ball up the wing, dodging stealthily past the defence.

"Oh no," muttered the spectator.

She glanced up at the gangly man. He was definitely a sub for the opposition, she thought, noticing the crest on his shirt saying St Ives 1sts. Abby craned her neck to see who else was on the sidelines. The Blues coach was at the far end, fists clenched in anticipation. A couple of blondes wearing their boyfriends' turquoise scarves stood clapping their gloved hands together, and then there was a line of strangers, whom Abby took to be with St Ives.

There was a loud thud, followed by the sound of a whistle and a tremendous, collective roar. Abby whirled back to face the pitch. The Cambridge boys were running about like lunatics – yelling, whooping and shaking their sticks. They were converging on Ben, leaping at him, hugging him and jumping on his back as though he were on fire and they were trying to put out the flames. It occurred to Abby that she'd just missed the most important part of the match: the part where her boyfriend scored the winning goal.

"Hey!" cried Ben, flinging his stick down as he saw Abby on the sideline. He was grinning like a little kid. This was Ben at his most adorable. "You came!" He wiped his glistening forehead and ran a hand through his hair, leaning forward to give her a kiss.

Usually a quick peck on the cheek would have done, but today she grabbed him by the collar and kissed him properly on the lips. Ignoring the wolf-whistles from the other lads, she locked her arms around Ben's hot neck and pulled his body close to hers.

"Woah – what was that in aid of?" he asked, beaming, as he finally pulled away.

Abby shrugged. "Just to say well done."

"Hmm, I should score goals more often," he remarked, chucking his astro-glove into the kit bag and kicking his boots off on the concrete.

"And to celebrate."

"Celebrate?" he frowned. "We were only playing St Ives, Abby – not the bloody Netherlands!"

"Well, we've got something else to celebrate, too."

"Eh?"

She extracted the crumpled, off-white paper from her pocket and passed it over.

Ben's pale blue eyes narrowed.

"Go on—" she motioned for him to look at the screwed up letter. "Read it."

With a quick glance at his team mates, who were all stomping towards the clubhouse, slapping each other on the back and laughing, Ben turned to study the piece of paper.

Abby watched his expression change. "Cray McKinley?" he said quietly. "What... the investment bank?"

Abby smiled.

"So..." Ben suddenly looked perplexed. "You applied to Cray McKinley?"

"Yeah." Abby's smile faded. She knew what Ben was thinking. *Why hadn't she told him about the interview?*

"Why didn't you tell me about the interview?"

"In case I didn't get the job," she said quickly. "Come on – let's go inside. You're standing around covered in cold sweat. We'll get a drink from the bar."

She bent down, picked up his kit bag and marched towards the clubhouse before he had a chance to object. This was the reaction she'd been dreading. Poor Ben. He'd spent the last two weeks filling out application forms for management consultancy jobs, and he hadn't received a single response. Now here she was waving her offer letter at him – an offer of a job at Cray McKinley. He was bound to feel a bit outdone.

Abby was sitting on a bar stool playing with the ice cubes in her drink and wondering how to make it up to him when Ben emerged, hot and damp from the changing rooms. He grabbed her round her waist and pressed his lips against hers.

"Cheers–" he said, grinning, holding up his Coke.

She smiled and raised her glass.

"So! Investment banking, eh?" he said.

Abby looked at him sheepishly.

"After you told me that I shouldn't apply for management consultancy because the city was 'fucking boring'."

"I didn't say it was 'fucking boring'," she replied carefully. "I said the people who *worked* in the city were fucking boring."

"And now you suddenly find them interesting?"

"No – I still find them boring, but I think *I* could work there and be different."

Ben smiled and shook his head.

"What?" Abby didn't like people taking the piss.

"No – nothing!" he laughed. "You're probably right!" Ben waved at the barman and held out his glass for a top-up. "What's the starting salary?"

"Forty k," she mumbled into her Coke.

Ben slammed the glass on the bar and held onto it. The barman leapt backwards and busied himself with some bottles.

"Forty k?!" Ben repeated, staring at Abby. "That's shit-loads!"

She smiled awkwardly. "I know."

Ben's hand slithered off the glass, and the barman swooped forward to whisk it away.

"What do they make you *do*, for that kind of money?"

"Well, the work's supposed to be hard, and the hours are quite long, but I reckon I'm quicker and more efficient than most, so I won't turn into one of those zombies who spend their whole lives in the office."

"You'd better not," Ben warned.

Abby smiled and swivelled on her stool so that her knees were nestled between his.

"I can't believe you didn't tell me, Abby – when was the interview?"

"Last Wednesday. When I said I had a basketball match in Surrey."

Ben nodded, looking quite hurt.

"Don't worry," she said, putting a hand on his thigh. "I haven't got any other secrets – I just didn't want everyone getting their hopes up. Didn't want to look like a failure."

"Abby, *I'm* the one that's applied to seven consultancies and heard nothing back from any of them!"

Oh dear. Bad choice of words. "Well... that's management consultancy for you. It's a nightmare to get into. Banking's much easier," she lied, although Ben didn't look convinced. "And it's only November. Most people haven't even thought about applying for jobs – you're well ahead of the game."

He nodded reluctantly, and took his drink from the barman.

"What about your MoD offer?" he asked suddenly.

Ben had a point. Abby had worked for the Ministry of Defence every summer throughout university, and they'd paid her thousands of pounds in sponsorship. If she turned down their graduate job offer, she'd have to pay a lot of that money back. But Abby had thought this through.

"Stuff the MoD," she said dismissively. "I never wanted to work for them. I can pay them back with the sign-on bonus from Cray McKinley."

"Sign-on bonus?"

17

"Yeah – I get one of those 'golden handshake' thingies. Eight grand. I could write off my student debt *and* pay back the MoD with that."

Ben ran a hand through his wet blonde hair. "Eight grand...?"

"The MoD was dull," she said. "Slow-moving. Boring projects. Stupid people. Crap money. And I *hated* being a small cog in a big machine."

"Cray McKinley's a big machine too," he pointed out.

"Yeah, but at least small cogs get the chance to become big cogs there, if they're good enough."

"I guess," he agreed sceptically. "But careful, Abby – it's a man's world, investment banking. There're stories every day in the press about sexual harassment and stuff, and–"

"Ben," she cut in. "*Physics* is a man's world."

She knew she was right; being a female in a man's world had never held Abby back. In fact, being an *attractive* female in a man's world gave her a distinct advantage. It would be just the same at Cray McKinley, she felt sure.

"Speaking of which," she said, checking her watch. "I should go – I've got a lecture."

They both drained their glasses and stood up.

"Well played today," she said, looking up into his eyes.

"Well *done* today," he replied, nodding at the letter she was still clutching.

Abby pushed up onto her tiptoes and kissed him, then with an affectionate smile, dashed off.

4

MIKE SIFTED through the stack of mail in his letterbox. Having removed the letters addressed to Matt Cunningham, the geek in the year below, and the correspondence from Avenues, the country's largest introduction agency – the rugby lads' idea of a joke – there were four envelopes in his hand. Two looked like college junk mail, one was a bank statement, and the other was a heavy, A4 package – thick, cream woven paper with a London postmark. This was the one he'd been waiting for.

Stuffing the other three into his kit bag, Mike tore open the anonymous envelope and pulled out the sheaf of paper. Yes, this was it. Cray McKinley headed paper. Multiple pages, he noted. A good sign.

'Dear Michael,' it began. Mike didn't bother with the blurb. He just wanted a yes or a no. Scanning the first paragraph, his eyes stopped on the word 'delighted'.

'...to offer you a position at Cray McKinley,' he read.

Mike felt a surge of something rush through his body. This was it. This was confirmation of the glittering career that lay ahead for him in London. He had a job offer from Cray McKinley, the best-paying firm in the city. This was the moment he'd been daydreaming about for the last two months. He was going to be an investment banker. Mike looked around to check that nobody was watching, then punched the air. *Yes*. Life didn't get much better than this.

He ran towards the clubhouse with newfound energy. It was as though he'd just taken an ecstasy pill; he felt capable of anything. The urge to do cartwheels along the edge of the pitch was so strong that he nearly hurled himself onto the touchline, but remembered just in time that he couldn't actually do cartwheels, and made do with sprinting to the clubhouse door.

"Afternoon!" he boomed, trying to control the excitement in his voice.

"Mickey! Not like you to be late!" It was the other Mike speaking – Minnie. When Mike Atkins had joined the squad a year ago, things had got a bit confusing on the pitch. So right at the start of this season, they'd been allocated nicknames: Mickey (Mike Cunningham-Reid) and Minnie (Mike Atkins). Minnie had never really taken to his name on the team, but being scrum-half and several inches shorter than the captain, he didn't have much say in the matter.

"Minnie, what are you *wearing?*" Mike asked, staring at the little player, who was sporting a pair of red knee-length shorts in a floral design and a yellow T-shirt saying *Dude*. The thin white socks only made it half way up his stumpy shins.

"Oh, er, yeah. Sorry – my kit's dirty."

"But you knew we had practice today!"

Jenkins, the bulky full-back leaned across. "His mummy's taken it home for a good wash," he whispered loudly.

Mike shook his head and dropped his kit bag on the floor. He felt like laughing. Everything seemed funny this morning – even the state of his scrum-half.

"Looking smug, Mickey," commented James, or Hooker as he was known, for more reasons than one. "Get laid last night, did you?"

Mike raised an eyebrow cryptically and said nothing. The boys could think what they liked. Another day, the answer might have been a yes, but today he was smirking for a different reason. Mike wasn't sure whether to tell his team mates about the job offer or not. Some of them were applying for positions in the city, and having trouble even getting to the interview stage. As captain, he had to tread carefully. He wanted admiration and respect from the lads, but he didn't want resentment.

"Where's Jim and Dan?" he asked.

Jim and Dan were the latest recruits to the squad, both of them second-years. They were nimble and accurate, and the fastest wings

Mike had ever played with, but it was their attitude off the pitch that was worrying the captain. They just didn't act like part of the team.

"Anyone?" he pleaded. "Has anyone seen Jim or Dan?"

Blank looks from all the boys.

"OK. I'll call them. Greg's already out there, so get kitted up and start doing laps."

Greg was the new coach. He had withdrawn from professional rugby with a hamstring injury after only six months in the game, and now devoted most of his time to the university team.

"MY GOD! LOOK AT THAT!" roared BFG – the Big Fat Goon. The flanker was holding up a double-page spread – 'spread' being the operative word – from a magazine he'd found stuffed between the slats of the bench. The players converged on the naked woman like kids around an ice cream van.

"C'mon guys, get out on the pitch!" Mike ordered, booting the lads out the door. He wasn't really cross. Nothing could make him cross today.

Finally, the squad was complete. "Just one more lap!" yelled Greg from the touchline.

"Alright for you," gasped BFG, dropping to the back of the pack. Mike pushed forward, to be running alongside Chris, his best mate from school. It was strange playing with Chris again after so many years. Mike had persuaded him to trial a few months ago, after a spate of injuries had left a hole in the team, and he'd played as centre ever since. They jogged around the edge of the pitch listening to the sound of their own breath and the squelch of the mud under their feet.

"How's things?" Mike panted.

Chris looked up. "Good. You?"

"Good, yeah…" He just had to share it with someone. "Did I tell you I applied to Cray McKinley a few weeks ago?"

"The merchant bank?"

"Investment bank – yeah. I just heard back this morning–" Mike filled his lungs. "Got the job!"

"Really?" Chris gasped. "That's fantastic, mate! Awesome."

They were nearly back at the clubhouse. A writhing mass of bodies had formed around the coach, stretching, bending, crouching, twisting.

"Right lads," yelled the coach. "We've got a full squad today, so we're gonna start with fitness, do some ball-skills then move into a game. It'll be hard work, OK?"

Mike divided the wandering players into groups. They were like sheep, he thought as he pushed them into place. They'd do anything he told them to. But he didn't begrudge that. He loved his position on the team.

Greg had not been exaggerating when he'd said 'hard work'. After twenty minutes of drills, the students were staggering about at the side of the pitch, spluttering, panting and gasping for air. Mike lay flat on his back in the mud, staring up into the white-grey sky, hearing nothing but the thumping pulse in his ears. His lungs were aching from all the sharp intakes of cold air, and his muscles felt stretched and worn. There was no denying it, though. Greg was a fucking good coach.

It was at Wellington College that Mike had earned the nickname Sticky Mickey, for his ability to cling to the ball. And by some quirk of fate, here he was again on a Wednesday afternoon, passing and catching with his school friend Chris. The drill was easy, and neither one of them needed to concentrate. Pass, switch, catch, pass, switch, catch... They could have done it with their eyes shut.

"So what'll you be doing in this job of yours then, Mickey?" shouted Chris as he hurled the ball backwards.

Mike glanced cautiously from side to side; he hadn't had a chance to explain that he wanted to keep this quiet.

"Corporate finance!" Mike shouted, as softly as he could.

"Chalk and diamonds?!"

"*Corporate finance!*" Mike articulated, increasing the volume slightly. "You know – transactions and stuff!"

"Oh!" Chris lurched forwards to receive Mike's pass, which had been uncharacteristically weak.

"Come on you two!" yelled Greg. "*Think* about what you're doing!"

"What's the pay like?" Chris called. It was the question Mike had been dreading.

"Dunno – haven't checked."

It was true – he hadn't actually checked. But he knew roughly how much Cray McKinley paid first-year analysts, and he wasn't about to shout that across the playing field. According to his mate in the London office, it was somewhere between forty and fifty grand a year. And that was before bonuses.

"Haven't checked?! Why the hell not? I bet it's thirty grand or something!"

Chris was planning to stay on for a teachers' training qualification. City salaries were a mystery to him.

"I'll check the letter after training," Mike muttered as they trotted back towards an angry Greg.

"That was *sloppy!* You can do better than that. From now on I wanna see *accuracy*. You hear me? *Accuracy*. Good passing, good catching, good tackling, good kicking... You get the picture. Now get into threes."

Four drills and one sprained ankle later, the coach seemed somewhat pacified.

"OK, that's enough lads!" he called. Then, almost inaudibly, he added: "You've worked hard today."

That, in Greg's terms, was a compliment. There were a few raised eyebrows among the boys before they trampled off the pitch, supporting the hobbling BFG.

Despite the pain of the last ninety minutes' exertion, Mike still felt fresh and bursting with a special type of energy that overrode his physical tiredness. He and Chris hung back from the rest of the team as they headed towards the showers.

"So!" Chris looked expectantly at Mike. Mike could sense what was coming. "This job..."

"Yeah — the thing is Chris, I know some of the boys inside were—"

"What will you be doing? Where are the offices — London?"

"Well, actually I applied to the Paris branch, so that I could..."

"Paris?! What, France?!"

"Well, that's where Paris was located last time I checked. But listen—"

"I just meant... Why there? Surely Drake McKinsey has offices in *this* country?"

"Cray McKinley," Mike corrected. "Yeah, they have offices in

London – that's where I had my interview – but y'know, I've just spent four years working for a degree in French, so I figured I might as well use it. But hey, Chris, there's guys in the..."

"That's really brave, Mick," Chris said admiringly. "Starting a new job with new people, in a new country... I don't think I'd wanna do that."

Mike laughed. "Oh, I dunno. It's not *that* brave," he said modestly. "Most of the meetings are conducted in English." They were entering the changing rooms, and he was desperate to change the subject. "How's the new bird – Sophie, is it?"

"Awesome." Chris grinned, and stripped down to a pair of old, yellowy Y-fronts. He started rummaging around in his kit bag. Mike grimaced and looked away, hoping Sophie never got to see him like that.

As he stood under the lukewarm trickle of water, the glorious feeling returned. Mike thought about the life that lay ahead, and wondered what he'd be doing in one year's time. Would he be chairing a meeting between Cray McKinley and one of its global clients? Catching a plane to some financial hotspot on the other side of the world? Shaking hands with the Chief Executive of a multi-million pound superpower? He remembered the words of the woman he'd met at the graduate recruitment dinner: 'A job at Cray McKinley is whatever you make of it. For the real high fliers, there's potential for you to go as high as you like.' Mike smiled. He was a high flier. And he was going all the way to the top.

He stepped back into the changing room, towel round waist, dripping and shivering slightly. A raucous discussion was breaking out.

"No, he hasn't even *looked!* I know!"

"It'll be fucking big bucks, I tell you."

"Oh, here he is! What's all this then? Cray McKinley?" BFG was barely masking his contempt.

"Oh, um, yeah. Just heard this afternoon. I don't know any details yet though – it's early days." Mike pulled on his boxers and dived into the kit-bag for his jeans.

"Details?!" roared Adam, the Edinburgh fly-half who'd apparently applied to every city firm in EC1. "Mate, you don't need *details*

24

– it's *Cray McKinley*. Nobody thinks twice about an offer from them!"

"Yeah, maybe," said Mike quietly. This was beginning to get a bit awkward.

"So, Corporate Finance, eh?" It was Minnie, coming from the other end of the changing room, tugging his over-sized kit bag behind him, floral board-shorts hanging out. Word was obviously spreading.

"Well, like I said, I haven't made up my mind yet."

"When did you interview, mate?" Minnie asked, with excessive emphasis on the last word.

"Only a couple of days ago. They're pretty efficient."

"Was it hard, the interview and everything?" Adam pressed.

"Well, yeah. It was tricky. Lots of questions, a numerical test, team-building – you know the sort of thing."

"Did you have to fill out an on-line application form?" asked BFG.

"How many jobs did..."

"When did you apply?"

Shit, thought Mike. They were really bitter.

"How many applic–"

"Look, sorry guys," he cut in, swinging his bag over his shoulder. "I've gotta run."

5

ABBY WAS AWARE of the bleeping noise, but she couldn't open her eyes. She lay there, motionless, willing it to stop. It was getting louder. She still couldn't open her eyes. Any slight movement of her head on the pillow caused a thumping sensation in her ears.

Bleep-bleep. Finally, she rolled over and slammed her hand down where she expected the button to be.

Peace. Her eyes remained shut. It felt as though someone had poured glue into them during the night. Poking a finger into the corner of one of them, she prised it apart. Her lashes were crusty with yesterday's mascara, and her face felt itchy and dry. There was a horrible taste in her mouth, as though she'd eaten a mouthful of compost the night before. This was getting too much. She had to slow down. The human body wasn't designed to run on three hours' sleep a night and a diet of pretzels and alcohol.

Slumped like a dead-weight in the huge double bed, Abby stared at the only thing in the room that was moving. The fan. It wasn't so much spinning as *edging* round, with no obvious effect on the temperature. Abby hadn't yet mastered the air conditioning unit, so it was all she had. Her body felt greasy and hot. She shifted sideways onto a cooler patch of sheet, and contemplated switching on the TV. American chat shows, Abby had discovered, were the best way of getting her out of bed in the mornings. As she summoned the energy to reach the remote control, there was a knock on the door.

"Hi Abby," called a soft male voice. "You up?"

With great effort, Abby managed to put a face to the voice.

Mousy, freckles, friendly smile. It was Alan. Fellow trainee. Suite next door.

"Mmm. Yeah," she croaked, pulling a sheet up over her naked body.

"You told me to check you were up this morning. You feeling OK?" He was smiling; she could tell by the sound of his voice. What had she got up to last night? She had vague memories of a cocktail bar in Lower East Side, then some bar near Union Square, then… another bar? A club? The drink had blotted out large portions of the night. She'd have to ask the boys.

"Yeah, I'm fine," Abby lied. The effort of speaking was making her head throb. "See you in the lobby at quarter to?"

"Yup – see you there. That's… Seven minutes!"

Seven minutes? Abby frantically kicked off the sheet and propped herself up on the pillow. Shit. She must have been drunk when she set her alarm. Water. That's what she needed. Her head felt as though it might explode.

With a shaky hand, Abby filled her third glass, and poured it down her throat. She staggered, naked, through to the bathroom and turned on the power-shower – the anti-hangover machine. She longed to stand there for another hour, feeling the force of the boiling water between her shoulder blades, massaging the shampoo into her scalp and washing away the grime from the night before, but this morning there wasn't time. She was due at a lecture in twenty minutes, and it wasn't just any old lecture. It was the introductory lecture by Stanley Conway, President of Cray McKinley International. This was the one time she couldn't be late.

Abby stared into the gigantic walk-in wardrobe, where her clothes skulked inadequately at one end. She was experiencing that slow, indecisive, fuzzy-brain sensation that always came after a big night out. What should she wear…?

Seven forty-four. Abby had one minute to get down twenty-eight floors, preferably with some clothes on. She grabbed some jeans and a top and pulled them onto her damp body. It was only as the door slammed behind her that Abby realised she'd forgotten the most important thing.

"Hey Sean!" she called to the guy coming out two doors down.

"Hold the lift for me, will you? I'm just coming!"

Sean smiled and rolled his eyes, keeping one foot in the jaws of the elevator while Abby ran back for her kit. Saturday afternoons were the best part of the week – she wasn't going to miss basketball.

They bounded through the lobby together, just in time to see the contrasting silhouettes of Alan and little Joe disappearing into the morning sun.

"Oi, wait!" Abby yelled through the revolving door, not caring about the disapproving looks from the fat women behind the Concierge desk. She clattered down the shallow steps and walloped the boys on the back.

"Hey!" cried Joe, his expression changing from one of shock to one of amusement. "Didn't think you'd make it this morning."

"I *always* make it, don't I?" Abby replied indignantly, glaring down at him.

It was true. Abby always made it to lectures. Late, maybe. But she always made it. They'd been in New York for nearly a month, and she hadn't missed a single one. It was a habit she'd picked up at Cambridge. Physicists went to lectures at nine o'clock every day, six days a week, and Abby had been no exception.

"Shall we take the yellow line?" asked Alan with a raised eyebrow. It was a private joke among the trainees. There were two subway lines – red and blue – that ran down to Wall Street where the Cray McKinley headquarters were located. The third alternative, which avoided the heat, the stench and the risk of being accosted by homeless madmen, was to take a yellow cab. This was 'the yellow line'.

"Definitely." Abby nodded, sticking her hand out into the street. "I'll vomit if I go underground."

The driver, a small Hispanic man with wild black eyes and nicotine-stained teeth, seemed to have a peculiar infatuation with beads. There were small, wooden beads everywhere Abby looked: hanging round the man's neck, dangling from the rear-view mirror, draped around the door frames, lying along the dashboard and alarmingly, strung from the top of the windscreen in front of his face.

"Wall Street?"

"Ye-es!" the Hispanic man replied keenly, as though Sean had been offering him a spliff.

"We're going to Wall Street?" Sean confirmed, looking slightly anxious.

The man turned to him with a yellow grin, and slammed his foot down on the accelerator.

Abby was thrown back in her seat, and remained there, slumped in the corner, her head rolling uncomfortably on a string of beads. The air in the taxi was musty, and smelt of stale tobacco.

Alan looked sideways at Abby's half-closed eyes, and laid a hand on her arm. "Don't worry," he told her. "I'll get him to open a window. Er, abierto ventana? Ventana abierto?" he said hopefully.

The driver threw his head back, let out a peal of coarse laughter then swerved into the middle lane of traffic.

"Ventana abierto?" Alan pleaded, with a frantic winding-the-window-down gesture followed by a mime of somebody throwing up.

The man nodded, chuckled some more, and lit a cigarette. Abby concentrated on looking out of the window as the cab filled with sickly brown smoke.

Finally, the trainees hurried into the cool, vast atrium of the Cray McKinley headquarters. There were two familiar faces waiting for the elevators: one white, one black, both square-jawed and handsome with impeccable sets of teeth. Tao and Rod, both from Princeton, were fellow graduates heading for the New York office.

"Hey, Abs, how you doing?" Rod smiled, looking her up and down in a way that made her feel slightly uncomfortable.

"How're you *feelin'*, more like?" asked Tao.

Abby began to wonder what she might have done last night. She didn't even remember seeing Tao or Rod. "Er, fine. A bit dodgy, but I'll live."

"*Dor-dgy! Dor-dgy!*" cried Tao. "She feels *dor-dgy!* That is *so funny!*"

Abby smiled. She'd forgotten how hilarious Americans found that word.

Scanning the lecture hall for somewhere to sit, she spotted Brad and the other Aussies in the corner of the room.

"How's it going?" asked Brad, grinning. "Feeling a bit ropey this morning?"

Abby looked at him sheepishly.

"No bruises in strange places...?"

"Huh," Abby snorted, and decided it would be wise to ask what on earth had happened last night. "Brad, could–"

A hush fell on the auditorium, as a man entered through the left-hand stage door.

"*Here's the big man himself!*" hissed Brad.

The man was indeed big. He was enormous. Probably forty years old, and almost completely bald, this was their President. Abby stared. He looked as though he spent his entire salary on food. All around the room, people were glancing at their neighbours, trying to catch a raised eyebrow or a sneaky smile. The guy was *huge*.

"Hi. And welcome," Stanley Conway drawled, in a slow, nasal Mid-Atlantic accent. "I am proud, <pause> and excited, <pause> to be here today."

Abby groaned under her breath. She couldn't believe she'd got out of bed to sit through an hour of this.

"I'm standing here, <pause> looking at three hundred pairs of eyes, <pause> and I'm thinking: <pause> these are the eyes of our future! <pause> The future of Cray McKinley! <pause> And that makes me happy. <pause> Because you are not just any old people. <low-pitched chuckle> No! You are the smartest, sharpest, most talented young people this city has ever seen! And I can tell you something.... <long pause> You've come to the right place to start your careers!"

Abby got out her notebook and drew a horizontal dashed line on the back page. "*Hangman!*" she whispered.

Brad smiled and took the pen.

"When I joined the firm, and that was a long time ago, <pause for obligatory laughter> there were two things I wanted to learn about the firm –"

"*Where the canteen was?*" muttered Abby, adding an arm to her stick-man.

"–Firstly, what I'd be *doing* in Corporate Finance. <pause> And secondly, how much I would earn!"

More false laughter rippled around the auditorium. Abby watched as Brad filled in the remaining letter of O̲ B̲ E̲ S̲ I̲ Y̲.

The speech droned on. The back page of Abby's notebook became a dense mass of scribbles, and after twenty minutes, she and Brad ran out of games to play. Bored and tired, she flopped onto the desk and let her eyes roam around the room.

The front row was filled with Malaysians, as usual, all of them fast asleep. They slept through all the lectures, and they came top in every test. She wondered how long it would be before Tze-Han, who was sitting at the end of the row and leaning at a precarious angle, toppled into the aisle.

The middle block was populated with keen Americans – the source of most of the irritating questions. On the far left were the Scandinavians, their blonde hair shining like halos on top of their conscientious heads.

Abby's sleepy gaze was drawn towards the back row: The Lads' pad. Marcus occupied the middle seat and was reclined with his feet up on the one in front. Sean, Alan, Danny and Joe, his disciples, were arranged either side of him, playing their favourite game: firing scrunched-up lecture notes at Americans. Right at the end of the row, nonchalantly handing ammunition to the boys, was the dark-haired guy with incredible eyes. Mike with the double-barrelled surname. His looks were really his redeeming feature, thought Abby, thinking back to last week's basketball match when he'd practically trampled her into the tarmac. He was a complete tosser.

She let her eyelids drop shut. Stanley Conway's voice was smooth and monotonous, and quite relaxing as a background noise. Abby's limbs began to feel heavy, and then numb. There was a nice cool breeze circulating around her face.

She was standing on an escalator. It seemed to have no beginning or end – it just went on for ever. There were other people on the steps above her and below, all of them very serious-looking and dressed in suits. They were brandishing briefcases, newspapers and umbrellas like weapons over the side of the escalator, taking a swipe at anything that came within reach. Abby peered over the side. It turned out that the things being walloped were not in fact things, but *people*.

The escalator was transporting them through an infinitely large factory, where workers dressed in overalls were going about their business – welding, cutting, fixing and soldering – and suffering regular blows to the back of the head from the men in suits.

As Abby looked on, she felt a stab in her back, and turned round to find an angry man in a pinstriped suit poking her with his umbrella. He seemed to be indicating that she too should be lashing out at the workers. Abby didn't want to. She tried to ask the man why they were doing this and who all these people were, but she'd been stripped of her vocal chords.

Abby turned her back on the pinstriped man, and gazed out at the industrious scene. There was another jab in the small of her back, and then another in the side of her ribs. The man was poking her again and again.

"Abby! Abby!"

The man was using the butt of his newspaper now to prod Abby in the ribs. It was beginning to hurt.

"Abby!"

She opened her eyes. Brad was holding a wad of rolled-up lecture notes and smiling.

Regaining her bearings, Abby looked at the stage. Stanley Conway had been replaced by a table. She squinted. Behind the table were four very unremarkable faces, which were beaming up at the roomful of trainees like children's TV presenters who'd forgotten to go to Makeup before coming on set.

"*What's going on?*" whispered Abby.

Brad nodded towards the front. "Peer group panel. They're Cray McKinley analysts."

"Oh." She scrutinised them again. Analysts, he'd said. That meant they weren't much older than Abby. But most of them could've passed for thirty-five. "What're they doing here?"

"Answering our questions." Brad shrugged. "According to that HR woman, they've turned off all the video cameras and stuff, so we can say what we want."

Abby snorted. She wasn't so sure. All through the Cray McKinley training course, they'd been scrutinised like kids serving time in a juvenile delinquent centre. There were CCTV cameras all over the building, and when someone misbehaved in a lecture – usually one of the back row Brits – the footage was flashed up as a warning at the end of the day. Apparently, reports were being compiled on each analyst, detailing his or her conduct throughout the course. It was scary stuff. She doubted they'd miss out on an information-gathering opportunity like this.

"Hi there," said the first analyst, whose face was so fat it was difficult to make out his eyes. "I guess we'll start by introducing ourselves. I'm Jimmy. Graduated from Harvard two summers ago." His jowls wobbled as he sat down.

Rising to his feet was a tall, blonde guy with an exceedingly large chin. A long time ago, thought Abby, he'd probably been in good shape, but the man looked stodgy and weak. "Hank Nailer," he announced. "Second-year analyst in Investment Banking, New York. Studied Finance at Princeton."

"*Hank?!*" Brad muttered under his breath. "*Hank the Yank. I bet he likes a good—*"

"Rosalind Whittaker." The girl stood up. She was fair, with an unmemorable face and long, fuzzy hair the colour of weak tea. Standing under the harsh stage lights, her makeup did nothing to conceal the bags under her eyes. She glanced nervously around the lecture hall. "Hi. Second-year analyst in Leveraged Finance, New York. I have a Masters in Economics from Stanford."

Abby and Brad exchanged unimpressed looks. The last member of the panel — a tall, lanky man with ginger hair and freckles — was someone she recognised. He'd been shipped over from the London office to help with the training programme, and last week had spent a whole homework session explaining Discounted Cash Flow to Abby and Justine, the other girl heading for Corporate Finance UK.

"Hi," he said in his calm, Scottish accent. "Patrick Gilligan." He waved at the rows of trainees and then sat down. Abby smiled. She liked the guy. He didn't bother trying to impress.

There was a series of predictable, pointless questions that Abby had come to expect from the American trainees.

"How d'you ensure you keep to deadlines?"

"Does it help to do an MBA?"

"What's the best part of your job?"

"What does it take to be promoted at Cray McKinley?"

And then something unusual happened. One of the Brits asked a question. The Brits *never* asked questions. She looked up at the back row. It was Joe.

"I know you all work long hours," he began quietly, "but how long is 'long'? I mean, what can we really expect?"

A silence fell on the auditorium. All eyes turned to the stage. This was the question they'd all wanted to ask.

Jimmy the piggy-eyed analyst looked up first and broke into a grin. "Well. I'd say that an average day's work would start at 9a.m. and finish anywhere between 9p.m. and, well… sometimes I just work right through, two days running. It depends."

Murmurs travelled around the room as the trainees digested his response.

"If I've pulled an all-nighter, I usually try to get away by eight the next night, to catch up on sleep," the analyst explained.

Hank Nailer jumped in. "That's on weeknights. Weekends are usually different; Friday nights I like to leave before bars shut and a few of us go grab a beer after work. I usually work just a five-hour day on Saturday – they're kinda sacred – then a normal working day on Sunday."

"Yeah – Sundays are the best day," added Jimmy enthusiastically. "At least, for me they are. On Sundays I get to drive my X5 into work and I get a spot in the Cray McKinley parking lot!"

Abby stared at the repugnant, grinning analyst. He *had* to be joking.

Rosalind Whittaker looked up. "Our hours vary, week on week. On average, I guess we work a fifteen-hour day. It looks kinda bad if you're seen to be leaving the office before midnight."

There was more murmuring as trainees quietly refuted what had been said. And then, as quickly as it had swelled, the noise level dropped.

"…a little different outside New York," Patrick Gilligan said, his voice barely coming through. "Those of you going to London will certainly find that it's more about *work achieved* in the office than *time spent* there." He smiled pointedly at the three Americans. "Face-time doesn't happen so much in Europe. If you're done for the night at 7p.m., you *leave*. You don't hang around to impress."

A quiet snigger rippled through the room. Abby was liking the guy more and more every second.

Someone raised a hand.

"How much spare time d'you guys actually get then?"

Jimmy smiled zealously. "Well, put it this way: if you have a girlfriend, dump her now!"

If that was a joke, thought Abby, it wasn't very funny. Nobody else was laughing either.

"Yeah," agreed Hank. "You don't get much spare time, it's true. I haven't had a weekend off in four months."

Rosalind nodded.

Everyone looked at Patrick, waiting for his retort. Surely things weren't like that in the London office? *Come on – tell us it's not that bad*, urged Abby. Eventually, he spoke.

"Well, it has to be said, a whole weekend off is a rare thing at Cray McKinley."

Suddenly there was an almighty clunking sound from the front of the room. Abby looked down to see Tze-Han clambering back onto his seat.

"OK guys!" cried Jimmy. "That's it from us!"

6

THE FOUR GRADUATES SAT behind the boardroom table on the thirty-fifth floor. It was their final assessment: the presentation to the Board of Directors. Or, more accurately: the presentation to three senior Cray McKinley bankers who were pretending to be a Board of Directors.

Mike could feel the beads of sweat forming on his upper lip, despite the coolness of the air-conditioned room. He'd barely eaten or slept in twenty-four hours, and was feeling sick. He looked down at the trembling presentation in his hands, and prepared to speak, hoping he could trust his voice to come out at the right pitch.

"Hi, I'm Mike." It was fine; his voice sounded deep and steady. "As Olivier said, I'll be going through the DCF model. If you turn to page four of our presentation, you'll see an overview of the valuation technique we used."

The listeners' eyes glazed over.

"Unlike Olivier's analysis, the DCF method gives an absolute valuation of the company."

One of the bankers was reclined, full-tilt on his black leather chair, fiddling with a pen. The other two were slumped over the table, one gnawing at the side of his finger, one trying to shorten his watch-strap with one hand.

"Turning to page five, you'll see—" Mike stopped, and swallowed.

There was no page five.

He rubbed the corner of page four between his fingers. Nope. The glossy, comb-bound, colour presentation which they'd spent literally all night working on – which they had checked meticulously before submitting to Graphics, and finally completed at seven o'clock that morning – was missing a page.

Mike looked at his team mates. Nathalie was smiling into space. Olivier was flicking frantically through his copy, in search of the elusive page five. Benoit had flipped straight to page six, and using improvised eyebrow sign language, was encouraging Mike to do the same.

"Er, right. We appear to be missing page five. So moving on…"

The panel of bankers looked up from their respective daydreams and grumpily whipped over their pages.

"Obviously, it is essential to match the cashflows to a suitable discount rate. The weighted average cost of capital has been calculated on page seven…"

He was back on track. Mike had been allocated the easiest part of the project to present. The other members of his team – Olivier, Benoit and Nathalie – had all studied Finance together in Paris, and knew a lot more about valuation than he did. He'd been perfectly happy last night when they'd decided to take on the more complex parts of the analysis.

"…so that completes the DCF part of our presentation. Nathalie will now wrap up with a summary of our findings." He nodded briskly to the timid French girl, who obediently started to speak. He sank into the padded chair, enveloped in blissful relief. The stress started to ebb from his body, and he felt his muscles beginning to relax. It hadn't gone too badly, he thought, apart from the Page five fiasco…

The sharp jab in his left thigh made him wince, and his elbow slid sideways on the slippery table. Benoit shot him a warning glance. Mike forced himself upright.

"Sank you for listening," Nathalie concluded in a whisper.

The men sitting across the table snapped out of their trance-like states, and looked blankly at one another.

"Right," said one of them. "Right, thank you. Could you make your way back to the reception area, and call in the next group?"

Mike led the foursome out of the room, wondering whether the half-hour 'meeting' had really justified all the hard work, stress, or lack of sleep. They might as well have been talking about the different ways to cook turnips, for all the bankers cared.

The last night had been unbearable. After a day of heavy lectures and end-of-training assessments, they'd been divided into teams and set their assignments at six o'clock. Mike had been grouped with the other analysts heading for the Paris office. After an infuriating hour spent going round in circles – in French – the four of them had finally set to work.

By one o'clock in the morning, they were tired, hungry and irritable, and had stepped out into the sticky heat of Wall Street to find a deli. Back in the training room, they'd discovered a discrepancy in their calculations, and bickered until a neighbouring group had asked them to bugger off. The air conditioning had apparently finished for the night, and the sweaty trainees felt wretched. It was four o'clock by the time they'd finalised their presentation, and of course, being one of the last groups to finish, there'd been a two-hour queue in Graphics. They'd had just enough time to hail a cab, race back to the hotel, jump in the shower and put on their suits before diving into yet another taxi and heading back to the office.

"Vous l'avez trouvé comment, ce meeting?" he asked, as the team plodded wearily down the corridor.

"Pas mal," Olivier replied pensively.

"Vous voulez prendre un verre, pour le fêter?" asked Benoit, surprising them all. A celebratory drink was the last thing Mike felt like. His eyes ached, his breath stank and his body was desperate for sleep – not alcohol.

"Je veux bien! Ce bar-là vous dit?" replied Nathalie. Mike frowned. Nathalie didn't seem like the drinking type.

Bowing to peer pressure and ignoring the throbbing pain in his head, Mike strode into the Wall Street bar, which was crammed full of rowdy young men on their liquid lunch breaks, shirt sleeves rolled up and top buttons undone. As he elbowed his way through the hair-gelled masses, he picked out an English accent. It belonged to the largest trainee in the yeargroup – a six-foot giant called Marcus. He was navigating his way back from the bar, brandishing three full jugs of lager.

"Alright! How's it going?" he bawled, on seeing Mike. "We finished at eleven – been drinking ever since! You done then?"

"We just finished," Mike shouted. "Feel like shit – didn't get any sleep."

"Nah – me neither. But hey!" he roared, leaning towards Mike. "IT'S OUR LAST DAY IN NEW YORK – SO LET'S GET DRINKING!"

He motioned for Mike to follow in his slipstream, and headed for the corner of the bar. It looked like a cage in London Zoo: tables upturned, drinks spilled, glasses broken and Brits clambering all over the furniture. They were undoubtedly the noisiest people in the bar.

"Mike! Comeandsitdown!" slurred Danny, pushing himself up.

"You've been here a while, haven't you?" Mike guessed, picking up the chair that had clattered to the ground.

"Yep! Since ten!" he proclaimed proudly. "We were the first group!"

It showed. Danny was inebriated. The little lad staggered off muttering something about 'restrooms' and Mike sat down in his place. He had to remember not to get too drunk this afternoon; he was meeting his gorgeous, blonde, New York girlfriend at four on 21st Street.

"Drink up, boys!" bellowed Marcus from the other end of the table.

Mike looked at the fresh glass of lager sitting in front of him, and downed it in one. There was some catching up to do, after all.

"Right! Loser buys the next round!" cried Joe, holding a pool cue in front of Mike's face.

Joe had become one of The Lads right back in the first week, when he'd let the other guys look over his shoulder in the accounting exams. Today was one of the rare occasions he was out in New York without his girlfriend. Zoë and Joe were almost insepa-rable. They'd met back in school, and been everywhere together since: a year in Australia, three years at Warwick, and now a summer in New York, ahead of a lifetime together. Zoë was like a female version of Joe: short, attractive, intelligent. Mike smiled, grabbed the cue from his mate and followed him to the table, filling his glass on the way.

Ten minutes later, it became evident that someone had sabotaged the game of pool, replacing all the red balls on the table with over-sized replicas that wouldn't fit in the pockets. Mike just couldn't get them in. This wasn't a problem he usually had. In fact, he hadn't potted a single ball all game, and Joe was already on number four.

"Aaaaaah! Not so cocky now!" yelled Danny, waggling his finger at Mike and sloshing lager down his top.

Mike took another swig of beer. He was being made increasingly aware of the pain in his head and the soreness behind his eyes. Inspect, align, shoot, pot. That's what usually happened. But the last bit just wasn't happening.

Another swig of beer.

Joe potted his fifth ball.

Another swig of beer. The fizzy lager was refreshing, and seemed to be numbing the pain. Finally, Mike potted a red. Then another. Then another. He drew level with Joe, and then potted another. Two minutes later, Joe was storming up to the bar with a fifty dollar bill in his hand.

Danny slammed his hand down on a chair, and patted it repeatedly.

"Siddown, Mike. I wanna ask you something."

Mike took the seat, as instructed, and looked at the scruffy drunkard.

"Now, this bird of yours. Miriam. Where did you get her?"

"Miranda. You were *there* when I met her, Danny – that night in Tribeca Grand. You remember – when Marcus went missing, everybody went looking for him, Sean got kicked out, and then those two fit blondes sat down at the table? One of them was Miranda."

"Oh yeah, I remember," Danny replied, clearly not remembering anything of the sort. "So what's she like? Apart from her tits, I mean."

"Nice," Mike told him, looking forward to four o'clock when he'd get to see those lovely tits again. "Very nice. She used to be a model. Now she works for a magazine or something." He didn't actually know what Miranda did for a living, he realised, slightly ashamed; her career aspirations weren't her main attraction.

"God, it's so *unfair*," whinged Danny, mumbling into his beer glass. "Why are New York girls so much nicer than Londoners? And how come *you've* got yourself an American girlfriend?"

"Well, you know..." Mike smiled. "Looks, charm, wit, English accent..."

Danny didn't laugh. He was scanning the bar for women. "Now *she's* fit, that one," he commented, pointing with his glass towards a blonde who was ploughing her way to the bar. "She's a trainee – I've seen her in lectures. English. Marcus knows her."

As they watched, the girl thrust a tanned shoulder at the barman, planting her elbow on the bar.

"Now *that's* how you get served!" remarked Danny admiringly as not one but two barmen lunged towards the blonde. Mike didn't comment. He'd noticed her around – it was difficult *not* to, with legs like that – but he'd kept his distance. She was one of those irritating, giggly flirts who knew exactly how attractive she was.

"I bet she wouldn't go out with me if I *begged* her," moaned Danny, still staring at the girl as he drained his beer.

"Ah, don't get hung up on birds like her," Mike advised, shaking his head. "I bet she's got a string of men in tow; she probably sleeps with a different one every night. She's a tart, mate – forget it."

Danny looked at Mike as though he was mad.

The bar was getting more and more crowded as the afternoon wore on. Mike's headache was returning, and he found himself needing ever-longer swigs of beer to relieve the pain.

"Right then! Drinking rules!" announced Marcus, standing up at the end of the table. "And we'll need another round – Mike? You haven't got one in yet, have you?"

It was true. Mike hadn't paid a penny all afternoon. He fished out a crisp fifty-dollar note from his pocket and for the first time in several hours, looked at his watch.

A flutter of panic rose up inside him. Three forty-two! That meant… that meant… His brain was struggling to do the maths. That meant he was supposed to be on 21st Street in eighteen minutes. He hurriedly dropped the money onto the table.

"Sorry guys, I've gotta go. I've said I'll meet my bird tonight. There's fifty for the next round."

"LEAVING?!" "MEETING YOUR BIRD?!" "SIDDOWN!"

The young trainees were not going to let Mike leave quietly. The protests were coming from all directions, and they were getting louder.

"IT'S YOUR LAST FUCKING NIGHT IN NEW YORK! YOU CAN'T SPEND IT WITH YOUR BIRD!"

"YOU WUSS!"

"FUCKING LOSER!"

Mike rose to his feet, ignoring the uproar.

"Guys, I'm not gonna see her for months, so—"

He broke off suddenly as the room turned white, then grey, then room-coloured again. He grabbed hold of the table. The alcohol was obviously just hitting his brain.

"You OK mate?" asked Marcus, the only person to notice him wobble.

"Fine," he muttered, completely drowned out by the noise of the insults. He decided it would be wise to leave the rest of his beer, and planted the half-finished pint on the table. There was a sharp 'crack', followed by a tiny yelp as Danny noticed a shard of glass land in his lap.

"Shit – sorry mate!" cried Mike, watching the beer drip onto Danny's groin as the splinters were extracted. His coordination was obviously slightly off-kilter. Mike decided to do the decent thing and run away.

Lounging in the back of the yellow cab, Mike watched the street numbers flash past. He smiled to himself. The lads were so jealous of him, with his sexy New York girlfriend. And rightly so. Miranda *was* fit. Even Mike had never been out with a girl as cute as Miranda – he'd never even met anyone like her. In fact, if Mike was being completely honest with himself, Miranda was way out of his league. She was a cheerleading honey. A babe. But now was not the time for honesty. The girl was his – for one more night, at least.

Leaning against the rattling window, Mike realised he'd actually miss the lads, when he went to work in Paris. He'd miss them in the same way he already missed his uni mates. Back in Edinburgh, just like here in New York, he had been something of a hero, a person that everyone looked up to. He wasn't the *leader* of the pack, exactly – he left that role to people like Marcus Mackenzie – but he was the one that people wanted to *be* like. They wanted to be as strong as him, as good-looking, as sharp, as successful. Everywhere he went, Mike was admired, and he'd become accustomed to having guys – team mates, friends, fellow trainees – idolise him. Somehow though, he knew that things would be different when he started work in

Paris. He'd be a first-year analyst, the lowest of the low, in a foreign country, doing work that was new to him, in a firm where *everyone* was a hero.

The taxi sped away leaving Mike at the side of the road, wondering why the driver had seemed so ecstatic about his one-dollar tip. It was only as he entered the bar that he realised he'd given the man a sixteen-dollar tip for a journey that had cost four. Oh well, he thought. What was a few dollars, now that he was an investment banker?

The dress was the first thing he noticed as soon as he walked in. It was a shimmering, light blue affair with a low-slung back that showed off her tan. Miranda was perched on a stool, sipping a Margarita and attracting attention from every pair of eyes in the bar. She swivelled round as Mike approached, revealing a pair of bronzed, neatly-crossed legs and those glorious tits, which were pressing against the silky material of her dress. Mike wanted to take her back to the hotel room that instant.

"Miranda. You look *beautiful,*" Mike whispered as he slid his arms around her tiny waist.

"Ow!" cried Miranda, hopping onto her right foot whilst trying to grab the left one which Mike had crushed under his.

"I'm so sorry –" Mike gasped, putting out a hand to steady her, and somehow managing to plough it into one of her breasts.

He was silenced with a warning look from the injured blonde. "It's – it's alright," she whimpered, trying to simultaneously massage her damaged foot and tuck her breast away. "I'll be fine."

"I'm *really* sorry, my darling." He knew how much she liked being called 'my darling', in a proper British accent. "Let me get you another cocktail."

He leant over and kissed Miranda on the lips.

"Mike?" she snapped, pulling away. "Have you been drinking?"

"No – er, n– well, I had a beer just now with the boys. We finished our vi– fi– financial valuation presentations this morning."

"You're drunk!"

"No – just tired. Didn't sleep last night," he explained. Then quickly added: "Working, I mean. We worked right through the night."

Miranda squinted at him with suspicious eyes through strands of fine blonde hair.

"You sure seem drunk to me."

"Look, I'm *not drunk*, OK?" he told her, rather louder than he'd meant to.

Miranda's eyes widened again, and she stared silently back at him. Suddenly, Mike was overcome with lust. Never mind her irritating questions or her silly whining; the girl looked fucking hot. Mike wanted to rip off that tiny little dress, to see her naked, to let his hands roam over her smooth brown skin, to touch those tits...

"Why don't we go to my hotel room?"

"What?"

"My hotel room. Come on. Let's go." He picked up his wallet.

"We only just got here, Mike – what are you talking about? I thought we were gonna go for dinner or something, take a walk, maybe go see a show–"

"No, let's grab a taxi and go back to my hotel," Mike suggested. He knew that girls liked a man who took control.

"Wha–"

"Come on. Let's go." He grabbed her hand and pulled her off the stool – rather a gallant gesture, he thought.

"What are you *doing*, Mike?" she asked, stamping her foot and wrenching her hand free. "I don't *wanna* go to your hotel room at four o'clock in the afternoon. I don't *wanna* spend our last night together doing what *you* always wanna do..." There were several people staring now, but Miranda didn't seem to notice. "And y'know what? I don't wanna waste any more of my time with you. You come to New York, you – you charming English *gentleman* – and you take me out, splashing your dollars around on fancy restaurants and cocktail bars, when all the time, you're thinking about the one thing *you* want from me, huh? You don't have a clue, Michael Cunningham-Reid, do you? I'm a *person,* in case you hadn't noticed, with feelings and ideas and opinions and–" Miranda seemed to have run out of words. "Oh, whatever." She flapped her hands in his face. "I'm through with you."

She stormed through the bar, weaving briskly between tables of Friday afternoon drinkers who'd been watching her performance.

Everybody, including Mike, sat silently for several seconds, hearing the traffic screech to a halt as Miranda strutted across the street.

"Jeez, you need a drink," said the barman, the first to break the silence. "Lemme fix you something strong."

"No – no, it's fine," Mike replied, stepping hastily away from the bar. "I've got to – I've got people to meet."

He marched through the roomful of dumbstruck New Yorkers and flagged down a yellow cab.

Typical, thought Mike as he watched the now-familiar street numbers flash by, heading back towards Wall Street. That was just *typical* of a stupid, blonde, American ex-model. Silly bimbo. *'You don't have a clue'?* Yeah right, Miranda. *You're* the one without a clue.

7

THE CONFERENCE PHONE was already blinking in the middle of the table when Abby crept into the meeting room. The four men glanced up briefly as she pressed the door shut, then re-focussed on their draft documents.

"Right. We're all here at this end. I've got Geoff Dodds, Rupert Larkham and Frederick Jensen with me—"

"Hi" the men chorused.

There was a muffled squawk from the little grey device.

Abby slipped into the empty seat, wondering if they'd bother to introduce her.

"OK. Let's get started."

Evidently not, then. The man in charge was Charles Kershaw, Senior Vice President in Corporate Finance. Thirty-one years old, he was one of the youngest SVPs in the firm. He was probably one of the fittest, too. In between running a succession of multi-million pound global transactions, he squeezed in thirty miles each week on the treadmill, and a minimum of two hours on the weights machines. It was a fairly safe bet that if Charles Kershaw was not at his desk, he'd be down in the office gym — any time of the day or night. Aside from his obsessive fitness regime, Kershaw had nothing to distract him from his work: no wife, no children, no friends.

"We'll start with section two. Page seventeen," he barked, flipping open his copy of the presentation.

Abby stole a glance at Kershaw's face. He was actually quite attractive, she thought, if you liked the premature grey look, and ignored the dark rings around his eyes. He had a horribly aggressive manner, but he was also very successful. She wondered whether the former was a prerequisite for the latter. Hopefully not. She'd never have the nerve to act like him.

There was a rustle of papers in the meeting room and a crackling sound from across the Atlantic.

"Just to let you know, it'll be Frederick Jensen putting together the pitchbook at this end; he's a second-year analyst here and he's worked on a couple of IPOs before."

"Hi." Frederick said curtly. The half-German analyst never said much more than one word at a time; Abby had learnt this in her first week. He obviously felt it was inefficient to waste time on niceties. Evidently, he also felt it was inefficient to waste time on his appearance, she thought, noting the light sprinkling of dandruff on each of his shoulders.

"*Hi* there Frederick," drawled one of the American bankers – Chad or Josh, according to the agenda.

"So. Page seventeen," Charles Kershaw prompted. "This section is fairly standard. We've got an introduction to the team: myself, Geoff, Rupert and Frederick at the top – representing Corporate Finance London – then Chad and Josh in Palo Alto at the bottom."

Abby noticed that her own name was not on the list. It was hardly surprising, she supposed, considering her small contribution to the project so far. Her role was to 'help Frederick prepare the pitchbook', but she didn't feel she had 'helped' him particularly. In the run-up to the conference call, she'd sat at her desk, trying to look helpful while Frederick whirled around the office, whipping out reports, flicking through drafts, making urgent-sounding phone calls, tapping through spreadsheets and rushing up to the print room. It wasn't that she hadn't wanted to do all that stuff – on the contrary; she was *dying* to get involved – it was just that whenever she'd offered her services, Frederick had looked at her blankly and said, 'It's fine.'

"I think we should overlay this onto a global map," said one of the Americans.

Geoff Dodds, the director on the deal team nodded pensively, and started making an irritating *ca-lick ca-lock ca-lick ca-lock* noise with his biro against the table. "Hmmm… Chad may be right. We've got to *differentiate* ourselves on this pitch, you know; *think outside the box*."

Abby thought it was questionable that overlaying text on a global map would serve to differentiate Cray McKinley from other banks, but she kept quiet. Geoff Dodds, she was beginning to realise, was rather odd. He was a bit like Mr PotatoHead to look at: eyes too close together, ears sticking out and a face that just slipped straight down to his neck, with no chin. He spoke in his own language – always 'raising the bar' and 'touching base' and 'kicking the tyres'.

"We can talk about graphics later," Kershaw said irritably.

Geoff looked rather put-out. "Well, it's always worth running these things up the flagpole; see if anyone salutes…"

"Yes – quite so," Kershaw nodded. "Frederick, make a note of that."

Frederick already had.

Abby pointlessly scribbled 'Map' in her notes.

"Take a look at page eighteen," said a crackly American voice. "I'm thinking we need to update it to reflect our trans-Atlantic strengths; maybe go back a few years to find some more relevant case studies."

Kershaw motioned to Frederick to make a note of that.

Frederick already had.

"Yes–" Dodds cried keenly. "We *must* leverage our core trans-Atlantic synergystic linkages, especially on the institutional side."

Abby stopped mid-scribble. 'Link core gymnastic averages,' she'd written. She wished for a moment she was Frederick Jensen.

Frederick was always right. He was a lowly second-year analyst, but he was also the golden boy of the department. Quick thinking, intelligent, diligent and thorough, Frederick Jensen was destined to make Director by the age of thirty. Abby was beginning to despise him.

"So, page twenty, everyone," prompted Kershaw, rushing them through the pitchbook. He was probably itching to go to the gym, ahead of a long night in the office.

Charles Kershaw was a workaholic. Despite his senior rank in the firm – which granted freedom to wander into the office midmorning and leave work at six – he would frequently be seen at his desk in the early hours. Last year he was reported to have come in one Friday morning and worked right through to the Sunday, then taken a cab to the start-line of the London Marathon and run it in three and a half hours. Then, it was alleged, he'd jogged back to the office, showered in the gym, and got back to the deal he'd been working on.

The page-turning continued, and the analysis became more technical. Abby kept hearing the words 'seeds', 'hedges', 'allotment', 'greenshoe' and other gardening-related terms. Her list of *things to look up on Google* was growing exponentially.

At one point, the lanky VP sitting opposite Abby whose name was Rupert Larkham made a retching noise and uttered, "Well, they're hardly going to be allocated a *smaller* proportion, if they submit via the bookrunner, are they?!"

"Ahahahahaha!" chuckled Dodds.

Kershaw let out a burst of compressed air through his lips.

"HARDLY!" cried one of the Americans.

Frederick Jensen snorted.

Abby looked around the room with a *hah – how absurd!* look on her face, then buried herself once more in the draft. She was totally lost.

Sometimes the men would exchange a smug glance or a despairing look in reaction to something coming out of the speaker-phone, but nobody would ever look at her. It was a relief to Abby when Kershaw suggested they 'wrap up', and pressed a button on the machine to make the lights go out.

The men stood up, banging their papers on the desk and clearing their throats authoritatively. Abby hung back with the intention of cornering Frederick and enquiring about her forthcoming duties, out of earshot of the senior bankers. Her plan backfired, however. As she fumbled through her pages of notes, a queue started to form just inside the door.

"Come along, come along," muttered Kershaw, wafting his papers in Abby's face.

She stumbled back into the open-plan office, and busied herself at her desk. Frederick marched past, eyes fixed firmly on the floor, scratching the back of his head. She spied on him through a gap between filing cabinets. He re-aligned his notes so that they tessellated perfectly with the other items on his desk, rattled his mouse, then proceeded to toggle between applications with alarming speed. It was incredible, seeing how quickly the android worked; his monitor was flickering like a malfunctioning TV.

Abby wondered whether it would be better to approach him now or later. Or never. It wasn't easy, this shadowing thing. Especially as her shadowee clearly didn't want to be shadowed. Frederick was only about Abby's age, yet in terms of rank, he was years ahead. He just seemed to know *everything*, and he clearly had no time for pesky little first-years trying to follow him around.

Then there was the other, more pressing issue playing on Abby's mind: not how to shadow Frederick Jensen, but *why* she was shadowing him. She desperately wanted an assignment of her own. She was intelligent and competent, and she'd been trained by the best corporate financiers in the world – or so they'd told her – *so why was nobody trusting her to do anything?* In her first three weeks in London, she'd achieved a total of about four hours' work.

Still staring at the back of Frederick's head, Abby made a decision. She wasn't going to get anywhere in Corporate Finance, she reasoned, if she didn't show how good she was. If she wanted to prove herself to the rest of the department – which she did, passionately – she would have to find herself a project. And in order to do that, she'd have to succeed in 'shadowing Frederick'.

"Hello."

He glanced up at her briefly, then stared back at the spreadsheet, impulsively touching his bald patch – *bald patch! At the age of twenty-three!* – with a bony finger. Abby stole a glance at the skin on the back of his head. It was flaky and slightly inflamed.

"I'm supposed to be helping you on this IPO project; I just wondered what I could do," she said bluntly. She'd given up being polite.

"Yah," he uttered, finally turning round and looking at Abby's feet. "I need some dividend information for the company and its peers."

Abby nodded, flabbergasted. She didn't know what to say. Not only had Frederick responded to her question, but he'd responded positively. They were virtually having a conversation!

Five minutes later, Abby was back at her desk, staring at a page of unintelligible squiggles. As far as she could tell, the gist of her instructions was: trawl through the annual reports looking for dividend information, then draw up a presentation in PowerPoint. It was, Abby knew, another Pointless Task. It was exactly like the last one, and the one before that. It was something to occupy the new girl, to keep her out of the way. 'Go and look up...', 'See what you can find in...', 'Search through all the...' It was infuriating. Her first Pointless Task had been to create a directory of 'useful contacts in London' for Geoff Dodds – essentially an exercise in copying and pasting from a telephone directory. It was a far cry from the world of fast-paced, high-level deals she'd envisaged when she'd accepted the job.

Waiting for the tree's worth of documents to print, Abby skim-read the email sitting in her inbox.

To: Cray McKinley Corporate Finance, London (all)

You will be aware that Cray McKinley is currently under-going a significant restructuring programme, centring on Europe, Middle East and Africa. As part of this programme, the Paris office will be closing down, and the employees relocated to other branches of Cray McKinley.

The following addition(s) will be made to your depart-ment, taking effect from Monday, 10th October:

Name: Mr Michael Cunningham-Reid
Level: First-Year Analyst

It is anticipated that these changes will have minimal impact on the employees of Cray McKinley. Please address any queries on this matter to Annabel Boyden, Human Resources.

Michael Cunningham-Reid. The name sounded vaguely familiar, but she couldn't put a face to the name. Michael. A French guy called Michael. Nope. She remembered Benoit and Olivier, but she couldn't remember a Michael.

Then it came to her. Mike: tall, burly with dark hair and a broken nose. The arrogant Brit with amazing eyes who'd opted to work in the Paris office. The rugby lad who'd knocked her over in their last game of basketball. Abby's heart sunk. This would not have 'minimal impact' on her at all. This would be disastrous. Mike Cunningham-Reid was an arsehole.

8

"COULD YOU TYPE these up, too, Michelle? It's pretty urgent. Give it priority over whatever you're doing."

Mike liked having a secretary. Back in the Paris office, they'd had to share Josette between all twelve members of the department, so she'd never really helped Mike during the entire month he'd been there. Come to think of it, Josette had never really helped anyone with anything, usually being too busy reading her horoscope or emailing her friends. Michelle wasn't like Josette. She was hard-working and efficient. She wasn't as attractive as some of the Parisian secretaries – in fact she was rather plain – but at least she got things done. And Mike was only sharing her with three other bankers, two of whom spent most of their time in the States.

Michelle looked up apologetically. "Sorry Mike, it's nearly five o'clock. I'm leaving in a minute. Try Tiki – she's on 'til six."

Mike tutted and walked away. He always forgot that secretaries left at five. To him, that was only halfway through the working day; the girls had barely taken off their coats, slurped the froth off their cappuccinos and logged onto Hotmail before it was time for them to go home.

"Mmmm... Mmmm," muttered Tiki, idly studying the finger-nails on the hand that wasn't holding the phone.

Tiki Morgan, unlike Michelle, was not hard-working *or* efficient.

"Mmmm..."

Mike stood by her desk, looking down on the dumpy, toad-like secretary.

"I *know*..."

He moved closer.

"No way…"

He waved the piece of paper in front of her face.

"Mmm — exactly," she muttered, absent-mindedly plucking the sheet from Mike's hand.

He leaned forwards to catch her eye.

"Oh my God…"

Without meeting Mike's gaze, Tiki laid down the paper and gave a quick thumbs-up in his direction.

He bent down and cleared his throat next to her ear.

"Mmm," she went on. "Hold on a sec, will you?" She cupped her hand over the receiver and glanced up irritably as if to say *this had better be important*. Then, on meeting Mike's gaze, Tiki's expression melted. "Oh, hi! Sorry — didn't see ya there!" she cried with a fat grin on her lips. Her fingers brushed his forearm.

"It's just typing," he said, moving his arm out of pawing range. "But it has to be done tonight. Is that gonna be OK?" He waited for her to nod, and walked off.

The presentation was coming on nicely. It was a pitch for a major UK telecoms acquisition that had just been announced. Most of the work was being carried out upstairs in M&A, Mergers and Acquisitions, but Daniel Greening, the head of Corporate Finance, was playing an important part in the pitch, and needed an analyst to work on his slides. Mike was that analyst. *After less than a week in the London office, he was working for Daniel Greening.* It was a huge responsibility, but also a great honour.

This time a week ago, Mike had been wandering down the Champs Elysées. He'd stopped to admire the twinkling lights on the banks of the River Seine, and thought about buying a print of Paris from one of the shivering artists. He'd climbed the stairs of his apartment block, and exchanged bonjours with Mme Favé for the very last time. It was frightening to think how quickly things could change. Just as Mike had started to settle into his new Parisian lifestyle, that existence had been wrenched from under his feet, and he'd been catapulted to the London office at two days' notice. It was time to forget his old routine and move on.

Mike was working on a top-level transaction for one of the most influential men in the bank, and it was only his first week. But he wasn't going to let this go to his head. It was an important project, and he had to get it right. The deadlines were tight. Greening wanted a first draft couriered out to his weekend home first thing in the morning, which meant working through the night. But Mike didn't mind; it had to be done.

"Ah, Michael Runningham!" a voice rasped. "It is Michael, isn't it?"

Mike looked up to find a sweaty face peering down at him as if he were some rare species of plant. Limp strands of ginger hair were plastered across the man's forehead.

"Er, Cunningham-Reid. Michael Cunningham-Reid. Pleased to meet you." The handshake left Mike's palm hot and clammy.

"I'm Archie," the man wheezed. "Archie Dickinson. Managing Director in Corporate Finance." He paused to draw breath. "I sit just the other side of Melissa, there—" he pointed at Michelle, who smiled subserviently back— "so you might be hearing from me when I need an associate to do—"

"I'm not an associate-" Mike explained quickly. "I'm an analyst."

"Oh – beg your pardon! I assumed you were an associate!" Archie Dickinson rolled his eyes and did something strange with his jaw so as to make his chin disappear into his neck. "Well, good thing you told me that! Oh, I remember now – you're the analyst who started in the Paris office, aren't you?"

"Yes that's right," Mike nodded, pleased that his name meant something to the MD. "I came over on Monday."

"Ah, *le gai Paris!*" cried Dickinson with a theatrical flourish. "I was over there in summer – the Cray McKinley golf weekend!"

"Oh – a company golf weekend?" Mike asked, pretending to care. He wondered whether the man would actually make it round a golf course without an oxygen tank.

"Yes yes – there's one every year! This year it's in Las Vegas! You play, do you?"

"I do, yes." Well, it was partly true; his father occasionally dragged him around the local course in Surrey with a couple of old

55

ex-RAF bufties. Mike knew how important it was to keep in with the Managing Directors.

"Well you must come along this year then!" Archie cried, slapping Mike on the back. "*Must* come along this year!"

Mike righted himself and watched the MD lumber off. *Managing Director?* The man was a blithering idiot. How could he possibly have climbed all those rungs of the ladder?

The soft, Scottish accent came through before the flash of ginger hair. Now here was a man who'd know about Archie Dickinson, thought Mike.

"Hello," said the associate, dropping a pile of papers on his desk and looking down at Mike. "Still here?"

Mike grunted and nodded unhappily. Had it been anyone else asking, he would have slipped in a comment about how much work he had on, how important his assignments were and how late he was likely to be working tonight. But Patrick didn't play games like that.

It was great sitting next to Patrick Gilligan. He was one of the only down-to-earth blokes in Corporate Finance. He was also a great source of information.

"Patrick? Can I ask you something?"

"Sure. Rights issues again?"

"Nope."

Patrick raised an eyebrow.

Mike glanced quickly over his shoulder. "*How the fuck did Archie Dickinson become an MD?*"

A little blast of air escaped out of Patrick's mouth. "Ah, yes. Good question." He sat down in his chair and pulled himself eye level with Mike. "His nephew, Andrew Dickinson, is a massive Cray McKinley shareholder in the States," he explained quietly. "He keeps his uncle in a job."

Mike nodded. That made sense.

"And now," said Patrick, rising to his feet again, "I'm off for a couple of pints with the boys. Coming?"

Mike shook his head grimly. A cold lager was exactly what he felt like right now, but there was no way he could spare the time. And right now, he wanted to know what this email was supposed to mean.

From: Graphics Department (London)
To: Cunningham-Reid, Michael (London)
Subject: C701-222-01

Please find attached your completed presentation, Job Number C701-222-01. To send this to Printing, simply forward this email to *New Jobs, Printing.*

Kind Regards,

Graphics Department
Ext. 2101
Cray McKinley International

Clearly, somebody had made a mistake. He'd already *asked* them to print his presentation – almost two hours ago – and now they appeared to be telling him it hadn't been done. Mike stared at the words as Patrick logged off. Phoning Graphics, he knew, was a waste of time. He would be put on hold for ten minutes only to be told that no operators were available, and that he should call back later. He marched out of the office and headed for the lifts.

"Hi."

The pretty young blonde on the front desk jolted and looked up.

"Could you tell me if my job is ready for collection please? Job Number C701-222-01."

The girl let out a long sigh, and typed something into her computer. She had long, multi-coloured fingernails that made a clattering noise on the keyboard.

"Hmm, that's weird," she muttered in a soft Australian accent. "I've got no record of that number on here. Sure that's the number?"

"Positive. I've just received an email saying my presentation is complete," Mike said, his confidence already waning. There were so many people working in the Printing department here that nobody seemed to know what was going on. At least in the Paris office, there'd been some collaboration between the four members of the Print team. Here, it was mayhem.

"An email? Let's have a look..." She clicked her mouse, then sat, drumming her fingernails on the desk, waiting for something to happen. "Nope, I can't see that job number here. Who was the email sent from?"

"Who?" Mike repeated, agitated. "Well, it was just an automatic email from Graphics."

"Ah – that's the problem then," the blonde replied, smiling. "This is the Print Room. Your job hasn't left Graphics yet. We're different departments."

Mike frowned. "But I specified on my original submission that I wanted it *printed* on completion!" He'd sent them the presentation two hours ago; how hard could it be to print ten copies?

"Yeah, this happens a lot," she nodded, wearing a look of false concern. "There's a procedure you have to follow. See those pink forms over there? You have to fill out one of them to get something printed, and hand it in here. Otherwise Graphics will just email you the completed file when it's done."

Mike was beginning to lose it. Didn't anyone have any common sense around here? Had they ignored his instructions? He stormed over to the rack of pink forms, and whipped one out of its slot. Filling in the boxes in huge, rounded capital letters, he thrust it towards the girl, who had resumed her noisy typing.

"Oh thanks," she mumbled without looking up. "That's great. You'll get an email from us – that's the *Printing* department – when it's ready.

"Thanks for your help," Mike muttered irritably, and strode off. His anger subsided as he marched back to the lifts. It wasn't *her* fault his work hadn't been printed. It was just one of those annoying things about working for a large company: everything was done with *procedures*.

Mike flung open the glass doors of Corporate Finance and headed back to his desk. He stared at his screensaver, wondering what to do. His encounter with the Graphics – sorry, *Printing* – woman had put him in a bad mood. He'd have to wait forty-five minutes for the first batch to be finished before he could courier it out to Greening's home in Kent.

There weren't many people around; the senior bankers had packed up and gone for the weekend, and most of the associates had slipped away too. On the far side of the room, a second-year analyst sat scratching the back of his head. He was half-German, and never had much to say. The girl was there, too. Abby – the other first-year analyst. She was sitting right behind Mike, typing with gusto – probably emailing her mates, he thought. She never did any work, as far as Mike could tell. She spent a lot of time at her desk – always there by eight in the morning and often the last one to leave – but she never seemed to be *doing* anything. Not once had Mike seen her consult a director or hand over work to an associate. He wondered how she occupied herself for fourteen hours a day.

It was obvious why Abby was here, of course. She was a statistic. Everybody knew that Cray McKinley had to keep their male:female ratio down, particularly in Corporate Finance. This girl was here to improve the gender balance. There were plenty like her all over the bank – cute, leggy, bimbos who didn't really *do* anything, but helped to boost the firm's reputation as an Equal Opportunities Employer.

The typing stopped, and Abby strode past to fetch something from the printer. Mike looked her up and down as she passed. He had to hand it to Cray McKinley; she certainly was attractive. Blonde hair, dark skin, nice bum, long legs: eye-candy. That's what she was. He remembered her from lectures in summer – the girl that everyone fancied. But there was something different about her now. In New York, she'd been annoyingly chirpy, giggling and flirting the whole bloody time. Now, she was quiet and sullen. She never smiled. Obviously the moody type.

As she passed him, Abby pulled off a sheet from her stack of print-offs, and offered it to Mike.

"Here. You might wanna look at this. It's the weekly deal-sheet. Explains what's going on in the department. You missed the Monday morning meeting, so you probably didn't get one."

Mike took the sheet and nodded. He'd actually been given a deal-sheet already by his secretary, but he didn't want to appear ungrateful. He looked up at Abby and thought about making some sort of introductory remark, but as he did so, she turned her back on him and strutted back to her desk. *Definitely* the moody type, he thought, swivelling round and dropping the page in the recycling bin. He'd met girls like her before. Girls with too much attitude and not enough intellect. Girls with hormones all over the place.

Looking warily about the office, Mike sauntered over to the photocopiers, trying not to attract attention. He leaned into the gap between the machines and pulled out a squashed blue sports bag. He'd discovered this hiding place the day before. It was handy because this part of the office was shielded from the main section by a row of frosted-glass panels. If you walked to the end of the corridor, there was a door that led straight to the second set of lifts, and you could escape from the office without being seen.

★ ★ ★

"Alright, Mike! Didn't expect to see you down here so early!" Marcus waved from one of the running machines. Mike smiled wryly at his reflection and wandered over.

"Had a bit of a 'misunderstanding' with one of the printing girls," he explained, raising his eyes to the mirrored ceiling. "Needed to vent some frustration."

"Oh, tell me about it! I dunno where they get them from, some of them. Don't know their arse from their elbow, do they?"

"Huh." Mike stepped onto the next machine, and started jabbing at buttons. He wouldn't have put it quite like that, but that was Marcus for you.

"So how're things going in your first week here?" Marcus panted as the gradient on his imaginary hill increased.

"Not too bad, actually. I'm working for Daniel Greening at the moment. Quite a big project." Mike glanced at his mate as he started to jog.

"Daniel Greening?" Marcus gasped, staring back at him. It was exactly the response Mike had hoped for. "What, the head of Corporate Finance? Fuckin' hell. That *is* big stuff. What's the deal?"

"Well, it's just a pitch at the moment," Mike said casually. "It's M&A work really, but Greening wants to help out with the book, so I'm doing his slides."

"Cor – not bad for your first week!" Marcus exclaimed. He

sounded properly impressed. "Hey listen mate, when are we gonna have that Welcome Back Mike thing we talked about?"

"Oh yeah – had a few ideas about that, actually." Mike looked at Marcus' brutish face, waiting to catch his eye. "I was thinking..."

"What?"

"Well, I was thinking we could do something a bit different."

"Different from what?"

"From getting steaming drunk in a bar then throwing up on the pavement and losing your keys in the gutter then stumbling around looking for a cab and ending up walking home and sleeping on your kitchen floor."

Marcus raised his eyebrows at Mike in the mirror. "Controversial, mate. What did you have in mind?"

"Track racing."

"Eh? As in, Formula One?"

"Yeah. You can do circuit racing at Brands Hatch in proper little cars. What d'you reckon?"

Marcus smiled, pressing a button on his machine. "I reckon it's a fucking awesome idea." He wiped his forehead and flicked off the sweat. "Expensive, but fucking awesome. It's been ages since I had a play with some decent wheels." Marcus slowed to a jog, and then launched himself backwards off the treadmill. Moving round to Mike's machine and leaning across, he added, "*Or decent bodywork.*" He tipped his head sideways.

Mike saw what he was referring to. He'd seen it already, two days before. With a slender waist and toned, tanned legs, the brunette was in her early twenties, and wearing a tight black running vest and a pair of tiny red shorts – hotpants, really – which barely covered her tight little buttocks.

Mike fiddled with the weights at the back of his machine, lingering for longer than was strictly necessary to snatch a last glimpse of the bum before lying down. He tensed his triceps, inhaled deeply, then bore the strain of the sixty-kilogram load. His evening trip to the gym made an invigorating break in his otherwise dreary routine. Weights were the hardest – but also the most satisfying – part of his regime. He always spent at least ten minutes working on his arms, chest or legs. He'd picked up the habit at university. Today, the workout seemed especially beneficial. He pressed against the metal bar, his muscles shaking under the strain. A trickle of sweat ran from his forehead into his hair, transporting away some of the stress and anxiety from his first week in London.

"See you in the canteen!" shouted Marcus as the doors slid shut.

Mike lowered the metal bar and lay on his back, panting. Yes, London was the place to be. This was where he belonged after all.

9

"HAVE A GOOD EVENING, chaps!" cried Geoff Dodds as he swaggered towards the exit, swinging his umbrella.

Abby snapped out of her daydream and looked at her watch. Six fifteen. *Lucky git.* She was beginning to understand how the system worked at Cray McKinley. Basically, the more senior you were, the fewer hours you were expected to spent in the office. Managing Directors generally wandered in at nine-thirty, and breezed out at six. Directors like Geoff worked a similar day, although occasionally they'd stay on 'til seven or eight. VPs (Vice Presidents, the next rung down on the ladder) worked a fairly standard eight-til-seven. Associates were pretty low down in the pecking order, so tended to work at least a fourteen-hour day, often more. *Analysts,* however, at the bottom of the ladder, were subject to a different set of rules altogether. As far as Abby could tell, they worked until their work was done. If that meant putting in thirty-six hours without a break, then that's what they had to do. It was just one of the facts of life for a junior investment banker. *Except, of course, if you didn't have any work.*

The printer finished whirring, and Abby lugged the wad of annual reports over to her desk.

"Nice bit of bedtime reading you've got there," quipped Jon Hargreaves, the associate-cum-comedian who sat next to Abby. She gave an obliging chuckle.

The office was emptying out now, with only the junior members of the department left. Abby preferred it like this; the senior bankers were intimidating. Although they never said anything to her out loud, she felt sure they were laughing at her. She hated the fact that Stuart Mackins, the Managing Director known for his fiery temper, had an office directly overlooking her screen, and could see every word and number she typed. He and the other MDs probably got together and discussed the junior analysts, praising the Fredericks of the department and mocking the Abbys. Today, thankfully, Mackins was long gone. He'd blustered out at about five o'clock muttering something about a ballet.

"Right, I'm off for the night. Can't stand any more sixteen-hour days in here!"

It was the comedian again. Whether or not he expected a response Abby couldn't tell, so she opted for a good-humoured grunt.

That was the other thing she'd noticed. Everybody appeared to be playing the *I-work-longer-hours-than-you* game. The bankers, particularly the junior ones, were all trying to prove how hard they were working. 'I guess my brain's not functioning too well on two hours' sleep!' they'd say. 'Not sure if I remember where I live, it's been so long since I went home!' Another way of playing the game was to send out a department-wide email in the early hours of the morning. It didn't really matter what the email said, just as long as the time-stamp showed how late you were working.

Abby's phone was ringing. She looked at the display and fixed a phoney smile on her lips.

"Hi Sean!" she cried, her voice coming out exceedingly high. "How's things?"

"Oh, alright. Tired – I didn't get to bed 'til three last night."

Oh God. Even Sean was playing the game.

"Really? You poor thing!" she sympathised. "Are you on a big deal?"

"Well, potentially big, who knows. Anyway, we're going down to eat now – coming?"

"Yep, definitely. I'll see you downstairs in two minutes."

The thought of food – and more importantly, a break from staring at her computer screen – cheered Abby up, although she knew it would be a strain seeing the boys again. Whenever they met up, she had to pretend to be the happy, bossy, fun-loving girl that everybody knew. She couldn't bear to let them see how unhappy she was right now.

She recognised the hulking figure up ahead. "Hey, Marcus!" she yelled, breaking into a run.

"Whoah! Easy!" Marcus laughed as she smacked into his shoulder.

"You heading to the canteen?"

"Yeah, damn right," he growled. "Got a long night ahead of me, if last night's anything to go by."

Marcus was playing it too.

"A late one?" she asked.

"Well, two-thirty. Not too bad. What about you? Are you on some awful Corporate Finance thing?"

"Oh, mine's alright – I haven't been kept in too late so far," she answered truthfully.

"Let's see what delicacies they have in store for us tonight," Marcus grumbled, picking up a tray.

Everybody moaned about the Cray McKinley canteen, but really, it wasn't that bad. And it was all free, of course. That was one of the perks of the job for an analyst – that and a free cab-ride home.

Avoiding, as she always did, the grease-spattered hot counter, Abby veered towards the sandwiches. It wasn't really healthy to eat sandwiches for two meals a day, but she couldn't bear the idea of battered cod with deep-fried chips after a day spent slumped at her desk. She was doing less exercise now in a week than she used to do in a day at Cambridge, and she could feel the effect on her body. Her arms, once toned from shooting goals and hitting serves, were becoming soft and weak. And her fitness was slipping, too; just running up the tube station escalators now made her breathless.

"Hey, Abby" Alan's freckly face was beaming as he beckoned her over to his table.

She glanced from Alan to Sean, then back again, torn.

"Er–" She shot an apologetic look in Sean's direction, and squeezed in next to Alan.

"How's life?" asked Danny, who was ploughing his way through a mound of mashed potato.

"Not too bad," she lied. She could hardly start moaning about her lack of work in front of her over-worked peers.

"Doing anything exciting?"

"Oh, an IPO pitch for next week – I wouldn't say 'exciting', exactly."

"Well, mine's a live deal now!" George piped up from the end of the table.

Nobody liked George. He was small and cocky, and Abby couldn't help wondering if he might have a bit of a complex about his height.

"What are you working on?" Alan asked. Someone had to.

"The GE Insurance rights issue," George replied proudly. "It was announced last week – you might've heard of it."

Nobody said anything. Of course they'd heard of it.

Alan got up to leave. "Sounds exciting. Anyway, I've gotta crack on. I'll see you around,"

"See you Alan," Abby smiled. "Hope you're not in too late. Oh–" she was distracted by the mass of curly black hair wavering at shoulder-height behind Alan. "Justine! Sit here!" she yelled, patting the empty seat.

Justine Brown was the only other girl in the year who'd gone into Corporate Finance. She was four foot nine and skinny, but what she lacked in size she made up for in personality. Abby and she had become quite close, having spent many hours together in Abby's New York hotel room, grappling with numbers and financial terms.

It felt good, all of a sudden, to be sitting in the Cray McKinley canteen at half-past seven on a Thursday night. Perhaps not as good as it would have felt to be snuggled up on the sofa watching a film with Ben, but it felt... well, OK. She almost laughed, thinking back to her earlier despair. Fancy getting that worked up over a silly project! She must have been hungry after all.

"...and anyway, he told me it was needed that afternoon–" Justine was telling her, "–even though the meeting was on Friday morning!"

"Really?" Abby tutted, and made a start on her yoghurt.

"...not that bad really, well, I guess I worked *quite* late, like four a.m. on Monday, then three a.m. on Tuesday..."

So Justine was playing the game, too.

"...promised to have it on his desk first thing Thursday, but then he told me the meeting was only next *Wednesday!*"

"Wednesday?!" Abby repeated incredulously. She wasn't really listening. Deep down, something was troubling her. Everybody, it seemed, was slogging away at high-profile client projects to meet urgent deadlines, except her. The other first-years had all been launched headfirst into the world of global mega-transactions, while Abby was stumbling along at the bottom of Corporate Finance, shadowing a second-year analyst on a dubious-looking pitch. She felt like a fraud, sitting there at the table. She didn't deserve to be there. She wasn't earning her free dinner or her taxi-ride home.

Justine finished her outrageous story and looked up expectantly for a response.

"Unbe-*liev*able, Justine." Abby shook her head. "I should head back upstairs. But see you down here tomorrow I guess!"

Justine grunted and waved goodbye with her fork.

Abby's part of the office was almost completely empty. In fact, the only person still there was Frederick Jenson, the android. He was gazing intently at a cell in his spreadsheet, scratching his flaky scalp. Abby watched him in disgust.

Slowly, without taking his eyes off the screen, and without removing his hand from the back of his head, the young man stood up. Then he tore himself away from the spreadsheet, and walked briskly towards the door.

He wouldn't be gone for long. Abby knew his routine. He would rush out of the office at high speed, and then, exactly four minutes later, he would return – again at high speed – carrying a sandwich, a flapjack and three bananas. There were two reasons, Abby presumed, why he came straight back to the office. Firstly, it meant that he didn't have to waste time eating downstairs – he could shovel the food into his mouth whilst staring at his screen. Secondly – and she guessed that this was the primary reason – *he didn't have any friends to eat with.*

She picked up the phone.

"Hi Ben, smec."

"Babe! How's things? You on your way home?"

"No. I'll be in for a while," she said grumpily.

"How long's 'a while'?"

"I don't know," she replied, wishing she did. It all depended on how long the Pointless Task was going to take.

"I've just done some food—"

"I've just eaten – sorry."

"Oh."

She could hear the disappointment in his voice, and wanted more than anything to be there with him. "I'm really sorry Ben – there's nothing I can do. I'm probably gonna be here another few hours. I wouldn't wait up if I were you."

"Hey – I'm not going to bed while you're still stuck in the office!" he protested.

Abby smiled. Ben was so sweet. "It's up to you. But I won't hold it against you if you go to sleep."

"Do you *really* have to stay so late?" he asked, sounding like a little child.

The guilt and the irritation hit Abby at once. She felt bad about the lifestyle she was inflicting on Ben, but she was cross that he just didn't seem to understand.

"Ben, I've *told* you. I wouldn't do it if I had the choice!"

He went quiet.

"I have to get the work done," she explained.

"Mmm," Ben conceded. "You are OK, though? You sound a bit stressed."

Abby smiled and shook her head. That was a typical Ben-style understatement.

"I'm fine. I'll see you in bed."

"See you Abs. Love you."

"Yeah, bye," she said quickly, as the android marched back into the office.

Abby replaced the receiver and slumped forwards, rubbing her eyes. This was getting to be a bit of a problem. Ben didn't understand how things worked at Cray McKinley. At his company, someone who stayed 'til seven p.m. would be heralded some kind of workplace hero. He thought she was *choosing* to work this late. 'You're going overboard in this new job,' he kept telling her. 'You'll make yourself ill.' She'd tried several times to explain that *all* the analysts at Cray worked this hard – that she didn't have any say in the matter. But Ben didn't get it.

Frederick Jensen strutted past Abby's desk, head down, and stormed over to his. She got back to her reports, and tried to forget he was there. The work was demoralising, particularly as the bankers on the deal were likely to toss her work in the bin without even looking at it. She was fed up with her role as Pointless Tasks Facilitator. She was wasting her time. Nobody cared about dividend information for an IPO pitch – even Abby knew that – but there was nothing she could do. She could hardly turn down the work.

By eleven o'clock, the text-boxes were swimming around on the screen in front of her, and Abby's eyes were aching. She'd finished the number-crunching and was putting the final touches to her meaningless set of slides. All of a sudden, she was desperate to leave. To walk out of the building, to rip off her clingy nylon tights, release her hair from its stupid, tidy ponytail, kick her shoes off and *run*. She didn't care where – she just wanted to run. Away from her computer, away from Corporate Finance – away from that hideous, scaly *thing* that was sitting four desks away, scratching its head and staring. After weighing up the options, however, and deciding that running around the streets of London barefoot in the dark at pub closing time was probably not a good idea, Abby settled for a Cray McKinley cab. Maybe she'd go for a run one morning. Maybe she and Ben could run together... Maybe this weekend... Maybe find a park... She was falling asleep.

10

"AROUND A HUNDRED AND TWENTY miles an hour is usually what good drivers can reach on the straights, if it's their first time racing."

Mike looked around at the other lads' faces. Marcus was nodding slowly in a way that suggested he was planning to do a lot more than a hundred and twenty. Alan was anxiously gnawing the side of his thumb, glancing between the instructor and the wall-sized circuit map. Danny, whose head was poking out of a fire-proof boiler suit that was about four sizes too large and completely obscuring his hands and feet, was mouthing the words *one hundred and twenty* in a flabbergasted way at Mike.

"There are no speed limits on the track," the instructor went on. "You can go as fast as you like. But remember what I said. There's speed, and there's stupid speed. *Don't* attempt the impossible. There *are* rubber tyres around most of the bends—" he gave Marcus a lingering look – "yes, *most* of the bends – but we'd rather we didn't have to extract you from them. Remember the rules. And listen to your instructors. They've been doing this a lot longer than you have." He paused to scan the set of eager faces before him. "OK. Off you go. The instructors are waiting by the cars. Have fun!"

After a moment's hesitation, there was a flurry of helmet donning, sleeve rolling up and in Danny's case, trouser-hoisting. Joe led the way out to the cars, looking quite the part in his snug little racing suit (the only Small, much to Danny's annoyance) and matching black gloves. Mike had a feeling that Joe was going to be irritatingly good at this. He was one of those guys who tended to be good at everything – but you couldn't resent him for it; Joe was too nice.

George was leaning over a railing in the spectators' area, looking down on the row of shiny sports cars awaiting them. He had no helmet and no boiler suit. "Enjoy," he muttered sulkily as the others jostled past. "Will do," Mike replied, grinning smugly.

George wasn't allowed to race, as he'd forgotten his driving licence – deliberately, Mike suspected. George was the sort of guy who couldn't bear to lose at anything. He was also a terrible driver – as they'd discovered when the New York hire car had mysteriously developed a dent the day George had parked it – and it was exactly his style to pay two hundred pounds for a day at Brands Hatch and then spend it sitting in the stalls, peevishly watching the others have fun.

Mike's instructor was a Frenchman called Sebastian, who spoke how Mike imagined him to drive – aggressively.

"So. You do a slow lap first, to get to know ze course. Next lap, faster. Ze next lap is when you can overtake your friends. OK?"

Mike nodded, his hand reaching down to release the handbrake.

"No." Sebastian shook his head fiercely. "Not yet." He waved his hand briskly around the Renault's interior. "You are in a very powerful vehicle. You must make sure you are comfortable before you drive."

Mike nodded. "I'm comfortable."

Sebastian shook his head again. "Seat," he barked, motioning towards Mike's seat. Mike obediently wriggled around in his seat to demonstrate that he was comfortable in his seat. He noticed Marcus' car pull away just behind them. "Mirror," Sebastian said, pointing. Mike made a show of tilting the mirror in various directions then returning it to its initial position. "Gears." Mike waggled the gearstick violently and raised his eyebrows at Sebastian, as Joe's car pulled out and zipped away.

"OK. You are ready now."

"*No shit,*" Mike muttered, under his breath. It was like his first ever driving lesson. And this part was only really the warm-up. It was a precursor to the thirty minutes that was the main point of the day: driving the one-seater. The proper racing car. This little jaunt with the instructor was just an exercise to verify that he could drive.

Mike pulled out, and found the back of his head hitting the headrest with considerable force. "Fuck!"

He eased off the gas, glancing quickly at the speedometer. Clearly this was no average Renault; they'd reached forty miles an hour in approximately two seconds.

"Powerful vehicle, I told you," said the instructor quietly.

Right, thought Mike, pressing his foot down hard once more. He'd had enough of Sebastian's condescending remarks. This was not going to be the 'slow lap' that the patronising little man was expecting.

Mike could feel his pulse rate quicken as they hurtled along the first straight, overtaking three other cars – including Marcus', Mike was pleased to note – and heading for the bend up ahead. The track was narrower than Mike had imagined. It was just like a normal road, without markings. Perhaps he was cutting it fine, overtaking so close. He could feel his body being pressed back against the seat by the g-force, his foot still firmly on the accelerator. The car hugged the road as though it were on tracks. They were travelling at over a hundred miles an hour.

"Slow down," Sebastian instructed, sounding irritatingly calm.

Mike toyed with the idea of speeding up, but was becoming increasingly aware of the right-hand bend up ahead. There were black tyre-marks all over the road where cars had spun off into the sand. This was scary stuff. Mike was determined to stay in control.

The adrenaline pumped round his body as they approached the bend, still travelling at nearly ninety miles an hour. Fuck. They weren't slowing down quickly enough. In fact, they were heading straight for the bank of red and white tyres ahead.

"Take ze outside of ze bend," Sebastian told him, still sounding perfectly placid and not at all like someone who knew he was about to die.

Mike veered to the left, his hands gripping the wheel so tightly they felt as though they were part of the steering column. They were doing seventy, and the bend was practically upon them. There was no way they'd make it round. Mike clung to the wheel, desperately treading the brake pedal into the floor and wondering what it would feel like when they slid into the bank of tyres.

"No more brake," the instructor said.

Are you fucking mad? Mike thought, continuing to brake. The bend was even sharper than he'd imagined. He found himself holding his breath as the stack of tyres zoomed towards them, looking frighteningly solid. In desperation, he released his grip on the steering wheel and yanked it round, wondering which side of the car would hit the wall first and hoping it would be Sebastian's.

"Stop braking," the instructor told him again. "You should *accelerate* out of the bend."

Out of the bend? Mike blindly released his foot from the brake and realised that they were indeed *out of the bend*. Somehow. They weren't buried in a pile of red and white tyres, or entwined in a mass of twisted metal. They were pootling along a perfectly straight stretch of road at a dignified sixty-five miles per hour, slowing down all the while. In a state of shock, Mike changed down a gear and put his foot down.

"Good," said Sebastian gruffly. "And ze next bend, you will do without my help."

Help? Mike risked a quick glance at the instructor. Was he serious? Sebastian's two-word commands had hardly *helped* Mike to navigate the bend.

Then he realised. Dual controls. The instructor had been doing all the work. Mike pulled away, vexed and determined that the rest of the circuit be executed without a single touch on the instructor's brakes. He caught sight of Joe's car up ahead, and put his foot down harder. As he did so, he felt a strange sensation in the back of his seat. A juddering. A rattle that hadn't been there before. Mike glanced across at Sebastian to see whether he was feeling it too. He wasn't showing any sign of discomfort. Shit. Maybe the car was falling apart. No – that was silly. These things were built for professional racing. They didn't just shake themselves apart.

The juddering stopped, then he felt it again. A distinct vibration, right behind his left buttock. With horror, Mike realised what it was.

"What are you doing?" Sebastian demanded, as Mike released one hand from the steering wheel.

"Oh, er, nothing." The device continued to vibrate as Mike fumbled in the folds of his boiler suit. The speedometer was reading one hundred and five.

"Both hands on ze wheel!" he yelled, just as Mike managed to retrieve the BlackBerry. He dropped it in his lap and regained his grip on the steering wheel.

"What is zat?" asked Sebastian, staring at the little grey gadget.

"Someone's trying to call me," Mike explained, easing off a little as the track curved gently to the left.

"You have your mobile phone on?!" Sebastian exploded. "You are travelling at a hundred miles an hour, and you are wanting to answer your mobile phone?!"

"It's my Black-"

"Pull over here." He jabbed at the stretch of grass alongside the track. "Now!"

Mike braked hard as the BlackBerry buzzed distractingly against his groin. He glanced at the screen. *Withheld Number* was flashing up at him ominously. Shit. This meant one thing: work.

"Well, are you going answer it?" asked Sebastian angrily.

Mike was torn. Was he going to answer it? If he did, it would almost certainly mean curtailing his weekend. If he didn't... well... If he didn't, it might mean curtailing his career. The only reason analysts were provided with BlackBerrys was so that they were contactable all the time. *All* the time. That was the deal. They'd been lectured on Communications Etiquette in their first week of training. Cray McKinley rules said that Mike had to take this call.

"Hello?"

The instructor watched him as he absorbed Charles Kershaw's words. Mike half-listened to the Senior VP's advice, his mind drifting back to the row of shiny sports cars back at the pits. They did a hundred and *fifty* on the straights...

"Yes, absolutely," he nodded into the receiver, sensing the instructor's disgusted gaze on the side of his face. "Not much, no – I can get to the office by two-thirty." His mind flicked between the slick little one-seaters and the PowerPoint pitchbook that Kershaw was referring to. "No problem," Mike said with a heavy heart and a phony smile. "I'll see you in less than an hour!"

11

ABBY FELT BEN'S HAND reach under the duvet and pull her towards him. She lay there, snuggled up against his chest with one leg hooked around his.

"Morning," he muttered into her hair.

Abby made a tired noise, and closed her eyes again. Weekends were a time for sleeping and recuperating.

"Time to get up babe."

"Not yet," came the muffled reply. "We're sleeping in."

"You'll be late," he warned.

"Uh?!" Abby started. "What day is it?"

Before Ben could answer, she wrenched off the duvet and rolled over to look at the alarm clock.

"Monday?"

"'Fraid so."

Abby felt a horrible plummeting sensation. No. It couldn't be Monday. She felt terrible. Exhausted. There was no way she could get out of bed.

It wasn't even as if she'd been partying all weekend. She hadn't consumed a single molecule of alcohol.

"Knackered?" asked Ben, rolling over and covering her with his warm body. "What time did you get in last night? I didn't even hear you."

"Dunno," Abby replied, knowing exactly what time she'd got in. It had been one-thirty, the same as every other night that week.

"Mmm, you work too hard," he said predictably, brushing a lock of hair off her face and giving her a sympathetic look.

Abby lay still, saying nothing. She felt agitated now that she knew it was Monday morning, and slightly trapped by Ben's embrace. His comments were beginning to annoy her. 'You work too hard,' 'You work too late,' 'You're never here'... He didn't understand the nature of her job.

"I hardly see you any more," he murmured, watching her face as he ran a finger lightly from her shoulder down to her waist, and up between her breasts.

She didn't move a muscle.

"And we hardly ever—"

"Ben, I'm *sorry*," she interrupted, unable to hear him say it: *And we hardly ever have sex any more*. It wasn't her fault; she was just too exhausted the whole time. "I can't help it – that's how things are at work. It's the same for everyone. Practically all the analysts were in this weekend."

Ben nodded as though he didn't believe her.

"Ben, it's *true!*" Abby told him, pushing him off her with a shoulder and sitting up in bed. "That's what it's like at Cray McKinley. I can't just leave the office at five o'clock every day like you can – I'd lose my job! And right now, I'm on a massive transaction – the first proper one I've had in eight weeks. I've gotta get it right. *That's* why I was in all weekend. Sorry."

Ben stayed where he'd been pushed, looking hurt. Abby felt a wave of guilt wash over her.

"Look, I'm *sorry*, Ben," she said imploringly. "I *wanted* to see you this weekend, but I had to get this model built for today's meeting, and I'd never've got it done in one day."

It was true. She really had to work this hard. The financial model was still nowhere near complete, and the bankers needed it by one o'clock this afternoon. Abby wasn't even sure if she'd get it done by then.

"We'll do something together next weekend," she suggested hopefully.

"I've got a hockey match in Wales."

Damn. She should have remembered that. "Sorry, yeah. Of course. Well, maybe I'll have some weeknights free," she offered, knowing full well there'd would be no chance of a clear evening for at least the next two weeks.

* * *

The westbound platform was deserted. Abby walked to the edge and looked down the track. She could just about make out the tail-lights of the District Line train shrinking into the darkness. Great. It was going to be one of those days. She had no idea when the next one might be. Stepney Green had no form of notification system – probably because any system they tried to install would be vandalised or stolen within the week. In Stepney, everything was a stealable item – even your dustbin, as Abby and Ben had discovered.

An icy cold draught was biting at her extremities. Rainwater was dribbling through the roof and spattering onto her shoes. A pigeon flapped past her face, and Abby stepped backwards, into a puddle. She shook her umbrella and dropped it onto the concrete. Next year, she told herself, they'd live somewhere nice.

The time on the swipe card machine said seven forty-five as she bleeped through the door. She was the first person in, as always. Everything was exactly as it had been six hours earlier. The combination of tinted windows and fluorescent white lighting made it impossible to tell the difference between day and night inside Corporate Finance. Not that there was much difference, for analysts.

She unlocked her workstation. There it was: her masterpiece. The product of a weekend's labour. The Project Coral financial model. Looking at it now, with fresh eyes (well, relatively), it didn't seem very substantial. A spreadsheet of formatted numbers – that was all it was. But behind the numbers were formulae, macros and a great deal of thought. And if she could just sort out this one last problem, it would be one hell of a financial model.

It didn't feel like a Monday morning. For the last two months, Monday mornings had been a time for quiet contemplation – and emailing – of the weekend's events. Silently, she would engage in raucous conversations about the hilarious antics of Friday and Saturday night. 'Does anyone remember conga-dancing into the kitchen and kidnapping the Head Chef?' 'Did Kate disappear with that Moroccan guy wearing clogs?' 'What happened to Phil during that game of Suck or Blow?'... It would keep Abby occupied for most of the morning. Today though, there were other things to think about. The senior bankers on Project Coral were leaving for their meeting at one o'clock. There was no time for mindless banter.

What was wrong with the model? The company valuation seemed totally off.

Frederick Jensen strode through the office, scowling at the floor. Now *he* was a person who'd know what was wrong. Not that she'd dream of asking him. She watched as he placed his jacket over the hook of the coat stand, checking that the folds were symmetrically arranged, then turned briskly and headed back to his desk. She wondered if he might be mildly autistic.

By eight o'clock, the office was swarming with bankers, the almighty Daniel Greening among them. "WIP meeting, people? WIP?" he bellowed, swaggering about and oozing authority.

The Work-in-Progress meeting was a weekly dose of tedium for all members of Corporate Finance. It was, as far as Abby could tell, an opportunity for the senior bankers to listen to the sound of their own voices in a room full of important men (no secretaries, obviously), and a chance for junior bankers to practice standing in respectful silence. In the seven WIP meetings Abby had attended so far, she hadn't uttered a word.

Every Monday it was the same routine. The analysts and associates would file into the conference room and loiter at the back, allowing the directors to settle around the table, pouring cups of coffee and nibbling on warm croissants. Daniel Greening would enter, welcome the group, and then make his standard joke about cost-cutting and the lack of refreshments for analysts. Everybody would titter politely, and then the meeting would commence. Each banker at the table would give a long-winded update on the state of his current transactions, which would typically degenerate into a mind-numbing story about one particular client or project, only finishing when the next person butted in.

Joining the flock of suited men, Abby headed towards the third floor meeting room. Just before they reached it, she cut sharp right and dived into the Ladies'. Nobody would notice her absence. They never noticed her presence, after all.

She looked in the mirror, killing time as she waited for the office to clear. It was a horrible sight. She looked like a figure at Madame

Tussaud's before the face had been painted on: waxy and plain. Even her hair looked waxy. It was lank, straight and dull. Abby had never seen herself like this. It was disconcerting. Was it a permanent thing? No – surely not. It was just tiredness. She'd be fine after a good night's sleep.

Lara, Abby's secretary, was alone in the office when Abby returned. She was pulling faces into a makeup mirror, applying a thick layer of plum-coloured lipstick.

"Not in the WIP meeting?" she articulated using only vowels.

"No – too much to do." Abby tried to keep the resentment out of her voice.

The lip-painting job was complete. Lara snapped shut her makeup case and swivelled round to face Abby.

"Good weekend, then?" she asked chirpily. Lara was always chirpy, even on a Monday morning.

Abby gave a vague nod, settling back down at her desk.

"Gorgeous weather, wasn't it? Real Indian summer!"

"Yeah!" Abby cried, not having the faintest idea what the weather had been like, or how an Indian summer differed from any other sort of summer.

Lara smiled brightly. "Get up to anything exciting?"

"Er, not really. Spent most of it in here, actually." Abby snarled at her computer screen.

"Oh, poor you! That's miserable. I'd better let you get on." She reached down and fished out the Sun from her handbag.

Abby was still staring at the macro when the room started filling up again. Snatches of conversations floated over to her as the men streamed past her desk.

"…ruddy good idea! <snort> Should've happened *years* ago! <wheeze>" "…choppy day in the markets, though…" "…ugly as sin – she looks like she's been run over by a tractor!" "Bloody hell no! It's the bloody *analyst* who's responsible!" "…take it to the next level! Got to keep pushing the envelope…" "The share price is holding up well despite the sliding sector-"

Something slotted into place in Abby's mind.

Share price. Share price. Project Coral. Share price. *Of course! That was it!* Suddenly, she knew what was wrong with the model. It was the share-price macro on the first sheet; it was bringing in the wrong figures from Bloomberg! She looked back at the spreadsheet. *Yes.* That was it. The share prices were all wrong! The only issue now was how to fix the macro.

"Ah, Ms Turner," droned her irritating neighbour. "You've decided that you're too important to attend the weekly WIP meeting, have you?"

Trust Jon Hargreaves to have noticed. "I – I had to press on with this," she stammered. "Did I miss anything?"

Hargreaves let out a puff of air and flashed a horrible grin. "What do *you* think? Does *anything* ever happen in Greening's meetings?"

Jon's sarcasm was wearing, but at least this time it wasn't being directed at her. It usually was. He thought he was being funny with his stupid snide remarks, but the truth was, he was really quite horrible. 'Didn't they teach you anything at Cambridge?' he'd ask. 'Why don't you stick to making tea?' 'I won't ask you to get me a sandwich – it might end up like some of your work: four hours late and completely wrong! Ahahahahaha!' Abby sometimes felt quite hurt, although she'd never let it show in the office.

"I'm sure it was inspirational, as always," she replied, smiling along with the joke. She swivelled her chair towards her desk, signalling the end of their exchange. Jon Hargreaves was tactless, irritating and childish, but he was also three years her senior. He wasn't someone she wanted to antagonise.

Visual Basic, Abby began to realise, was not as difficult as she'd imagined. It was just a simple computer programming language, like the ones she'd used at university. Within forty minutes, the macro was fixed, and her model appeared to be working. Launching her wheelie chair backwards, Abby headed for the metal filing cabinet. She opened the bottom drawer and flipped through her New York training manuals. 'Financial Modelling: Part III'. That was it.

She'd have to be stealthy, looking things up in her training notes. It wasn't something people did in the office. She felt like a schoolgirl, copying homework from an example they'd done in class. But this was Abby's first financial model; she had to get it right. And she was determined to do it on her own. There would be no crawling to Frederick Jensen or Patrick Gilligan to ask for help on this. She slipped the manual onto her desk, flicked to the appropriate page, and then buried it under a mound of papers.

"Lara?" Abby asked, a productive hour later. "Can I ask a favour?"

"Sure!" she replied, beaming. "Is it typing?"

"No – it's um, er," She always felt awkward asking Lara to do things for her. Lara was several years older than Abby, and had been at the firm for longer; it didn't seem right telling her what to do. "Have you ever put together a COFI before?"

"A coffee?" Lara laughed. "Black or white?"

"No – a COFI – a Company File of Information," Abby explained, guessing that that was a no.

"Oh, I think I might've done actually!" Lara replied, looking genuinely excited. "Is that one of those information packs with annual reports and share-price graphs and stuff?"

"Yes – that's it!" Abby nodded keenly.

Lara was great. Not only was she was helpful, efficient and bright – probably brighter than most of the people she worked for, come to think of it – but she was also keen to take on new work. "If I give you the sources, could you put together a COFI on this company?"

"Course I can!" Lara replied, gleefully snatching the paper from Abby's hand. "Leave it to me."

Turning back to her desk, Abby gave her spreadsheet a final glance, before pasting the results into her presentation. *There,* she thought proudly. *Not bad, for a first proper assignment.* It was nearly midday – she had an hour to get it printed and bound.

"Nah probs, darling," said the coarse voice at the other end of the phone. "I'll have it done in half the time. Gimme ten minutes, and it'll be wivya!"

Gary in the print room had a bit of a soft spot for Abby, and she knew it. He always made sure her jobs were given priority treatment, even when she insisted there was no need to rush. He called her up personally when her work was ready, and he often got one of the print room runners to deliver it to her desk. Abby didn't complain. He was harmless enough, and it was handy to know that her work would always be ready on time. There had to be *some* advantages to being a woman around here, she thought.

As she put the phone down, Abby heard an unpleasant wheezing sound coming from nearby. She knew what it was, even before she turned around. It was that hideous, fat, ginger MD – Archie something-or-other – the one that had mistaken her for a secretary in her first week. She looked reluctantly over her shoulder. Yes, as predicted, there was the huge, clumsy figure crawling towards her like a three-toed sloth. His trousers were held around the over-sized belly with a pair of gaudy red braces, and the white, tailored shirt did nothing to hide the sweat-patches under his arms.

"Ah, morning Andrea!" he panted, leaning against her desk for support.

Abby looked at him sourly. It had been Annie the last time, and *Audrey* before that.

"Got some letters that need typing," he gasped. "Only Melissa's not at her desk, so I thought I'd ask you–"

"Um, I'm not actually a secr–"

"Splendid, splendid. Thanks," he breathed, sticking his blotchy face in front of hers. "I think Melissa's at the doctors or something <wheeze> and I really *must* have these done this morning."

"Sorry – I'm not a–"

"Marvellous." He waddled away, grunting and spluttering.

Abby let out a loud sigh, which came out as more of a groan, and closed her eyes momentarily. Why did he assume she was a secretary? And why hadn't she had the nerve to put him straight? Abby wasn't a girl who got trampled on. What was happening to her? She heard a snigger and looked up.

Lara was shaking her head, grinning. "He won't learn," she said, reaching across for the papers. "We're all the same to him."

Abby smiled gratefully. It suddenly occurred to her that she hadn't eaten for almost twenty-four hours. No wonder she wasn't thinking straight. She had just enough time to nip to the third floor café and grab a roll while her books were printing.

She recognised the dark skin and angular jaw-line of the man ahead of her in the queue. As usual, he was wearing a well-cut suit with gold, ostentatiously large cuff-links. It was the new analyst from the Paris office.

Abby had barely spoken to the guy since he'd joined the department. Or rather, *he'd* barely spoken to *her*. She'd tried to be friendly, but he just didn't seem interested. He looked straight through her every time they passed, and when she tried to smile at him in WIP meetings, he just turned the other way. It wasn't that he was shy – Abby had seen the way he acted downstairs with the lads, and with the other men in the office – it seemed that he just had something against her.

Abby's eyes were just about level with his broad shoulders, and she felt sure he was aware of her presence, but he didn't turn round. She shifted sideways a little. She could see the profile of his chiselled features, his dented nose. There was no *way* he hadn't noticed her now. She had to say something.

"Oh – it's you!" she cried. "Hi Mike!"

He turned nonchalantly towards her, and then feigned surprise, stepping backwards and looking at Abby as though she had the bubonic plague. "Hi," he said. "How's things?"

"Good thanks," she replied, forcing a smile. "What about you?"

"Not too bad."

It was like French role-play back at school, Abby thought. "Have you got a lot of work on at the-"

"Oh – excuse me. Hi, yes. Granary bread. Stilton and chutney, no tomatoes…"

Abby bit her lip, determined to keep her cool. *What was wrong with the guy?* It happened every time. He made her feel clumsy and awkward. He was so tall and suave, standing there in his posh designer suit, undoubtedly one of Daddy's purchases, looking every bit the banker. And it wasn't just the way he dressed that annoyed her – it was the way he behaved. He was so damn cool. So cocky and self-assured. He seemed to just command respect, even from his superiors. *Bloody public-school boy,* thought Abby, staring at his dark, perfectly-waxed hair. That, she decided angrily, was the last time she made an effort with him. There would be no more begging for conversations with Michael Cunningham-Reid.

Abby returned to her desk to find a beaming Lara, holding not just eight copies of the COFI, as requested, but a stack of presentations, still warm from the print room.

"Gary called to say they were ready, so I thought I'd pick them up," Lara explained. "I think he was a bit disappointed you weren't around to do it yourself." She grinned.

"Oh, *thank you!*" Abby cried, wanting to fling her arms around Lara and give her a big hug. "Just in time!"

Lara smiled. "Hope they're alright. You'd better check them."

Lara was right. Checking presentations was one of the most important parts of an analyst's job. It was quite common to see a wad of blank sheets or upside-down pages inside. According to Cray McKinley mythology, an analyst had once lost his job for failing to spot an extra page – a page from a gay porn magazine – comb-bound in the middle of a pitchbook. "I will. Thanks, Lara," Abby replied, struggling to convey her gratitude.

She flipped through the copies one by one, scrutinising each page for errors. The books looked good, she thought, admiring the crisp quality of the professional print-work. They were flawless. And not only that, but they were *all her own work*. This was her first proper project, and she'd completed it without a scrap of help.

"Have you got those presentations for us, Abby?" snapped Mackins.

Stuart Mackins was a Managing Director. He was head of the Project Coral deal team, and he was highly volatile by nature. His explosive outbursts in meetings were almost less frightening than his bouts of excessive good humour – which happened quite often, completely out of the blue. He was short and ruddy-faced, with slicked-back auburn hair that he smoothed down the back of his neck.

"Just checking them now," she replied, increasing the pace of her page-flicking.

It was one o'clock already. The other team-members were waiting by the lifts. Mackins was standing by the door with his brief-case, and Abby could feel his impatient gaze on the back of her head. Abby's flicking became frenzied. It was a futile exercise now, anyway. There was nothing she could do to rectify a slip-up at this stage. She flipped the last copy shut and scooped up the glossy white books, hastening towards the door. Mackins was propping it open with his foot, making a *hurry-up-I'm-waiting* gesture with his hand.

"Here you go," Abby offered, trying not to look flustered.

"Right. Let's go then," said Mackins, yanking his foot out from under the door and letting it swing back in her face.

"*Any time*," she muttered under her breath, plodding back through the office.

12

STUART MACKINS STORMED into the meeting room, banged the door shut and flung his briefcase onto the floor. He threw himself into the directors' chair at the head of the table, and slumped forwards, rubbing his eyes.

"Oh God," he groaned, removing his hands from his face and blinking rapidly. "What a day."

The other two men in the room sat silently. They knew better than to cross Stuart Mackins when he was in a mood like this.

"What a day," he repeated. "What a *fucking* day."

He shook his head slowly and sat up straight, then looked around irritably for his briefcase, which was resting upside-down against the filing cabinet. Wheeling himself backwards, he snatched it up and walloped it on the table.

"Right," he said purposefully "Let's have a look at this fucking model."

He whipped out a wad of well-thumbed paper and a Cray McKinley biro, and dropped the briefcase back onto the floor. The other two men obediently opened their files.

"Shouldn't the analyst be here with us?" Charles Kershaw asked quietly. "It's her model, after all."

Mackins snorted. "Good point. Why isn't she here? Where the *hell* is she? I suppose she doesn't understand punctuality, just like she doesn't understand anything else in Corporate Finance?"

"Maybe she wasn't on the email distribution list," Kershaw suggested, hoping that the MD would calm down soon. He hated wasting time like this.

It was the third man, Patrick Gilligan, who answered their

question, talking softly and avoiding eye contact. Being only a first-year associate, Patrick didn't really have the authority to speak out in meetings like this.

"She wasn't on the list," he said. "You only sent it to Charles and myself."

Mackins ignored him and slammed his palm on the table. "*Fucking* analysts." He ran a hand through his greasy hair. "We don't need her. Let's just sort out this fucking mess."

His temper was not cooling as quickly as Charles had hoped.

"We've just sat in front of the *entire* board of directors of our *largest* client company, and told them the company they're about to acquire is worth almost *double* what it's really worth. How the *hell* are we supposed to explain that to them when we see them again next week?"

"Listen, Stuart," said Kershaw carefully. "It's not that bad. Our valuation wasn't *that* far out, and I'm sure when we explain that we were using an LBO–"

"*Exactly!* An LBO model! For Christ's sake! How do we explain to the client that we were using the *wrong fucking model*? 'Our analyst is new here, she doesn't know what she's doing'? 'Sorry, we've got idiots working on our team – hope you don't mind'? Fucking hell Charles, this is a fucking mess." He shook his head.

Patrick Gilligan stared at his notes.

Charles Kershaw had another go. "Stuart, I think you're overreacting. If we meet them next week with our *correct* valuation, and explain that today's figure was a little way off, then they won't..." he trailed off. He was treading on thin ice. Stuart Mackins was right; this was indeed a 'fucking mess'. But there was no point in dwelling on it. Charles just wanted to see the matter resolved, as quickly as possible.

"One thing's for sure," Stuart began, his voice slightly steadier. Charles looked up hopefully. Perhaps this was the start of one of Mackins' jovial spells. "We need a new analyst on the team."

"NO!" cried Charles, horrified at what Stuart was proposing. They *couldn't* strike the analyst off the team just because of a misunderstanding like this. She was only a first-year – she was bound to slip up. They couldn't just *remove* her from the team!

"We need a new analyst." The MD looked Charles in the eye. "*Someone who knows what they're doing.*"

"Look, let's just focus on the main issue here," Charles said brightly. "The valuation we've given our client, and what we're going to tell them."

"OK," Mackins conceded. "Patrick, you'll have to revise the model. Can you do that tonight?" He looked at the young Scotsman for the first time that day.

"No!" Charles butted in. "You can't get Patrick to do that. He's an associate. The analyst should do it, and she can do it under Patrick's guidance, so that she gets it—"

"Charles!" cried Stuart, exasperated, "Why are you so fucking hung-up on getting this analyst to do the model here?"

Charles Kershaw squared up to the MD. "Because it's her *job*."

There was a moment of absolute silence, and then Mackins dropped his shoulders and started to breathe heavily through his nose. His cheeks were ruddier than ever. Charles wondered how long it would be before the man had another heart attack.

"I will *not* stand for incompetence on my deal team," he growled. He was seething. "Who briefed the analyst on this project?"

The men looked at each other.

"Who briefed her?" Mackins repeated, louder this time.

"I – I told her she'd be doing the model," Patrick offered.

Mackins raised his eyebrows expectantly, waiting for more. The only sound in the room was that of his heavy breathing.

"So you told her she was going to be doing the model, but you didn't actually *brief* the girl? What, she just went ahead and did her own thing?!"

Patrick Gilligan lifted his shoulders in a nervous shrug. "I – I thought you were going to send out an email with the brief from the client."

The breathing stopped for a second. Mackins looked at the table. He had failed to send out the email. That was the crux of the matter. Mackins knew this was true, and the other two knew that he knew.

Charles Kershaw broke the silence. "Perhaps we should concentrate on the model here, rather than dwelling on what went wrong?"

"Fucking hell," muttered Mackins, shaking his head. "Let's start from scratch."

"I'm sorry?"

"I said, *let's start from scratch*. New analyst, new model, new valuation."

"But—"

"No buts."

"But it wasn't her f—"

"I said, Charles, *no buts*. Get a new analyst on the team, brief him properly on the deal, and get him to build the model by Thursday."

Patrick Gilligan risked a quick glance at Charles Kershaw. The man's expression was stony.

"*Fine,*" Kershaw grunted, looking as though the situation was anything but fine. "We'll reconvene on Thursday then."

13

MIKE STARED at his screensaver, waiting for it to dissolve. For some reason, his motivation was waning tonight. He'd provisionally said he'd meet the Edinburgh boys in town for a couple of beers, but even now, he knew he wasn't going to make it. It was always more depressing, working at night when you knew that all your mates were out having fun.

"Cheer up! It might never happen!" Jon Hargreaves cried merrily, grabbing the back of Mike's chair and spinning him round. Hargreaves thought of himself as the office joker; everybody else thought of him as the office prat. Mike gave an appropriate grunt of appreciation and swung himself back to his desk.

The IPO presentation was open on his screen, but Mike couldn't quite bring himself to look at it. He checked his hotmail account. There was one from *Big Meat* entitled 'Thick and long' and one from *Herbal Remedies* promising 'A to FF cup in less than 8 weeks'. He deleted them both and checked his Outlook. One boring email.

> From: Kershaw, Charles (London)
> To: Cunningham-Reid, Michael (London)
> Subject: Fw: Re: Project Coral
>
> Michael,
>
> Tried to catch you this evening but you weren't around. Do you have spare bandwidth at the moment?
>
>   We are looking for an analyst to work on Project Coral, and wondered whether you could assist. You would be required to build a financial model of the target under the

guidance of Patrick Gilligan.

Attached is the project brief, as sent across by the client. This should give you some idea of what is required.

Please advise either way and we can meet to discuss.

Regards,
Charles

_____

Charles Kershaw
Vice President
Corporate Finance
Cray McKinley International

Suddenly, Mike's motivation returned. He was bursting with enthusiasm. Did he have spare bandwidth? Yes – plenty! For something like Project Coral, Mike had a whole *spectrum* of bandwidth!

Project Coral was a live transaction. A client project. He hadn't yet worked on a proper deal since joining the firm two months ago. His assignments had all been silly, meaningless presentations about how great Cray McKinley was. But this, this was *real* work. He'd be meeting the client, working with directors, building models – models! He hadn't done one of them since New York! This would be Mike's opportunity to shine. In fact – yes – he could do a bit of background research for the deal tonight, and impress the socks off Charles Kershaw when they met up in the morning. Sod the presentation for Geoff Dodds. Sod the IPO book for Rupert Larkham. Sod the charts for M&A. They could wait 'til tomorrow. Right now, there were more important things to do. Mike clicked on the message.

The client brief was not attached directly; it was attached to another email that Kershaw had forwarded.

From: Mackins, Stuart (London)
To: Kershaw, Charles (London)
Subject: Re: Project Coral

Fine – go ahead and ask the new analyst. Have attached

brief from client as requested.

Suggest bringing the deadline forward to Wednesday – I know this will be tight for the analyst, but will give us an extra day to discuss prior to second meeting with client.

Thx.

Rgds,

S

Stuart Mackins
Managing Director
Corporate Finance
Cray McKinley International

Mike frowned. 'New analyst'? Was there already an analyst on Project Coral? Mike thought back to Monday's WIP meeting where the deal had been discussed. He could picture the scene with clarity: Stuart Mackins sitting next to Greening at the top of the table, his stubby fingers jabbing at flakes of croissant as he described the ins and outs of the deal. Unfortunately, Mike couldn't recall a single word he'd said. He just remembered being fixated by the way Mackins' nostrils flared as he spoke.

Who was the analyst on Project Coral? Mike clicked on the attachment, wondering whether the client brief would shed some light on the matter. With the attachment was yet another email. Mike clicked on it.

From: Kershaw, Charles (London)
To: Mackins, Stuart (London)
Subject: Project Coral

Stuart,

Further to yesterday's meeting, could you please forward me the original Project Coral brief so that I can send on to the new analyst.

I propose to ask Michael Cunningham-Reid, the new chap from the Paris office. Seems competent enough – has worked for Greening and Dodds in the last month, received favourable reviews from both. I will make sure he knows exactly what will be required of him.

Patrick has advised current analyst she is no longer required.

Charles

Charles Kershaw
Vice President
Corporate Finance
Cray McKinley International

Mike stared in amazement. This email was not meant for his eyes. *Patrick has advised current analyst she is no longer required.* Well, there was only 'she' in the department. Abby Turner. The token female. The blonde who sat behind him. Abby Turner was being kicked off the deal team.

Kicked off.

Nobody got kicked off a deal team. It just wasn't something that happened. Mike's head was teeming with questions. What had Abby done wrong? How had she made herself so unpopular? What had they said in that meeting? Why had they chosen him to take over from her on the deal? What did the project involve? If only Patrick was at his desk; he'd be able to answer them all. But Patrick was up in M&A, and probably wouldn't be back for hours.

Suddenly, Mike felt apprehensive. Would he live up to the MD's expectations? This project was a tough one – not like the ones he'd worked on so far. Financial modelling was complicated, from what he could remember; he hadn't done any since boot camp in summer. What if *he* messed up, just like Abby? Stuart Mackins was a fearsome man; he was known for throwing chairs at analysts. It was important to stay in his good books.

Twisting round, Mike glanced nonchalantly at Abby's desk. It was empty. She was probably in a meeting or upstairs in Graphics. Or perhaps she'd gone off to cry in the Ladies, he thought, feeling a pang of guilt. He was being given the opportunity to triumph where Abby had failed. She'd been removed from the team, to make way for him. He felt quite sorry for the poor girl. But no. It wasn't *his* fault she'd messed things up. She obviously hadn't been up to the job. Really, they should never have put her on the team in the first place. She hadn't been hired for her financial modelling ability; it was hardly surprising she hadn't coped.

He turned back to Kershaw's original email and hit Reply.

14

IT FELT WRONG to be coming home by tube; company taxis had become a part of her way of life. But today, Abby had left early. Six o'clock, to be exact – an outrageous departure time for a first-year analyst – but Abby didn't care. She had things on her mind. Today had been the worst day of her career so far.

She plodded wearily up the concrete steps and barged through the ticket barriers, the words from Patrick's 'little chat' still ringing in her ears. She passed through the station in a stupor, almost tripping over the pair of legs that lay across the exit.

"Sparesomechange," slurred the beggar. In a daze, Abby fished out some coins from a pocket and dropped them into his palm. She paused for a moment on the pavement. It was a clear evening, and her breath was forming clouds around her face. The sky was a rusty brown colour, glowing orange towards the horizon. Everything looked slightly blurry; her eyes were watering in the cold. Or maybe there were tears – she couldn't tell.

She turned left – the wrong direction for her flat. Abby couldn't face going home just yet. Ben would be there, and she wasn't in the mood for his cheerful twittering or his sweet, doting remarks. She needed to be on her own.

The discount stores along Mile End Road were still open, pumping out exotic tunes and smells. Abby felt little guilt about leaving work so early; she was too angry and too depressed. Shoving her hands deep into her pockets, she stomped through Stepney Green, thinking furiously.

Things had never exactly been great in the office, what with her succession of pointless tasks and lack of recognition for whatever she did, but this... *This* just topped it off. She'd actually been *removed* from the project. Patrick Gilligan had taken her aside and told her she was no longer on the team.

"Look, I know you've worked really hard on this... we do appreciate your efforts... you did everything as well as you could've..." His Scottish accent reverberated around her head. The kindness and tact of his works made her cringe almost more than their implications. It was the way Patrick had been so *nice* about everything – that was the most embarrassing part. "It's not your fault; really it's not..." Yeah right. Of course it was her fault. Why else would they remove her from the team? It was like being dumped with the 'It's not you, it's me' line. The lying made the whole thing worse. She didn't want to be fobbed off with bullshit. She wanted to know the truth. What had she done wrong? Why had they kicked her off the team? Patrick had been too bloody kind to explain.

The parade of shops came to an end, and Abby found herself walking alongside what looked like university accommodation. Silhouettes moved around in cramped, well-lit kitchens, their laughter escaping through steamed-up windows. A bunch of young lads in hoods spilt across the pavement in front of her, their Adidas stripes standing out in the darkness. On another day, Abby might have felt threatened. But today it was the youths who should have been scared.

Ignoring the wolf-whistles, she barged through the hooded gang, shooting a murderous look at the guy who dared to ask if she'd like to suck his cock. She was fuming. Today, things had really come to a head. The Project Coral episode, she knew, wasn't the real issue. Project Coral was just a tiny part of a much larger problem that had been simmering for a while. *She wasn't commanding any respect at Cray McKinley.* Nobody trusted her to do anything substantial. She'd been at the firm for over two months, and she still felt as though she hadn't really achieved anything. And when, occasionally, she did get to take on a proper assignment, she fucked it up.

A set of steps led down to the tow path of Regent's Canal. It was unlit, shielded from the streetlight by a thirty-foot high hoarding. She lingered for a moment, peering down into the gloom and trying to make out the distinction between water and gravel. Only a fool would walk down the towpath in the dark, thought Abby. People got murdered. Women got raped. A female jogger had recently been stabbed to death only a mile away.

She took one last look into the blackness, and marched down the steps. It was a risk, but today Abby wanted to take a risk. She needed to do something reckless. She was in that sort of a mood. She almost *wanted* to be attacked. Pausing to wait for her eyes to adjust, Abby headed north along the canal. It was quiet away from the road, and seemed a few degrees colder.

Why was she doing so badly at work? She was bright, articulate and well-presented. She was confident and quick to pick things up. She had everything it took to make a good investment banker – or so she'd thought. So what was she doing wrong? Why were they treating her like the work experience kid?

Was it the way she behaved? Should she try to be more serious? More jovial? More subservient? More keen? Or maybe it was the way she looked. Abby had often been told she looked young for her age; perhaps they thought she wasn't responsible enough? Maybe *that* was why she didn't get any respect from her colleagues.

Or maybe *none* of the first-year analysts commanded any respect? They were at the bottom of the ladder; perhaps they were all feeling as worthless as Abby, but nobody was admitting it? She thought about Marcus Mackenzie for a moment. And the others: Joe, Alan, Sean, Danny, George… No. They weren't feeling the least bit worthless, she could tell. They were always boasting about the deals they were working on. And then there was Mike Cunningham-Reid. *He* wasn't suffering from a lack of respect at work. *He* was a bloody superstar.

There was a creaking noise nearby. Abby stopped dead in her tracks and listened. Her heart was racing. She clenched her fists, poised to hit back at her attacker. Silence. Abby held her breath. She could hear the pulse in her chest. Then there it was again – a quiet creaking. It was getting closer. She forced herself to exhale silently, keeping her fists tense. There was a soft crunching noise, as though someone was tiptoeing towards her on the gravel. Abby moved her hands up to chin-height, and then instantly felt very silly as the pair of ducks waddled past.

It dawned on her that she was being quite stupid, wandering along an East London towpath in the dark, on her own, trapped between a canal and a patch of wasteland. Abby turned and retraced her steps at a brisker pace. As her walking quickened, so did her thinking. Something was definitely wrong. The Project Coral fiasco was proof of that. Abby was not the successful high flier that she'd expected to be – that *everybody* had expected her to be – at Cray McKinley. Perhaps it was her attitude. She was bold and assertive – as bold and assertive as it was possible to be, with such enormous egos to contend with – and she thought she'd got the friendly / professional balance just right. So what could she do to improve? Short of a sex-change, how could Abby become the Mike Cunningham-Reid of Corporate Finance?

The hum of traffic travelled across the water, getting louder as she approached the road. Suddenly, the solution came to her, crisp and clear like the night air. She knew exactly what the problem was: *She cared too much what people thought of her.* That was the difference between her and the other first-years. They didn't take insults to heart. If someone criticised Marcus Mackenzie, he'd just throw it back in their face. Or Mike. Or any of the guys, for that matter. They didn't mull over what they'd done wrong; they simply got on with the next piece of work. It was no wonder they earned respect at the firm – they *expected* respect from their colleagues. That was what Abby had to do. She had to care less about what people thought. She had to have confidence in her own ability.

She was practically jogging by the time she reached the steps, her sense of purpose restored. OK, so Project Coral had been a disaster. Abby had gone down in Stuart Mackins' estimation – and probably in Charles Kershaw's and Patrick Gilligan's, too. But she could win them back. They'd forget. There'd be other projects. And there were plenty more bankers in Corporate Finance. Who cared what those men thought?

Abby strode through Stepney Green, heading straight for the flat. She was ready to face the world again. She was ready to face Ben's gushing praise. She thought she might even be ready to face a phone call to her proud, pushy mother.

15

THE AUDITORIUM was noisy for a Wednesday evening. Mike signed the register and sauntered down the aisle.

"How's things?" he asked, sinking into the chair next to Joe, near the back.

His neighbour grunted. "Bit busy. Not bad."

"What've we got this week?"

Joe waited for Mike to look up. "We've got *Health and Safety in the Workplace*. Yeah baby, yeah!" He gave a little shimmy of mock excitement.

The minutes passed. The noise level rose. The lecturer didn't arrive. There were about a hundred analysts in the room, none of whom were the slightest bit interested in health or safety in the workplace. Mike grew impatient. He had plenty to do upstairs, and he resented this compulsory waste of an hour.

"Oi! Cunningham-Reid!" hissed Danny from the end of the row. "Have you heard the news about Justine Brown?"

Mike frowned absent-mindedly and scribbled on his notebook, trying to get his biro to work.

"You know – the short, skinny bird. Nice tits!" Danny hissed.

"I know who she is, mate. What about her?"

"She's shagging her boss!"

Mike looked up. "Really? Who?"

"Philip Oversby!"

"What – the Managing Director in Leveraged Finance?" Mike frowned. If Danny was right, then this really *was* news.

"Yes! Apparently they're at it like rabbits! Joe heard – he's in their department, aren't you Joe?"

Joe nodded tolerantly. He seemed a little subdued this evening.

"It's true!" Danny yelped. "Everyone knows!"

The other lads were watching Mike's reaction. He nodded slowly, eyebrows raised.

"Isn't Philip Oversby married?"

"Yes!" Danny hissed. "With a two-year-old kid! And apparently this isn't the first time it's happened. He's had loads of the girls here – his last secretary, two of the Graphics girls… and Kate Menzies, the blonde associate in M&A."

Mike thought for a moment about Philip Oversby. He was one of the most senior men in the firm – a Managing Director in Leveraged Finance and a close friend of William Arnold, Head of Investment Banking Europe. But he was also very ugly: tall and lanky with almost no hair. How did he have such success with women? And attractive ones, too?

"How–" A sharp pain in Mike's forehead stopped him in his tracks. He whipped round and saw a small paper aeroplane dive to the floor at his feet. Picking it up, Mike scanned the rows of analysts to locate the perpetrator. Finding no obvious suspect, he hurled the missile forcefully into the middle of the room.

The release of the plane coincided neatly with a sudden hush that fell on the auditorium. With horror, Mike watched as the projectile soared through the air in an upwards arc, then stopped, hovered, and fluttered down to the floor, landing in the middle of the aisle a few metres ahead of the oncoming speaker. Mike ducked down and set about rummaging in his bag.

The short, bespectacled speaker stepped over the offending article, keeping his head held high. He looked a bit like a mole, Mike thought, eyeing the man from between the chairs: wide forehead, beady eyes and stubby, turned-up nose.

"Welcome, analysts," the little man said from the front. "And thank you for coming down tonight."

"*Like we had any choice,*" muttered Joe.

"I'm Malcolm Snubbs, and I'm here to talk about the health and safety aspects of your work here at Cray McKinley."

"*Don't think he liked your paper aeroplane,*" Danny whispered loudly. "*Not healthy or safe enough!*"

Mike rolled his eyes. It was going to be a tedious hour.

The first mobile phone went off at twelve minutes past six, and a tall, oafish third-year crept to the back of the room, hunched over as if that would make him less conspicuous. *"What – the reports? OK, I'll be right there!"* he hissed, lumbering through the doors. Two more followed immediately after, adopting similar postures and holding similar conversations with similarly imaginary people.

"Now, you may be thinking that there are very few health risks associated with a computer-based profession such as yours..."

The analysts started texting, playing Snake and passing notes along the rows. Some of the more diligent analysts had brought work with them to the lecture, and were using headphones and fingers to block out the noise.

"Hey – what happened with Zoë last night?" Mike asked quietly. He was referring to a conversation he'd overheard between Joe and his girlfriend. The guys had been eating in the canteen when Joe had taken the call, and Mike had noticed something funny about him when he'd returned to the table.

"Oh – that." Joe shook his head as if to say 'it's not worth talking about', and then looked up, obviously changing his mind. "We've split up."

"What?!" Mike gasped, rather too loudly. The analyst in front of Joe – a greasy-haired second-year – turned round and glared at them both. Mike glared back.

"Yup, it's over. Wasn't working," Joe told him, staring morbidly at the ground.

"But mate – you were *perfect* together! How many years was it? Five? Six?"

"Eight and a half. We met when we were fourteen."

Joe stared at the ground, not blinking. His jaw was locked forwards and his lips were barely moving.

"Fuck, Joe. What happened?" Mike hissed, wishing they were somewhere else.

The greasy-haired analyst turned round again. Mike mouthed *'WHAT?'* at the guy, which did the trick.

"Oh, she didn't understand the demands of my job, I didn't understand the sacrifices she'd made... blah blah blah, the usual stuff."

"Mate, I'm sorry. Is it really over?"

"Yep. She's moved out." Joe blinked, but didn't move. Mike thought he might have seen something glisten in the corner of Joe's eye, but he didn't want to stare. Poor Joe. Zoë had been a part of his life for *eight and a half years*. That was almost longer than Mike could remember. How could something like that come to an end?

"And now," Mike heard the speaker announce, "to illustrate these points, I'm going to show you a short video."

There was a chorus of groans. Joe sighed despairingly and looked up at the ceiling. The auditorium was momentarily silent while the analysts waited for something to happen.

A woman appeared on the screen dressed in a green, flared trouser suit and platform shoes. She sat herself down in front of a bulbous monitor and began to type in a ludicrous, up-and-down manner. The camera panned across to a wiry young man with a side parting and a bushy black moustache.

Suddenly, there was a loud crashing sound as though a rhinoceros had been let loose on the set. The camera reeled back to the woman, who was now standing up, her hands raised to her cheeks, mouth wide open.

The greasy-haired analyst in front of them wriggled in his seat, dislodging the *I'm a twat* note that Joe had carefully affixed to his back. Joe scowled in frustration and turned his attention to the packet of custard creams that was being passed down the row.

The man with the moustache ran across the office towards the source of the loud noise, which turned out not to have been a rhinoceros after all, but an extremely large filing cabinet which had fallen to the ground.

Mike closed his eyes. He tried to make a list of the things he had to do back upstairs. There was the first-round pitch for Larkham, the introductory pages of that rights issue book... he was having trouble holding onto the thoughts. He drifted into a state of semi-consciousness, the dialogue washing over him like a lullaby.

His head rolled forwards and he pulled it upright. It lolled forwards. He pulled it up again. Forwards... back. Forwards... back. Forwards... back. His conversation with Joe kept replaying in his mind. *It's over... wasn't working... the usual stuff... didn't understand...*

It was gutting. Those two were *made* for each other. Joe was only half a person without Zoë.

It was obvious why they'd split up. No relationship built on fleeting contact at random hours of the night could be expected to remain intact. Not one where lives were fitted around project deadlines; where anniversary dinners were interrupted by an unexpected trip back into the office... Not one where every precious half-hour together was spent in conflict, tired and grouchy.

It was depressing. If Zoë and Joe couldn't make it, then nobody could. The piggy-faced New York analyst had been right, thought Mike, remembering back to his advice: if you have a girlfriend, dump her now.

"...hope that's given you a few things to think about," Malcolm Snubbs beamed stupidly at the sleepy audience. "And I hope you'll all pick up a *health and safety in the workplace* worksheet as you leave. Thank you for listening."

16

ABBY DIVED UNDER her desk, feeling a vibration against her foot. "*Hello?*" she hissed, aware of Jon Hargreaves' inquisitive gaze boring into the side of her head. She hated taking personal calls at work.

"Oh, hi. It's me – Justine," said a quivering voice that she didn't recognise. "Can you talk?"

The voice did sound a bit like Justine's, come to think of it – only a weak, low-wattage version.

"Sort of. Why are you calling me on my mobile? Aren't you in the office today?"

Hargreaves leaned closer, one eyebrow raised.

"Well, no, yeah," Justine stammered. "I am in the office – it's just... I had to call from a different floor – oh, it's a bit complicated. Have you eaten yet?"

Abby wiped the mayonnaise from the corner of her mouth and stopped chewing. Something seemed to be wrong. "Well, sort of."

"D'you fancy meeting for a coffee or something?" Justine asked shakily.

Something was definitely wrong. Nobody went for a coffee in the middle of the working day – especially not first-years.

Hargreaves started nodding his head at her, lips pursed, brow furrowed. Abby tilted her body away, and found herself staring straight into Geoff Dodds' groin. It was moving about in front of her, left, right, left, right, as the man spouted unintelligible crap in the direction of Jon Hargreaves.

"You and I need to touch base," he cried, making trigger-fingers and pointing them at Jon. "There's some easy meat to be had–"

Abby stole a glance at Jon, who was so busy eavesdropping on her conversation that he was oblivious to Dodds' performance.

"Yeah," muttered Abby, cradling the receiver. "Second floor café?"

Her neighbour slid closer and started nodding his head at her, frowning exaggeratedly.

"Um, could we make it somewhere else?" Justine asked pleadingly. "Starbucks or Nero?"

"...*helicopter vision*. I'm thinking: look at this thing from thirty thousand feet!"

"Sure – whatever," Abby replied, watching out of the corner of her eye as Dodds' monologue became more animated. Hargreaves still hadn't noticed him. "Let's say Nero in five. See you down there."

Abby checked her watch. Ten past one. She'd have to be quick. She had two pitches to finish by five, and things were already looking tight.

"Thanks, Ab. See you there."

The line went dead.

Weird. It was so unlike Justine to even call her up, let alone ask her for a coffee. She wasn't the type to waste time nattering.

"Hmm," said Hargreaves, his lip curling up on one side. "Working hard, are we?"

"So whaddaya say, Jonny-boy?" asked Dodds, clicking his fingers and lurching towards Jon. "Hey?"

Jon Hargreaves looked up, finally noticing the man.

"Um, er, well–"

Abby saved her work and pushed back her chair, with a quick parting glance at her neighbour. She walked briskly through the glass doors, hugging a random selection of papers against her chest as though she was going to a meeting.

★ ★ ★

There was a light drizzle in the air, so fine that it was difficult to tell whether it was actually falling or not. Justine shuffled in behind her as she pushed on the steamed-up café door.

"You OK, mate?" Abby asked.

"Yeah, fine," she muttered, her head bowed.

It was the most absurd reply she could have given. She looked anything but fine. Dark shadows ringed her small, bloodshot eyes, and her skin was wane. "Thanks for coming out."

"No probs. What're you drinking?" asked Abby, ushering her friend towards the counter.

"No – I'll buy," she said, expressionless. "Latte?"

Abby nodded. "I'll get us a table."

She perched on a stool by the window and wiped a patch in the condensation. A bus chugged past, slowing as it passed the café and blotting out what little light there was. It accelerated away, leaving a plume of smoke in its place. The looming office blocks across the road were blending in with the blotchy sky. It was on days like this that Abby hated living in London.

"Here you go." Justine plonked the coffees on the ledge, spilling some but not seeming to notice.

Abby looked at her friend's raw eyes. "So, what's up?"

Justine finally registered the question. "Oh, God..." She cringed. "I'm in a bit of a mess. I needed to talk to someone."

"Yeah, I guessed." Abby smiled sympathetically. "What is it?"

"Well," she started reluctantly. "You know the first deal I worked on – the SRL buyout?"

Abby nodded.

"Well, the deal closed two weeks ago, and..." she trailed off.

"Mmm?" Abby prompted. The clock said one twenty-five.

"Well, after the deal was done, we had the closing dinner. I wasn't supposed to be going – analysts don't usually get invited – but the associate on the deal had to go home to sleep, so Philip Oversby – he was the MD on the team – told me I should go along in his place."

Abby nodded again.

"Anyway, the dinner was at Coq d'Argent – that posh restaurant by Bank. All the clients and lawyers and bankers on the deal team were there–" Justine paused to slurp off some cappuccino froth. She was stalling for time.

"We all got a bit drunk – well, very drunk. Everyone was

wasted. But when we got up to leave, I suddenly realised I was the only girl there, and I think some of the men wanted to go to a strip club or something. They weren't gonna *say* it, but I think that's what they wanted to do."

"Fairly standard procedure," Abby nodded grimly.

"Yeah. Well, I started to say my goodbyes and walked over to the lifts in the restaurant, and Philip Oversby – he's the MD–"

"Yes, I know," Abby cut in, wishing Justine would get to the point.

"Oh. Yeah. Sorry."

There was an awkward pause.

"Well, he joined me in the lift, and said that the other men were 'doing their own thing', and would I like to go for a drink with him, just to 'see the night off?' If my boyfriend didn't mind, that was. Well, obviously I told him I didn't *have* a boyfriend, and that I'd love to go for a drink. It was a Friday night, and I didn't really feel like going home at eleven o'clock. It's not like he's a dirty old man or anything – I mean, he's my boss, right?"

Abby grimaced. It was so obvious what was coming.

"So we got in a cab, and he took me to this swanky club-type place in Mayfair. Not a club as in a nightclub – I mean a club as in… a gentleman's club. You know – old men and butlers and stuff. Well, we had a few shots at the bar there, and I suddenly felt *really drunk*. You know – when you don't trust yourself to stand up, and you feel a bit sick, and–"

Abby nodded. She knew only too well.

"I realised I was gonna have to go home. I told Philip, and he said no problem, he'd get me a cab."

Justine started stirring her coffee furiously, staring into the vortex.

"So the taxi came, and Philip opened the door for me, and then… he got in with me. I thought maybe he was gonna see me home then take the cab back to his place, but he, well…"

Justine looked around the café nervously, then lowered her voice to a whisper.

"In the back seat, he sat really close to me, and kept looking at me, sort of, weirdly. And then he put his hand on my leg – I was

106

wearing a skirt – and, well, his other hand... oh God, it was *awful*. He was touching me all over, and saying things, and kissing me – he was practically on top of me in the back of the cab–"

She looked up at Abby. "I didn't know what to do! I mean, he's my boss! I just sat there – well, *lay* there, while he put his hands up my skirt and stuff – urgh! – and *then, he got out the cab with me!*"

"At your flat?"

"*Yes!*"

Abby grimaced sympathetically. Justine was so naïve at times.

"Well, anyway, I won't go into details. It was awful. He left on Saturday morning – I pretended to be asleep, but I wasn't. I hardly slept at all, the whole night. It was horrible, hearing him breathing next to me in bed – *my* bed! – I felt so *dirty*, Abby. I wanted to *die.*"

"Did you–"

"Yes!" Justine looked close to tears. "I didn't have any choice, did I?"

"And then he stayed the whole night?"

Justine took a shaky breath. "He got dressed and crept out about six o'clock."

Abby looked at her. She was a wreck. "Does anyone else know?"

"No!" Justine gasped. "I haven't told anyone – apart from you. No, nobody knows. So you can't say a word! Please!"

"Justine," Abby replied solemnly, "I'm not stupid."

It was a wonder that Justine had kept it to herself for as long as she had, thought Abby. Two weeks was a long time to keep something like that bottled up.

"Sorry – yeah, I know." Justine clasped both hands around her mug and frowned into her latte.

Abby shook her head. "I can't believe an MD would *do* something like that."

Justine was silent.

"I mean, God, if someone found out, like if you *were* to let on, like try and press charges or anything... he could lose *everything*. He'd never get another job," she mused.

Justine glanced up nervously, then continued to squint at her coffee

Abby watched her. "Are you OK?"

She rubbed her sore eyes. "Yeah. Only…" Justine looked up apologetically. "The week after it happened, I avoided Philip completely. It was hard, 'coz he's in the corner office, right by the door. I had to use the back entrance to get to my desk, and everyone must've wondered why I was doing it, but I had to. I couldn't bear to look at him. Then he went to the States on business for a week – last week – and things went back to normal. But that's when the text-messages started."

"Text-messages? From him?" Abby hadn't realised forty year-olds were capable of text-messaging.

"Yeah. My mobile number was on the working-party list for the SRL deal, obviously. He sent one or two every day. Sometimes they were harmless, sometimes a bit flirty. But now—" she slid her phone across towards Abby– "look."

AM BACK IN UK. GET
YR WORK DONE 4 2NITE.
MEET ME @MY CLUB, 8PM.
HAVE BOOKED A RM. P

Abby stared at the message, then at Justine, then back at the message. "Oh. My. God."

"I know."

"This is really serious, Justine. He's your *boss*. He's an MD. He's like, high up in Cray McKinley. He's a powerful man. You can't mess this up, or you'll be out of a job. A *career*."

Justine snorted and gave a wry smile. "Yeah, thanks. I know."

"Sorry," Abby smiled back. Of course she knew.

They sat in silence for a moment. Abby wasn't sure what to advise. She finished her coffee and stared pensively out of the window, where a young woman was waiting to cross the road. A taxi roared past, splashing gutter-water up the woman's legs. Abby had never really agreed with the argument that the city was sexist. She'd always believed that if you were good at your job, then it made no difference what chromosomes you had.

Women were different, yes. They wore different clothes, had different skills, went about things in different ways, but it was no real disadvantage being a female at a firm like Cray McKinley. Women who filed sexual discrimination cases against their employers weren't doing anyone – particularly other women – any favours, because generally, in Abby's opinion, they'd done something to bring it upon themselves. But now, thinking about it from Justine's point of view, the whole thing suddenly seemed horribly unfair. Justine had had no choice but to open her legs to Philip Oversby. He held her career in his hands. And for the same reason, she now had no choice but to keep quiet about what had happened. Running to HR would be the quickest way out of a career in banking.

"OK," Abby said firmly, taking control.

Justine looked up at her, eyes full of hope. Her body language was changing, slowly; her shoulders were no longer hunched up around her ears.

"When did he send you that text?"

"Today – just before I called you. I don't think he's coming into the office, though. Thank God."

"Right. And the other messages – did you reply to any of them?"

She shook her head.

"Good. That's good. I think what you need to do is think up a reply to this latest message, which shows that you're not keen, but which doesn't offend him. That's the *last* thing you wanna do – offend him."

"Mmm." They sat in thoughtful silence.

"OK. How about, 'Can't meet you, have started seeing someone'?"

Justine screwed up her nose. "No – I told him I didn't have a boyfriend, and I can't just pretend to have picked one up in the last week."

"Hmm, OK."

There was another pause.

Abby sniggered. "How about, 'Would love to meet you tonight, but just remembered you're a lanky freak with a funny walk and no hair'?"

Justine smiled weakly.

"Oh, OK, I've got it!" cried Abby. "How about, 'I'm sorry, forgot to tell you – I'm a lesbian'!"

"Huh – and that's supposed to put him *off?*" For a moment, the old Justine was back.

"Good point." Abby smiled back.

They looked at each other, suddenly serious again.

"OK," said Abby. "I really have got it: 'Last time was fun,' – that makes him feel good about himself – 'but let's leave it at that.' Firm, but not rude."

"Yeah, I guess. That might do it," Justine agreed doubtfully.

"Come on. You've got to sort this out," Abby told her. "Send this, and then strut about the office as if nothing ever happened. Show him you're strong. Show him you don't care. If he gives you any more funny looks, just give him a breezy smile back, as if you don't even know who he is."

Justine sighed, and pressed *Reply*.

"Go on, Justine," Abby goaded, as her friend's finger hovered over the *Send* button. "I'm gonna sit here until you've done it."

Finally, the message was dispatched into the airwaves.

"Thanks," Justine mumbled.

"Now let's get back to the office, and you can forget about the whole affair."

Justine looked up and scowled at her.

"Sorry," Abby grinned. "Bad choice of words."

★ ★ ★

There was somebody sitting at Abby's desk when she skulked back into the office, still clutching her papers.

"Oi," she said, rattling the back of her chair. "What's wrong with *your* seat?"

Mike swivelled round, looking – Abby was surprised to observe – a little bit flustered.

"Oh. Er, sorry. My Excel – it kept – kept crashing," he stuttered.

She nodded, with a condescending smile on her face. For once, the tables were turned – now *he* was the bumbling idiot. Abby was enjoying her rare position of power.

"I had to, um, use another computer, and yours was free–" Mike ran a hand through his dark hair. For a moment, he actually looked quite sweet – all wide-eyed and blinking, like a teenager caught watching porn.

Abby glanced at the screen, mildly suspicious. It was indeed an Excel spreadsheet – not porn – though he'd minimised the worksheet so she couldn't see what he was doing.

"Do you want to swap machines for a bit?" she offered brightly, making a mental note to look at the list of recently opened files as soon as she sat back down. "I can use yours as long as PowerPoint's working on it?"

"Er, no. I'm done now, thanks. I'll – I'll just shut everything down."

Abby shrugged, and watched him as he did just that.

17

'GOOD NEWS FOR THE RETAIL SECTOR – BAD NEWS FOR THE CONSUMER'

'CRAY MCKINLEY WRAPS UP ANOTHER RETAIL DEAL'

'MACKINS DOES IT AGAIN FOR CRAY MCKINLEY'

The newswires were buzzing with updates on the merger. Mike watched in awe as they popped onto the Bloomberg screen, headline after headline.

Skimming the articles, he felt an overwhelming sense of pride, tinged with relief. Project Coral had resulted in one of the largest retail mergers the UK had ever seen, and Mike had helped to make it happen. The last four weeks had been bloody hard work and he was glad they were finally over, but he'd done a good job. Stuart Mackins was a happy man.

Mike leaned back in the chair, clasped his hands behind his head and hoisted his feet up onto the desk. Staring at the flickering screen, he allowed his eyes to glaze over. He hadn't gone to bed last night. There hadn't been much point. The whole team had been working 'til five a.m., and the announcement had hit the newswires at seven. Mike and Patrick Gilligan had stayed in the office, sleepily checking through figures together and waiting for seven o'clock to arrive.

Until about midday, Mike had been surviving on an electric, nervous energy that was fuelled by the thrill of the deal and the lack of sleep – and the four cans of Red Bull. Flitting from job to job –

printing, reading, copying, faxing – he'd been on the go all morning. But now the activity had died down, Mike was flagging. He was experiencing the afternoon wave of fatigue that always hit him after an all-nighter.

"You basking in the glory, mate?" Jon Hargreaves asked, tapping the screen with a biro as he swaggered past.

Mike gave a nod and a phoney grin, wondering when the associate had become a 'mate' of his. Yes, he *was* basking in the glory, as it happened, with every right to do so. He'd worked like a slave for the last four weeks, and deserved a few minutes to reflect on his achievement.

He was falling asleep. Mike swung his legs back down to the floor, and slumped forwards on the desk. He thought about sneaking down to the gym to take a shower. For some reason, at about three o'clock in the morning, the Cray McKinley heating system had started pumping hot, sticky air all through the department, turning Corporate Finance into a massive sauna. Even padding around in bare feet and an unbuttoned shirt, Mike had found himself sweating, and now his skin was coated in a dry, salty sheen, which was making him itch.

Patrick Gilligan stopped by the terminal to peer at the over-active newswire. He was looking remarkably bright-eyed and alert, thought Mike, considering his lack of sleep.

"You coming down to The Swan then?"

"What, *now*?" Mike looked at him incredulously. "It's four o'clock!" Nobody ever left the office before the markets closed, and analysts – well, analysts were *always* the last to leave.

"Aye, and we've just completed the largest retail merger in the history of retail mergers!" the Scotsman replied, grinning. "Grab your jacket – I'll see you there. The others have already gone down!"

Dragging himself back to his desk, Mike realised just how tired his body was. Every part of him ached: his limbs, his head, his eyes, his stomach. He wondered about the permanent damage he was doing to himself. It felt like an action re-play of his last day in New York. Mike shuddered as the memories flooded back. The noisy Wall Street bar, the drinking games, the slurred conversations, the – oh God – Danny vomiting in the pocket of the pool table, Joe throwing

113

a dart in someone's beer, then some sort of run-in with the NYPD. The combination of tiredness, hunger and alcohol was clearly a dangerous one. The Swan was not a good idea.

★ ★ ★

"Ah, you made it, Michael!" Stuart Mackins cried, running a hand through his oily hair as he looked up at Mike. "What're you drinking?"

"Oh, er, just an orange juice for now," Mike replied quietly.

"An *ORANGE JUICE?!*" he bellowed.

Men all over the pub turned and stared at Mike.

"Oh, actually," he said hastily, "I'll have a lager."

"That's more like it!" Mackins reached up and slapped him on the back.

Mike grabbed his pint and retreated as quickly as he could. Stuart Mackins was a formidable man to work for, but not the sort of person Mike hung around with out of choice. His mood-swings were exasperating. He was like a small child; one minute hurling his laptop onto the floor, the next cheerfully doling out drinks to all and sundry. He was also an alcoholic.

The Swan was a dingy little pub, but it backed straight onto the Cray McKinley building, and had pretty much become a part of the firm, like the in-house cafeterias and gift-shops. This particular afternoon, a large proportion of the clientele consisted of Project Coral team members. Charles Kershaw, the young, ambitious VP whose job it was to sit through Mackins' tantrums was standing nearby, talking aggressively with a couple of M&A bankers. Mike ventured closer.

"...exactly the point! They hadn't even *considered* flowback!"

Mike veered away, not sure he wanted to join the conversation after all. *Where was Patrick Gilligan?* He scoured the bar for a glimpse of ginger hair.

A number of balding, middle-aged men in suits were milling round Mackins at the bar. These were the clients. Among them was Martin Cooper, CEO of the newly formed entity that was now one of the largest retail conglomerates in the world. He was a powerful

114

man. Mike drifted closer and tuned in to what he was saying.

"...a deal like this, I suppose you have to work all through the night, don't you?"

Stuart Mackins laid a hand on Cooper's back and pressed his ruddy face up close. "Dear God, no," he exclaimed loudly, shaking his head. "*We* don't work all through the night! We have *analysts* to do that for us!"

The bankers and clients erupted in hearty peals of laughter, nodding and shaking their heads. Mike turned away. *Where on earth was Patrick?*

It was just as Archie Dickinson blustered into his field of vision brandishing two pints of rust-coloured liquid topped with yellow froth that Mike caught the sound of a curled 'r' above the hubbub.

"Thank God!" Mike shouted, pulling up a chair next to Patrick, who was sitting with two associates Mike vaguely recognised from M&A. "I thought I was gonna be stuck listening to Archie Dickinson's wheezing and spluttering all afternoon!"

Patrick snorted and lit a cigarette. "What's he doing here anyway?"

"Fuck knows." Mike shrugged. Patrick had a point; Archie Dickinson had made no contribution whatsoever to Project Coral.

Patrick let out a stream of grey smoke from the side of his mouth. "I wish the old fool would just hurry up and retire."

Mike nodded. He got on well with Patrick. He was quiet, for an associate, but highly competent. And a good man to work for, as Mike had discovered during his first week on the deal. Sitting next to him was another plus for Mike. Patrick was a mine of information, and unlike most people at Cray McKinley, he was willing to share it. Probably the best thing about him was the fact that he never revealed Mike's ignorance to the senior bankers – the men who mattered. In Stuart Mackins' eyes, Mike was a bright young star. He was the man who had heroically stepped in halfway through Project Coral, and hadn't put a foot wrong throughout. Nobody knew how much help he'd had from Gilligan.

Mike finished his pint and bought the next round. He was beginning to relax. It was a good feeling, knowing that the deal was over, and that he wouldn't have to go into work until Monday morning. *Monday morning!* He had a whole weekend away from the office! No more spreadsheets, no more PowerPoint slides... he wouldn't know what to do with himself.

Mike, Patrick and the M&A bankers – who were both called John – sat in the corner of the pub, supping on their pints and trying not to talk about the deal. The conversation got deeper as the men got drunker, and by beer number six, they'd solved a good number of the world's problems.

"Exac'ly! They need something t'fill page three, don't they?" slurred Tall John, trying to look Patrick in the eye.

Short John turned to Mike, looking suddenly hostile.

"What happened t'the blonde bird?"

Mike frowned, feeling strangely uncomfortable. He knew – despite the alcohol – exactly who John was talking about.

"You know – th'one that was on th'team before you!"

"Oh, her." Mike looked across at Patrick, who shot him a warning glance. Mike wasn't sure what to say. Somewhere in his muzzy, addled brain was something making him feel uneasy. "Er, well, I think she rubbed Mackins up th'wrong way... He got in one of his strops over the model, and demanded a new analyst on th'team."

"Too bad," moped John. "She was *fit*."

"Oh! I know who y'mean!" cried the other John, suddenly remembering. *"REALLY FIT!"*

Mike nodded briskly and looked around. "I'll get another round in – same again?"

"You'd better be quick," warned Patrick. "Last orders just went."

Mike squinted at his watch. Ten past eleven. They'd been down there for nearly seven hours! No wonder he felt drunk.

The pub was emptying out, and the group of Project Coral bankers had shrunk to half its original size. Leaning on the bar waving his twenty-pound note in the air, Mike felt something pulling down on one side of his body.

"You don't want another pint here, Michael! You're moving on with us, surely?" Stuart Mackins was practically hanging off Mike's shoulder, swaying backwards and forwards as he tried to focus.

Mike looked down at him. "Moving on?"

"Yes! C'mon–" he reeled closer to Mike's chest, then lurched away again, grabbing onto the bar for support. "We're going to catch a show!"

The thought of Stuart Mackins organising a group booking to go and see *The Lion King* was so bizarre that Mike burst out laughing.

Mackins looked confused for a moment, then began to chuckle himself. "Oh – you're new to this, aren't you?" Mackins swung himself closer to Mike and grinned wildly at his chin. "We're going to a club!" he explained, performing an unsightly wobbling action that caused the layers of fat to jiggle on his stumpy frame.

Mike finally understood what he meant. "Um, well," he stammered, "I was – we were – just gonna have another round here, then follow on." Mike waved his arm in a large arc to attract Patrick's attention.

"No, no, no–" Mackins protested, wagging his finger at Mike and grabbing onto his arm. "We're all leaving now – c'mon. AND TH'REST OF YOU!" he shouted over his shoulder at the three associates. The man was practically sweating alcohol through the pores in his ruddy face.

"Hey, guys!" Mike shouted over his shoulder as he was prised away from the bar. "We're going to – er–" He felt himself being guided away and pushed, head-first, through the doors of The Swan. His lasting memory, looking back, was of Patrick shaking his empty glass as if to say *where's my beer?* and of the two Johns staring gormlessly at one other.

* * *

"No – put your money away! You're not paying," Mackins scoffed, as people started fumbling in their wallets.

He delved into his pocket, pulled out a bundle of notes held together with a small silver clip, and without even counting them, stuffed half the wad into the hand of the towering doorman. The doorman flashed a brief smile at Mackins and stepped graciously aside.

Mike began to feel nervous, despite the fuzzy, warm feeling that

117

had crept up on him throughout the afternoon. He'd never been to a strip club before, and although he liked to think of himself as a bit of a lad, he found the idea rather intimidating. What would happen inside? Would he have to *do* anything? Would it be horribly vulgar? Would the girls waggle their bits in his face? Would they embarrass him? *What if he got a hard-on in front of his boss?*

Mike followed Mackins in. His attention was drawn immediately to the two silver poles, shining out of the darkness at one end of the club. Rippling against one of these poles was a platinum blonde with breasts the size of watermelons. She was wearing nothing but strategically placed scraps of black lace, which did little to hold in her magnificent tits. Mike tried not to stare.

Mackins led the other five men to a cluster of sofas and armchairs right next to stage. Mike was reassured to find that the music was just like the stuff they played in normal clubs. Dance music. He looked across at the middle-aged trio huddled on the sofa. They looked as uncomfortable as he felt. In fact, the only man who seemed at ease was Stuart Mackins, who was reclining in his chair like a Roman emperor waiting for his grapes.

"I'm Mandy," said a soft female voice. "What can I get you, Sir?"

A voluptuous brunette was standing over Mike wearing a long, low-cut, sparkling gold dress which had a slit all the way up to her left hip.

Mike swallowed. "Gin and tonic, please," he replied as smoothly as he could. He turned his attention back to the stage, where the dancer was rippling provocatively against the metal pole: shoulder, breasts, waist, hips, shoulder, breasts, waist, hips… Mike wasn't sure how long he'd been staring, but at some point the waitress returned, leaning down absurdly low to hand him his drink.

Mike reluctantly dragged his eyes off the stage, and allowed them to wander up to the girl's. She was gorgeous. A lock of brown hair was wafting across her face in the current of the air-conditioning. He found himself wanting to brush it aside – to touch her.

She was looking at him strangely.

Perhaps she *wanted* him to touch her, he thought.

She raised an eyebrow and smiled expectantly.

Mike started to smile back, then suddenly realised what she was waiting for. He fumbled around in his jacket pocket and handed over a tenner, hoping that would suffice. Was he supposed to tip, too? Should he stuff another note down her cleavage or tuck one into her knickers or something?

"Thanks," she breathed, fluttering her eyelashes and slipping sexily away.

Mike sat back in his chair. No schoolboy errors so far.

The blonde on the stage had stopped rippling, and was standing with her back to the room, legs apart, touching the pole in front of her with both hands. As the music pumped, she let her hands slither down the pole, bending at the waist and wiggling her lovely lace-clad arse at the men. Through her legs, Mike had a perfect view of her tits, which were hanging upside down, spilling out of the flimsy black garment.

Slowly, the dancer slid her hands up the pole once more and spun round, revealing those gorgeous, now totally unrestrained breasts. She stood facing the audience, completely naked except for the G-string. It seemed she was looking straight into Mike's eyes. He stared back, starting to fantasise, though he wasn't quite drunk enough to think that her gaze was significant. These girls were *trained* to make people feel special. Mike knew that. And anyway, surely she couldn't see *who* she was looking at, what with all those lights in her face?

Stuart Mackins leaned forward in his armchair and tried to tip him a wink. Mike ignored him. The girl took a small step backwards, still staring in Mike's direction, and grasped the pole behind her head. It all seemed so natural to her. She lowered her body slowly towards the ground, her hands slithering down above her as if she were handcuffed to the pole. Her legs were open wide as she crouched with her back to the metal, still staring – quite intently, or so it seemed – at Mike. Mackins let out a dirty growling noise, and tapped Mike on the elbow.

Releasing herself from her position at the base of the pole, the dancer rolled onto her hands and knees and rocked gently in time with the music. She rose gracefully to her feet and took hold of the pole again. Mike watched, awe-struck, as she proceeded to climb. Her hair swung wildly from side to side as her long legs twisted and flicked. Mike let out a contented sigh. His earlier feeling of nervousness and – what was it? Guilt? – had gone. This wasn't scary at all. And it wasn't seedy, either. It was just pleasant. Very, very pleasant.

To Mike's annoyance, someone moved in front of his armchair just as the dancer began her descent. He threw an irritable glance at the figure, and found himself helplessly staring.

Standing in front of him was a girl more striking than anyone he had ever set eyes on. Dressed in a tiny piece of silky red fabric, she had dusky skin and jet-black hair, which fell in thick waves over her shoulders. Her eyes, instead of being the dark brown colour that was natural for Indian girls, were ice-blue – obviously contact-lenses, but Mike didn't care. She was different from all the other girls in the club; skinnier, more petite – but still with a lovely pair of tits.

Mike wondered who she was. She wasn't a waitress – he could tell from the way she was standing. She was poised: long, slender arms hanging down by her sides, lean shoulders held back slightly, pushing her breasts up out of her silky little dress. Sitting back in his armchair, Mike's eyes were just about level with the girl's bronzed thighs. He wanted to reach out and stroke them.

"Hi," she said slowly, looking down at Mike with her piercing blue eyes. "I'm Rita."

Even without the heavy makeup, she would have been stunning.

"Mike," he told her, instinctively offering his hand. "Pleased to meet you."

There was a movement somewhere to his right. He sensed something edging towards him in the darkness. A bouncer. Of course. Mike had heard about the no-touching rule. He hastily withdrew his hand.

"Yeah, lovely to meet you, too," Rita replied, smiling seductively and ignoring Mike's blunder. "Have you been here before?"

Mike wasn't sure what was happening – she seemed to be chatting him up. He concentrated on looking up into the girl's eyes, despite his urge to stare at her tits.

"Um, no – not *here*, no."

"It's nice, isn't it?" she asked provocatively, tossing her long black hair off her face and letting it fall around her bare shoulders. "I like it."

Was she starting a conversation with him? Mike had presumed she worked at the club, but on second thoughts, perhaps she was just here as a guest? Mike was a good-looking guy; maybe Rita fancied him? No – that was ridiculous, he told himself, glancing at the breasts that were pressing against the thin fabric of her dress. The girl was a goddess.

"You want a dance?"

The question conjured up a vision of the pair of them sweeping across the stage together in a choreographed quickstep or Viennese waltz.

"It's ten pounds a song," she explained.

The vision disappeared, and Mike reached into his pocket again.

"Thanks," she said, rolling the note expertly and tucking it into the hem of her dress.

She moved towards Mike so that her smooth, golden thighs were only inches away from his face. Leaning forward, revealing a generous amount of cleavage, she took hold of his hands, which had been clasped in his lap. Mike did his best to stay calm, wondering what on earth was going on.

With the softest touch, she laid his hands flat on the velvet armrests, and then – to Mike's distress – gently prised his knees apart so that his thighs pressed against the sides of the chair. Mike had never felt so exposed in his life.

The beat changed. Something came on that Mike recognised – an R&B song with a heavy bass. Rita was standing right in front of his carefully parted legs. She was moving ever so slightly, rolling her hips rhythmically with the music. Mike let his eyes wander freely over her body: her long legs, her narrow waist, her smooth, toned shoulders and of course, her tits. She was unreal. The beat thumped harder, and Mike could feel the bass vibrating through the frame of his armchair.

Rita's movements became more pronounced – she was rippling from her shoulders down. With her high heels still planted between his feet, she leaned across him, and placed her hands delicately on the arm of his chair, one either side of his wrist. Mike was transfixed; she was so close he could actually smell her scent.

Rita was watching him as she teased, rolling her body in small circles right in front of his face. Moving one hand across Mike's lap – her breasts swinging so close he could actually feel the air move – she turned to the other arm of the chair, and performed the same routine, still gazing at him with her incredible eyes. Mike didn't know where to look.

Retreating from the arm of the chair, Rita swivelled slowly on her stiletto heels so that she was standing with her back to Mike. There were those thighs again – long, slim, golden thighs that looked even better from behind. Her arse was only inches from his face, rolling sexily from side to side inside the red silk. With one arm raised above her head, Rita ran her other hand all the way down her body, starting at her finger-tips and moving over her lips, lightly touching her breasts, brushing her waist and skimming the inside of her thigh. Mike willed her to turn round so he could see the full effect.

And then she did turn around. Facing her client, Rita started to play with the hem at the top of her dress. She tugged lightly at the delicate material, pulling it down, over her body. All the way. Mike watched, entranced, as she revealed first one, then both of her beautiful tits. They were even better than he'd imagined. He felt something stir. *Shit*. He was getting an erection. He didn't dare look down at his lap.

Bending towards him, Rita allowed the flimsy garment to slip right down to the ground, then stepped neatly aside, pushing the little heap away with her foot.

Rita was wearing nothing but a red G-string. Mike sat, mesmerised as she rested her hands on the arms of his chair once more, leaning towards him. Her tits were just *there,* in front of his face. Mike was desperate to put his hands back in his lap. He felt sure she could see what was happening down there. Then she lowered herself, and it was her wolf-like eyes he was staring at again.

Through the material of his shirt, Mike felt Rita's hair brush against his shoulder. She was so close. Her moist lips were almost touching his. Then suddenly she dropped away, sliding her hands off the armchair and crouching between his knees. He watched her run her fingers over her body, and saw her nipples harden. *Oh God.*

Things were definitely stirring down there.

The girl rose to her feet and turned her back on him again. For a few seconds, she let him stare at her firm, gyrating buttocks. Then, looking over her shoulder at Mike, gave a slow, deliberate pout. Stooping to pick up the little scrap of red material that was lying on the floor, she disappeared into the darkness.

18

From:	Nicky Turner
To:	Turner, Abby (London)
Subject:	Re: Happy 18th!

Hi Abby!

Thanks so much for the bday card – got it this morning. Can't WAIT to see you tonight – can you believe, the last time was back in June before you went to NY!?! Really excited about you coming up – you'll finally get to meet Richie!

Gimme a call when your train gets into Oxford – I'll come & meet you. SEE YOU LATER!!!

Nicky xxx

PS. Did I tell you I've got a college grant to cover the cost of my birthday dinner? On the grounds that it'll be a 'good bonding experience' for the year-group!!!

Abby skim-read the email and smiled. She loved her little sister. Loud, bubbly and constantly high, Nicky was like a mini-Abby. And she knew how to get what she wanted. *'Good bonding experience'?* Abby sniggered to herself.

"Particularly amusing work-related email, Abby?" asked the in-house comedian.

"It's from my sister," she replied truthfully. "It's her eighteenth today."

"Ah, I see," Jon Hargreaves nodded, eyebrows dancing up and

down. "Eighteenth, eh?" He jerked his head from side to side as if to say *would I have a chance?* "Is she fit?"

"Yes." *Not that I'd ever let you near her,* she thought. Aside from the fact that he was ten years older than Nicky, Jon was the most repellent man Abby knew.

Actually, second-most repellent man, she thought, remembering Archie Dickinson.

No – third-most. Stuart Mackins came second.

Turning back to the pitchbook on her screen, Abby continued to rearrange the logos on the final page. It was a job for Graphics really, but she had an hour to kill, so she didn't mind doing it. She reckoned she could slip away at six today. Most of the directors left early on Fridays, keen to return to their weekend homes in the country. And if anybody did remark on her early departure, well frankly, who cared? It was her sister's eighteenth birthday, and Abby was going up to celebrate.

"Hi Abby. Has your secretary gone home?"

She looked up. Michael Cunningham-Reid was towering over her, fists planted firmly on the end of her desk. She stared back at his handsome face, determined not to look intimidated.

"Lara?" she said brightly. "Yes – she just left. I'm not sure who's doing the late shift today – maybe Tiki?"

"Cool – thanks." He nodded and strode off.

Arrogant git, thought Abby, watching him march over to Tiki's desk and shake a piece of paper in her face. He treated women like dirt. Secretaries, graphics girls, printers, analysts... he talked down to them all. 'Get me the files.' 'Type this up.' 'Check how long it will take.' He was so damn *rude.* Abby found herself wondering what Mike's girlfriend was like – assuming there was one. Beautiful and pathetic, she decided. Probably one of those rich girls with a horsey-pony name – Flavia or Petunia or something. She'd wear pearl earrings and pastel-coloured dresses and–

"What's your capacity like?"

Charles Kershaw was poking his head round the meeting room door, looking in her direction with an impatient look on his face. Abby tried to think of a neutral response.

"Oh, er, well–"

"Good. Can I have a word?"

"Absolutely." She nodded. "I'll be right there."

Charles Kershaw, despite Abby's dismal performance in Project Coral, was one of the only men in the department who trusted her to do 'proper' work. He actually seemed to have a certain amount of respect for her, in fact. Admittedly his assignments were only ever last-minute, do-the-best-you-can tasks, but at least they weren't generally pitches. She picked up her notebook and grabbed a pen.

"Excellent. Now I'm sorry to do this to you on a Friday evening, but…" He rummaged around in the pile on his desk. Abby waited anxiously.

"Ah, here it is." He waved a piece of paper in the air. It looked like a print-off from a spreadsheet. "This is the list of companies. I need you to do some comps. Have you done comps before?"

Abby wondered whether it would be better to lie; the only time she'd ever done 'comps' was in New York, and she'd totally forgotten what they were. "Er, no but–"

"–but you can learn?"

"Yes – we were taught how to do–"

"Good, good. So. Here's the list. There are only a couple of tricky ones I think. Patrick Gilligan was doing this you see, but he's snowed under with Project Vesper at the moment."

"Right." Abby applied her most professional tone. "Have you got a – a template you want me to follow?"

"Template?" Kershaw gave her a strange look. Abby wished she hadn't said anything. "I think you'd better see Patrick if you have any questions," he advised, the doubt already evident in his voice. "He'll be able to help you."

"Yes of course. I will. Thanks." Abby nodded. "Um, when does this have to be done by? Monday?"

"Ah. Now this is the problem, you see. We need it by midday tomorrow."

"Tomorrow's Saturday," she pointed out. Nobody ever had Saturday deadlines – not even in this place.

Kershaw tutted. "Yes, I know. It needs to be emailed out to myself and the rest of the team – I'll give you the distribution list – sometime before midday tomorrow. We've got a conference call with the client, you see. It's all a bit of a rush."

"Oh I see," Abby replied, performing some mental arithmetic. She had a total of nineteen hours in which to complete the task, get to Oxford and attend her sister's eighteenth – in any order that worked.

"Well, I'm off now," he said, picking up his briefcase. "I'll be on my BlackBerry if you need me. Otherwise, Patrick should be around. OK?"

"Fine!" she sung. "Have a good weekend, then!"

She strutted out of the meeting room, head held high, then flung herself down at her desk.

Fuck. Staring at the print-off, Abby evaluated her options. Option number one was to finish Kershaw's assignment this evening, then hop on a train to Oxford and arrive at her sister's party just a little bit late. Realistically, that was never going to happen. This was probably eight hours' work – maybe more – and the last train to Oxford left at eleven.

The second option was to make a start on Kershaw's work, go to Oxford as planned, wake up early the next morning, travel back to the office and finish it off before midday. That would be tough, but just about possible, Abby reckoned. She'd need some guidance from the talented Mr Gilligan, but she thought she could just about do it.

Option three, which was by far the most disagreeable but also the most likely, was to miss her sister's birthday altogether and work through the night on the stupid damn project. *Why had he given it to her at five o'clock on a Friday afternoon?* He must've known about it *hours* ago! Why was it that directors had the authority to just walk out at the end of the day like that, leaving their analysts to sweat through the night? 'I'm off now!' 'I'll be on my BlackBerry!' What a *joke*. As if she'd dare call Charles Kershaw on a Saturday morning, asking for help on some comps!

"I've emailed you the distribution list, OK? Good night!" cried Kershaw as he swept through the office.

Good night? Oh, yes, it was going to be a really *good night*. A real corker of a Friday night. Abby seethed. Did he have any idea what it was like to be an analyst? Probably not. Most of the senior bankers joined the firm at VP level, missing out the gruelling years at the bottom. Charles Kershaw didn't have a clue.

Option Two, Abby decided, was the one to go for. It was ambitious, and it meant knuckling down for the next three hours, but she wanted to give it a shot. It was her sister's eighteenth, for God's sake. She *had* to make it to Oxford.

Abby texted her sister to say she'd be late, and turned to the sheet on her desk. What was a 'comp' anyway? It was another New York training manual moment. She wheeled herself backwards.

'Doing comps', it turned out, was just a fancy phrase for looking up figures in financial reports and putting them into a spreadsheet with a few formulae. Easy. There were only eleven companies on the list. Things weren't that bad after all. If she worked quickly, she calculated, she'd make it to Oxford by ten o'clock – maybe even in time for dessert.

The first comp took longer than she'd hoped. It was nearly six by the time she'd found all the figures and worked out what to do with them. Abby looked down the list and panicked. *She had to work faster.*

Half-way through the third comp, the phone rang.

"Hi Abby? It's me. Alan. You coming down to eat?"

"No – sorry. Bit stressed tonight. I'm skipping dinner."

"Oh, really? Want me to bring you something from downstairs?"

"Er, no, I'm fine thanks," she replied distractedly, one-handedly flicking through an annual report.

"Sure? It wouldn't be any trouble."

It seemed increasingly likely that Alan fancied her, Abby thought awkwardly. "Thanks, but I'm fine. I've got some, er, sandwiches that my *boyfriend* made me."

There was a slight pause at the other end. "Oh. Right. Well, see ya."

Abby felt a bit bad, but she didn't have time to worry. Looking down, she buried herself in comp number three.

By eight o'clock, Abby was nearly crying with frustration. She'd hit a brick wall. The data for the fourth comp just didn't seem to be in any of the reports. No matter how hard she looked, Abby just couldn't find the figures. She flipped the pages one more time. No –

the information just wasn't there. There was only one thing left to do.

She headed for the associate's desk. He seemed to be engrossed in something on his screen.

"Hi Patrick. Sorry to be a pain, but…" Abby waited for him to turn round. He didn't. "Could I ask for some help on these comps?"

Suddenly the young man spun round to face her with an idiotic grin on his face.

"Oh, *you're* the lucky one doing Kershaw's comps! Lucky you! Luck – laaaark – lucky you!" he cried, sounding rather like a chicken. His eyes were glistening.

Abby nodded timidly.

"I wondered who was doing them! Had to step down from that project on Monday, 'coz of *this* little baby." He pointed at his screen.

"Monday?" Abby echoed.

"Aye, Monday. Why?"

"Oh, well, it's just he only gave me the comps a couple of hours ago," she explained. "Told me it was a bit last-minute."

"Ah, that's Charlie Kershaw for you!" he cried, sniffing loudly. "Curly Charlie Kershaw! Helpful as ever! He's known about this lot all week! Now, what's the problem?"

He was on something, thought Abby. Nobody could be this happy on a Friday night without the aid of drugs.

"The Swedish company," she told him, dropping the reports onto his desk. "I can't find the figures. Their interim reports are totally different to the UK ones."

"Ah, yes," Patrick nodded energetically. "Trust the Swedes to do things differently, huh! All countries have their own ways of reporting. Now let's have a look…" He bent eagerly over the first report, looking like an archaeologist with a hunch that the pile of dung in his hands was the relics of an ancient coin collection worth several thousands of pounds.

"Ah yes, ah yes…" he murmured as he pored over the figures.

Abby watched, agog. *He was actually helping her.* That was unprecedented. Nobody ever helped anyone at Cray McKinley.

"Thank you *so much*, Patrick," she said, walking away ten minutes later with a complete set of Swedish data and a newfound faith in mankind. Cocaine or no cocaine, Patrick Gilligan was her saviour.

At nine o'clock, Abby was back in the depths of despair. There was nobody else in the office. She was tired, hungry and miserable, and she'd only just finished the fifth comp. She wasn't even half way. If she didn't leave the office now, she'd never get to Oxford before midnight.

She admitted defeat.

"Hi Nicky, it's me."

"Abby! At last! Are you at the station? Shall I come and meet you? We've just finished the main course, but I could tell them to wait a bit and—"

"No—" she cut in. "Nicky, sorry. I'm not at the station. I'm still in the office."

"What? You're still in London? You'll never make it up here if—"

"Look Nicky, I know. I'm sorry. I just can't get away. I've got this—"

"But maybe if you leave *now*," she suggested, "you could get the last train and—"

"Nicky! NO!"

The twittering voice at the other end fell silent. There was a long pause. Abby felt horrible. She'd never shouted at Nicky before.

"I'm sorry, Nick. I just—" Abby couldn't finish her sentence. Her throat was all clogged up. Her jaw was locked in the half-open position and her lip was shaking uncontrollably. She tried to speak again, but there was a lump in the back of her mouth. She sat, unblinking, waiting for the tears to start spilling down her face.

"Abs? Are you OK?" Nicky asked quietly.

Abby made a strange noise. She couldn't get past the lump.

"Abby, it's alright. I don't mind you can't come up — I know your job's really important."

Suddenly the lump was gone, and Abby could speak again. The tears were streaming down her face and dripping onto the pile of reports.

"No it's *not* alright, Nicky — it's awful! I wanted to come up to see you tonight — I haven't seen you in months, and you're my sister!

130

I haven't seen you since I started this... this *job*, and now I'm not gonna get to–" she stopped to rub her eyes, and lost the thread of her thoughts.

"Abby?"

"Oh, God, I'm sorry. It's your birthday. You shouldn't be listening to me blubbering on about my crappy life. Go and get drunk with everyone–"

"No, don't be silly. Tell me what's wrong," Nicky said sternly. Strangely, she seemed to have taken on the role of big sister.

Abby wiped her eyes again and thought for a moment. *What was wrong? What was the matter with her?* She didn't actually know.

"Don't worry about me, Nicky. I'm fine."

"Come on Abs, tell me," she urged.

Abby knew her sister was trying to help, but the truth was, the sound of her strong, familiar voice – the voice that Abby once would have recognised as her own – was making things worse. Abby and Nicky used to be so close; now they barely knew each other.

"I'm *fine*. I'm just–" *Just what?* Just *not fine at all*. She wasn't herself any more. A year ago, she'd been happy, popular, talented, successful... And now... Abby hated the person she'd become. Boring, lonely, helpless, weak... The tears were welling up in her eyes again, and the lump had returned.

"Is it Ben? Is something up between you two?"

Oh God! Ben. That was just another part of her life that had fallen apart. Their relationship was a disaster. They lived together yet they rarely spoke, and when they *did* speak it was just to argue. There was no spark between them any more, and she couldn't remember the last time they'd had sex. "No – it's not Ben–" she managed.

"Then what, Abby? I *know* there's something," Nicky persisted.

"Oh, Nicky it's everything!"

Suddenly, it all came flooding out. "It's me, it's Ben, it's work... it's everything! I'm tired. Permanently tired. And miserable! I'm *useless* at this job, Nicky. I'm not just saying that – I am. I can't do anything right, and everybody hates me. I don't wanna stay, but I don't have any choice. I'm trapped. And anyway, I'd probably be crap at anything else. I'm not *good* at anything. I can't remember the last time I did something *right*."

She took a gulp of air. "And I never get to go out any more – I don't have time. My friends don't bother calling me, 'coz I'm never around, and when I am, I'm too knackered to even talk. I'm becoming *boring,* Nicky! And I'm *sick* of pretending to be happy when I'm not. Mum and everyone - they think I'm some sort of 'high flier', when actually I spend most of my time doing pissy little projects that don't even get looked at!"

She couldn't stop herself. "I don't have *any* life outside work – I don't even have time to *think!* I'm always here! Always in the office! I *hate it!* I *hate* this place, and I hate the people. They're all horrible. I don't fit in. I feel shit. And I look shit, too. I haven't done any sport for *weeks,* Nicky – I haven't even had time to go for a run! It's awful – and now I'm stuck in this shitty office, faffing about with an Excel spreadsheet when I should be in Oxford with *you!*"

There was a moment's silence, then Nicky made a *phhhhhhh* noise down the phone that sounded like a breathing exercise at the end of a yoga class. "You done now?" she asked. Abby could tell she was smiling.

"Yeah. Thanks." Abby smiled too. "I'm done now."

"Good. Sounds like we've got things to talk about. I'm gonna go and eat my dessert, now – and yours, come to think of it – but give me a call soon, Abby, when you get a chance."

"I will. Thanks Nick. Thanks."

"Will you stop saying 'thanks' alright?!"

"OK – sorry." Abby wiped the tears from her face.

"And that!" yelled Nicky. "Stop saying 'sorry', too!"

"Sorry – argh!" Now she was laughing. "I'll speak to you soon, Nick. Happy birthday."

19

BOLLOCKS, THOUGHT MIKE, looking around the empty office. This was not how he'd intended to spend his day. He'd been looking forward to this for weeks – a Saturday afternoon and night on the lash. He hadn't seen some of the Edinburgh boys since uni.

A year ago, Saturday had been his favourite day of the week. He would wake up at nine or thereabouts, lie around having lazy sex with whichever girl was in his bed, shower, eat, and jog to the clubhouse. Most weeks, he'd walk off the pitch victorious, but either way, he'd spend the afternoon drinking in the clubhouse bar. Now *that* was what Saturdays were for.

It was nearly midnight. They'd be somewhere in Soho now – Mike had no idea where. He'd tried calling them several times, but been greeted with a succession of voicemail bleeps. They wouldn't be picking up now; they'd probably be too drunk to hear their phones – let alone know how to operate them.

Mike half-heartedly dialled Chris' number again. Of all the boys, his old schoolmate was the one most likely to pick up. If there was anyone remotely coherent at this hour, it would be the reliable Christopher Lloyd.

Voicemail.

Mike banged his phone down on the desk. He was never going to find them. The lads would be rolling about in each others' arms, singing the night away in some crowded bar. They would have been drinking for nearly eight hours; it would have been pointless to try and play catch-up – even if he could track them down. Slowly and angrily, he logged off and swept his old drafts into the bin.

Damn this fucking job, he thought for the very first time. Up until now, he'd only ever been mildly annoyed by having to miss nights out. But now, he actually felt resentful. He hated Cray McKinley.

It had been a fucking long day, and Mike was dying for a beer. Who could he call? His flat mate Jack was away, and the Edinburgh lads were a lost cause… who else? Some of the other first-years had been working today – he'd seen them at lunchtime. He tried Marcus. Voicemail.

He tried Danny. Voicemail. Perhaps he should just head into town on his own? Mike was torn. The idea of an ice-cold pint of lager was very tempting, but the thought of drinking it alone in a bar, surrounded by drunks on a Saturday night, was not. He tried Joe. Voicemail.

This was getting embarrassing. Did he *have* any friends in London? Lifting his jacket from the back of the chair, he realised there was one other option. It was walking towards him, laden down with a stack of freshly-printed pitchbooks.

"Huh. Still here then," he grunted in Abby's direction.

"Oh yes! So I am!" she cried, looking down at her body as if surprised to find it there.

Mike ignored her sarcasm. "You done for the day?"

"Yeah. *Finally*," she muttered, dropping the presentations onto her desk. "It's been a shit one. I'm outta here – need a drink."

Mike hesitated. What did that mean? Did she already have plans for the night? Was she suggesting they go for one together? She was unpredictable, this girl. Sometimes she was as sweet as honey, other times – like now – she was a sarky bitch. He wasn't sure he could bear the humiliation of being turned down for a casual drink. Although, he really fancied a beer…

No, thought Mike, he'd just go home and go to bed, and forget this day ever happened.

"What about you?" Abby asked brightly. "Are you done?"

Friendliness, all of a sudden! The girl was schizophrenic. "Er, I guess – um, yeah." So how about a quick pint on the way home? *Go on – say it.*

"You don't sound very sure about that," she laughed.

"Well–" God, she was irritating. Why was he justifying himself to her? "I just, I'm, er, I'm supposed to be meeting mates in town and I don't know if I really want to. They're all gonna be pissed."

"Oh, right, I see." Abby nodded slowly.

They looked at each other.

"So, I might just grab a beer in Soho anyway—" *Oh, what the hell.* "D'you fancy a quick drink on your way home?"

"Yeah, why not?" Abby replied lightly, zipping up her little bag and swinging it onto her shoulder.

Mike stopped fumbling in his pocket and looked up. *Unbelievable.* She was actually smiling.

"Cool," he said flatly. "Let's get a cab then."

★ ★ ★

"Cheers!" Abby shouted above the din.

Mike reluctantly chinked his glass against hers. He was already regretting his choice of drinking buddy.

"Have you been here before?" she asked. She made it sound as though they were in one of London's most exclusive night spots.

Mike looked around him disdainfully. "No," he sneered. A gaggle of drunken women trooped past beneath a beer-stained wedding veil.

Abby grinned. "What – don't say it like that. It's cool. I love the Sports Café!"

"Abby," he said patiently. "The music is shit, the beer tastes like piss and the people—" he waved his hand in the air just as a pair of spotty lads in Burberry caps happened to stumble through the door – "well, look. It most definitely is not 'cool'."

Abby shook her head, still grinning. "You're such a snob, Michael *Cunningham-Reid.*"

He shrugged. He didn't care what she thought of him. One more drink, and he was out of here.

"And anyway," Abby went on. "I didn't hear *you* come up with a better suggestion."

"Look, if it hadn't been half past twelve on a Saturday night, I would've taken you to my club," Mike replied. "But I'm not sure when they lock the doors." *And I'm not sure how well you'd fit in there,* he nearly added.

Abby screwed up her nose. "Your *club*?"

He instantly wished he hadn't mentioned it. "Well, not mine personally, but I'm a member. Adam Street Club."

"Where's that?"

He looked at Abby. "Er, Adam Street?"

She glared at him. "Yeah, thanks Mike. I guessed that much. I meant, *where's Adam Street*?"

"Just off the Strand."

"So how d'you become a member of *Adam Street Club*?"

He looked at her carefully. She was clearly taking the piss. "Recommendations from other members. School friends, in my case."

Abby nodded slowly. "That figures," she said.

"What d'you mean, 'That figures'?"

"Bloody old boys' network." She tutted. "Which school did you go to?"

"Wellington," he replied sheepishly, wishing for the first time in his life that he'd attended an East London comprehensive.

Abby rolled her eyes up to the ceiling and took a long swig of beer. She was really beginning to annoy him now.

"Come on," said Abby, planting her now-empty glass on the table. "Drink up."

Mike reluctantly lifted his pint, but was instantly distracted by the commotion on the other side of the bar. Six men in their early twenties were clambering onto a table by the window, tugging and twisting at each others' beer-stained shirts in an attempt to winch themselves up.

For a moment, Mike felt sure he was looking at his Edinburgh rugby mates, but closer scrutiny revealed otherwise. The first man to secure his position on the table let out an almighty roar, and started beating his chest like Tarzan. Then, with his back to the window, he looked down and started to fiddle with the buckle on his jeans. Mike shook his head. He knew exactly what was coming.

"That'll go down well with the bouncers," Abby noted calmly, motioning to the two well-tattooed giants guarding the entrance to the bar.

Mike watched with a deliberately scathingly expression as the smallest of the drunkards fell forwards into the window, trousers at half-mast, leaving smeary marks on the glass and landing in a little heap on the floor. It was interesting to observe the spectacle from a sober viewpoint, thought Mike. Pulling moonies at innocent passers-by had been one of his favourite occupations back at university; the rugby lads did it all the time. Suddenly, Mike felt rather ashamed.

"Uh-oh." Abby nodded towards the doorway.

The reverberations had roused the bouncers. The shorter skinhead was swaggering purposefully towards the table of lads, who began to jump ship. Bodies were flying everywhere. One of the mooners had crowd-surfed his way to safety, landing on a pair of middle-aged women. Another had tried to hop onto a neighbouring table, misjudging the distance and finding himself soaking up a waterfall of beer.

"What makes guys *do* that sort of thing?" Abby asked, shaking her head and staring incredulously at the spectacle.

"Ah, it's beyond me," said Mike, also shaking his head. "Absolute idiots."

She squinted at him, and drew her head back. "Are you telling me you've never pulled a moony?"

"Me?" asked Mike, frowning indignantly.

"No, I guess you didn't," she replied flatly. She sounded almost disappointed. "I'll go get that beer."

Mike started on his second pint, and sat trying to think of something to talk about. Abby was obviously doing the same. Ten seconds passed, and they simultaneously took another sip of beer. Mike played with the condensation on the outside of his glass. It was strange. He didn't usually have difficulty chatting to girls. He took another swig, and wondered if he were desperate enough to talk about work.

"So. You play rugby, then?" asked Abby finally.

"Did," he corrected. "Don't get the chance any more."

Abby nodded.

They listened to the din around them.

"How d'you know I played?" he asked, mainly for something to say.

She looked at him. "Mike, you went to Wellington. You're friends with Marcus. You have a broken nose. You're built like a—" She reached out as if to touch his shoulder, then faltered, and withdrew her hand. "Well, you are the archetypal rugger-bugger."

He shrugged, pretending he couldn't care less. Trust her to bring up the broken nose.

"I tried rugby once," she said.

Mike nearly spat his mouthful back into the glass. "You?!"

She shrugged. "Yeah. Why?"

He swallowed his beer. "No offence, Abby, but you're not exactly made for rugby. You're…" he looked down her figure, lingering on her gazelle-like legs.

"Yeah, maybe. Wasn't very good, anyway," she went on. "I kept trying to pass the ball forwards, like in basketball."

"Basketball?" he repeated, reluctantly lifting his gaze from her legs.

"Yes – *basketball*. You know – the game where you have to put the big orange thing in the round metal hoop? I believe you played it once in New York?"

Mike snorted. Her sarcasm was already wearing thin.

"I played at uni," she said.

Ah, thought Mike. *Uni.* Now here was a subject he'd been meaning to bring up. Abby had studied physics, apparently – although where, he didn't know. Physics. She must've had universities *begging* to take her on. Physics was one of the most male-dominated subjects there was; universities were desperate to take on more women. No doubt Abby Turner had been the token female on her course, just like she was the token female at work.

"Which uni did you go to?" he asked casually.

Abby took a sip of beer and mumbled something into her glass. "Sorry?"

She lowered her glass and muttered something that sounded like 'Cambridge'.

Cambridge? Could she really have gone to Cambridge University? Then Mike remembered: there were two 'universities' in Cambridge. He nodded and smiled understandingly.

Abby looked embarrassed. *Rightly so,* thought Mike. *Cambridge*

University indeed! She probably played that game every time.

"What about you?" she asked quickly. "Where were you?"

"Edinburgh."

"Oh – I *love* Edinburgh!" she trilled. "Went up there on tour last year!"

"Tour?"

"Yes–" she pointed to her left breast.

Actually, Abby had very nice tits, but he wasn't quite sure why he was being encouraged to look at them.

"The winter tour," she prompted.

And then he noticed the crest on her shirt. *CUBT – Tour of 2004.*

"Really pretty place," Abby prattled on. "And the people are so friendly up in Scotland…"

CUBT. Cambridge University Basketball Team? Lucky it wasn't Netball, he thought, and nearly made a witty remark, then suddenly realised what this meant.

Cambridge University Basketball Team. She'd gone to *Cambridge University.* Not East Anglia ex-Polytechnic or whatever it was called. She'd gone to Cambridge. The real thing.

"…much up there?"

Mike looked at her.

"Well do they?" she asked again.

"Do they what?"

Abby rolled her eyes. "Do they do much *rowing* up there?!" she articulated, extremely loudly and clearly the way Mike's mother would talk to a foreigner.

"Uh, yeah, a bit," he muttered.

Cambridge University. He couldn't believe it. Bloody Token Females! It made him angry the way people like Abby Turner wangled their way into the top institutions, just because they were girls doing science. They were denying the worthy, intelligent people – like Mike, for a start – of well-earned places.

"…year in France?"

Mike registered it was a question, and mumbled something non-committal.

"Oh of course! That's why you were in Paris to begin with!"

cried Abby, with enthusiasm that was obviously false. Mike wished she'd just shut up.

OK. So she'd gone to Cambridge. Now Mike had a fresh challenge in mind.

"So… You did physics at Cambridge?"

"Yeah."

"Isn't that *really difficult*? Physics at Cambridge, I mean?"

Abby frowned at him suspiciously. Perhaps he was overdoing the flattery.

"I heard it was one of the hardest courses there was," he told her.

She pouted thoughtfully, narrowing her dark brown eyes. "Hmm. I'm not sure about *hardest*…"

"Well that's what I heard. But obviously you did OK?"

Abby shrugged. "Yeah, I guess."

Say it! Say what you got, for God's sake! "What did you end up with?" he asked, sipping his beer.

"Oh, I got a first, but—"

"A *first?!*" Mike spluttered, then quickly composed himself. "Well *done!*" he cried. "That's incredible!"

Quite literally: incredible. How could Abby Turner have got a first from Cambridge? By sleeping with the examiners? By bribing some poor, sad, sexless geek to take her exams for her?

Something was beginning to dawn on Mike, and it was making him feel uncomfortable. Either Abby had fluked her way into Cambridge, fluked her way to a first in physics and fluked her way into Cray McKinley, or – and this is what Mike had issues with – Abby Turner was actually very bright.

"…where I first played basketball," she went on.

Mike looked at her blankly.

"—which is why I was no good at rugby."

He decided he'd better say something.

"I never see you down in the gym," he commented.

"I hate gyms."

"Why?"

Abby laughed. "I've heard what certain men say about the girls down there – I don't fancy being discussed like a piece of meat in Lycra!"

Mike snorted and took a swig of his pint. Self-righteous little cow. How dare she imply that he was lecherous?

"Don't look so hurt!" she laughed again. "You're not the only ones, you and Marcus – all the guys do it!"

"You're saying women *don't* do it?" Mike retorted, tilting his head and raising an eyebrow.

"What – score out of ten on tits and legs? No, we don't. Not usually…" She shrugged. "Another beer? You're falling behind."

Mike had never met a girl as quick as Abby at drinking beer. Or buying it, for that matter.

"With shots?" Mike noted.

"Yeah – some drunk guy bought them for me. I told him I needed two – one for my friend, the tall, leggy brunette."

Mike couldn't help smiling. "I've never been described like that before."

"Oh, shit–" muttered Abby all of a sudden. "Is it really one fifteen?"

Mike looked at his watch, wondering how 'a quick drink' had turned into four. He felt quite light-headed. "Ten past – does that matter?"

"Oh – I was supposed to call my boyfriend when I got out of the office, that's all. It's OK – I'll do it now." She got out her phone.

Mike slipped off to the gents.

Boyfriend?

Abby Turner had a boyfriend?

Mike had assumed she was single – that she got through dozens of men every week – hopping from bed to bed like a rabbit. It was the way she behaved: flirting and giggling with the first-year guys, fluttering her eyelashes and flicking her hair. She probably had men queuing up to sleep with her. *She had a boyfriend.* Mike pushed the thought to the back of his mind and squeezed through the crowds.

"He's not answering, anyway," she said, tucking her phone away. "Out with the hockey lads. Hey, did you know there's a dance floor in this place, Mike?"

Mike grimaced. Dancing wasn't really his thing.

"Oh – go on!" she cried. "I haven't been dancing since New York!"

"I don't think, um... I'm not drunk enough yet," Mike stammered, wishing he could think up a better excuse. The truth was, *he couldn't dance*. Rugby, yes. Dancing, no. Dancing was for girls.

"Right," Abby said decisively.

She jumped off her stool and marched off.

"Wha–"

She was gone. He frowned. Abby was pushing her way through the hordes of men, heading, he thought, for the bar.

Mike sat there sipping his fresh pint, watching her arse, wondering what she was up to. She was actually quite entertaining, he had to admit. She was loud, rude and uncouth, and she had something of an attitude problem, but she was also a bit of a laugh. She wasn't like the other girls Mike knew.

Abby was back, cradling four shot-glasses full of thick, greeny-brown liquid.

"Here you go – two each!" she announced, beaming proudly.

"What..." he asked, peering at the cloudy shots, "*are* they?" He'd had never seen anything so revolting in all his life. And he'd seen some fairly revolting drinks in the rugby club bar.

"Surprise. Try one."

He stared at the lumpy concoctions. "It looks like curdled penguin bile, Abby. I'm not drinking that."

"Just *try one*," she urged, thrusting a glass into his hand. "They taste better than they look – I promise. We used to drink Clover Leaves all the time at uni. I know they *look* grim, but they're actually quite nice – and very alcoholic. Go on."

Mike took hold of the glass suspiciously.

"*DRINK IT YOU LIGHTWEIGHT!*" she shouted, tipping her head back violently and chucking hers down her throat.

Right, thought Mike. That did it. Nobody called Mike Cunningham-Reid a lightweight. He rose to his feet with a glass with each hand, and drained both of his drinks simultaneously, without splashing a drop. They were actually surprisingly tasty.

"Excellent – drunk enough now? Come on–" she said forcefully. "Let's dance."

She tried to grab his hand.

"No – I've just thought–" Mike interjected, remembering conveniently that he *did* have something to say.

She growled angrily. "What?"

"Y'know your mate Justine?"

She dropped her shot glass on the table and looked up. "Ye-es?"

"D'you know anything about her and Philip Oversby?" he asked, leaning towards her.

Abby looked at him blankly. She clearly didn't have the faintest idea. He raised an eyebrow.

"What... You mean...?" she muttered.

"Yep. Apparently they're all over each other. *Everybody* knows. He's been telling the guys in Leveraged Finance – Riaz and the other associates. Joe–"

"Hang on–" Abby interrupted, looking horrified. "Philip Oversby's a Managing Director! He wouldn't–"

Mike smiled triumphantly. He was definitely winning *this* round. Abby didn't even seem to know about the affair! "Apparently she sends him dirty text-messages. He's shown them to everyone. 'Last night was great', that sort of thing."

"No! That wasn't–" Abby frowned for a moment, then looked straight into Mike's eyes. "He's been *showing* people?"

"Yep," Mike replied smugly. "It's all over Cray McKinley. Surprised you hadn't heard. They're really... experimental... apparently."

"No... I – I hadn't heard..." Abby's voice was faint. She was obviously wondering why Justine hadn't told her. The girls were supposed to be friends, after all.

"OK," Mike said, changing the subject. "How about this for a deal: I buy another round of... penguin bile, we drink them over there, and you can strut your stuff on the dance floor while I prop up the bar."

"Sounds good," Abby nodded, coming out of her trance.

They fought their way to the bar.

"I told you – I'm not dancing," he warned as he paid for the next tray of lumpy green drinks.

"Fine!" shouted Abby, who was already twizzling into the spotlight.

Mike watched as she strutted across the tiny stage, flicking her long blonde hair as she spun round to face them. She was such a show-off. But fair enough, he thought. She did look hot. Mike drained his second shot, smiling as he heard the man next to him thump his mate in the chest and mutter, "fuckin' hell – look at that!"

When he looked up, a group of spotty lads in football shirts had swamped the dance floor and were hanging off each others' shoulders, sloshing beer and shouting. They looked young – probably only eighteen – but there were lots of them. Abby was nowhere to be seen.

Mike planted his shot glass on the bar and took a closer look. Then he saw her – sandwiched between two ugly football fans who were grinding against her body. Abby looked distraught. She was lashing out at the guys, but one of them had grabbed her arms, and was wrapping them firmly round his waist. She was trapped. Mike left the bar and stepped up onto the stage.

"Get. Off. Her," he mouthed at one of the assailants, jerking his thumb over his shoulder and staring down at him.

The guy stared back, looking more confused than angry, and to Mike's relief, loosened his grip on Abby's waist. His smart-ass friend did the same. Abby twisted angrily away from them, and barged her way off the dance floor. Mike followed, quite relieved that both Abby and his pride had survived unscathed.

"You OK?" he asked, once they'd reached a quieter part of the bar.

"Fine," she huffed.

"Wankers."

"*Wankers.*"

Suddenly, Abby smiled. "You're right. This is a shit-hole." She grabbed Mike's hand. "Let's get outta here."

Mike felt himself being tugged through the noisy bar until finally, he breathed in cold, fresh air.

Abby was still holding his hand as they spilled onto the pavement. "Thanks for that," she said.

Mike looked down at her face. For once, she wasn't smirking and she wasn't scowling. She was just staring straight up at him. He wondered why he hadn't noticed before how unnaturally dark her eyes were, for a blonde.

Then Mike did something impulsive.

"D'you fancy a nightcap back at mine?"

She hesitated.

Oh God, thought Mike, regretting his invitation. Suddenly, the nightcap seemed like a very bad idea. This was Abby from work. Abby who sat behind him in the office. Abby who sat behind him in the office *who had a boyfriend.* What was he doing, asking her back for a nightcap?

"Er, I'd better not," she replied, disentangling her fingers from of his.

A strange combination of relief and disappointment washed over him.

"Had quite enough curdled penguin bile for one night!" she said, giggling awkwardly.

For a moment they stood there in silence, then it was broken by a loud scuffling noise. They turned round. A dishevelled drunk tumbled out of the bar.

"YEAHFUCKINYEAH-WHA'EVER-YERFUCKIN FUCKER!"

Abby turned back to Mike and smiled. "I think I'll just hop in a cab."

She stepped into the road with her hand held out. A taxi pulled up immediately.

"Well, goodnight. Thanks for the drinks," she said, lingering on the curb.

"Er, goodnight." Mike moved forward to kiss her on the cheek.

It transpired, too late, that Abby was aiming for Mike's other cheek. After a moment of indecisive head-wavering, they collided mid-way, and kissed on the lips. Abby let out a strange *'huuuuh'* noise as she withdrew and stumbled backwards into the cab. Mike stood there, motionless, as the cab pulled away.

He'd just kissed Abby Turner.

He turned on the spot and set off down Haymarket, trying to straighten out his thoughts. OK, they hadn't *kissed,* exactly, but there had definitely been lip contact. *It was nothing*, he told himself. *Just a drunken act of mal-coordination. Nothing.* He stepped off the curb and hailed another cab.

20

"KEEP THE CHANGE," Abby slurred as she thrust a twenty-pound note through the glass partition.

She'd asked the driver to stop one block away from her flat, so that the noise of the engine wouldn't wake Ben – a nice touch, she thought.

"Mind the step!" the cabby warned as the pavement came hurtling towards her.

She staggered to her hands and knees and looked around, dazed. Her left shoe was lying in the gutter.

"I'm fine!" she assured the driver, reaching behind her and slamming the cab door shut.

He didn't drive off. Abby cursed. That was *all* she needed: a bloody chivalrous cabby. She wiped the grit off her hands and tapped on the passenger window. He wound it down a little.

"I'm fine, really – you can go now," she told him.

"I can't *go*," he informed her patronisingly, "while you're still attached to my car, can I?"

Abby looked down, and noticed the seatbelt wrapped around her waist. She untangled herself and shoved it back in the cab. Finally, the driver put his foot down and roared off.

Scooping her belongings off the curb and into her bag, Abby brushed herself down and chased her foot back into its shoe. She walked carefully along the edge of the road, determined not to trip.

The key wasn't going into the lock. She stabbed again, but still it wouldn't go in. Clearly someone in her block of flats had changed the locks while she was out. Abby cursed, and tried one last time, this time using her front door key rather than her bike lock key, which worked much better.

There was only one flight of stairs separating Abby from her bed. She felt queasy, drunk and overwhelmingly tired. As her foot reached the top step, her hand went out instinctively towards the hallway light switch.

There was a loud cracking noise, followed by a THUD, THUD, THUD, THUD: the sound of something large and heavy smashing its way down the stairs. Abby fumbled for the light switch and flicked it on.

Shit. Most of the vacuum cleaner was lying in pieces on the ground floor, while the nozzle and tubing remained on the first floor, wrapped around her foot. She'd have to have words with Ben about leaving things in stupid places.

A figure appeared in the bedroom doorway, his blonde hair tousled with sleep. "*Abby?*" he whispered, although it was doubtful the neighbours would still be asleep. "*What are you doing?*"

"What does it *look* like I'm doing?!" she hissed, removing her leg from the plastic tubing. "I'm chucking the hoover down the stairs – you left it on the landing!"

"Abby, *you* left the hoover on the landing. You said you'd do the hallway tomorrow. Are you drunk?"

"No!" she barked. "Ow!" The nozzle bounced off her foot and cartwheeled down the stairs. The cheek of him – accusing her like that!

"Where've you been, Abs? It's nearly three o'clock!"

Abby barged past her boyfriend, carrying the redundant piece of tubing through to the kitchen.

"I was working late 'coz of a stupid pitchbook thingy, then I went for a couple of beers with the guys from the office."

It was only adding an 's'. Ben got jealous when she went out – however innocently – with another guy. And in this particular instance, she wasn't sure how innocent it had been. She'd just kissed Mike Cunningham-Reid. And then nearly gone back to his place! What had she been thinking?

"Couple of beers, eh?" Ben laughed at her. "You're swaying all over the place!" He followed her as she went to fill a glass from the tap, and tried to put his hands around her waist. She shrugged him off, and marched purposefully towards the bedroom.

"No I'm *not,*" she stated, banging her hip on the doorframe. "I had a couple of pints, and one or two Clover Leaves – I had to. Mike had never had one before."

Christ. Her hip was hurting like hell. Maybe she'd broken it.

"Who's Mike?"

"Oh, just one of the analysts at work–"

"What – Mike Fanningham-Wobblebottom? The pompous fuckwit? Was he there?"

"Mike *Cunningham-Reid*, yeah. And he's not a fompous puckwit – pom- fom- anyway. He's quite a nice guy."

He was more fun than her grumpy sod of a boyfriend, she thought, slamming her glass of water onto the bedside table. He was acting like her bloody mother!

"Why weren't you answering your phone?" Ben asked, as he collided with her in the bathroom doorway. She ducked under his arm and locked herself in.

"Why wasn't *I* answering my phone?!" she yelled. "It was *you* not answering your phone!"

There was no reply from the other side of the door. He must have realised that she had a point.

She emerged two minutes later, her skin feeling raw after an overly-aggressive face wash. Ben crawled under the covers and folded back the duvet on Abby's side of the bed. She ignored this gesture and started meticulously hanging her clothes in the wardrobe. She was cross with Ben. He didn't have the right to accuse her of being *drunk,* just because she was late home on a Saturday night. And it was *his* fault she hadn't spoken to him; *he'd* been the one ignoring his phone.

"Abby," he said quietly. "I tried phoning you back – when I missed your call."

Having finished aligning the coat hangers, Abby bent down to pick up her bag, and emptied the contents onto the end of the bed. A surprising amount of grit fell all over the duvet.

Abby pulled out her BlackBerry.

11 Missed Calls. Ah. Shit. Abby glanced sheepishly at her

boyfriend, then started industriously brushing off the gravel.

"We were in a noisy bar," she explained. "Couldn't hear my phone."

"Where were you?" Ben asked brightly, propping himself up in bed. "Somewhere in the city?"

"No – Haymarket."

"Really? Same here! We were in *Tiger Tiger* 'til about midnight."

Oh God. Tiger Tiger was about twenty yards from the Sports Café. Their paths must've practically crossed! *What if Ben had seen her with Mike?*

"I thought you were going to be out all night with the boys," she said casually.

"Well, not all night – they wanted to go back to Brian's to watch porn or something. I came home about one – thought you'd be back by then."

"Oh right. I see." Abby placed the folded garments in the chest of drawers. Now he was trying to make her feel *guilty*.

She undid her dressing gown and slipped into bed.

"Why's my pillow all wet?!" she demanded.

"Er, maybe because you just sloshed water all over it?"

Abby grunted. She could feel Ben's fingers tickle the side of her stomach. She rolled away from him and curled up in a ball on the other side of the bed.

The fingers followed her over.

"*Ben!*" she hissed. "*You've got cold hands – get off!*"

He did as he was told. There was a short silence, then his voice again – deep but very quiet.

"So you didn't get my messages?"

"No – what did they say?"

"Oh… nothing. Don't worry about it."

She knew what the messages would have said: *I love you. I miss you. Call me.* She couldn't bear it when he got all soppy like that. *What was she supposed to say? I love you too? I miss you too?* The truth was, she was no longer sure that she *did* still love Ben. So much had happened in the last few months: leaving university, spending summer apart, starting new jobs, meeting new people… things weren't the same any more.

Abby could feel his fingers lightly stroking her hair on the pillow. She closed her eyes, and felt herself drifting off. She quickly fell into the semi-conscious state where reality blurs into dreams.

"Good night, Abby," she heard faintly.

"Mmm, g'night M- Ben."

21

MIKE STARED at the email. This had to be a mistake.

He scrolled down to the bottom of the page, and back to the top again. There was no doubt about it; the email was definitely intended for him. And they wanted him to work on the Pharmacolt acquisition – the deal on everybody's lips. They wanted him to replace Patrick Gilligan on one of the largest transactions the bank had ever advised on.

He couldn't understand it. It wasn't that Mike didn't think he could handle it; he knew he was good, for a first-year analyst. But Patrick Gilligan was an associate – a highly competent associate – and this was an important piece of work. The deal was worth millions to Cray McKinley, so why were they about to replace a capable investment banker with a fresh-faced graduate like Mike? Was Patrick stepping down from the deal team? Had Mike been recommended to replace him, following the success of Project Coral? He'd have to ask Patrick when he got in.

Something caught Mike's eye: a wild, frenzied flapping movement, just outside the glass doors that led to the lifts. A tall man in a suit was performing some kind of African dance in the lobby, waving his hands above his head, leaping energetically from one foot to the other. Mike squinted at the peculiar spectacle, and realised the man had ginger hair. He wandered over to find out what Patrick was up to.

"Ah, thanks mate!" the associate gasped. "Been trying to catch someone's attention for nearly ten minutes!" He smoothed down his rumpled trousers. "Fockin' swipe-card's gone wrong; wouldn't let me through the turnstiles downstairs, either!"

Mike shook his head understandingly. It had happened to him once, and the receptionists had taken twenty minutes to verify that he was the real Michael Cunningham-Reid.

They returned to their desks.

"Strange…" Patrick muttered. "That's a weird error message."

Mike leant sideways.

'Patrick Gilligan is not a valid User ID for this workstation. Please contact your Systems Administrator.'

"Hmm… that *is* weird," agreed Mike. "I've never seen that one before. Sure you got your password right?"

"I'll try again." Patrick frowned. "Nope – still get the same message. 'Not a valid User ID' – huh."

Mike grinned mischievously at his neighbour. "You know what this means…" He was teasing. It was a standard joke in the department. Redundancies were happening all over the firm, and there were constantly rumours flying around about 'who'd be next to get the chop'. Often, a failed log-in would be the first sign that someone was about to lose his job.

"Aye, very funny," replied Patrick with a thin smile. He knew as well as Mike did that he wasn't about to lose his job. He was one of the hardest working associates in Corporate Finance, and he had a queue of directors begging for him to work on their deals. There was no way they'd be letting go of Patrick.

That reminded Mike.

"I wanted to ask you something. Why did you step down from–"

Patrick silenced him with a palm and started muttering into his handset.

"…very weird… says *not a valid User ID*… could you look into it… aye…"

Mike turned back to his desk. He felt distinctly unmotivated, and slightly distracted. The lack of motivation was perfectly normal for a Monday morning, but the distraction – the thing that was niggling away at the back of his mind – was not. He opened up the annual report on his desk, and half-heartedly flicked through it to find the financials. Then he forgot what he was looking for.

He checked his notes. *Ah yes.* Letting the document fall open at the balance sheet, he absent-mindedly scanned the page for Intangibles. It was no good. Mike couldn't concentrate. The niggle was getting worse. He'd been fending it off, shoving it to the back of his mind, ignoring it for over a week now, but he knew it was time to face up to it.

Abby Turner.

That was the problem. It was Abby, the girl sitting six feet behind him. He could picture her now, sitting bolt upright as she always did, her glossy blonde hair tied back in a ponytail, her brown eyes staring determinedly at the screen. Mike had a sudden, compulsive urge to whip round and look at her, but he forced himself not to.

Abby and Mike hadn't spoken to each other for nine days. They hadn't even made eye contact. It was getting ridiculous. Everywhere he went, she was *there*: the lobby, the snack bar, the drinks machine, the meeting room... she was almost impossible to avoid. But avoiding her was definitely the best thing to do. The thought of talking to Abby after that night in the Sports Café made him cringe.

And again, he found himself thinking about it. He'd asked her back to his place. Had he been out of his mind? She was a girl from the office, for a start. Mike had always sworn that he'd never get involved with a colleague – it was just asking for trouble. But worse, she was a tiresome, irritating, loud-mouthed know-all – not his type at all. *And she had a boyfriend.*

A muffled grunt came from under Patrick's desk. The associate appeared to be rummaging amongst the cables on the floor.

"IT guys not coming up to help?" Mike asked.

Patrick slid out a little way, just enough for Mike to see his face. It was very pale.

"You OK, mate?"

"Yeah, fine..." Patrick muttered vaguely, retreating into his hole. He seemed to be tidying the area under his desk – bringing out papers, folders and notebooks and cramming everything into a white polythene bag. Wriggling backwards and balancing on his haunches, he started yanking open his drawers, one at a time, pulling out little scraps of paper and stuffing them into the plastic bag. Mike turned back to the report on his desk.

It was nearly eight o'clock. Mike looked around for the usual signs that the Work-In-Progress meeting was about to begin: Daniel Greening muttering 'WIP, people? WIP?', associates loitering by the meeting room door and directors milling about aimlessly before their moments of glory. But strangely, today there was no such activity. The directors were seated at their desks and the Head of Department was nowhere to be seen. The office was exceptionally quiet.

Mike jolted. Tiki's flabby face had appeared at the side of his monitor.

"Psst!" she hissed needlessly at Mike, who was already staring straight back at her. Tiki was flapping her hands about and pointing frantically at something the other side of Mike's monitor. She looked like a sign-language translator on speed. For some reason – and this was unprecedented, Mike thought – she wasn't making any noise.

What? he mouthed, shaking his head blankly and wishing she'd leave him alone. Tiki appeared to be pointing at Patrick. Mike looked from Tiki to Patrick and back to Tiki again. *What?*

The girl started acting out a peculiar mime behind the monitor. *Scrubbing? Scooping? Flying? Cleaning?*

Suddenly it became clear.

Clearing out. Patrick was clearing out his stuff.

Mike glanced again at his neighbour, who was sweeping pens, key-rings, small plastic toys and other useless office junk from his desk into the bag. Finally, it hit home.

Patrick really *was* being made redundant.

The tubby young secretary waddled back to her desk with a final sidelong glance at Mike, which he chose not to interpret. He swallowed, and stared at his screen. Suddenly, the morning's events all fitted together. So *that* was why Patrick was being taken off the Pharmacolt deal. *That* was why his swipe-card wasn't working. *That* was why he hadn't been able to log on. And *that* was why Daniel Greening was lying low.

Mike fixed his gaze at a spot straight in front of him, unable to move. Poor Patrick. Surely it was the last thing he – or anyone – had expected. *Why* Patrick? It didn't make sense.

Propping himself up in his chair, Mike looked around at the other members of the department. They were all sitting behind their computers, peering, squinting, frowning, chewing pens. There was very little movement. The office was like a morgue; no Monday morning banter, no churlish grumbling and no idle chit-chat from the secretaries. *Everybody knew.* The other members of the department didn't need someone like Tiki to tell them what was happening; they'd seen it all before.

Mike couldn't move. It seemed insensitive or... well, wrong. He couldn't even bring himself to pretend to work, like his colleagues were doing. He just stared straight ahead. How would it happen, he wondered? How would Patrick leave? Would there be no goodbyes? Would he just walk out the door, and never come back?

A uniformed security guard was standing in the doorway, waiting to escort Patrick away.

The Scotsman stood up slowly, hugging the bulging bag to his chest. He uttered something under his breath that sounded like *'see ya'*, but Mike couldn't think of a reply. What would he say? *'Bye mate!'? 'Have a nice day!'? 'Enjoy your life!'?* Everybody continued to hide behind their monitors.

Why had they picked on Patrick? Perhaps there would be more cuts to come? Mike wondered whether his own job was secure. Was he at risk, too? No, he decided. He'd be alright. For a while. It was a well-known fact that Cray McKinley never cut at analyst level – especially not from their first-year intake; it gave them a bad reputation with the universities.

The glass doors swung shut behind the security guard, and people started to breathe again. Still nobody spoke, but something changed. The air cleared. Secretaries resumed their typing, analysts got back to their spreadsheets and directors stood up at their desks, looking around for the signal from Daniel Greening.

Mike looked down at the balance sheet in front of him, but his eyes – and his mind – kept wandering. A stack of papers and training manuals sat next to Patrick's keyboard, and there was a tidy pile of Cray McKinley stationery on the edge of the desk. A rolled-up Post-It note had stuck itself to the side of one of the books, and leaning across to pick it off, Mike read *'Renew gym membership, Weds.'* Mike smiled wryly. *They saved you the trouble*, he thought, flicking it into the bin.

He couldn't concentrate. It wasn't Abby Turner on his mind any more – it was Patrick. *Why Patrick? Why Patrick?* It seemed totally illogical. Patrick had been one of the best associates the firm had ever employed – anyone who'd worked with him could vouch for that. And he'd been *nice,* too, which was rare. It was almost unheard of at Cray McKinley. In fact, thought Mike, perhaps that was it. Perhaps his niceness had been his downfall. Patrick had been *too* nice. Quiet, modest, helpful, kind… all the things an investment banker didn't need to be. There was no room for a man like Gilligan in a place like Cray McKinley.

"Ah – here's a spare one!" cried Stuart Mackins, whirling past Mike's desk and yanking Patrick's chair into the gangway. "Need a few extra for the WIP meeting–"

"Guess this is up for grabs, is it?" a voice piped up. Jon Hargreaves was clutching Patrick's Rolodex, plucking out business cards one by one and dropping them into the bin.

"WIP MEETING! WIP!" boomed Daniel Greening.

"…bring everyone up to speed on the IPO, so we can really get the ball rolling…" Geoff Dodds was barking into his phone.

"Ah!" shouted Larkham triumphantly, reaching across and grabbing Patrick's calculator. "Been looking for one of these!"

Within seconds, the desk next to Mike's was bare. It was as if Patrick Gilligan had never existed.

22

ABBY CAME OUT of a restless sleep, and rolled over to look at the clock.

Two-fifteen. *Why on earth was she awake at two-fifteen in the morning?* She lay there, listening. Was there somebody in the flat? The bedroom was quiet except for the sound of Ben's gentle breathing. She listened some more. There was a faint rattling noise coming from the radiator at the end of the bed, and the sound of a car engine idling in the street. Which was odd, thought Abby, at this time of night. She hoisted herself up onto the cold plastic windowsill and squinted into the pool of yellow light.

A taxi. Abby's heart started to thud. It was a Cray McKinley taxi. That's what had woken her. Abby slipped out of bed and felt her way to the bedroom door, pulling her dressing gown around her as she went. Ben rolled over into the space she'd just left and mumbled something that sounded like 'horses in tupperware' but Abby didn't look back. She scurried across the landing, hurling herself down the stairs in an effort to reach the door before the driver rang the bell.

"Hi!" she gasped breathlessly, looking into a very hairy armpit.

"Oh, hi. Miss Turner?" The cab driver let his hand drop, sending a blast of salty body odour her way.

Abby looked at him. "Yes."

"Taxi for you?"

She frowned. "I don't think so, no."

"Well, that's what I've got down 'ere."

Abby sighed. "I *did* book one, but that was to come home about four hours ago."

157

"Huh," he frowned. "I'll have to check me books then. Abigail Turner, eh?"

"Yes," she confirmed irritably.

"Hmm. And you ordered a taxi to get home?"

"Yes."

"Four hours ago, ya say?"

"Yes. And it came. Four hours ago. And took me home." Abby was getting angry. It wasn't the first time the cab company had cocked things up.

"Tell ya what – I'll radio HQ. They'll know wha's going on."

The fat man waddled back to his cab and switched off the engine. For a few seconds, the street was eerily silent. Then Abby heard the crackle of his radio, and an electronic beep. She heard the beep a second time. And again. It was only after five or six beeps that she realised it wasn't actually coming from the cab. It was coming from inside her flat.

"Hello?" she panted, banging her head as she picked up her BlackBerry from under the kitchen table.

"Abby, it's Anthony. I've been trying to call. You weren't answering."

Shit. She'd broken one of the Cray McKinley golden rules: *Always answer your phone.* No matter what time it was, how drunk you were, how tired, who you were with, what you were doing… you *had* to answer your phone.

"I'm sorry–"

"There should be a cab arriving any time now," he said gruffly. Abby stumbled back down the stairs and started waving at the driver, who was arguing into his radio. "We need you to come back to the office. There are some figures that need checking on Project Buffalo. When you get in, open up your spreadsheets and give me a call."

The line went dead before she could reply.

When Abby finally caught the man's attention, she realised she was revealing quite a lot of cleavage through the gap in her dressing gown. "Sorry – could you wait here please?" she asked, hastily re-tying the belt. "I am getting in after all. Won't be long – thanks."

Ben was awake when she crept back into the bedroom.

"What's going on?" he asked groggily, squinting at her in the half darkness.

"Oh, I was just performing a private dance for a middle-aged cab driver."

Ben screwed up his face. "Uh?"

"Sorry. It's work. They need me in the office. Don't worry – just go back to sleep," she said, switching on the bedside lamp and angling it away from him.

Ben groaned and pulled the duvet over his head. "It's half two in the morning, Abby," he mumbled through the fabric.

"Yeah, I know. They've got some 'figures' that need checking or something. God knows..." Abby sighed as she flicked through the suits in her wardrobe.

The tuft of blonde hair popped out again. Ben's eyes followed her as she flitted about, throwing on clothes, rushing to the bathroom and packing things into a bag.

"Right, I'm off. See ya. Not sure when I'll be back – probably tomorrow evening." She glanced briefly at her bewildered boyfriend. A shaft of light was pouring through the gap in the curtains, shining on his sleepy blue eyes.

"Come back to bed," he moaned.

Abby slipped backwards out of the room before she said something she'd regret. Ben was getting on her nerves. He had no idea what it was like for an analyst at Cray McKinley. If he said the words 'you work too hard' one more time, she thought, she'd actually resort to violence.

The taxi was warm and stuffy, and Abby felt herself drifting back to the world she'd just left behind. She was having a horrible dream about a fairground ride that was run by Stuart Mackins and powered by a flock of pigeons – one of whom looked a lot like Joe from work.

"Nice area, Stepney, innit?" said the driver, trying to make eye contact in the rear view mirror.

Abby came to and grunted, thinking that 'nice' was probably the last word she'd use to describe Stepney Green.

"Mate o'mine, Tony, lives round 'ere."

She grunted again. Clearly he was one of those cabbies who liked to bond with his passengers.

"White 'orse Lane. Not far from 'ere."

Abby felt her head rolling forwards. She pulled it back up with a jerk, and pushed her fingers into the corners of her eyes.

"Lived with 'is nan, till she died."

Abby made an effort to nod. It was all too tiring. She tried to throw herself back into Project Buffalo mode. Her head lolled forwards again and she felt herself slipping away again. On Abby's request, the driver pressed a button on the dashboard to let in some air from the outside world, and started telling her about his mate's nan's cat.

The night air hit Abby's face like a splash of cold water. *Project Buffalo*. That's what she had to focus on. Project Buffalo was a small-scale UK Media acquisition. She wasn't really supposed to be working on the deal – it was a job for the guys up in M&A – but she'd somehow become involved, and now Anthony Dawson, the associate on the deal team, had started treating her as 'the analyst' on the team. It was flattering, really, to be considered such a valuable asset. She almost felt useful. Finally, thought Abby, she was earning her free evening meal and her free cab-ride home. Or, more accurately, her free cab-ride *in*.

"Then he got another cat-door put in, see…"

The events of the deal floated slowly to the front of Abby's mind. Everything had been going well until the previous week, when a multinational media giant had thrown a spanner in the works by launching a rival bid for the target company. Since then, Project Buffalo had been teetering on the brink of failure. The M&A bankers had worked almost solidly for four days and four nights, trying to think up ingenious ways to out-bid the new opposition. It was a near-impossible task, but they were giving it their best shot. Project Buffalo was one of the few live transactions on the Cray McKinley books, and one of the firm's only potential sources of revenue. They had to try and resurrect the deal.

"…two hundred quid, just for the bleedin' extension!"

Abby had gone home early the previous evening. She'd felt guilty, leaving at ten while the M&A guys worked on through the night, but her brain had practically ground to a halt; there'd been little point in sticking around. That, thought Abby as she rested her head on the vibrating door frame, had been a mistake.

"Turned out, the cat didn't even exist! The old girl was a fruit-cake…"

She pushed her head further into the stream of cold air, and wondered what 'figures' Anthony had been referring to. What would they want her to do? It would have to be something quite urgent, she thought, if they'd sent a cab round for her in the middle of the night… She tried to whip up some fresh enthusiasm.

★ ★ ★

The luminous strip-lights hurt the back of Abby's eyes. Her head was throbbing, her hands were shaking and her skin felt sweaty and hot. The four hours' sleep had been worse than none at all; it was as though her brain was stuck in the half-on, half-off position.

"Hi, it's Abby," she announced. "I've got all the spreadsheets open – what should I be looking at?"

"Good," Anthony replied brusquely, "I'll just put you on speakerphone. We're all up here – I'll let Tim explain what's required."

Tim Sanders took over, his deep, authoritative voice sounding distorted and strained on the internal line. Or maybe just tired. The M&A bankers had been hunched over the same speakerphone five hours ago when she'd left. They'd probably been there ever since. Abby wondered what they'd been saying in her absence. She felt sure that her 'early night' had not passed without comment.

She replaced the receiver, and stared at her scrawled page of notes. It had all seemed quite clear when Tim had explained it, but looking through her improvised shorthand scribbles, Abby began to have doubts. '2nd qtr deprec. figs – intm rep. not annl… Cashfl. Diff 4 yr2, & amort. Intang." It wasn't clear at all.

It was something to do with the figures in the financial model – she understood that much. She was supposed to be emailing a new model up to the bankers sometime before 4 a.m. That gave her just over an hour.

The hot, gritty brown liquid on Abby's desk didn't taste anything like coffee, but at least it was caffeinated. Abby was beginning to understand why there were so many of these drinks machines on every floor. For the seven hour period between when the canteen shut and when the in-house coffee shops opened, they were the only source of stimulant. The only legal source, at least.

Nearly an hour later, Abby kicked off her shoes, stretched her legs and let out a satisfied sigh. The model was complete, and was winging its way through the Cray McKinley email system to the bankers up on the fourth floor. She reached forwards and picked up the phone.

"Hi. I've just sent you the revised model – is there anything more I can do at the moment?"

"Hmm. We've just got your email." Anthony sounded weary. "We'll have a look at it and get back to you, OK?"

"Yep – no problem. Thanks."

Abby put down the receiver and stared at it. *Thanks? THANKS?* What was she saying? Why was she thanking them for ruining her night? Leaning back in her chair, Abby let her eyes flicker shut.

The caffeine was obviously working. Despite her tiredness, Abby couldn't doze off. Her brain was buzzing with thoughts – bizarre, illogical, pointless thoughts – that disappeared before she'd even had time to focus on them. Project Buffalo, the taxi driver, the financial model, that night in the Sports Café...

She blinked. She'd spent the last two weeks trying not to think about that – about him – but here he was again, popping into her head when she least expected. Abby sat up straight and waited for her mind to wander onto something else. It didn't. She glanced around the office, looking for something that would distract her: files, monitors, speakerphones, desks... Abby had a sudden urge to walk over to Mike's desk and pull open his drawers – just to see what he kept in there. Loose change? A tie? A spare shirt and deodorant for when he worked through the night?

Abby jiggled her mouse, cross with herself for thinking such ludicrous thoughts. She shouldn't be wasting her time thinking about Mike Cunningham-Reid. He was an arrogant, chauvinist know-all, and he didn't warrant space in her head.

Scrolling through her address book, Abby wondered who to email. Tao and Rod would be at their desks, surely. It was only midnight in New York. But they'd be busy; they wouldn't have time to chat. Brad would probably be strolling back to the office after a ten-minute break in the sunshine. Abby was tempted to give him a call – they'd hardly spoken since they said goodbye in summer – but again, he'd probably be busy. She wished the bankers would hurry up and call her back.

Sod this, Abby thought, twenty minutes later. She was feeling hot, tired and angry. She didn't like being excluded. After all, she was part of the deal team; she had a right to know what was going on.

At first glance, the fourth floor seemed to be deserted. Abby felt like an intruder, her footsteps standing out above the gentle hum of office equipment on standby. Then she became aware of another noise. A tap-click-tapping of fingers on keyboards. Looking around, Abby realised that the vast, open-plan office was not deserted at all; it was dotted with figures. Every so often, she caught sight of a hand going up to massage a neck, or a pair of glasses being removed. M&A was alive with analysts – although 'alive' was probably too strong a word, she thought.

Anthony's desk was vacant, but his screensaver hadn't kicked into life. She heard a door slam behind her and looked round.

"Ah, hi!" shouted Anthony, beaming as he returned from the gents. "Sorry – we forgot to call you back, didn't we?"

Abby watched as the young man bounded over. He seemed incredibly energetic, considering it was five o'clock in the morning.

"Well, we checked out your model – it's fine. We need to add the data for the XLM subsidiary, but I'll do that myself. Other than that, it's done and dusted."

Abby wondered, looking at the speck of white powder just beneath his left nostril, if this was a Freudian slip. "Oh right," she said. "So, I'm free to–"

"Go home – yes. If you think it's worth it. But, er–" he hesitated, and glanced furtively in the direction of Tim Sander's office. "I'll tell you what–" He lowered his voice, and pressed his face very close to hers. "It'll earn you a few extra brownie points if you just call Tim yourself and let him know you're still around – you know, ask if he needs you to do anything, that sort of thing... Show you're keen."

"Er, thanks," Abby replied, not sure how to respond, and distracted by the white speck. "OK, I'll... I'll do that."

She headed for the lifts. Was *everyone* on cocaine in this place? Was that how people survived? And what was all that shit about brownie points? Was he serious? Abby couldn't tell. She knew Cray McKinley was a competitive place to work, but she was loath to believe that it operated on a brownie point scoring system. Surely she didn't have to grovel to Tim Sanders with a pointless can-I-do-anything-to-help phone call? No. She wasn't going to do it.

Abby looked at her watch. Five thirty. Definitely not worth going home. She'd already sought out a dormitory: a glass-walled office in the corner of the room, once home to a Managing Director who'd been made redundant back in summer. The black leather sofa would be perfect. Dragging her coat from the back of her chair, she padded over to her makeshift bedroom.

The room was hot, and the fluorescent strip-light above her head bore straight through her eyelids, but Abby didn't care. She buried her face in the soft, furry jacket lining and slipped straight into an exhausted sleep.

It seemed only a matter of minutes before she heard the bleeping of her phone alarm. Abby propped herself up on the sticky leather sofa and delved into her coat pocket. Her head was pounding, and she could feel strands of greasy hair plastered to the side of her face.

She jabbed at the handset to silence it, and then, just in time, realised what was going on.

"Hello?" she croaked, taking in the *Withheld Number* on the screen.

"Abby," barked a voice she now recognised as Tim Sanders'. "I've been looking at this model." He sounded cross. "I'm talking about the subsidiary part – the XLM subsidiary."

She forced her brain into gear. "I didn't do that part of–"

"It's riddled with errors," he went on, spitting the words down the phone.

Abby held the receiver away from her ear. "No – I didn't actually do that part of the–"

"You've got the Cost of Sales wrong on the P&L, your five-year projections are way out of line, and I don't know *where* you got your dividend figures from!"

"I–" It was no good. She couldn't compete with the MD for volume.

"The XLM part will have to be re-done. It makes a mockery of the whole model! I'm getting Anthony to re-do that part of the model; I just wanted you to know what was happening up here."

Abby heard a click, then silence.

She lay back on the sofa, trying to work things out. There was only one explanation, really. Anthony had messed his part of the model up, and now Tim Sanders was blaming her. But how weird; Anthony Dawson was on her side, wasn't he? He'd tried to help her suck up to Sanders! Or had that just been the effect of the drugs? Had Anthony persuaded the MD that it was her fault? There was no way of knowing. She couldn't call anyone to find out; Tim would be seething with rage, and Anthony... well, he was an associate. She couldn't just pick up the phone and make accusations – she was only a first-year. Her head was throbbing and her eyes ached; she was in no state to pass judgement on anything.

Abby was hitting the leather cushions with a lever-arch file, trying to restore them to their initial, un-dented state when she started to sense that she was being watched. She glanced over her shoulder, awkwardly lowering the folder to waist-height.

"Oh, er, hi," she stammered.

"Morning," Mike said, smirking, she thought – although she couldn't bear to look him in the eye.

"I was just, er, smoothing down – um–" Abby motioned in the direction of the sofa. "The, er, cushions."

"Right," he said, with a smile in his voice.

Abby stooped to pick up her coat from the floor and blustered past him, cheeks glowing.

Standing alone in the Ladies, staring at her pallid but now slightly blotchy reflection, Abby re-lived the moment again in her head, just to torture herself. She'd been bashing the sofa with a file, for Christ's sake. What must he have thought? She looked terrible, too, she realised, scraping a greasy blonde strand off her cheek. Not that it mattered, of course, what he thought. But it was frustrating to have been caught off-guard.

The icy water smacked against Abby's face, almost numbing it with cold. She cupped her hands one more time and let the last few drops trickle down her neck. Leaning forwards, she stared at her reflection in horror. She knew how unflattering the harsh white lighting was, but this was not an illusion. *She looked hideous.* Her eyes were dull and lifeless; they'd shrunk so much that it was hard to tell what colour they were. And her hair – it had almost turned brown with grease. She turned sideways and shook her head vigorously until she felt a hammering sensation in her ears. That distributed the lankness a little.

Two Nurofen and a thick layer of foundation later, Abby was back at her desk. The other analysts and a couple of associates were in – among them the witty Jon Hargreaves.

"Ah, morning Ms Turner, nice of you to turn up!" he cried.

Abby turned to face her monitor and pretended to focus on an email.

"I've been hearing about your slacking, you know – I just met Anthony Dawson downstairs. You're not exactly flavour of the month up in M&A, are you?"

Abby swallowed, and glanced nervously at her neighbour.

"Not a good idea, getting in Tim Sanders' bad-books, Abby. *Not* a good idea." He tutted and shook his head, smiling smugly.

Abby was mortified. "Er, I'm not exactly in Tim Sanders' bad-books... it's just... there was a bit of a mix-up–"

"Huh! That's not what I heard! Nipping off home for a good night's sleep, then dumping them in it with a fucked-up model?" – he drew a sharp intake of breath – "I wouldn't want to be in your shoes, that's for sure!"

Abby looked up at the associate just in time to see the conceited little face disappear under the desk. Jon started to shine his shoes. Before she had time to think up a response, her phone rang.

"Abby it's me. Justine. Wasn't sure you'd be in yet–"

"Hi," Abby whispered. "Listen, I'm kinda snowed under with–"

"Have you got a minute?" Justine pleaded. "I just need to check something with you,"

Abby gave in. "Yeah, go on," she replied in a hushed voice. This was not the sort of thing she liked to discuss in front of her colleagues – especially not her nosy shoe-shining neighbour.

"It's about you-know-who."

"Yeah, I guessed. What?"

166

"Well, I've been thinking... about what you said. About what you said Mike said. D'you think it really is Philip spreading those rumours? I mean, I can't believe—"

"Listen, Justine," Abby hissed. "Believe what you like. I told you what I heard, and I can't think where else the stories would've come from."

"Maybe it was some—"

"Justine! Think!" she urged through gritted teeth. "*You* haven't told anyone, *I* haven't told anyone, and nobody *else* saw what happened that night. So it *must've* been him!"

"Yeah, but the text-messages – he *can't* have been showing people. I didn't send—"

Abby groaned despairingly. "Anyone can send himself a text-message and change his name to 'Justine' in his phone book!"

Justine made a whimpering noise.

"He's an arsehole, Justine – a *married* arsehole! Stay away from him!"

"Sorry – yeah, you're right. It's just, he called again yesterday and—"

"For God's sake. You didn't, did you?"

"No – I told him I was busy. But what if he calls again?"

Abby flipped. "*THEN TELL HIM TO FUCK OFF!*" she hissed. There was a short silence at the other end, and Abby regretted her choice of words. "No – don't tell him to fuck off. That was a stupid idea. Sorry. I'm just tired. Ignore you-know-who. Pretend there's nothing going on. I don't know what he hopes to achieve here, but he's making a fool out of you. Just get on with your life and... forget he exists. If you wanna meet for a coffee some time, let me know. Just not today – things are really manic right now."

"OK, thanks," Justine mumbled. "Sorry for bugging you."

"That's cool – any time!" Abby cried with excessive cheer.

The shoe shining operation came to an end just as Abby replaced the receiver. Jon Hargreaves turned to face her, his head cocked expectantly to one side.

"Hmmm, Agony Aunt Abby, eh?" he quipped, pursing his lips and nodding his head.

Abby shot him a hateful glance and turned back to her screen, wondering how much he'd heard.

"Well!" Jon muttered, standing up at his desk with a patronising grin on his face, "I hope you do a better job of sorting out your girlie problems than you do your financial models!"

★ ★ ★

Abby could smell the spices as she trudged up the stairs. Ben was cooking one of his curries. Usually this was a good thing. Today, though, it would only make things worse.

"Hi babe!" he yelled from the kitchen.

"Hi," Abby sighed and plodded in.

"How was your day? You must be knackered!" he cried, trying to plant a kiss on Abby's evasive lips.

"It was shit. The worst yet." She dropped her bag on the kitchen floor and stood motionless in the doorway.

"Well, don't worry. I've done us a curry. Chicken madras – your favourite!" Ben lifted the lid on the simmering yellow mixture. It did smell good.

"I've eaten already," Abby lied, avoiding Ben's doting gaze. "I ate at work."

"Oh, come on Abs – since when've you turned down a second dinner?" He dropped the ladle into the bubbling sauce and hopped across the kitchen. Smiling, he poked his head into the curve of her neck. She stepped aside irritably, shrugging him off.

He frowned. "What's up?"

"Nothing. I'm just tired." That was partly true, but it wasn't the only problem.

"You'll feel better with some of this inside you–" he motioned to the pot on the stove.

"I'm not hungry. I told you – I've eaten." Abby stared at the ground.

"You work so hard, Abby," he muttered, turning his attention to the saucepan of rice. "You should go easy on yourself – chill out a bit!"

Abby felt the irritation flare up inside her. "Ben, I'm an *analyst* at

Cray McKinley. If I could 'chill out a bit', I would. But I don't have that choice. I just do what I'm *told* to do!"

"Look – I'm sorry, I was just thinking–"

"No, Ben, you *weren't*." She waited for him to turn round. He did, with hurt in his eyes. "That's just it. You *weren't* thinking. You weren't thinking about my life, because you can't. And I know it's not your fault, but you can't even *imagine* what it's been like today – or any other day. And... well, I don't know what's going on in *your* life, either." She sighed unhappily.

Ben was staring at her. He hadn't blinked. Abby hated herself, but she knew she had to go on. "I'm just not a part of your life any more. It's my fault, totally," she said, knowing it wasn't making things any better. "I wish–" Abby felt a lump rise up and lodge in the back of her throat. She was finding it difficult to speak. "I wish it wasn't–"

She forced the words out. "I wish it wasn't like this, Ben. But I feel like we hardly even know each other any more. And–"

There were tears in his eyes; she could see them glistening. She'd never seen Ben cry before.

"It's not the same," Abby said quietly. A warm droplet ran down the side of her nose. "There's nothing between us any more; I just don't see the point–"

"What are you saying?" Ben whispered, breaking on the last word.

"I'm saying it's over." She shrugged miserably, tears pouring down her cheeks. "I'm really sorry, Ben. It's over."

23

"TELL YOU WHAT, THOUGH," said Jon Hargreaves, sending the magazine skidding across the meeting room table, "that's *nothing* compared to the arse I saw yesterday – the new bird on the Equities trading floor."

"Which one?" Mike asked, thinking he knew exactly who Jon was referring to.

"Right in the corner – you *must*'ve seen her. Samantha something-or-other – she's Scott Newman's secretary. Nice pair of legs, too."

Mike obliged with a throaty laugh and flicked through the pages of FHM. He was just about to start a conversation about Halle Berry's tits when the heavy door swung open.

"Good morning!" cried Carlos Gonazalez-Torres in his thick Spanish accent. He planted his briefcase on the table and stared, goggle-eyed at his two younger colleagues.

"Morning Carlos," Hargreaves replied with a brief nod at the short, bespectacled man.

"Morning," mumbled Mike, stuffing the magazine between his legs.

"So! How are my little associates doing? Eh?" the Spaniard asked, grinning inanely at the men.

Mike started to mumble something about being an analyst, not an associate, but stopped himself. It didn't do any harm to have people think he was an associate. He was doing Patrick Gilligan's work, after all.

"You have for me the book, yes?"

Mike passed him a glossy colour copy of the latest Pharmacolt presentation, still warm from the print room. He was rather proud of his achievement. It had taken him most of the night to complete, but it was an impressive piece of work. Well, Mike thought so, anyway.

"Excellent." Carlos nodded, and set about arranging his pens in length order on the table in front of him.

There was pause as the three men tried to come up with appropriate small talk. Mike looked at his watch and frowned. Ten thirty exactly. Daniel Greening was bound to be late. He did it on purpose, Mike suspected, to assert his authority. But Rupert Larkham, the pedantic VP who complained when the text on a memo was one font-size too small – he was never late for anything.

The door swung open on cue, and in lurched the stick insect-like figure.

"Morning," muttered Larkham.

"Mister Rupert! Good morning!" Carlos cried, reaching across to Mike's pile of presentations and sliding one across the table.

The door was flung open one last time, and Greening's almighty presence filled the room. Behind him was another figure – a much smaller figure, who slipped in like a shadow behind him.

Mike stared. What was *she* doing in the Pharmacolt meeting?

"Righto. Let's get started. I've brought another analyst on board, just to ease the workload at the bottom. Most of you know her– um–" Greening flapped a hand in her direction.

"Abby," she prompted, glaring at the Head of Department. Mike winced.

"Yes – Abby," Greening said irritably. "She'll be helping with the groundwork." He looked pointedly at Mike as if to say *be grateful*. "Now let's get going on the book. I want to keep this meeting brief; we've got a lot to get through."

Mike flipped open the cover of his presentation and looked down at the familiar first page. 'An Introduction to the Acquisition Process.' The words blurred. He was tired. Greening started to talk, but Mike wasn't listening. He stared at the presentation, trying to jam his brain into gear. *Concentrate*. Out of the corner of his eye, he saw Abby tuck a lock of hair behind her ear, and lean forward to write something down.

Mike felt a surge of emotion run through him. Anger, he

thought. He was angry with Abby for walking into his meeting – onto *his* deal – when he'd been managing perfectly well without her. He was annoyed that they'd chosen her, of all people, to join the team.

"Michael? Did you say you'd add that into the presentation this week?" Greening was looking at him.

Mike plummeted back to the meeting room. "Yes."

"Good. Put that in the next draft, and we'll have a look at it on Wednesday," Greening instructed, drawing a large red tick on his copy and flipping several pages in quick succession.

Mike glanced around the table, searching for a clue as to what he'd just agreed to do. Rupert Larkham was idly stroking his jaw, Jon Hargreaves was taking apart a biro and Carlos Gonzalez-Torres was drawing a fish in the corner of his page. Abby was scrawling all over her copy like a graffiti artist. *She'd* know what had to be done, thought Mike, baulking at the idea of asking her for help.

"Right. Target multiples," Greening continued, addressing the senior bankers in the room and turning away from the analysts.

Mike looked down at the page in front of him. *Target multiples*, he read. *Target multiples. Target multiples.* He read the same line seven times. It was just words. Mike planted his elbows firmly on the table and pressed his fingers into his skull. *Concentrate. Focus. Think about target multiples.* Abby was frowning at a table of figures, absent-mindedly tickling her bottom lip with a finger.

"…and the model will need amending to reflect these changes," Greening went on.

"Oh, modelling!" Jon Hargreaves interjected with an over-zealous grin. "I'm sure we won't have any problems there; we've got Abby Turner! Abby *loves* modelling, don't you, Abby?"

Mike looked up, appalled. That was below the belt. It wasn't fair to hurl insults at members of the team – especially not in front of the Head of Department. Mike wasn't even sure what Jon had been insinuating, but he could tell from the tone that it wasn't compli-mentary. *How dare he?* Mike felt a sudden urge to reach across and thump Jon Hargreaves. He managed to hold back, and glanced at Abby. She was returning Jon's comment with a lofty smile, her eyes loaded with hatred.

"And now, we talk about the section on Pharmaceuticaaaaaals?" asked Carlos.

"Ah, yes of course. Thank you Carlos." Greening looked up and tapped his pen at the man like a sorcerer waving a magic wand. "Now, I suggest that the two analysts–" he nodded at them– "divide the work between you. Most of the information will be in previous presentations; it'll just be a matter of finding it. Have either of you worked on a Pharma transaction before?"

Both analysts shook their heads.

"Well, you'll find–"

"No–" Hargreaves interrupted shamelessly, "but I think Abby's worked on a 'farmer' before! Ahahahahaha!"

Everyone looked down at their books.

"Well," Greening resumed once Jon had calmed down. "You'll find it's not all that different from any other. Like I said, you can pull most of the data from old presentations – it'll need updating, of course – but if you get stuck I'm sure Jon or Rupert will be able to help you." He shot Jon Hargreaves a stern glance.

Mike nodded earnestly, hoping that it wouldn't come to that. Asking Hargreaves for help would be the last thing he ever did. He was beginning to wonder how Abby stayed sane, sitting next to the fool.

"Right. I think that just about covers everything. Any questions?" asked Greening, heaving his considerable bulk out of the chair. It was hardly the time to bring up a question.

"Good. Next draft, eleven o'clock Wednesday."

He yanked the door open and strutted out.

"Excellent, excellent," muttered Carlos Gonzalez-Torres, clipping his briefcase shut and following in his wake.

Rupert Larkham, who had barely uttered a word throughout, suddenly turned to the junior bankers.

"You helping Michael out then?" he asked, peering at Abby curiously as if she were a Girl Guide trying to attain her *Helping People Out* badge.

"We're working together, yes," she said curtly. "I think Mike was replacing Patrick Gilligan on the deal team, so he needed an extra pair of hands."

"Hmm, right," Larkham muttered disinterestedly before strutting through the door.

Jon Hargreaves let out a long 'Urrrrrrrrrgh' sound as he stretched back in his chair.

"Everything OK then, analysts?" he asked, his head flicking between Abby and Mike like a tennis umpire's.

"Fine." Mike replied, preventing the words 'you condescending bastard' from tumbling out afterwards.

"Well, I might just leave you to it then!"

The first-years watched Hargreaves' tiny body swagger out of the room. Mike couldn't wait for him to leave. Although, at the same time, he was slightly apprehensive about being alone in the room with Abby.

"So," Abby muttered, flicking through her copy of the presentation.

"Hmm." Mike tried to catch her eye but she seemed to be engrossed in something on the back page.

"Looks like you've made a good start," she said, not looking up. There was a pause.

"Why don't–" "Why don't–" they both said at once.

Abby let the book fall shut, and reluctantly looked at Mike.

"Go on–"

"No – go on," he urged.

"I was just gonna say, why don't we split the work into Transaction and Pharma – like Greening suggested? I don't mind which I do."

Mike nodded. He wasn't really concentrating. For some reason, he was wondering what Abby's boyfriend was like. He played hockey – that was all Mike knew. He was probably attractive, and fairly tall, and he'd have to be fairly tolerant–

"Mike?"

"Sorry – what?"

"Which section?"

"Oh – I don't mind."

"Right." Abby looked up briefly with a what-is-the-matter-with-you look on her face, then shook her head brusquely and flipped over a page. "I'll do Pharma, you can do Transaction. Oh, and you're adding that Interloper page for Wednesday's meeting, aren't you?" she asked.

"Er, yeah." So that was what Greening had been on about.

"I'll leave that to you then. Can I just borrow–" Abby leant across and picked up Mike's highlighter, her arm brushing against his hand.

There was a click and a blast of air as the door was flung open behind them. Their knees collided as they simultaneously spun round.

"Ooh – sorry!" cried Stuart Mackins. He looked surprised to see them. "Just wondering if the meeting room was free, but obviously you're... *busy!* Sorry – didn't mean to interrupt!" He gave Mike a strange look, and blustered out.

Abby frowned. "*Interrupt?* What, did he think we were having rampant sex on the meeting room table or something?!"

Mike's laugh sounded forced and rather stupid. Abby looked down at her book.

"Um, right," muttered Mike, reverting to an über-businesslike voice. Is that everything?"

"Think so," she replied, not moving.

After a moment's hesitation, they picked up their papers and stood up.

Jon Hargreaves passed them as they re-entered the main office. "All sorted, kids?" he asked, tapping Abby on the shoulder with a pen and smirking.

She made an admirable attempt at smiling back.

"How d'you put up with that?" Mike asked softly, as soon as they were out of earshot.

Abby smiled and shook her head. "He's got SMS," she whispered.

"Eh?"

"SMS," she said. "Small Man Syndrome. He's got a complex about his height."

Mike chuckled and looked back at Hargreaves, who was jabbing at a pile of documents on Lara's desk and firing instructions at the poor girl. Abby was right; he did seem to have SMS.

"Right. Well I'll get going on the pharma section – I might have to ask for some help on a couple of things," she told him.

"Right," he muttered. "Excellent."

They headed for their desks.

Suddenly, Abby was back by Mike's side. She put her mouth right up to his ear. "I guess we can always ask *Jon* for help if we get stuck," she whispered, giggling.

Mike watched the blonde ponytail flick round as Abby spun away. Something had just occurred to him. He suddenly understood why he hadn't been able to concentrate. He could finally pinpoint that feeling – that distracting, frustrating sensation that had absorbed him for nearly a month. He knew exactly what the problem was. *He fancied Abby Turner.*

24

"BLOODY HELL, JUSTINE! What've you got in here? Bricks?" Abby stopped for a moment to rest her load on the back of the paisley sofa. Her arms felt inches longer after their day lugging furniture across London.

Justine grunted. "This is the last one, I promise."

Abby let out an exhausted sigh, and looked around at their new lounge, which was stacked high with boxes. "That's enough for one day. Let's leave the unpacking 'til tomorrow."

"Might need to track down the box with the bedding in," Justine pointed out.

"Hmm. Oh and which room d'you want? Upstairs or down?"

Justine shrugged. "Don't really mind."

"I hate that phrase! You found us this place – you get first pick of rooms. Now decide!" The roll of duck-tape glanced off Justine's shoulder and bounced into the hall.

Justine shrugged again. "Toss a coin?"

Abby growled in frustration. It wasn't like Justine to be so apathetic. "OK. Heads you're upstairs, tails your downstairs." They watched the twenty pence piece twirl down to the threadbare carpet.

"Heads," Justine noted, as though she really couldn't care less.

Abby looked at her friend. "What's up? You look a bit... low. Is it the thought of living with me?"

Justine smiled weakly and shook her head. "No, I'm fine."

"Is it the Oversby thing again?"

Justine's eyes flickered nervously up to Abby's.

"Oh God," Abby groaned. "What's he done? Is he coming onto you again?"

"No… it's just–" She looked up with a worried expression. "People are talking. I know they are. I heard some of them in the canteen the other day."

"Saying what?"

"I don't know – they stopped as soon as I got near them. It was a load of associates from M&A. That's the worst thing – I don't even *know* what people are saying! The rumours are just flying all over the bank… I can't do anything about them!"

They stood in the kitchen doorway looking at each other.

"I'm gonna tell HR," Justine announced.

Abby drew a sharp breath. "Careful, Just. He's a powerful man. He's an MD, and you're an analyst. Who d'you think they'll believe – him or you? You might end up losing your job."

Justine ran her fingers through her wild black hair. "But what else can I do?!"

Abby just looked at her. She couldn't think of anything helpful to say.

"OK," said Justine, sounding a little calmer. "I'll leave it. I'll see what happens. Hopefully the rumours will just fizzle out; people will get bored of them soon, won't they? But if he makes another move… if he sends me one more text message, or gives me one more dirty look, I'm going straight to HR. I don't care if I lose my job."

Abby smiled. This was the Justine she knew: strong, ballsy, resilient. Although it did seem a bit rash, putting one's career on the line because of someone like Philip Oversby. "Come on then – let's open the wine. Where's the box marked fragile?"

They found it eventually, beneath the box of polished stones that Justine insisted would be good 'Feng Shui'.

"Have you got a corkscrew?"

"Ah…" Abby grimaced. "Um, the thing is, I haven't really got any kitchen stuff."

"What – none at all?"

"Er, well, Ben does all the – did all the cooking. He enjoyed it. I left everything with him in the flat."

Abby suddenly felt all emotional. This was the first time she'd actually thought about what she'd left behind. She wasn't going back to the flat. She'd never hear Ben's eager footsteps again as she put her key in the lock. She'd never feel his soft stubble against her chin, or trip over his hockey kit in the hallway. She'd never find one of his gourmet meals in the fridge with a note saying how much he loved her. She'd never fall asleep in his arms on the sofa, knowing she'd wake up wrapped around him in bed... Justine was looking at her.

"You OK?"

Abby nodded. She wondered what Ben was doing now. Probably stripping the flat of traces of her: taking down photos, rearranging furniture, taking her books to the charity shop...

"You miss him, don't you?"

The image of Ben running towards her, victorious, after the Blues hockey match last year was suddenly painfully vivid: messy blonde hair, sparkling eyes, the most ridiculous grin on his face. He'd run, full-pelt towards Abby, so wrapped up in the moment that he'd forgotten to remove his mouth-guard, and nearly broken her front teeth with his kiss.

She nodded. "I miss how it was. How it used to be."

"But that's exactly it," said Justine softly. "It wasn't like that towards the end, was it?"

Abby bit her lower lip. She couldn't push the image out of her mind.

"That's why you split up, isn't it? Because it wasn't the same any more. It wasn't working, was it? You did the right thing, Abs. It might not feel like it, but you did."

"Thanks." Abby nodded. It certainly didn't feel as though she'd done the right thing.

Justine had located a bottle opener and was boring her way into the cork.

They held up their over-sized wine glasses and Abby managed a smile.

"A toast!" cried Justine. "Here's to getting on fine without men!"

It was exactly as the sharp, tannin flavour hit Abby's taste buds that her phone started to ring.

Justine watched with a pained expression as Abby finished the call. "Let me guess. Work?"

Abby nodded glumly. "Life doesn't get much better, eh?"

Mike was alone in their part of the office when she arrived. He was poring over an Excel spreadsheet and obviously hadn't noticed her come in.

"Hello." Abby said loudly, slinging her bag on the desk. Mike jumped.

"Hi," he said, turning to face her. Abby couldn't help taking a second glance. He looked different. It wasn't just the dark rings around his eyes, it was something else.

"So what's going on?" she asked.

Mike sighed. "It's the Pharmacolt deal."

"No shit."

Mike stood up. "We're really screwed."

"What d'you mean?"

"The bid's turned hostile."

"Eh?"

"The bid's turned hostile," he repeated.

Abby rolled her eyes irritably. "I heard you the first time, Mike. What are you talking about? *The bid's turned hostile* – what's that supposed to mean? That it's leapt out and bitten Daniel Greening on the arse?" She glared at Mike, and to her astonishment – and annoyance – noticed he was laughing.

"Not quite," he said, grinning.

"Well then what?" Abby demanded. "You can speak to me in English – I'm only an *analyst*."

"OK, OK!" Mike cried, holding his hands up in the air. He came over and rested his forearms on the top of Abby's monitor. "Basically, the board of directors of the target company have decided they don't want to be taken over after all, so Pharmacolt's just gonna go ahead and acquire them regardless… hence the term 'hostile'."

"So…"

"So we have to help them do that." Mike finished.

"So…" She still didn't see what they were supposed to be doing.

"So we have to re-do everything we did last week, but with the new terms. *By Monday morning*."

"By Mond–"

"Yep. Ridiculous, I know." Mike shrugged and pulled away from her screen.

"But – why wasn't I told about this when–" when *you* were told about it, she wanted to say.

"Um, well, it's my fault. I mean – it's my fault you're in, I mean–" he looked at his hands.

She raised her eyebrows impatiently. He continued to look at his hands. That was when she realised what was different about him today. He seemed more humble than usual. Less bolshy.

"Well, I got a call from Larkham this morning, telling me the news and explaining what we had to do. But it didn't seem like too much work, so... I didn't call you in. I thought I could do it on my own. But it turns out I, er, I can't. I should've phoned before. Sorry."

"Mike, you're an idiot," Abby told him crossly, although actually she was flattered he'd called her in at all. "You should've phoned earlier. You'd never've got it all done before Monday!"

"Yeah... sorry."

For a moment, Abby felt bad. He'd obviously been struggling away for hours on this, and here she was having a go at him for trying to do it alone. "So shall we divide up the work the same as we did last time?"

"Yeah, might as well. Oh – and I found something you might like to see." He reached over and picked up some papers from his desk. "A presentation Patrick was working on before he got... kicked out. Here."

Abby flicked through it. Then she took a closer look. It appeared to be an almost exact replica of the presentation they were working on.

She looked up at Mike. "Oh."

Mike nodded.

"Would've been helpful to have seen this thing *before* we wasted the last two weeks of our lives," she remarked.

"Would've been helpful if Patrick hadn't been made redundant."

She snorted and returned the presentation to Mike. "I guess they could hardly've kept him on though."

"Why not? He was the best bloody associate they had in Corporate Finance – they were *mad* to let him go!"

Abby looked at him as though *he* were the mad one.

"What?" he asked. "Why are you pulling that face?"

"Well they had to get rid of him, didn't they? They couldn't make an exception for one associate, just because he was good at his job."

Mike frowned. "What're you talking about?"

"Well, they could hardly overlook the fact that he'd been doing coke on Cray McKinley premises – that it was all a figment of Philip Oversby's imagination, could they?"

Mike shook his head quickly. "I'm sorry. You've lost me. Philip Oversby? As in, MD in Leveraged Finance? What's he got to do with anything?"

Abby rolled her eyes in despair. Why was he acting so dumb? "Philip Oversby was the man who caught Patrick doing a line in the gents," she reminded him.

"Did he?" Mike asked, looking flabbergasted.

Oh wow. He really hadn't heard. Surely everyone had heard? "I can't believe this, Mike. You sat next to the guy! Didn't you know why he got the sack?"

"He got made redundant... it was a headcount thing, wasn't it?"

Abby smiled and shook her head. It was nice to have one up on Mike for a change. "They *called* it redundancy, for his sake. But it wasn't a headcount thing. He got the sack. Apparently he'd been working all night on the Transcom deal, and he'd gone to the gents' for a quick line of coke to keep himself going. Philip Oversby barged in for his morning dump, and found Patrick bent over the sinks. Didn't have a clue who he was, obviously, but took down his name and had him fired." She shrugged. "Firm policy, apparently: *no drugs.* Or at least, *no getting caught doing drugs.*"

"Poor guy," muttered Mike, shaking his head.

Abby watched him as he slowly came out of shock. He was definitely different today, she thought.

He finished shaking his head and looked at her. "Right."

She smiled. "Right."

"Let's decide what needs doing."

"You'll have to go through the new terms of the deal with me," she said, feeling strangely excited about the prospect of working through the weekend with Mike Cunningham-Reid.

"OK." He nodded. "I'll go get my notes."

25

"AH, MICHAEL, come in, come in," Greening coaxed. "Sit down." He waved his hand nonchalantly at the huge black chair that occupied a large proportion of his office.

"Thanks," Mike muttered nervously as he was sucked into the folds of creaking leather.

"Oh – shut the door behind you, would you?" he demanded, just as Mike reached near-horizontal position.

Mike dug his fists into the soft, yielding leather and levered himself upwards, catapulting himself towards the door and knocking it shut with an unintentionally loud bang.

"Now. I think you know why I've called you in here today," Greening looked sternly at Mike, who was perching himself carefully on the edge of the seat and doing his utmost to appear relaxed.

"Mmm," Mike nodded. He knew exactly why he'd been summoned into the Head of Department's office; it was because the Pharmacolt deal had fallen through.

"It's no secret that we're going through a rough patch in Corporate Finance," the man began, leaning forwards as though he were giving a sermon. "There's a lot of belt-tightening going on in investment banking right now."

Something lurched inside Mike's stomach. Was this the introduction to a redundancy speech? Had he slipped up so badly they were going to get ride of him?

"There has to be. Transactions are thin on the ground at the moment. Occasionally, a good one comes along, and everyone works their socks off – or at least, they *think* they're working their socks off – but half the time the deals just–" Greening threw his hands in the air as if he were scattering birdseed onto his desk– "come to nothing."

That wasn't fair, Mike thought angrily. He *had* worked his socks off on the Pharmacolt project. It wasn't through lack of effort that the deal had fallen through! And he'd taken over from an associate, too. How dare Greening imply he'd been slacking off?

"It's especially hard when we're having to let go of so many people. Good bankers, too, some of them…" He looked straight into Mike's eyes.

Oh God. This was it. They really were getting rid of him.

"It's the same at every bank – it's not just Cray McKinley," the huge man continued, propping one foot up on the handle of his desk drawer and stretching back with his hands behind his head.

Just hurry up and do it then, thought Mike. Skip the consolation crap.

"The Pharmacolt transaction was…" Greening squinted and pursed his lips. Mike held his breath. A disaster? A shambles? A perfectly good deal until the analyst fucked it up?

"…probably never going to be the billion pound deal the press had hyped it up to be."

Mike frowned. He couldn't believe how the man was dragging this out. Why hadn't he just arranged for Mike's swipe-card to be cancelled, the way Patrick's had been? At least that had been quick. Humiliating, but quick.

This was unfair. He'd only messed up once in his three months at Cray McKinley, and it hadn't been that big a mistake. OK, maybe it had. But he was a first-year! There should have been someone more senior, overseeing his work… Jon Hargreaves! *He* should have been checking Mike's work. It was *his* fault the deal had fallen through!

"…shame about the Pharmacolt deal, but not really surprising…"

Greening was still talking, but the words were washing over Mike's head as though they were in another language. He was busy coming to terms with the fact that he no longer had a job.

He tortured himself with a series of *what if* scenarios: What if he'd gone to Hargreaves for help? What if he'd listened more carefully in meetings? What if he'd never agreed to work on the deal? What if he'd joined a different department? Or never accepted the job at Cray McKinley in the first place?

As Greening droned on, Mike started looking ahead to his gloomy future. How would he explain this to the boys? He could just imagine what they'd say when they heard: 'Couldn't hack the pressure!' 'Wasn't cut out for the city!' 'Kicked out in his first three months!' Oh God, the humiliation! Nobody got made redundant so soon. Nobody! *Especially* not someone like Mike.

"But I digress," Greening said suddenly, leaning forwards and letting his feet drop to the floor.

Yes you do, thought Mike, hoping his time had finally come, but at the same time, hoping that he'd misread the signs, and that Daniel Greening wasn't planning to sack him after all.

"The Pharmacolt acquisition was a complicated one, and relatively taxing for a junior analyst, wouldn't you say?"

Mike nodded slowly as if contemplating the question on a very deep level.

"And as such, it's a good opportunity to assess team members' abilities," he continued. "Now you're probably aware that we keep a fairly close eye on our employees at Cray McKinley, particularly the new recruits—"

Mike nodded.

"...and as well as the annual appraisal system in place at the bank, there are many forms of ongoing evaluation that are conducted throughout the year."

Were there, Mike wondered? He hadn't realised he was working under such close scrutiny. What else had they observed? Did they monitor their employees' whereabouts using swipe-card information? Did they listen in on phone calls? Watch them on CCTV? It was like being a contestant on Big Brother, he thought, still nodding.

"I know it's not easy to give a fair analysis of a colleague's work when there's not much between you – in terms of seniority, I mean – and when you are peers from the same year-group—"

Mike looked at him earnestly, wondering what he was on about.

"But I'd like you to give us some feedback on one of the members of the team. *Honest* feedback, please."

Mike nodded sagely. Where on earth was this conversation leading? Perhaps he wasn't losing his job after all?

"Because," Greening went on, "we've had reports – well, *a* report – on the analyst in question, and we just need to clarify a few things. It wasn't entirely… favourable. Shall we say."

The analyst? Mike had to give feedback on 'the analyst in question'? Suddenly he understood. This meeting wasn't about him at all. It was about Abby. Abby Turner was 'the analyst in question'. The knotted feeling in his stomach slackened off a little.

"I'm talking about Abigail Turner of course," the man confirmed, leaning forwards on his desk and clasping his hands together. "I understand there was some confusion arising when… when Ms Turner came on board?"

Mike mumbled something, keeping poker-faced while the thoughts tumbled around inside his head. What was Greening saying? That Abby had come along and messed things up? That it was all her fault? That she was responsible for the collapse of the deal? It would be nice if that were the case. But the truth was, Abby hadn't put a foot wrong throughout. In fact, she'd been instrumental in getting the work done on time – however futile her efforts had turned out to be.

How had Greening got it so wrong? Someone had given him a 'not entirely favourable' report on Abby Turner. Hmm. Mike had a fairly good idea who that was.

"Just your impressions," prompted the Head of Department. "I can assure you that anything you tell me now will stay within the confines of these four walls, Michael."

"Um," he started, trying to arrange his thoughts. Surely there'd be no harm in going along with the story as it was? It wouldn't exactly be lying; it'd just be… saying nothing. Letting them think what they liked. That way, Hargreaves – or whoever it was making the accusations – wouldn't be seen as a liar, Mike would get to keep his reputation as the first-year genius, and Abby… well, she'd be alright. She was used to taking the blame. It happened all the time for first-years.

"Well," he began cautiously. "Abby is a competent analyst–"

Greening arched one eyebrow, clearly waiting for the inevitable 'but'.

"–but I didn't really work that closely with her on the deal," Mike lied, suddenly losing his nerve. "So I can't really say any more than that."

Daniel Greening snorted loudly. "Don't be ridiculous, Michael. You were the analysts on the deal team! Of *course* you worked closely with her! A summary – that's all I need. A brief summary of Abby Turner's capabilities, so that I can match them up with the report I received from J– from the member of the deal team."

Hah! So it had been Jon Hargreaves after all! The bastard. Mike felt the rage bubbling up inside him again. Why couldn't he just leave Abby alone? Mike looked Greening in the eye.

"Actually, Abby Turner is a *very* competent analyst, and it was all *my* fault the deal fell through."

The Head of Department rolled his eyes and tutted. "Come on now, Michael. This is no time for chivalry. I don't want you owning up to things you never did just because there's a young lady involved!"

"No – it's true!" Mike squawked. He cleared his throat and went on in a very deep voice. "No. I was responsible for the confusion when the deal went hostile. *I* made the mistake. Abby had nothing to do with it – she just helped me out with the number-crunching and the presentation." He could hardly believe he was sitting here arguing his way into Greening's bad-books.

"I see." The Head of Department rested his elbows on his desk and carefully pressed the tips of his fingers together. He sat like this for a while.

Mike waited anxiously for some kind of reaction. Seconds passed. Possibly minutes. Mike was so tense he couldn't move. *What had he done? Why had he owned up? Why? What would Greening think of him?*

At last, He spoke. "Well, thank you Michael, for letting me know. I respect your honesty." He gave a brief nod of approval. "That will be all."

26

THE WOODEN DOORS flapped shut, and Abby felt a gust of cold air follow her in. She glanced around at the pinstriped figures, wondering – not for the first time – why she'd agreed to meet in The Swan. Everything about it was tatty. The peeling wallpaper, the grimy windows... even the bar itself, tucked away in the dingiest corner, draped in mangy strips of recycled tinsel.

Abby was aware of a dozen pairs of eyes undressing her as she walked through the pub, two of which belonged to Barry, the ruddy-faced barman. He was standing proudly behind the row of tarnished beer-taps, his hands clasped under the bulge of his belly as though it were a sack of potatoes.

"Evening darlin'!" He beamed, his gaze sliding down to Abby's breasts.

"Hi Barry," she replied, casting an eye over the fat man's T-shirt and settling on the dubious brown stain stretched across the front.

He leaned forwards so that his stomach bounced gently against the edge of the bar. "What can I getcha?"

"Pint of Stella, please – oh – and a double vodka and coke." She breathed in a lungful of musty air.

"That's three pound exactly."

Abby passed over a ten-pound note. "Is that all?" she asked, smiling and frowning at once.

"The Stella's on me, darlin'. My pleasure."

"Oh!" cried Abby, sounding surprised. "Thanks!" It happened every time. She curled her fingers around the coins as they dropped into her palm, and felt something shoot in front of her face.

Abby watched the projectile as it soared through the air, setting a

188

paper chain swinging and then plummeting to the floor. It looked like a sausage roll. Wiping the grease off her nose, Abby slowly turned to face her attacker. Attackers. Or more accurately: traders. She watched as another airborne nibble was lobbed across the pub.

The air suddenly became saturated with savoury bar snacks. Crisps, peanuts, pretzels, cheese straws – the full range of Barry's buffet menu was raining down on the floor around her. Guarding her eyes from the line of fire, Abby slid to the other end of the bar and hid behind a plastic holly wreath.

The barman moved towards her as though he wanted to impart a valuable pearl of wisdom. "Mind yourself, darlin'," he advised.

"Is it someone's birthday or what?" Abby asked, picking a flake of pastry from her hair.

"One of 'em's leaving," Barry explained. "That one there—" he pointed.

Abby followed the line of his flabby arm. The trader in question was clambering onto a rickety bar stool, shouting something unintelligible at his mates. He looked exactly like the rest of them: good-looking but stocky, probably in his early thirties. He was wearing a crisply ironed pink shirt with the top buttons undone and the cufflinked sleeves rolled up.

"ARRRRIGHT, LADS!" he slurred at the top of his voice, and promptly toppled backwards off the stool. There was more barging, more shouting and more pretzel throwing.

"OK GUYS!" he yelled into the testosterone-filled air as he clambered back onto the stool. "I'VE GOT SOMETHING T'SAY!"

Abby watched as the hefty figure teetered and reeled on his precarious podium. She wondered what sort of a leaving speech the man would pull off in his current state.

"SOMETHING T'SAY!" he repeated loudly, swinging his arms around in increasingly large circles like a swimmer doing butterfly.

"Scott Newman…" he said, once he'd regained some of his balance, "is GAY!"

A ferocious jeering erupted from the crowd beneath him, followed by a torrent of raucous abuse directed at one of the traders – presumably Scott Newman – and another shower of crisps and peanuts.

Abby took a swig of her pint, watching the wooden doors hopefully.

Miraculously, as she watched, they burst open, revealing her little friend Justine.

"Thank God!" Abby yelled. "Get this down you, and we're out of here!"

"What's going on?" asked Justine, taking the drink and looking over at the scene.

"Traders," Abby explained.

They watched as someone else clambered onto the wobbly stool, then bellyflopped onto the makeshift buffet table – three pieces of rickety furniture shoved together and covered in what looked like blue toilet paper – scattering the remains of the food.

"OK, I'm done!" yelled Justine, slamming her glass on the bar. "Let's make a run for it!"

Abby picked up her bag.

"What can I get you naaaaaah?" said a voice that was too close to Abby's ear for her liking. Barry was leaning over the edge of the bar – as far as his belly would allow – grinning zealously at the girls.

"Oh – we're just on our way–"

"Nah – it's on the house. Same again?" Barry growled, pressing his face right up to Abby's and then, as she recoiled, up to Justine's.

"Er, well–"

It was too late. The double vodka – which looked suspiciously like a quadruple vodka – and coke was already splashing into the tumbler.

The girls smiled politely and accepted their free drinks.

"After *this* one then!" Justine mouthed, gulping down at least two of her shots.

Abby found it hard not to stare at the commotion on the other side of the bar. It reminded her of a nature programme she'd once seen about baboons. *'See how the larger male lurches and swaggers in an attempt to assert his dominance, and the smaller, less experienced primates try to imitate his actions. See also how the younger mammals amuse themselves by foraging for food, pushing and squabbling when a peanut is unearthed, and competing for attention from the head primate...'* One of the baboons had broken free from the pack and was standing a few feet away, peering aggressively at Justine.

"Wha're you doing over here?" he demanded, leaning against the pillar for support. "Come'n get some champagne – s'free, c'mon."

He pointed to the opposite corner of the bar where a group of similar apes were showing off their food-juggling capabilities. Behind them, it was just about possible to make out a cramped arrangement of tables covered in more blue toilet paper, and – yes – row upon row of full champagne flutes.

The little man tugged at Justine's arm, causing her elbow to slip off the bar and a large proportion of her drink to slosh down her leg.

"Oh – sorry!" the baboon yelled, bending down to inspect the stain on Justine's trousers. For a moment he looked genuinely concerned, but then he obviously remembered the reason for his visit. "I'll get you some champagne – wait there!"

The creature bounded away, leaving Justine to mop up the spillage.

"You OK?" Abby asked.

"Fine!" she replied happily. "He's quite cute, isn't he?!"

"Cute?! He's a pissed, hairy, dribbling, greasy–"

"Shh!"

The little baboon was on his way back. With champagne. And with more baboons in tow.

"Here y'go!" he roared, thrusting champagne at the girls. "Lemme introduce you to some of the boys–" He flung his arm out to the side, hitting one the shorter men in the chin. The man reeled backwards and dropped out of sight and the other traders moved in to fill the gap.

"I'm Dave," said the first baboon. "We work at Cray McKinley – just next door. We're trade–"

"Yep, we know. We work there too." Abby replied curtly.

"Oh right." Dave looked a bit put out. "Well, this is Dan, this is Scott... Jason, Angus, Eddie, Zacco, Luke... oh, and this is MadDog–" He made way for the smallest, scrawniest man in the group and gave his hair an affectionate ruffle. The lad looked about twelve years old, and more like a cathedral chorister than a Cray McKinley trader.

The men roared with laughter and slapped the little choirboy on the back, howling *'Maaaad Daaawg! Maaaad Daaawg!'* as though it was funny.

After a while, the hooting died down and the spotlight swivelled back to the girls. Except that Justine had disappeared.

It didn't take long to spot the wavy black hair. Perched on a stool in the corner of the bar, nestled between two identical pink shirts, Justine was guzzling champagne and chattering away as though she'd known the men for years. Abby sighed, resigned to the fact that she'd lost her friend for the evening.

Things could have been worse, she thought. It was Thursday night, she was surrounded by men, and there was an endless supply of free champagne.

Scott Newman, the equities trader who had – wrongfully, it would seem – been pronounced gay, tapped Abby on the shoulder.

"Hey Abby. Your mate – what's her name?"

"Justine. Why?"

Abby saw the look on his face, and suddenly realised what was coming.

"Isn't she the one shagging Philip Oversby?"

Several traders moved closer.

"No," replied Abby. "She works in Leveraged Finance with him – that's all."

"So that's a yes, then," said Scott, smirking.

Abby narrowed her eyes at him. "No, it's a no."

If she hadn't had so much lager and champagne swilling around inside her, she might have become quite aggressive. How *dare* they insinuate that poor Justine was voluntarily sleeping with Philip Oversby? It was people like Scott who were fuelling the rumours that were making Justine's life hell. But Abby wasn't in the mood for hostility. She felt mellow and slightly drunk, and she couldn't be bothered to start a fight. The traders obviously sensed that she wasn't going to give anything away, and moved onto talking about Justine's tits.

The cosy, alcoholic cocoon in which Abby had enveloped herself was suddenly ripped apart as the doors burst open again.

Don't see me, don't see me, willed Abby, shifting sideways so that her face was obscured by a large silver bauble. Jon Hargreaves swaggered up to the bar.

"Oi, *MATE!*" yelled Scott Newman, right next to Abby's ear. With a sense of foreboding, she peeked out from her hiding place. Hargreaves was making straight for their group.

"Abby," started Scott, "this is a mate of mine, Jon Har–"

"I know," she cut in. "We sit next to each other."

"Hi." Jon grinned irritatingly at Abby, shooting a quick glance at the V of her blouse and then turning his attention to Scott. "Mate, I brought along a little straggler – found him in the office and couldn't bear to leave him there on a Thursday night…"

He stepped aside, making room for the 'little straggler' who happened to be a good foot taller than Jon Hargreaves.

"This is Mike – he's a first-year. Mike, this is Scott Newman – equities trader."

Abby felt a surge of hope. *Mike Cunningham-Reid. Somebody interesting.*

Mike leaned forward to shake Scott's hand, and nodded at the other traders in the circle. He winked at Abby and mouthed 'hello' with a *poor you* look on his face.

"A first-year in Corporate Finance, eh?" asked Scott, standing on tiptoes and poking his turned-up nose in Mike's face. "How're they treating you there? Wishing you were on the trading floor yet?"

"It's alright," Mike shrugged.

The little chorister returned from his drink-fetching errand and handed Mike a glass of champagne. Mike drained it in one, earning the approval of Jason and Scott, then leant across Abby to plant his glass on the bar. "*Knobheads,*" he murmured under his breath.

She spluttered into her drink, and suddenly found herself giggling uncontrollably.

"What's up?" asked Newman, clearly hopeful that he might have inadvertently said something funny.

Abby disguised her convulsions by breaking into a hearty coughing fit. "I'm – I'm fine!" she stammered, fending off the arms and hands that were hovering around her like flies.

"She needs another drink!" shouted one of the aides, motioning for the choirboy trader to fetch more champagne. He scampered off.

The next hour was even more painful than the last. Scott now had three people to impress, and was working his way through a series of racist jokes that all the traders seemed to find hilarious.

Abby was itching to break free. Several times she peered round the bar to see if Justine had managed to escape, and on every occasion it looked more and more obvious that the girl had no intention of escaping. The pink-shirted traders had trapped her behind a row of champagne flutes, and she was obligingly working her way through them.

"Right then lads!" bawled Scott, slumping backwards against a pillar and holding up his glass, "And ladette," he added, winking mischievously at Abby. Then, raising his voice several decibels, he roared: "S'NEARLY LAST ORDERS, SO LET'S MAKE THIS OUR LAST! HERE'S TO ANDY WADE, WHO'S FINALLY LEAVING US TODAY!" At which point, everybody within earshot – which was everybody in the pub – lifted their glasses and simultaneously tipped back their heads.

"AND WE'RE NOT STOPPING HERE!" he bellowed, "WE'RE GOING ON TO…" he looked down at the nearest person, who happened to be Jon Hargreaves. Jon stared gormlessly back at his open mouth. "WE'RE GOING ON TO… TO TEXTURE!" He dropped his voice again and added, "useless cunt," in Jon's direction.

Abby's heart sank. Texture was one of the most pretentious clubs in the city – no, in the whole of London. It was a place for people to flash their cash and show off their new look-at-me-I've-just-come-back-from-a-luxury-ski-holiday tans. It wasn't really a club – just a meeting point for posers.

"Come on!" yelled Newman, slinging his little arm around as many people as he could and peeling them away from the bar. "We'll lead the way!" He herded Abby, Mike, Eddie, Luke and Jon Hargreaves through the door.

The crisp night air was refreshingly cold on her bare arms and face, and it was then that she realised she'd forgotten her jacket.

"Go on ahead – I'll catch you up!" she called, darting back into the pub and ploughing her way through the second wave of drunkards. She was half hoping that the men would forget about her, so she could just sneak off home. A night on the piss with a bunch of traders she didn't like in a club that she couldn't stand didn't really appeal.

When she emerged from The Swan a minute later with her crumpled coat and handbag (which she'd also left behind), she was relieved to see that the others were already half way up the road, zigzagging their way to the club. Justine's petite silhouette was among them. Excellent, thought Abby. Nobody would miss her now.

"Hello."

Abby whirled round.

"Oh! It's you!" she breathed, her heart still hammering against her ribcage.

Mike was leaning against a lamppost, smiling. His eyes were glinting in the glow of the streetlamp, and he looked... well, he looked like an aftershave ad or something. Gorgeous.

"I'm hanging back," he explained. "Didn't really fancy being part of the drunken lurch."

"Ah," Abby nodded, suddenly brimming with excitement. Maybe the club wouldn't be that bad after all? There was something intriguing about Mike Cunningham-Reid, she thought, and it wasn't just his good looks.

"Shall we?" He offered his arm.

She smiled up at him and looped her arm through his. Which was just as well, because three steps later, she was dangling off Mike's forearm, trying to work out which way up she was.

"Sorry!" she cried, scrambling to her feet and brushing the grit off her trousers. Smooth, thought Abby. Very smooth.

"D'you want me to *carry* you to Texture?!" Mike asked, laughing as they started all over again.

Yes please, thought Abby, imagining the feel of his muscular arms around her body, as she rested against his chest... oh dear. She was obviously drunk.

They walked slowly, not wanting to catch up with the baboons up ahead.

"Bunch of tossers," Mike muttered.

She smiled. "Yep. Doesn't surprise me that Hargreaves is 'in' with that crowd."

"They're right up his street, aren't they?" Mike laughed. "He's a wannabe trader, Jon Hargreaves."

"Have you ever been to Texture before?" Abby asked, letting Mike steer her round a traffic cone.

"No – have you?"

"Yep, twice."

"What's it like?"

"Horrible."

"What sort of horrible?"

"Horrible music, horrible barmen, horrible posers wearing horrible shirts... oh, and there's a horrible entrance fee – fifteen pounds or something."

"Oh," said Mike. "Sounds horrible."

They walked on, listening to the soft crunch of stones under their feet. Without any exchange of words, they came to a gradual halt, and looked at each other.

"Shall we–" they both said.

She waited for Mike to go first. He looked at her. She waited some more.

"Shall we go somewhere else then?" he suggested, finally. "If it's that horrible, I mean."

Abby shrugged. "Yeah. I'm not mad keen on Texture... or the barrow boys. Or Hargreaves." She paused. "What else is open at eleven o'clock round here?"

"Um, well..." Mike looked around. "I dunno."

"Well, we could always go back to mine for a drink," Abby found herself suggesting. "It's just round the corner, and Justine's – well–" Oh God. This was coming out all wrong. It was sounding like a come-on. "She's–"

"Yeah, let's." Mike put her out of her misery. "But, won't your boyfriend–"

"Oh, er, no." She looked away from his eyes. "We... we split up."

He nodded. "Oh. Right. Sorry."

"I live with Justine," she explained. "Justine Brown. The one that–"

"I know who Justine is."

Abby stopped babbling. They started to walk on, still arm in arm. It was a while before Abby recovered from her embarrassment and pointed out that they were going the wrong way for her flat.

★ ★ ★

The thoughts were hurtling around Abby's head as she led him up the steps. This was Mike Cunningham-Reid. He was a rude, arrogant public school boy. He was gorgeous, and he knew it. But there was something nice about being alone with him. Oh, but he was a colleague. Under different circumstances, perhaps she'd consider... no. Not with Mike.

Hell, she thought, forcing her key into the lock, they were only having a drink. That was all. Just a drink. After a good deal of twisting and coaxing, the key turned, and Abby tumbled into the flat.

Mike followed her in, rather more coolly. "Nice place," he commented.

She glanced back to check he wasn't taking the piss, as she did so, banged her elbow on the banister.

Mike reached out to steady her, smiling. "You're determined to hurt yourself tonight, aren't you?" he let his hand slip away from her waist.

Crouching in front of the fireplace with a hand on the bookshelf for stability, Abby inspected the measly array of bottles.

"Don't have a lot of choice, I'm afraid. We're not very good at building up a drinks cabinet here; we tend to get through everything the day we buy it."

Mike laughed softly and stepped closer.

"What d'you reckon? Red?" she asked, peering at the labels. Merlot, Merlot, Beaujolais, Chardonnay, Merlot, Old Man's Finger (one of Justine's acquisitions), Merlot, Merlot. It wasn't a great selection.

"Mike?" Abby glanced up over her shoulder. Mike wasn't looking at the bottles – he appeared to be looking at her. His lips were parted as though he was about to say something, but he seemed to be having difficulties getting the words out.

"Let's go for red then," Abby mumbled to herself. She turned back to the row of bottles and pulled out the most expensive-looking one. She could feel Mike's eyes boring into the back of her head as she scratched away at the foil, finally breaking through to the cork – excellent, real cork – and pulling off the plastic shrink-wrap.

Abby sprung to her feet and brushed past him, in search of a cork-screw. Above the clattering of tin openers, fish-slices, cheese graters and wooden spoons, Abby thought she heard Mike's voice. "Sorry – what did you say?" There it was – under the potato masher!

"What was that?" she asked again, returning to the lounge to find that Mike had barely moved.

Mike blinked and looked at her. He seemed distracted.

"Um, d'you want me to open the wine?" he asked half-heartedly.

Abby handed it over, and watched him plunge the corkscrew in. He slipped the bottle between his thighs and with seemingly no effort at all, pulled the cork free. As he planted the wine on the table, he looked at her, and she was almost sure he said her name – very quietly. She wasn't sure enough to respond.

"I'll get some glasses," she said, slipping back into the kitchen, perplexed. Mike had gone all weird on her.

She returned a minute later, brandishing a pair of hot, dripping wine glasses which she'd salvaged from a bowl of bolognaise sauce. He looked at her, and this time she was sure he said her name. "Er, sorry," he stammered. "I have to go. I just remembered – I have to be up really early tomorrow." He backed into the bookshelf. "Sorry – sorry about the wine; I didn't think."

"Wha-"

"Sorry." Mike picked up his jacket from the back of the chair, and stumbled backwards into the hall.

"I'll see you out," Abby said vaguely, unsettled by his sudden change of heart. Was it something she'd said? Had she offended him? Was it her choice of wine? Her messy house? Her clumsiness? She wandered towards the front door in a daze, pressing her back flat against the wall as Mike barged past.

"G'night," he mumbled, glancing over his shoulder but not meeting her eye.

Abby pushed the door shut and leant back on it, banging her fists against the frame. Tipping her head back, she stared vacantly at the ceiling, trying to make sense of the last ten minutes. She inhaled deeply to calm herself down, and caught the faint scent of Mike's aftershave in the air. It reminded her of that night – the feel Mike's stubble against her chin as their lips had accidentally touched, the stricken look in his eyes.

Abby thumped the back of the door in frustration. She dug her nails into the flesh of her palms and tensed the muscles all the way up her arms. The pain distracted her, but it didn't help her focus. Her brain was muzzy.

She couldn't work out why Mike had run away. First he'd been leading her along the street, inviting himself into her flat, acting all friendly and opening her wine. Then all of a sudden he'd bumbled out, muttering some half-baked excuse about an early start. What was she supposed to think? If she hadn't drunk so much, maybe things would be a bit clearer. It was so infuriating, not being in control.

Abby stood there, pressing her fists against the back of the door. The truth was, she'd wanted Mike to stay. Just for a drink, of course – nothing more than that. OK, maybe more than that. OK, yes, definitely she'd wanted more than that.

She made a decision. It was probably a decision she wouldn't have made under different circumstances, but Abby had alcohol in her bloodstream and thoughts whizzing around her head, and a burning desire, all of a sudden, to be with Mike Cunningham-Reid. She flung open the door, snatching her keys from the hook before leaping barefoot onto the main road.

As it happened, Abby didn't get as far as the main road. Somewhere between opening the front door and reaching the top step, she smacked straight into Mike's chest. She looked up in shock, and before she had a chance to register the intensity of his gaze, felt herself moving backwards, guided deftly by Mike's hands.

Abby stood against the wall in the narrow hallway, Mike's body pressing against hers. She felt his fingers tugging lightly on her hair, tilting her head up towards his. He kissed her, lightly at first, then harder, pushing his way into her mouth.

With distress, Abby realised that the front door was still wide open, and not quite within reach. The inhabitants – and employees, she thought anxiously – of EC1 were getting a good view of their embrace. As if reading her mind, Mike kicked the door shut with his foot, still kissing her, his body wrapped around hers. Abby could feel the heat of his chest through the thin shirt material. She pulled him close and combed her fingers through his hair. He was kissing her passionately, forcefully almost. She felt meek, as though she had no control – but for once, Abby didn't mind.

She was being pulled, slowly but deliberately, away from the wall. Mike guided them in a quarter-circle and pushed Abby backwards towards the lounge. As they reached the doorway, Abby tugged at Mike's sleeve, gently redirecting them. Thank God for the downstairs room, she thought.

He was hard – she could feel it against her groin, grinding against her through both sets of clothes. Mike pulled off his shirt and strad-dled her on the bed, his biceps propping him up. His skin was naturally tanned; there were no pasty white T-shirt marks half way along his arms. She reached up and touched his shoulder, moving towards the smooth, dark skin of his chest, over his ridged stomach and down, slowly, to the buckle of his belt.

She was vaguely aware of garments being kicked off, ripped off and thrown across the room, and the next thing she knew, they were naked, writhing and sliding against one another. Mike rolled her over roughly so that she was on top of him, her breasts hanging freely above him. Abby's nakedness made her feel unexpectedly powerful. She looked down at his hungry eyes, and felt him run a finger lightly over the curve of her waist, over her breast, up to her neck and back down to her breast, where he played gently with her nipple. The feeling of power drained away.

She heard his breathing become quicker and more ragged, and within seconds, she too was groaning. Abby's body arched and shuddered as her mind went numb with pleasure. And again it happened, and again and again, until both of them collapsed on the bed, exhausted, gasping and slippery with sweat.

27

MIKE OPENED HIS EYES slowly and stared at the ceiling.

It wasn't his ceiling.

He lay there, not moving. He'd done this before, but not for a while. There was a procedure to follow. The key was to remain perfectly still and quiet, until you'd worked out where you were.

There was a bleeping noise coming from outside – a lorry or a van reversing – and a continuous drone of traffic. He wasn't in Chelsea. The room was smaller than his own, and filled with a dull white light; the curtains hadn't been drawn. Mike's right arm was outstretched on the pillow beside him, and he could feel something weighing it down in the middle – a girl's head, he presumed.

Very slowly, he twisted round. There was a mane of blonde hair splaying out from under the duvet. He peered closer. Nestled in the crook of his arm was a little face. A cute face, Mike was relieved to see. Flushed cheeks, freckly nose and long, dark eyelashes. Her lips were turned up at the edges; she was smiling in her sleep.

Abby Turner.

Instantly, he remembered. He'd had sex with Abby Turner. He'd had *mind-blowing* sex with Abby Turner. The memory was vivid, all of a sudden. It had been the most incredible – and unexpected – Thursday night ever. This was Abby Turner, the other analyst in his department. And now she was lying next to him, naked.

Abby stirred in her sleep, turning towards him so that her cheek was resting on his upper arm, and one of her legs was pressing up against his thigh. She'd rolled so that she was half on top of the duvet, exposing her back to the air. Her skin was smooth, the colour of caramel. Mike's gaze travelled from her shoulder down to the dip of her waist, up over her hipbone and all the way down her long leg... He was getting hard.

She groaned very quietly, and her eyes flickered open. Mike watched her.

Confusion. That was her first reaction. Then she smiled, nervously, and pulled the duvet over her body.

"Morning," said a voice that belonged to Barry White.

"M-Mike-" she replied uncertainly.

"Yes, that's right – and you must be... Abby?"

She smiled, properly this time, and looked at him. Her knee was touching his thigh. Mike was practically rock-hard.

Abby suddenly looked at him, horrified. "Oh God – it's Friday! We've gotta go to work!"

"Hmm," Mike grimaced. He'd already come to terms with this. "Yes, I think maybe we should stagger our entry into the office – what d'you think?"

She giggled quietly and moved her head up his arm. "I'll give you a ten-minute head-start."

Mike was assessing his chances of a cheeky morning shag – he was feeling horny as hell. He wondered whether she'd be up for it.

"Get a move on, Mike – you'll be late for work."

So that would be a no, then. Reluctantly, Mike started to extract his limb from under her head. But Abby seemed to be pressing down, pinning his arm to the pillow.

"Er, Abby? Could I possibly have my arm back, please? I'm gonna need it today, you see."

She smiled provocatively at him, pushing her head harder into his bicep.

Mike's hopes rose. He left his arm where it was, and gently rolled on top of her so that he was cradling her head, staring into her sleepy brown eyes. He kissed her softly on the lips, and was surprised to feel her tongue dart straight into his mouth. He took this as a positive sign, and lowered his body on top of hers.

"Mike," she murmured, suddenly pulling away. "Seriously–"

He kissed her again. God, she was such a tease.

"Mike-" she repeated, more forcefully this time. "It's eight o'clock – we should be in the office!" She reached round and grabbed the duvet, whipping it off his back. The air was icy around him.

"Go and get dressed – I'll see you at work!"

28

JON HARGREAVES' CHAIR was empty when Abby slunk into the office at twenty past eight. She dumped her bag, quickly logged on and skipped across to the Bloomberg machine. Searching the headlines in the Construction & Building Materials sector was one of her daily tasks for the Project Mantra deal team. It was her responsibility to brief them each morning on news that could potentially impact the deal – a spin-off of a UK subsidiary from a US construction firm.

SHARES IN PLUMBING EQUIPMENT GROUP SOAR! UPMARKET HOUSEBUILDER RETURNS CAPITAL TO SHAREHOLDERS. PROPERTY GROUP DELIVERS ROBUST INCREASE IN FIRST HALF PROFITS. It wasn't the most exciting sector.

She downloaded the relevant news stories and emailed them to herself, stealing a quick glance at Mike's back as she returned to her desk. His shirt was creased and his jaw was dark with stubble. Abby grinned smugly. Less than an hour ago, that chest had been pressing down on her, those hands tangled up in her hair, those lips–

"Morning! Or is it afternoon?" Jon Hargreaves quipped, squinting at his watch. Another hilarious one-liner. "Thought you'd put in an appearance, did you?"

She realised she was still grinning, and disguised it as a yawn.

"Tired this morning?" he asked, settling down at his desk and prising the lid off his cappuccino. "Slight headache, perhaps?"

"Oh!" cried Abby, as though last night had had nothing to do with her lateness. "No, I… I was late because I had a problem with my washing machine! It was leaking all over the floor. Took ages to clean up the mess!" She threw her hands in the air, inspired.

"Ah, right..." He nodded slowly and pensively, clearly not believing a word. He could think what he liked, frankly. In fact, Abby *didn't* have a hangover – she felt on top of the world.

She turned back to her computer and opened up the email she'd sent herself. She could feel the grin spreading across her face again.

"You joining us in the Geoff's office, Abigail?" asked Charles Kershaw, stopping briefly as he rushed past her desk.

"Absolutely," she nodded assertively. "Just waiting for the articles to print.

"Good-good. Don't be late. Geoff's got a conference call at nine."

She hastily opened up the file and pressed *Print*.

Abby felt as though she were gliding through the office as she went to pick up her work. It was a very strange sensation. Perhaps this was what people meant when they talked about 'being on cloud nine'.

The printer was unhelpfully flashing *'Error F1'* at her, and for all her random button-pressing, Abby didn't seem to be having any effect. On the way back to her desk, she passed Geoff Dodds' glass-walled office. He and Kershaw and the other three bankers were already inside. Kershaw waved frantically as she floated past, tapping his watch and scowling. Abby waved back cheerily. It was only eight twenty-seven, for God's sake.

She bent over her desk and clicked on *Print*, opting for printer number four.

"So where did you get to last night?" Hargreaves enquired, swivelling round and blinking up at her.

"Oh, er..." Printer four didn't seem to be working either. Abby scrolled through the options.

"Did you get lost on the way to Texture?"

An orange rectangle appeared on her screen from the Cray McKinley instant message system.

Cunningham-Reid, M: Tell him you couldn't go to the club because you had an urgent analyst assignment, & had to get the legwork done last night.

Abby hit *Escape* and started gnawing at the side of her thumb, desperately trying to control the grin.

"Oh, I just um… I went to bed." She nodded. "Felt a bit tired."
Printer three started whirring.

"Pah!" Hargreaves shook his head. "You analysts have no stamina! Young Mike didn't make it to Texture either!"

"Didn't he?" Abby asked loudly.

"No! Very poor show from the analysts! Can't keep up with the traders – that's your trouble. Pity you didn't come along last night – you missed out on some quality action!" He shook his head, smiling woefully.

Oh no I didn't, thought Abby. "Ah well – next time!" she cried, breezing over to the printer and picking up her work.

29

"AND THEN, OF COURSE, there was the kafuffle with the estate agent... something to do with the new owners' paperwork... I mean, there shouldn't have been a hold-up at *their* end – they were first-time buyers! That was the whole reason we accepted their offer! Poor Denise was beside herself..." The analyst twittered on.

Mike was perched on the flip-down seat in the back of the cab, watching the globular drops of rain wobble their way down the outside of the window and run into the trough at the bottom. He wasn't really listening. He didn't give a shit about the plumbing problems in old Victorian houses, or the extortionate cost of solicitors these days, or the risk of being 'galumphed', whatever that meant.

And that wasn't the only reason he wanted the analyst to get out and walk. The real reason was that Mike wanted Abby to himself. He wanted to be in this cab alone with her, preferably going somewhere that wasn't the Corporate Finance Christmas do. His place, or hers, or a quiet bar... anywhere really, just as long as he could have another night like last Thursday.

Abby looked ravishing. Not that Mike was allowing himself to look. She was wearing a short, silky black dress – not trousers, for once – and she'd done something clever with her hair – twisted it into a loopy knot on the top of her head leaving a few long, glossy strands hanging down by her face. Mike kept his eyes fixed firmly on the droplets, aware of the orangey-brown blur of her cleavage in the corner of his field of vision. The cab lurched away from the lights, causing the water to splurge out of its trough.

"I mean, how much would you expect to pay for something like that?" asked the analyst, raising his eyebrows expectantly.

Mike shook his head obligingly and let out a 'phhhhh' noise.

"I mean, how much?"

Shit. It was a question. "Well!" Mike muttered, exhaling noisily through pursed lips, "*God* knows... the way things are at the moment!" He shook his head despairingly. "What d'you reckon, Abby? How much would you say?" Hah. She'd know what he was on about. She always paid attention.

"I'd guess at two hundred grand, for a location like that."

"THREE HUNDRED AND TWENTY!" the analyst cried jubilantly.

Abby and Mike looked suitably astonished, and stole a quick glance at each other.

"Three hundred and twenty!" Mike repeated, agog. "Who'd've thought it?"

They had arrived at their destination: a tall, inconspicuous brick building in a narrow residential street in Knightsbridge. *This was the famous Black's Gentlemen's Club? The club with the five-figure membership fee?* It looked like an ordinary town house. There was nothing impressive about it at all. There wasn't even a doorman. Mike couldn't help feeling – with some satisfaction – that Daniel Greening was being ripped off.

The door creaked open, revealing a shrivelled old man in a yellowy shirt and a faded dinner jacket.

"Welcome," the tiny man squawked. "You are with the Greening party, I presume?"

"Yes," they chorused.

"You are the last ones?" It was more of a statement than a question. Of course they were the last. They were analysts.

The butler led them up a dingy staircase lined with ornaments, candles and bowls of dust that probably once resembled pot pourri. The banister was waxy to touch, and the air stank of stale cigar smoke.

"You're in the dining room," the midget announced, and with a shaky hand, pushed open the door.

Once he'd recovered from the shock of the fat, naked woman staring back at him from the oil painting opposite, Mike took in the scene. Bankers were drifting around in twos and threes, clutching drinks, chuckling at jokes and trying their best to look relaxed. The low-pitched drone of polite conversation was punctuated by shrieks of laughter from the corner of the room, where the secretaries were getting drunk.

"Ah! The youngsters have arrived at last!" boomed Daniel Greening, powering towards them. He ushered the analysts away from the door and beckoned a timid-looking girl with a drinks tray. "Come along! Come along! Get these good people a drink!"

There was a deafening jangling noise coming from the doorway, followed by complete silence. For a moment, Mike thought his eardrums might have split. He turned his head gingerly to see what was going on. The decrepit butler was standing there proudly, wielding a bell the size of his head.

"Dinner... is served!"

Mike joined the other bankers as they plodded slowly in a clockwise direction, peering at name badges and trying to hide their disappointment when they realised who they were sandwiched between. In Mike's case, he didn't really care where he sat. There were so few people he actually liked in Corporate Finance that the chances of sitting near any of them were slim. Of course, there was *one* person he'd really like to be sitting near, but he wasn't holding out much hope. Which was just as well, really, because Abby and Mike had been seated as far apart as was geometrically possible.

Squinting into the darkness, Mike picked out the silhouette of Greening's sloping shoulders at the head of the long wooden table, and the puny outline of Jon Hargreaves on his left. Abby was squeezed between Hargreaves and – oh, poor girl! – the wheezing Archie Dickinson. Mike watched the man splutter into his glass, then lick his fingers and paste a strand of ginger hair across his forehead.

"Looks like you're the lucky ones!" cried Stuart Mackins, enjoying his privileged position at the foot of the table. He was addressing Mike and Tiki, who were sitting to his left and right respectively.

Tiki shrieked, pouting at her boss with her fat, wine-stained lips, and letting her gigantic boobs wobble up and down. Then, alarmingly, she slipped Mike a look which he thought was probably supposed to be seductive.

"PUT YOUR HAT ON!" Tiki demanded, pointing at the roll of green tissue paper that Mike had found in his cracker and carefully pushed under the butter dish. Grudgingly, he did as he was told.

"Ah, this is the bit we've been waiting for!" cried Mackins, rubbing his hands together gleefully and nodding towards the far end of the room, where something very strange was happening. Daniel Greening appeared to be donning a Santa Claus outfit.

Mike felt the energy sap from his body. Oh God. To think that this time a week ago, he was wandering through Farringdon with Abby, gently guiding her as she tripped over flagstones and prattled on. To think that only week ago, he was just hours away from ripping her top off, from seeing her naked, from feeling her fingernails dig into his back... and now, he was sandwiched between two of the most obnoxious creatures on Earth, watching his boss dress up as Father Christmas. Mike sighed, and watched Greening disappear inside the ominous, bulging sack labelled 'Secret Santa'.

"FIRST ONE IS FOR... TIKI MORGAN!" he roared.

A small brown package skimmed its way down the table, passing dangerously close to the flame of a candle. Tiki clutched at it, grinning stupidly. Suddenly the room fell silent. She prodded at the wrapping a few times, and then ferociously ripped off the paper.

Her smile vanished instantly. It was only because Stuart Mackins leant across and snatched it from her grasp that anybody got to see what it was.

"Give it here!" Tiki wailed, as Mackins dangled the white Extra Large Super Strength Reinforced Sports Bra between finger and thumb. There was a surge of laughter from all around the room. Mike tried to suppress a smile as Tiki stuffed her flabby breasts under the table.

"AND NEXT IS... STUART MACKINS!" cried Greening, cutting through the din.

A huge, brown parcel in the shape of an enormous lollipop was passed down the table. Mackins chuckled heartily as he read the label.

"It says, 'I know how much you miss your hunting days!'" It was a hobby-horse.

The MD rose to his feet and galloped in an ungainly circle behind his chair, beaming, ruddy-faced at the array of flashing disposable cameras. Tonight, thankfully, he was in one of his exceptionally good moods.

The hilarity continued. Tiki was uncharacteristically quiet, which was nice. Mike craned his neck to see what Abby had been given from the sack, but couldn't see past Archie Dickinson who was practising with his new set of rubber juggling boobs.

"MICHAEL CUNNINGHAM-REID!" Greening announced, pulling out a small, bulging parcel wrapped in pink. It crashed down on Mike's fork, which flipped up and hooked itself onto Tiki's gigantic bra that Stuart had hung from the lampshade. With minimal fuss, Mike tore off the paper.

Body Buffing Bronzer, Soothing Aloe Vera for younger-looking skin, Sleek Black Hair Gel, Non-Greasy Moisturiser, Raspberry Matt-finish Lip Balm ... Mike started to re-wrap the gift set. Obviously someone had put the wrong label on the present.

"That'll replenish your supplies!" Mackins teased, leaning over and brushing his knuckles against Mike's smooth forehead in a gesture of mock affection.

Mike frowned. Was this actually meant for him? Did his colleagues think he was vain or something? What a load of bollocks. He barely paid *any* attention to his appearance. The hair gel – well, that might come in handy, maybe, and possibly the moisturiser, too. But lip balm? Aloe Vera? Body buffing bronzer? Mike scowled at Mackins.

"Watch out, Mike!" Tiki yelled in a raucous voice that indicated she was back to her repugnant self. She was pointing at a mousy little waitress who was trying to insert a plate under his elbow. Tiki's over-mascara'd eyes were still on him as he started to eat, which Mike found rather disturbing. He turned to Frederick Jensen.

"So! You going back to Germany for Christmas this year?"

The analyst looked at him. "No."

Mike nodded his head expectantly.

Frederick looked back at his side plate and started methodically cutting his bread roll into pieces.

"Right," he said, turning in desperation to Stuart Mackins.

"THAT WAS BECAUSE THE BLOODY BOARD OF DIRECTORS DIDN'T WANT TO!" he was bawling down the table.

"OH, BUT I THINK THEY *DID!*" roared Charles Kershaw from twelve seats down.

"YOU THINK THEY HAD ANOTHER *BID?!*"

Mike sighed, and drained his glass. At least the wine was good. He stole a quick look in Abby's direction. It was difficult to see in the flickering candlelight, but there certainly seemed to be a lot more action down that end of the table. Daniel Greening was playing with his Work In Progress whip, and Lara was tottering about astride the hobby horse in a pair of painfully high heels, yelling 'Tally-ho!' and slapping her arse.

Two courses and several bottles of wine later, the room was unrecognisable. Chairs were strewn about randomly, some upturned, some stained, some water-logged (a consequence of Geoff Dodds' attempt at flame-throwing). Pieces of charred paper napkin were scattered about like bonfire debris (also due to Geoff Dodds' demonstration). The walls, too, appeared to be billowing in and out, like the sails of a ship, thought Mike. But that was probably just the wine.

"Port, Michael?" Mackins offered, already starting to pour.

Mike watched it slosh into his glass, and smelt the familiar sickly smell. He accepted the glass and pretended to take a sip. The nausea was taking hold.

"So Michael," said a voice coming from over his shoulder. He twisted round, wondering whether it would be wise to rush to the Gents before he vomited all over the table. *Hold it in. Hold it in.*

It took Mike a few seconds to work out who was crouching beside his chair. The man's head was wrapped in a colourful patch-work turban – which, on closer inspection turned out to be a pair of festive underpants – and his glasses were resting at a jaunty angle on the end of his nose. In fact, it was only when he started speaking that Mike identified the man as Geoff Dodds.

The director swayed back on his haunches, then pulled himself forwards again. "Tell us about you and young Abigail, then."

Several conversations seemed to peter out, and Mike became aware of heads turning towards him. He frowned.

"Ah, come on Michael!" Dodds slurred, squinting at Mike's eyes. "Don't go all coy on us!"

There were lots of people waiting to hear his reply. "What d'you mean?" he asked casually, wondering how anyone knew anything about him and Abby.

"Ah!" Mackins gasped loudly. "Been waiting for someone to bring that up! You two are at it, aren't you?"

"No," Mike replied, a little too quickly, perhaps. "No – what makes you think that?"

"It's obvious!" cried the MD, throwing his head back despairingly. "You give each other little 'looks' all the time – I've seen you! We all have!"

Mike put on the most carefree expression he could muster. "That's ridiculous!"

"Oh, denying it are we?" Dodds goaded, raising an eyebrow and causing his gaudy headgear to slip down over his face. He flicked it away with great panache.

"You're a fool," Mackins declared, with a dirty smile. "She's the best bit of skirt we've had in Corporate Finance for a *long time,* I can tell you."

"But you've never managed to get in her knickers..." Dodds rolled forward and peered down the table.

Mike nearly fell into the trap. He was drunk. 'Oh yes I have, you sad, lonely, under-sexed banker – I spent the whole of Thursday night in her knickers,' he almost blurted out. "Of course I haven't."

"No, of course you haven't, of course you haven't," Geoff Dodds muttered knowingly, looking around at the audience. "So how d'you explain her present?" he cried, full volume, grabbing the back of Mike's chair for support.

"Her what?"

"Her *present!* You know – her Secret Santa present! The chain-thing!"

Mike frowned. It was difficult to take him seriously with a pair of Y-fronts on his head. "Sorry – I don't know what you're talking about."

"She got a chain-thingy saying Abby loves Mike, didn't she?!" Dodds yelled, flapping his free hand about impatiently.

"Did she?"

"Yes! A NECKLACE SAYING ABBY LOVES MIKE OR SOMETHING!"

Mike couldn't resist a little smirk. So they'd guessed. It was quite funny, seeing how jealous everyone was. He wondered how they knew what was going on. Even *Mike* didn't really know what was going on. The directors seemed better-informed about his sex life than he was. Geoff Dodds reeled backwards onto the floor, and Mike took the opportunity to slip away to the Gents.

Easing back into his seat two minutes later, Mike sensed that something wasn't right. It was quieter than before. Emptier. In fact, his end of the room was completely deserted. He looked around anxiously, fearing that he might be the victim of some cruel practical joke, and was relieved to see that there were still people around – but they were all at the other end of the table. And they were all… all female.

A hearty slap on the back made Mike jump.

"Come along Michael!" It was Stuart Mackins. He had that horrible glint in his eye.

"Where–" Mike already knew the answer. There were a dozen young bankers loitering by the door. Mike thought back to the last time he'd been out with Stuart Mackins, and remembered the smooth, tanned skin of the scantily-clad dancers, their impossibly long legs, their enormous breasts… tonight, somehow it didn't appeal.

"C'mon, Mike!" cried one of the men. "We're leaving. *Now!*"

"Hurry up – it's nearly midnight!"

"Um, I don't think–"

"Oh, don't be silly Michael!" Mackins urged, giving Mike's shoulder a violent shake. "I'll pay!" And then, turning to face the other bankers, he yelled, "HE DOESN'T WANT TO COME OUT WITH US!"

"Hanging back with the girls!" shouted Kershaw, yanking the door open.

"Probably waiting for – wooeurgh!" cried Dodds, falling backwards through the door.

"THINKS HE'S GONNA GET LUCKY TONIGHT!" roared Mackins, using Mike's shoulder as a launch pad to propel himself towards the door.

Mike felt his cheeks burning. Should he go on with them after all? It did look rather pathetic, staying back with the girls. And he didn't want them thinking he was weird. The first few men broke away, and staggered through the open door. There was a noise that sounded like canon-balls being bounced down a wooden staircase, and then a loud groan coming from the ground floor.

"Well, have a good night, Mike," he heard someone sneer, and looked up just in time to see Jon Hargreaves' bony arse slip through the door.

Mike stared at his smeary glass. There was a layer of cigarette ash floating on his wine. Absent-mindedly he picked up his fork and started stabbing at the sticky lump of Christmas pudding. He stabbed again, and again and again, until there were enough holes to make it crumble in two, and Mike started mashing the fruity pieces with the back of his fork. *Mash, mash, mash, mash.* Why was he sitting here, drunk, alone, playing with his food? He'd just turned down the offer of a decent lads' night out in favour of moping about in a dingy old club. And Abby didn't even seem keen.

He leant forward, and felt something cold and wet seep through the sleeve of his shirt. Red wine. What was he doing? Why was he here? Abby wasn't interested. That much was obvious. The only time she'd come anywhere near Mike tonight was when she'd cavorted past astride a hobby-horse with four other girls, for God's sake. He gave up. He slipped the bag of cosmetics into an inside pocket, and with a final sidelong glance, hauled himself to his feet.

30

ABBY TWISTED onto her stomach and buried her head in the pillow. There was something funny about the flat this morning. It smelt different. It was warmer than usual, too. Justine had obviously left the heating on overnight.

Trampling her duvet down to the foot of her bed, Abby listened out for the bleeping of delivery lorries up in Smithfield, and the clatter of high-heeled shoes outside her window. She heard neither. It seemed lighter than usual in her room; perhaps she'd slept through her alarm. The sound of muffled voices came through the walls – adult voices, she thought. Then there was a rhythmic chopping noise, and the sound of laughter. Was it the weekend?

Abby lifted her head from the pillow and opened her eyes. They settled on the basketball on top of the wardrobe. Her brain jumped into gear. Her basketball was back in –

"Abby, dear! Are you up yet?" she heard her mother sing.

She was back in Gloucester. Abby fought to piece together the information. She was staying with her family. The voices belonged to her parents and – oh no – The Relatives. That meant... that meant... The church bells confirmed her theory. It was Christmas Day.

"Aaaaaa-beeeeee!" the voice cooed outside her door. "Wake up dear, it's late!"

A wave of grey-blonde hair flopped into sight, followed by a festoon of pearls.

"Morning," Abby mumbled, hoisting herself into a sitting position.

"Well, it is – just about!" her mother thrust a cup of tea in front of her face. "Merry Christmas!"

"Mmm, Merry Christmas," she managed, setting the mug down on her bedside table.

Abby's mum whooshed about the room, yanking at curtains, pushing drawers shut and straightening already-straight picture frames. "Are you not feeling well?" she asked, peering at her daughter with a look of impatient concern.

"Just tired," Abby sighed. That was an understatement. She'd slept for nearly twelve hours, and felt as though she could do with another twelve.

"Well hurry up and get dressed! Everybody's downstairs, waiting for you! Poor Pete and Maggie had an *atrocious* journey – apparently they had to stop off at Geneva, and their flight was delayed for *seven hours!* Can't *imagine* what that was like with the children…" She paused on her way out and looked over her shoulder. "Don't forget to bring down some things to show them, will you?"

The door clicked shut.

Some things to show them. Abby groaned out load and let her eyes drop shut. She knew what her mother meant. Some things to wave at The Relatives. Some things to demonstrate how successful she'd been this year. Every Christmas, going back as far as Abby could remember, there would be a moment just before lunch when she and Nicky would sheepishly sidle into the lounge, followed closely by their mother, holding a pile of 'things': Concert programmes from the County Youth Choir tour, Most Promising Basketball Player trophy, Young Designer Award, Grade 8 piano certificate, Cambridge acceptance letter…

Abby massaged her temples, her eyes still shut. She wasn't a kid any more. She didn't *do* things that earned her prizes or certificates. In fact, she didn't *do things*. Since leaving university, she'd barely set foot on a basketball court. She hadn't opened her sketchbook once. The only keyboard her fingers had touched was the one on her desk at work. She was in the real world now. She was a hot-shot city banker – or that's what her mother had told everyone. What 'things' could she possibly bring down to show them? A pay slip? A print-out of her CV? A list of the pathetic, pointless pitches that she'd worked on in her five months at Cray McKinley?

217

Her eyelids felt heavy, and Abby let them rest, just for a moment, while she collected together her thoughts. *Christmas day... the relatives were here... she had to take something down to show them...* Abby could feel the energy seeping out of her. Her mind started to wander. She fought to stay in control, but it was as if someone were dragging her down... down... down...

"ABBY!" screamed a voice, jerking her out of a shallow, uncomfortable sleep. Nicky was standing over her wearing a frilly white blouse and a pair of tight suede trousers. "Wake *up!*" she ordered. "What's the *matter* with you?! We always wake up *early* on Christmas Day – it's nearly half-past twelve!"

"Half-past...?" Abby muttered, dazed.

"Yes!" cried Nicky, flinging her hands in the air.

Abby began to embark on a sarcastic response when she felt her face being stretched by the onset of a gigantic yawn.

"So, are you coming downstairs?" Nicky asked, looking scornfully at her older sister.

Abby finished yawning. "Yep. 'Course. Just gotta put some clothes on. Nice cow-girl outfit you're wearing, by the way."

"Shut up."

"Where's your lassoo?"

"I said shut up." Nicky shot her a nasty look and flounced out the room, leaving the door to slam.

Abby perched on the edge of her bed, determined not to fall back to sleep. What *was* the matter with her? She'd never felt so exhausted in all her life – not even after a whole term of non-stop partying back at university, or after a summer in New York... Her head lolled forward, and she shook it violently, willing herself to wake up. There'd be no more sleeping. It was time to get up. And no, she wouldn't be taking anything down to show The Relatives. She simply had nothing to show.

The general hubbub got louder and louder as she crept down the stairs. She ran her palm down the tinsel-wrapped banister, fixing a wide, bright smile on her face as she reached the bottom. It was Christmas day. She had to at least pretend to be happy. The truth was, though, she just felt knackered.

The smell of turkey fat and bacon drifted out from the steamy kitchen. Peering into the fug, Abby picked out the lean figure of her father, bent over the chopping board wearing – as he did every year – his Christmas hat and apron. Coming from that general direction was a strange, mid-pitched whistling noise, like an old-fashioned kettle in a constant state of boiling, which Abby knew from years of experience was supposed to be *Good King Wenceslas*.

Her mother was flapping about beside him, opening cupboards, rummaging in drawers and muttering to herself. "What shall we put the carrots in? Ooh, I know – we can use that salad bowl the Gilliards gave us, can't we? Oh, not too thick, dear – don't want your mother choking! Now where did I put the sherry…"

Abby leant against the doorframe, watching the scene with fond amusement. They were so predictable, her parents. *Everything* was so predictable. She'd forgotten what it was like back home. Life was easy here. Undemanding. Simple. Things were exactly as they had been ten years ago – except without so much clutter in the hallway. Nothing had really changed. She wished for a moment she was back in this life. Back in Gloucester with mum, dad and Nicky. Back in her old bedroom. Back with her old personality – the one that had deserted her sometime after graduating.

Quite unexpectedly, Abby felt her lower lip start to shake. She stood there helplessly as the kitchen dissolved into a sea of greys and browns. As her eyes filled up, Abby tried to reason her way out of her sadness. It wasn't as if there was anything particularly *wrong* in her life… but there wasn't really anything *right*, either. What was the point? What was the point of her stupid, 'high flying' existence? She stared, unblinking, into the nothingness, letting the pressure build up behind her eyes.

Eventually, she blinked. The tears spilled out and rolled down her cheeks. The kitchen came back into focus, and emerging from the fuzziness at high speed was her mother, brandishing a tray of crisps and olives.

"Ah-ha! The sleeping beauty awakes at last!" She forced the tray into her daughter's arms. "Now take these nibbles into the lounge, will you? Everyone's dying to see you! And they all want to hear about your fabulous new job in the city!" Mrs Turner pushed Abby's shoulder in the direction of the lounge and flitted back to the kitchen.

With a heavy feeling inside, Abby wandered over to the hallway mirror. Balancing the tray on the radiator, she wiped her cheeks with a sleeve. They were slightly blotchy, but she thought she could hide that with a smile. 'Fabulous new job'? *What* fabulous new job? Looking back over the last five months, all she remembered was futile, meaningless work, thankless tasks and projects on which she'd tried so hard but still managed to mess up. She remembered the mistakes, the criticisms, the misunderstandings, the spiteful, belittling remarks... no, there was nothing 'fabulous' about her new job in the city at all.

What could she tell her family? They thought she was some kind of superstar. Her mother was bristling with pride. 'My daughter's an investment banker,' she told all her friends. 'She works in stocks and shares! It's one of those well-paid graduate jobs!' Mrs Turner didn't have the faintest idea what Abby did for a living, or what it was really like at Cray McKinley.

A warm, wet tear trickled down the side of her face. Abby looked at her red-eyed reflection, and made a concerted effort to pull herself together. She took a deep breath, and braced herself for the impending interrogation. With a surge of false confidence, she burst into the lounge.

"So, Ebby!" cried Australian Uncle Pete. "Tell us all about your new job in the siddy!"

This was her least favourite part of Christmas Day. And this year would be even worse than usual, because it would be a solo act. Nicky had already been done. Abby knelt on the rug and forced a smile. "It's great! I'm really enjoying it!" She was a good liar, but she knew that her words sounded hollow.

"So, what exactly d'you *do* every day?" Aunt Maggie asked, looking suitably excited.

"Oh, well, I'm in Corporate Fi–"

"Do you *dance?*" Abby's grandmother interrupted. The ninety-two year old was sitting primly beneath a large blue hat in the corner, wearing a matching dress that appeared to be on inside out.

Abby smiled kindly and bawled, "NO, I WORK IN AN OFFICE!" Then, turning back to her aunt and uncle, "I'm in Corporate Finance. Which means–"

"You should be a dancer, Nicola. It's in the blood, I tell you. Did you know, I was a dancer once? I used to dance on board a ship! We used to–"

"–DANCE FOR THE QUEEN, YES, I KNOW!" Abby cut in. Nicky looked up from pacifying the whimpering baby and sniggered. "So anyway, I'm in Corporate Finance, which means I help companies undertake transactions, like mergers and acquisitions and rights issues and stuff. We advise them when they're thinking of making a…"

She trailed off. Aunt Maggie's head was nodding rhythmically up and down while her eyes roamed aimlessly around the room. Abby may as well have been talking Cantonese. "We, um, we help corporations do deals."

"I see!" cried Maggie keenly, snapping out of her daydream.

"And where in London do you work, exactly?" quizzed Aunt Maud, a wizened old lady with crinkled brown skin which looked like a jacket potato that had been left in the fridge for a week.

"Oh, well the offices are right in the middle of–"

"Because it's so *dirty* in London these days, isn't it?" she went on, scowling at her niece as though the fault was entirely Abby's. "It's disgusting the way people drop their litter on the streets. And the *stench!* It's un*bearable* isn't it?"

"Um, well, the city itself isn't too bad; it's quite–"

"It's *disgusting! Disgraceful!*" Aunt Maud concluded, shaking her head accusingly at Abby.

There was an awkward pause while everybody nodded in agreement and wondered what to talk about next.

"Hey Ebby," her Australian aunt said finally, obviously feeling sorry for her. "I bit you're earning miga-bucks in your job, eh?"

Abby cringed. This was not the way she'd intended the conversation to go. "It's pretty good pay, yeah."

"I hear graduates are like gold-dust at these accountancy places," Uncle Pete added knowledgeably. "They earn something like forty k a year, isn't that right, Ebby?"

Abby squirmed on the rug, wondering how to get out of this. She probably earned two or three times what Pete took home from his surf-school business in Bondi.

"I, well I…" Her mind went blank. She needed to change the subject.

"Did you say you were a dancer, Nicola?" asked Abby's gran, suddenly sitting bolt upright in her chair and looking down at Abby.

"No – I'm a BANKER!" Abby replied, smiling at the impeccable timing. "I WORK IN FINANCE – MONEY AND FIGURES AND STUFF!" she shouted, pronouncing each word with extra clarity.

"Figures? Ah, you've got a wonderful figure, dear. Comes from the Wilson side of the family, that does! Long legs – that's what it is. I was a dancer, you know. I danced on board the–"

"Mmm, YES, I KNOW!" cried Abby. "D'YOU WANT ANOTHER DRINK?"

The little old lady smiled up at her granddaughter as the watered-down sherry trickled into her glass.

"Are we all alright for nibbles?" called Mrs Turner, hovering in the doorway and fanning her cheeks with a pair of festive oven gloves.

There was a general noise of agreement that sent Abby's mother scurrying around the room. "Have you finished with this? Shall I top up the crisps? Who's for another fig roll? Oh Nicky! Why didn't you tell me we were out of baby milk?" And then, totally without warning, Mrs Turner looked at her older daughter and asked loudly, "Have you told them about your bonus, dear?"

Abby glowered at her mother then mumbled something under her breath. She was beginning to wish she'd never said anything about that stupid sign-on bonus. Mrs Turner had got it into her head that the eight thousand pound lump-sum had been some sort of prize that was awarded only to the very best analysts.

"Speak up, Abby! Nobody can hear what you're saying!"

"Oh, er, it's just a bonus you get at the beginning of the year. *Everyone* gets one–" she shot another meaningful look at her mother – "a sort of golden handshake – golden hello-type thing."

"A golden handshake? That sounds exciting!" cried Aunt Maggie, clapping her hands together with glee.

Before Abby – or her mother – could elaborate, Auntie Sandra interjected. "So, d'you have a man in your life at the moment, Abby?"

It wasn't the lifeline she'd been hoping for.

"She's got that nice boyfriend—" Mrs Grover butted in, clicking her fingers impatiently. "Tall, blonde fellow... Hockey player... oh, what's his name?"

"Ben," Abby replied coldly. "But we're not going out any more."

"Oh! What a shame!" everybody chorused, wearing matching expressions of false concern.

"But he was such a nice chap!" cried Mrs Grover.

"Yeah well," Abby muttered, wondering how Mrs Grover had managed to form an opinion of Ben from the two-second glimpse she'd caught one day as he'd cycled past her kitchen window with a hockey stick on his back. "Some things just don't work out the way you expect."

The Grovers weren't actually related to Abby's family. They lived next door. Abby had no idea why they came over for Christmas lunch every year, or why they took such pleasure in their little point-scoring exercise against Abby and Nicky, but they'd been doing so for as long as she could remember. They were both in their sixties, both retired primary school teachers, and both extremely irritating.

"Ah, there's plenny more fish in the sea!" cried Aunt Maggie, slipping her hand affectionately onto Uncle Pete's knee. "Who wants to settle down at your age, anyway? You're *far* too young!"

Abby smiled gratefully.

"So what about the man situation in the office?" Auntie Sandra pressed, evidently determined to reduce her niece to tears.

Good question, she thought. What *about* the man situation in the office? Abby was desperate to know the answer to that. One minute, Mike was pushing his way into her flat and ripping off her clothes; the next he was sloping away from the Christmas do without even saying goodbye. She didn't know what to think. Perhaps it had just been a one-night stand. She hated not knowing, not making the decisions herself.

"Abby?"

"Er, no, there's no one in the office. Anyone for more sherry?" She rose to her feet with the bottle. Thankfully, four-year old

Tammy chose that moment to start attacking her younger brother with a fork.

"So!" Auntie Sandra resumed, once the bawling child had been pacified. "Are you still doing all your sport? You were ever so good at your baseball, weren't you?"

"Basketball," muttered Abby, not that her aunt knew the difference. "Well, no – I don't really get time any more."

"Oh, what a pity!" cried Sandra, with a hint of satisfaction in her voice. "Can't you play after work? Or at weekends?"

Abby almost laughed at the absurdity of the suggestion. "We, um, well we work quite long hours in banking," she explained patiently. "I can never guarantee I'll be out of the office before, say, ten o'clock at night, so it's impossible to commit to a team, you see."

"Oh." Her aunt looked puzzled and slightly suspicious.

"Ten o'clock?" Uncle Michael repeated doubtfully. He was an estate agent, and had probably never worked past five o'clock in his life. He exchanged a dubious look with his wife.

"So what exactly do you *do* 'til ten o'clock at night in this accounting place, then?" Mr Grover asked.

"Well, it's not actually accounting, it's investment banking, but–" she caught his eye and faltered. "Well, I help with the groundwork for the transactions we advise on."

Mr Grover nodded wisely, as if groundwork and transactions were things he was all-too familiar with from his days as a teacher.

Suddenly, the cloud descended again, and Abby felt sad and weak. What *was* she doing at Cray McKinley 'til ten o'clock at night? What was she doing now, sitting with her family, defending her job, defending the firm, defending the world of investment banking, when these were the very things making her miserable? She resented Cray McKinley for taking over her life. She loathed the fact that someone as pathetic as Jon Hargreaves had the right to ruin her weekends. She was letting her friends down so often now that they'd pretty much given up calling. She felt wretched. Abby's lip was starting to shake again. No – don't cry, she told herself. She couldn't bear to break down in front of The Relatives.

Abby stared at a fleck on the rug, frightened to blink in case the tears started flowing again. She was vaguely conscious of Uncle Pete making some remark about how hard young people worked these days. She heard the armchair creak as Mrs Grover leaned across to Aunt Maud.

"Sounds awfully dull, doesn't it?!" she hissed, loud enough for everyone to hear.

Aunt Maud tutted disapprovingly. "Don't understand why she's doing it – it's a man's job, isn't it?"

Abby continued to stare at the brown spot on the rug, wanting to jump up and shake the old biddies. *IT'S NOT A FUCKING MAN'S JOB,* she wanted to yell. *I'M PERFECTLY CAPABLE!* But to Abby's dismay, she found herself unable to do anything at all. She couldn't even stare at the splodge on the rug, as the world had turned watery and grey. A heavy droplet fell onto her thigh and seeped through the fabric of her trousers. She quickly tipped her head forward and hid behind the curtain of hair.

Someone was asking her a question – she could tell from the silence that had fallen on the room. Abby stayed behind her thick, blonde wall, letting the tears roll down her cheeks. The misery was so intense that she couldn't think about anything else. She wasn't even sure *why* she was miserable – she just felt totally numb.

"Isn't that right, Abby?"

She was clearly being scrutinised by The Relatives. At that moment, though, Abby didn't care what they thought. They could laugh all they liked, she thought miserably, feeling her shoulders starting to shake. Abby sniffed away a tear. They probably knew she was crying, but she no longer cared. Blinking rapidly, she prepared to shake away the veil of hair. As she did so, there was clattering sound coming from the doorway.

"Ooh, blimey!" came her father's voice, followed by another cacophony that sounded suspiciously like the hallway vase rolling onto the floor and smashing. "Oops. Never mind. Dinner's ready, everyone! Come and sit up!"

Abby kept her head down, hearing her mother sweep onto the scene.

"What have you done?!"

"Don't worry – I'll clear it up. It was a horrible old thing anyway."

There was a silence, in which Abby could tell that her dad was receiving one of those *you idiot!* looks from his wife. The vase in question, if Abby remembered correctly, had been a present from Aunt Maud last Christmas. She nearly smiled, despite herself. Dear old dad. Head down, Abby slipped out of the room.

"Ooh, Abby dear—" Her mother caught her as she slunk through the hallway.

Abby grunted, barging past and locking herself in the bathroom.

"I forgot to tell you," she called through the door. "Some post came for you yesterday. I'll leave it on the hall table, OK?"

Abby peered at her dripping, red face in the mirror. The cold water had cleared up the blotches, but her eyes still looked sunken and sore. *Too bad,* she thought. Her relatives were all too old or too insensitive to notice things like that.

It was a Christmas card lying on the hall table – from one of her school friends, she presumed – except, intriguingly, it looked more expensive than that. She poked a finger into the corner of the envelope, and tore at the thick, cream paper. The card was dark blue – square and glossy. Not like the ten-for-a-pound ones she exchanged with her friends. On the front was a little cluster of silver stars. Abby's heart began to thump. *It was just the sort of thing he'd choose.* She yanked the card open.

Dear Abby
HAPPY CHRISTMAS
Here's to seeing more of you in the New Year.
With love,
Mike

Abby's mood flipped from morose to ecstatic. *He'd sent her a card.* She stared at the evidence in her hands, turning it over, reading and re-reading the message inside. *Here's to seeing more of you in the New Year. With love* – that wasn't a standard colleague sign-off, was it?

Perhaps she was over-analysing, she considered. It was only a Christmas card, after all. But hey, it was a Christmas card from Mike! So it *hadn't* been a one-night stand after all. Abby was filled with a newfound happiness. Maybe things would be better after Christmas, she thought. Had they really been that bad before? She stuffed the card into its envelope, and skipped back to the dining room with an irrepressible smile on her face.

31

FOR THE FIRST TIME in weeks, Mike was excited about coming into work. It was as though he knew something good was about to happen. He was wearing his most expensive suit and his new shirt from Emmetts – a Christmas present from his father – and the extra few minutes he'd spent on his hair had evidently proved worthwhile, judging by the looks he'd received from the girls on reception. It was Abby's first day back at work.

He could hear her behind him now, typing quickly and furiously. Mike took a sip of his latte and waited for his machine to boot up. He wondered about sauntering over to casually enquire about her Christmas, but decided against it. They'd have to be discreet in the office, or rumours would start flying again. Bankers in Corporate Finance had such empty lives that a mere exchange of words or *looks*, as Dodds had pointed out – could spark a month's worth of gossip. Thank God for email, thought Mike, relishing the prospect of a morning's silent flirtation.

"Happy New Year all!" spluttered Archie Dickinson, leaning against Mike's desk for support.

Mike nodded obligingly and waited for the man to waddle off before wiping the spit off his keyboard. He opened up Outlook.

That was keen, he thought, jumping to the most recent message and ignoring the three from Stuart Mackins. She'd already emailed! It must have been the first thing she'd done when she'd got in this morning. Mike smiled. Today was going to be fun.

From: Turner, Abigail (London)
To: Cunningham-Reid, Michael (London)

227

Mike,

Have been advised to speak with you re. Project Mantra. Geoff Dodds tells me you put together a presentation recently including a section on Acquisitions in the Housebuilding Sector; if so, could you please email it to me, or direct me to it on the network? Alternatively, you could leave a hard copy on my desk.

Also, would you please email me the weekly transactions update you send out each Friday? Have been left off the distribution list. AGAIN.

A

P.S. Found gold cufflink under my bed. Presume it is yours; have put it in your desk tidy with paperclips/treasury tags.

Abigail Turner
Analyst
Corporate Finance
Cray McKinley International

Mike frowned, and read the message again. It seemed rather curt, considering they'd *slept* together. He skimmed it a third time, trying to read between the lines. Where was the flirtation? It was the sort of language she'd use with an incompetent bank manager! Perhaps someone had been watching her, Mike considered. Perhaps Jon Hargreaves, the nosy twit, had been peering over her shoulder. Or was she just taking the piss? She certainly had a cutting sense of humour. *Well*, thought Mike, clicking on Reply. *If that was the case, then two could play that game.*

From: Cunningham-Reid, Michael (London)
To: Turner, Abigail (London)

Hi A,

Do you not think that 'speaking' with me suggests an element of verbal communication? Or is that just my old-fashioned interpretation of the word?

The presentation to which Geoff Dodds is referring is the DeFilia pitch I did. It's on the network under DeFilia/Final Docs. It was a UK pitch, so not sure how relevant it will be to Project Mantra (which is a US spin-off, isn't it?) Can't think of any more useful presentations at the moment; not very well up on the US side of things.

Attached is the transactions update I sent out. Not sure why you're not on the distribution list; I send it to *Corp_fin_analyst_all*, so you should've received it. Perhaps you've been put in *Corp_fin_secretary_all* by mistake(!)?

Mike

P.S. Thanks. It is mine – I wonder how it got there...

P.P.S. Yes, I had a very good Christmas, thanks. You?

Michael Cunningham-Reid

Analyst

Corporate Finance

Cray McKinley International

Mike clicked on Send and turned his attention to Mackins' requests. As usual, the Managing Director was nitpicking over miniscule details: Make borders green, not blue. Change font on headings. Indent bullet points. It was always such trivial changes – and of course, senior bankers could never agree, so when Greening took a look at the final draft, he was bound to change everything back again.

Mike flicked back to PowerPoint and watched as the presentation slowly opened, glancing quickly at the corner of his screen. No reply from Abby. He drank some coffee and one-handedly scrolled to page four – Previous Acquisitions. It was time for some cutting-edge investment banking, he thought: *colouring the borders green*.

He'd just finished page four when the little envelope icon appeared on his control bar. He abandoned his font re-sizing.

From: Turner, Abigail (London)

To: Cunningham-Reid, Michael (London)

Mike,

Thanks, but I intend to stick with my own interpretation of the word, if you don't mind. Would prefer to keep verbal communication to a minimum.

DeFilia info & transactions update gratefully received. Found your suggestion about distribution list error highly entertaining, as I'm sure Cray McKinley HR will too.

A

P.S. From what I hear, you're *perfectly* well up on the US side of things – particularly the New York side.

P.P.S. I didn't actually enquire about your Christmas, but since you asked, yes, mine was great.

_____

Abigail Turner
Analyst
Corporate Finance
Cray McKinley International

Mike frowned again, fighting back the urge to swivel round and stare at Abby. Was she having a laugh? He could only assume so. There wasn't a single bit of flirtation in the whole email. And what was that P.S. all about? He hadn't worked on a New York deal in the whole time he'd been at the firm.

Aware of the fact that Abby had a perfect view of his screen from where she sat, Mike swiftly clicked on Reply, as though he couldn't care less. If she wanted to be all sarcastic with him, he was happy to play along.

From: Cunningham-Reid, Michael (London)
To: Turner, Abigail (London)

A,

Fine, will endeavour to endeavour to steer clear of verbal communication (although if you are hoping to avoid catching something, I would say that it's probably too late).

My comment about distribution list was meant as a joke – no doubt HR will understand that.

M

P.S. Haven't worked on any US transactions – what are you on about?

P.P.S. D'you fancy a drink sometime? I'm busy for the next few weekends, but how about end of Jan? Say Sat 31st? Have a rugby match in Twickenham that day, but maybe late eve? Or first week of Feb?

Michael Cunningham-Reid
Analyst
Corporate Finance
Cray McKinley International

It was worth a shot. He was only asking her for a drink, anyway – he wasn't asking her *out*. Mike got back to his presentation. The borders looked rather naff in green, he thought, but who was he to criticise? He set to work changing all the Times New Roman to Helvetica 65 Medium. No reply from Abby.

Stuart Mackins' office door was suddenly flung wide open, sending papers flapping across Mike's desk.

"Michael. You got my emails?" the MD barked.

"Yes," Mike replied, collecting up the loose leaves and putting them back in a pile.

"So you'll have it done by nine-thirty?"

"Er…," Mike faltered. The emails hadn't mentioned a deadline.

"For the meeting upstairs?" the man prompted impatiently. He was obviously having one of his bad days.

"Er… yuh." Mike nodded.

"Right. Make sure it's done properly – Daniel Greening and the M&A bankers will be wanting to see it. Run off six copies. No, make it eight. Fuck it – make it ten. In colour."

The door was pulled shut, sending the papers flying again. Mike turned back to his screen. The envelope icon was back.

From: Turner, Abigail (London)
To: Cunningham-Reid, Michael (London)

M,

For God's sake, anyone would think you didn't have

any work to do. I'm terminating this email exchange now. Please don't reply.

A

P.S. you know exactly what I mean.

P.P.S. I have no desire to go for a drink with you, January, February, or ever.

Abigail Turner
Analyst
Corporate Finance
Cray McKinley International

Jesus. Was she trying to be funny? Mike whirled round to face her. He just couldn't help himself.

There was a loud 'clang' as Abby's chair went hurtling into a filing cabinet. She snatched up a pile of reports from her desk and stormed through the office towards the photocopiers. As she passed him, she glanced over her shoulder and looked straight back at Mike with a cold, hateful stare. One thing was for certain, he thought. Those emails had not been a joke.

32

"HIYA!" JUSTINE CALLED from the kitchen. "How was your first day back?"

Abby stomped through the hallway, slamming the front door behind her. "Crap. What about yours?" She barged into her bedroom and flung herself down on the bed.

There was a clattering noise followed by a tiny yelp. Justine was evidently trying to cook. "Oops! Pretty good, actually – Philip Oversby's away all this week! Want a cup of tea? You know what, this must be the earliest we've both been in the flat together!"

Abby grunted and threw an arm across her eyes to try and block out the day. She wasn't in the mood for chit-chat or cups of tea, but she clearly didn't have much choice. The patter of Justine's dainty footsteps got louder and louder, then stopped abruptly.

"Oh." She hovered timidly in the doorway. "It's like that, is it?"

Abby reluctantly moved her arm and let out a long, shaky sigh.

"Here. Have some tea," offered Justine, as though tea were the antidote to all things evil. "Is it Mike?"

Abby grunted again, staring furiously at the ceiling. Of course it was Mike.

"Oh Abby, I'm sorry. I wish Joe had never said anything."

Abby looked at her stormily. "I'm bloody glad he did! Otherwise I'd never have known!"

Justine nodded apologetically and looked at the floor.

Abby groaned and flopped back onto the bed. She was so angry with Mike. And hurt. And ashamed. She felt fifteen again. He'd led her to believe there was something going on between them. She'd really thought there might've been. That night he'd come back to hers had been… well, she couldn't put it out of her mind. And then, just to fuel her hopes, he'd sent her that card. She'd spent the last two days in a state of anxious anticipation, almost desperate to come back to work. What an *idiot* she was. How *naïve*. Abby felt like punching the wall.

"Bet she's ugly," Justine said quietly, "Mike's girlfriend."

Abby shook her head, continuing to stare at the ceiling. "She's an ex-supermodel or something – isn't that what Joe said? Didn't you see her, when we were out in New York?"

Justine thought for a second. "No – did you?"

"No," Abby admitted. "But I bet she's stunning."

"Yeah, and a complete air-head," Justine retorted, obviously trying to make Abby feel better.

"Justine, *I'm* the air-head – for falling for Mike. What was I thinking? He's probably got loads of women on the go – all over the world! Why did I think I was special? He's just a typical good-looking guy. A lying, cheating, son-of-a-"

"Come on, Abs, don't beat yourself up over this."

"Why *not*? It's my own fault. I shouldn't have got mixed up with him."

"Just forget about him," Justine suggested unhelpfully.

Abby looked at her. "How? When he's still trying it on?"

"What?"

"He emailed today. Asking me out for a drink."

"Oh my God! What did you say?"

"Told him to fuck off, obviously."

"Does he know you know about the girlfriend?"

"Oh, he does now. I made that perfectly clear." Abby groaned in frustration. Her anger was directed more at herself than at Mike. She was cross that she'd let herself get so involved. Past experience had taught her to stay away from people like him. He was a player. A guy who got through women faster than he got through under-pants. He wasn't a man to get all hung up about. But unfortu-nately, the idea of going for a drink with Mike still appealed, even now. That P.P.S at the end of his email had ignited a spark of hope – hope that there *might* be something between them after all. It was pathetic, really. It was silly even to waste time thinking about it.

Justine pointed at Abby's cup of tea, which was going cold on her bedside table. "Come on. Drink up."

Abby rolled over and picked up the mug. It was time to stop wallowing in self-pity. She smiled unconvincingly at Justine, and noticed for the first time how different she looked. The five days off at Christmas had obviously done her some good. Her eyes were sparkling, her skin was radiant. She looked like the girl Abby had met back in summer. She was smiling, too. In fact, she could hardly *stop* smiling.

"Justine, what's with the—"

"Oh! I've been meaning to tell you—" Justine cut in excitedly, waving Abby's question away. "I was talking with Joe this evening in the canteen, and he's asked me if I wanna—"

"Hah!" cried Abby, suddenly working it out.

"What?"

"I know why you're grinning like a Cheshire cat!" Abby propped herself up in bed, prepared to postpone her chronic bad mood for a bit.

"What d'you mean, 'grinning like a—"

"It's Joe Cartwright, isn't it?"

Justine tried to frown, but it turned into another grin.

"Ah-ha!" cried Abby, finding herself grinning back at Justine. Joe Cartwright. The only other person in the year-group as smart — and come to think of it, as *short* — as Justine Brown. "Come on! Tell me!"

Justine shrugged. "There's nothing much to tell, really. We just... got chatting over Christmas, and found out we both do salsa—"

"Joe does *salsa dancing?*" Abby asked, staring incredulously.

"Oh – but you can't tell the guys! Joe told me not to tell anyone! He and Zoë used to do it. But he hasn't been for ages – since they... split up. So anyway, he asked me if I wanted to go to this club he knows. On Saturday."

Abby smiled. It was good to see Justine so happy. She hadn't been herself lately, what with the Philip Oversby fiasco. Perhaps a little romance with Joe would turn out to be just what she needed. It might even dampen the rumours, too.

"It's not like a *date* or anything," Justine said defensively.

"No, no — of course not." Abby nodded earnestly, watching her friend blush.

Justine tried to glare at her, but it came out more like a smirk. "Oh, stop it!" she cried, rushing out of the room, purple-faced.

33

"WELL, HAPPY fucking New Year everyone," Marcus grunted, raising his can of Red Bull.

One or two analysts around the table mumbled something in return and half-heartedly lifted their drinks, but most of them didn't bother. The mood in the canteen was glum.

"Two days into it, and we're already down here again," moaned Danny, stabbing at another chip. "Might as well not've bothered with Christmas."

"Feels like we never went away," said George. He never had anything new to add.

Suddenly Marcus slammed his can on the table. "BLOODY HELL – LOOK!" He pointed at the giant screen that took up the end wall of the canteen. Usually the TV was tuned to News 24, or occasionally BBC 1 if there were enough analysts lobbying to watch EastEnders. Today though, it was showing two voluptuous blondes in skimpy bikinis, rubbing up against one another in a jacuzzi.

The analysts stared.

"Lipstick lesbians!" one of them hissed.

"Are we watching the Adult Channel or something?" bleated Danny excitedly.

"It's Channel Four," George informed them in a monotone, his eyes not leaving the screen. "It's a trailer for that reality TV programme – the one where the girls have to live on a farm in Alabama for three months."

"Doesn't look like a farm to me," Marcus muttered vaguely, fixated by the erotic scene.

"I presume that's before they've left."

The voiceover was just loud enough to hear.

"*See whether dancers Miranda and Clara can pack up their bags and their mischief as they head for the sleepy town of Waverly, deep in the heart of Alabama...*"

The steamy jacuzzi was replaced by a small, crumbling brick outhouse with a corrugated iron roof. The analysts got back to their food.

Danny looked across at Mike. "Isn't that your New York bird?"

Mike snorted. "She was called Miranda, yeah. And she did have nice tits." He glanced up at the screen, hoping to catch another glimpse of the naked blondes. Disappointingly, it was filled with the sight of frying bacon, and then, panning back, a fat Alabama mother, waddling about the kitchen doling out eggs to obese children. "She doesn't really qualify as 'my bird' any more though," Mike admitted, thinking back to that disastrous episode in the New York cocktail bar – an episode he'd never had to explain to the lads.

There were a couple of quizzical looks from some of the guys around the table.

Mike shrugged. "We, um, well, we didn't exactly–"

"So, you've heard the news, then?" chirped Joe, appearing from nowhere with his trayful of food for the night ahead.

The analysts looked up at him blankly, conveniently losing interest in Mike.

"About the job in Corporate Broking?" Joe prompted.

Suddenly, Joe had everybody's full attention. Corporate Broking (or 'Corporate Joking', as it was known among analysts, due to its short hours, easy work and vast budget for entertaining clients) was a department they could only dream about. It was a holiday camp for first-years.

"Nobody's supposed to know yet," Joe confided, glancing around the canteen, "but I was talking to that work experience girl they've got in HR. She let it slip by accident."

"What – a vacancy for an analyst?" Mike asked. As far as he knew, they didn't bother with analysts in Broking; the work consisted mainly of taking clients out to lunch – something better suited to Managing Directors than to lowly analysts.

"Yep – they're gonna make it official in May. And y'know what? The pay's the same as what we get now!"

There was a short pause while the young men digested this information. Mike's brain started to whir. He wanted that job. Becoming a Corporate Broker could be the solution to all his problems. He would still have the salary he'd become accustomed to, but he'd actually have time to *spend* it. He'd get to go out at night instead of being trapped in the Cray McKinley canteen. He'd get to see more of his uni mates. He might even get to go away at weekends. Maybe he could join a rugby club, or even play for a London team... The excitement bubbled up inside him, but he was careful not to let it show. If Joe was right about this new position, then there'd be intense competition for the place.

"So don't they have any first-years in Broking at the moment?" he asked casually.

"No – didn't think they'd need any this year, but apparently they've changed their minds," Joe explained. "Guess I shouldn't really be telling you all," he added, grinning. "Don't want you all applying! Anyway, I'd better get back upstairs. See you around."

"And me," added Alan, following him out with George in tow.

The table emptied quickly, leaving just Marcus and Mike alone with their sticky toffee puddings. Mike shaved off a gooey sliver with his fork. He knew he should really be back upstairs, but he wanted time to think. Joe's tip-off had given him some ideas, and he needed to formulate a plan. And that wasn't the only thing on his mind.

They chomped their way through the syrupy sponge, pausing occasionally to slurp on their drinks. Marcus got through his in record time, chucking his spoon on the table and releasing a loud, throaty belch. "Good stuff," he muttered, leaning back in the chair. "So, how was your Christmas?"

"So-so." Mike turned his nose up and rolled his eyes. "Yours?"

"Alright, actually. Bit short, but not bad." Marcus nodded pensively, and a faint grin crept up one side of his face. It was a look Mike had seen before.

"OK, mate. Who is she?" he asked.

Marcus tipped his head to one side and clicked his tongue against the back of his mouth. "Someone I've had my eye on for a while, actually."

"Really? Who?"

"Huh – that's the thing." The cheeky grin vanished. "She's a mate of my little sister's. Lives down in Portsmouth."

"Ah." Mike frowned in sympathy. Marcus had no chance of holding down a long distance relationship. It was difficult enough for the analysts who *lived* with their girlfriends – let alone those who were hundreds of miles apart.

"And she's at uni in Hull," Marcus added gloomily.

"Oh." Mike's frown intensified. Their relationship was doomed.

Marcus sighed wearily. "Jesus, I hate this place," he muttered, cupping his head in his hands.

Mike looked across at his friend, nodding glumly. He felt the same way. They'd been at Cray McKinley for six months, and already he was beginning to loathe it. It wasn't just the work that made it so bad (although typing up pages of bankers' scrawl and fiddling with PowerPoint slides was not exactly stimulating); it was the company's attitude towards analysts. Nobody gave a shit about them. He couldn't remember the last time he'd been acknowledged – let alone thanked – for doing a good piece of work, for staying late, for cancelling his weekend plans. It was just assumed that analysts would put their lives on hold for their jobs.

That was the worst thing about Cray McKinley – the sense of imprisonment Mike felt the whole time. He spent every minute of every day in this goddamn building. And even when he occasionally escaped for some sleep, he was on call. It was like being a convict on parole. He couldn't walk free. He couldn't plan. He couldn't commit to anything. Or to anyone. Which brought him back to the other issue on his mind. He looked across at Marcus' miserable face, and suddenly felt desperate to confide in him.

"I'm having a similar problem," he said quietly.

"Oh yeah?" Marcus tilted his head in his hands.

"Mmm. Y'know Abby Turner?"

"Yeah – course I do!" Marcus chuckled. "There's only one fit, leggy blonde in our year-group!"

"Well…" Mike trailed off, hoping that his friend would get the idea.

"What about her?" he asked dumbly.

Mike hesitated, wondering whether he should say anything after all. Perhaps it was insensitive to tell a colleague. As he wavered, a look of understanding came over Marcus' face.

"Heh-hey! Are you telling me what I think you're telling me?!"

Mike nodded reluctantly. Telling Marcus had been a stupid idea.

"No shit! When? How? God, the boys'll be mad – Danny and Alan have been trying to get in with her all year! *Everyone* has!"

Mike winced. He should never have said anything. The news would be all round the firm within a couple of hours. "Mate…" he looked pleadingly at Marcus. "Don't mention it to anyone, OK?"

Marcus' face become dead-pan. "Sure." He nodded. "Don't worry. Won't tell a soul, I swear."

Mike looked at him gratefully. He trusted Marcus.

"So, what's going on between you two?"

Mike shrugged. "Well, that's just it. I dunno. We went to some leaving drinks just before Christmas, and ended up going back to hers, and well–" he looked at Marcus, who seemed to catch on this time. "That's when it happened. And then she took a week off for Christmas, and when she got back on Monday… well, I think I must've done something wrong. She's gone all cold on me. Rude emails and nasty looks – that sort of thing. It's weird, mate. I can't work it out."

Marcus shook his head slowly, looking up at the ceiling. "Women," he said. "Can *anyone* work 'em out?"

They sat there quietly for a moment.

"Playing hard to get?" Marcus suggested, after a thoughtful pause.

Mike shrugged. "Maybe. Didn't think she was that sort of girl."

"No, you're right. Abby Turner's got her head screwed on." He frowned. "Fuck knows. So you're not gonna talk to her about it?"

Mike gave him a scornful look. Of course he wasn't going to talk to her about it.

"No, right. Course not." Marcus nodded, conceding the stupidity of his suggestion.

There was another short pause while they pondered Mike's situation.

"Well, if you want my advice," said Marcus, tipping his head back and draining his can of Red Bull, "I'd steer clear of her altogether."

Mike's shoulders slumped. This wasn't the advice he'd wanted to hear.

"It wouldn't work, with you both being in Corporate Finance. Never does. Look at what's happened to Justine Brown."

Mike scowled. "Come on, mate! That's totally different! She's shagging a Managing Director. A Managing Director with a wife and kid! This is me and Abby. We're both first-years."

"Exactly. You're both first-years. You're rivals."

"No we're—" Mike stopped, not even bothering to argue his case.

Marcus looked at him and shook his head. "Your choice, mate. But think about what you're doing," he warned. "Don't mix business with pleasure."

Mike grunted. At the back of his mind, he knew Marcus was right. It was just asking for trouble, getting involved with a colleague – especially a fellow first-year. A fellow first-year in the same department. He and Abby *were* rivals, competing for the next rung of the corporate ladder.

"You're right," he said reluctantly. They simultaneously pushed back their chairs and stood up.

34

Abs,

Bought this as a way of communicating. Haven't seen you in over a week!

Hope things OK with you. Saw you in training on Weds, but you were busy arguing so I left you to it. You around this w/e? Am working most of it, but hoping to escape (Salsa Sat!) – fancy cinema Fri?

Just x

Hello!

Good idea. Keep forgetting who I share flat with. Things fine here – same as ever. Hate my job, hate my colleagues, hate my life. Nothing new.

Fri sounds good – work permitting. Lots on in Corp. Fin. at the mo – all pitching. Gripping stuff. Let's decide on the day. Will email.

A x

P.S. Mike C-R acting v weirdly. Seems to be *flirting*. Tosser.

FUCK FUCK FUCK!

Been put on new deal. Head of project PHILIP OVERSBY! Think he did it on purpose. Caught me at midnight & asked me for a drink (I made up some crap excuse)

Gonna go to HR about him. Nothing else I can do. He won't leave me alone. Will let you know how it goes...

Things looking bad again for Fri. This deal's taking over my life – SORRY!

J xx

P.S. Can't believe the cheek of that guy! What a twat! Feel sorry for poor NY gf.

FUCK! Asked you for a drink?! The man has no shame! Let me know how it goes with HR – BE CAREFUL JUSTINE. Remember, it's Analyst vs. MD. You know who they'll believe.

→ Bought some Pro-plus stuff. Help yourself. I NEED SLEEP!

A

P.S. M C-R totally ignoring me now. Men!!!

Grrr.

So much for the Fri night out. No chance 2nite, I'm afraid. If I'm out B4 midnight, I'll be heading straight for bed – sorry.

Went to HR, fat lot of good they were. Need 'evidence' of harassment. Texts no good. WHAT DO THEY EXPECT ME TO DO? Plant bugging equip. in office???

Joe says Oversby's showing associates dirty text-msgs from me. HELP!!! Have sent no such thing! Might apply to transfer depts. Or quit…

J

P.S. we've got one of your guys working on this deal – associate called Jon Hargreaves. Know him? Seems bit of a prick.

No – DON'T QUIT! You can't leave me in this shit-hole.

Bad news re. HR. Must be another way. Will have a think.

Fake text-msgs? WHAT A LOSER!

No worries about last night. Was working til 10 anyway.

Jon Hargreaves – you poor thing. Sits next to me. Complete prick. Avoid him if poss.

Enjoy salsa 2nite!

A XXX

Hmm. No note?

You dirty stop-out. So salsa ~~date~~ not-date went well then?

Look forward to hearing all – maybe later?

A x

P.S. would it help if Philip saw you with Joe? Perhaps you could engineer chance 3-way mtg?

Dirty stop-out? If only!

Never got near salsa club. Had to cancel. Was working on stupid pitch til 8am.

I HAVE IMPORTANT NEWS FOR YOU! Your phone was off – come wake me up as soon as you get in!

Jx

35

"LOOKS LIKE RAIN," the taxi driver remarked, nodding up at the ominous sky as he eased himself out. Agonisingly slowly, he opened the boot and reached inside for the kit bag. Mike yanked the strap from the dawdling man's hands, thanked him and set off across the car park.

It was exactly a year since he'd played at The Stoop. Exactly a year since the last Old Boys match. Exactly a year, he realised as the panic fluttered up inside him, since he'd last played rugby.

The Old Boys match was one of the highlights of the university calendar. Mike remembered how hard they'd trained at the end of last season, in preparation for the big game down in London. Extra practices, group fitness sessions, ten-mile runs... and still they'd lost 42-30. The Old Boys had been so much stronger than the Edinburgh fifteen. At the time, Mike had consoled himself with the fact that the opposition had been older and more experienced. They were men; Mike's team had been mere students. This year, it was his side with the supposed advantage. He tried to be encouraged by this thought.

The changing rooms were deserted. Mike found his way through the maze of concrete corridors to the place he remembered from last year. As he'd hoped, a scattering of abandoned clothes and a trail of soft, stud-imprinted mud led the way out to the pitch.

Discarding his office clothes on the bench, Mike jogged onto the field, his bootlaces flicking up at his ankles. The cabby had been right. The black cloud above the stadium was just starting to shed its load, the rain beating sideways on a wild, swirling wind. Mike ploughed through it, the icy droplets stinging his flesh like needles. It was a horrible day for spectating, he thought, looking up at the near-empty stadium.

"Mickey!" shouted a strained voice. Minnie was bent over at the waist, his head and shoulders jerking up and down as his hands failed to make contact with his toes. He'd put on weight since Mike last saw him.

"You missed the run!" gasped BFG.

Jenkins spat a mouthful of phlegm onto the grass and shoved his mouth-guard in. "'Bout bruddy time, Mick! Kick-offsh in two minutch!"

Mike hardly recognised the man. A year ago, Jenkins had been built like a weight-lifter. Now, he just looked fat.

"Yeah, sorry guys – been in work all night. Only–" Mike stopped himself. His team mates didn't want to hear that he'd only had two hours' sleep. They didn't want to hear that he'd spent his weekend miserably picking out figures from a stack of annual reports. That he'd consumed nothing but three cans of Red Bull since yesterday afternoon, or that he hadn't been to the gym in nearly a week. He was their captain. He had to show strength. "Only just made it!" He clapped his hands together authoritatively.

Mike looked around at his squad. It didn't inspire him with confidence. Jenkins, their ever reliable full-back, was wheezing and spluttering at the side of the pitch, his shirt visibly taut around his stomach. Squatty and Porker, the props whose combined strength had once lifted the team minibus six feet in the air, looked like a pair of pot-bellied pigs. Adam, their nippy fly-half and kicker, was sitting on the sidelines looking pasty and weak, as though this was his first trip outdoors in months. The only person who hadn't changed was Chris. Cheeks flushed, hair all over the place and in no particular style, he looked exactly as he had done a year ago.

"Who're we missing?" Mike demanded.

"Well we've got no wings, as Jim and Dan are still playing for Edinburgh–" Chris nodded towards the far end of the pitch, where a blur of blue, red and white was whooshing from side to side in some kind of high-speed warm-up exercise. Greg, their old coach, was standing on the touchline, barking orders at his new young protégés. Mike looked away, feeling betrayed.

247

"—and no James, either," Chris continued, glancing warily at Mike. "He called this morning."

"*WHAT?!*" he exploded. "NO HOOKER?! What the fuck's he playing at?"

"Says he was working late last night, and was too knackered to play," Minnie explained.

"WORKING LATE?" Mike studied the chipmunk-like face to check this wasn't one of Minnie's hilarious jokes.

"He's on some big transaction at work, apparently," Adam said, sounding full of admiration for the missing hooker.

Mike didn't comment. *Working late.* Some people didn't know the meaning of the phrase.

"And we're missing a flanker and a centre," Jenkins put in.

"—but we've got some subs from the bench!" Chris added enthusiastically.

Mike turned to the cluster of unfamiliar figures warming up a few metres away. Five subs? That was a third of the team! How were they supposed to compete with such a serious handicap?

"I'm Will," ventured one of the strangers, eyes darting all over the place except back at Mike's. "I think I'm playing left wing."

Mike suddenly became aware of how he was coming across. He was acting like Stuart Mackins on a bad day. Poor subs – they must have been wondering what they'd let themselves in for. Breaking into a warm smile, he extended his hand to the undergrads. "Great!" he cried. "So, we're supposed to trust you to play for the Old Boys, eh?" He gave a hearty laugh.

The subs grinned anxiously, and then shuffled closer to the team. They were a scrawny-looking bunch, thought Mike – probably from the bottom of the Thirds. He was particularly sceptical of the skinny little fellow who'd been chosen to play as their hooker; he seemed to be having trouble standing up in the wind.

"Are we all warmed up and ready to go?" Mike asked, rubbing his hands together gleefully as if he couldn't wait for the game to start.

There was a general mumbling which indicated that the boys were as ready as they were ever going to be, and a lethargic movement towards the pitch.

Jogging into position, Mike studied the members of the opposition. He couldn't help noticing how professional they looked in their Edinburgh kit. They seemed so much neater, smarter and keener than Mike's fifteen – jumping up and down, punching the air and psyching each other up with intimidating grunts just as he remembered doing a year ago. Mike's nerves ramped up. He felt like a soldier leading his troops over the edge.

The whistle blew, and the battle began. For several minutes, the ball just bounced from one set of slippery hands to another, skidding and slapping on the waterlogged grass, but it didn't take long for a stronger side to emerge. As expected, it wasn't Mike's.

The Old Boys struggled. Their passing was weak and their tackles were flaky. It was all they could do to keep up with the students, chasing them around the pitch like tired dogs trailing after their owners. Ten minutes into the match, they were losing twelve-nil.

Mike got angrier as the game progressed. The whole thing was a farce, he thought. How were they supposed to compete in such absurd conditions? They were playing in a hurricane, for Christ's sake. The pitch was like a paddy field, and the Old Boys were missing half their team! He pushed away the mat of hair that had plastered itself to his forehead.

After half an hour, Mike had all but given up. He plodded around in his mud-caked boots, just waiting for half-time. His tiredness kicked in. He hadn't noticed it up until now, but suddenly the lack of sleep, the hunger and the physical exhaustion all caught up with him at once. Mike felt weak, and he knew that his tiredness was affecting his mood. He ignored the ball as it passed within easy reach and fell straight into the hands of a cocky young student. *Fuck it,* he thought as it was carried off to the Edinburgh try-line.

There was a patter of applause from the frozen spectators as the students scored again and a roar of approval from Greg.

Finally, the whistle blew.

"Right," said Mike, cracking open his last can of Red Bull and looking around at the glum set of faces. "What do we think so far, guys?"

"Bit weak in the mid-field," offered Adam, after a lengthy pause.

"But it's not *too* bad, considering we haven't played together in ages," Minnie added hopefully.

"NOT TOO BAD?!" Mike bellowed, glaring at his little scrum-half. "ARE YOU PLAYING THE SAME GAME AS US, MINNIE?!" He took a final swig of Red Bull, crumpled the can in his fist and threw it down on the grass. "WE'RE LOSING NINETEEN-FIVE! AND WE'RE LUCKY TO BE LOSING BY ONLY *THAT* MUCH!"

Minnie looked hurt. The others gawped silently at their captain.

"OK," Mike went on, trying to sound more composed. He knew that shouting at the boys wasn't helping; he was just tired. "We can do better than this. Our mid-field is weak – you're right Adam – and our passing is lame. Minnie, you need to do more to bring the ball forwards, and Adam, you need to be right there behind him. Flankers, you're not going in for the tackles–"

Mike stopped abruptly and sighed. He couldn't be bothered. They were fighting a losing battle. The Edinburgh team were faster, fitter and stronger, and what's more, they were playing like a *team*. How could a bunch of flabby city graduates put up a fight?

"What about the defence?" one of the subs asked timidly.

"Well you need to be faster, for a start." Mike looked briefly at the sub then let his gaze rest on the enormous full-back. "What's *happened* to you, Jenkins?"

"Huh?"

"I said, what's happened to you? You used to be quick! And agile!"

"It's my asthma. I can't–"

"Bollocks!" Mike yelled. "Asthma my *arse!* You're just fucking unfit, Jenkins!"

The full-back snorted belligerently and flung his banana skin down on the ground. Mike looked around at his team. He couldn't catch anybody's eye. Fuck. This was no way to motivate a team. He took a deep breath.

"Listen guys, I know the conditions aren't ideal; the wind's pulling the ball right out of our hands, and kicking's a nightmare." Mike looked across at Adam, who was stomping about moodily on the sidelines. "But keep your passes short and low on the ground, and look up to see where the players are. Visibility's shit, I know, but at least it's the same for both teams."

Mike glanced up at the stormy sky, shielding his eyes from the downpour. There was no sign of a let-up; it seemed to be getting heavier, if anything. A strong gust of wind powered through the stadium, driving the rain at the huddled spectators, who were sitting, shivering beneath their umbrellas. They must have been utterly miserable.

"Right!" he cried, clapping his hands together in a vain attempt to convey enthusiasm. "So we know what we've gotta do, boys. The wind's blowing our way now," he lied, "so this half's gonna be easier. WE CAN DO THIS."

Mike bounded back onto the pitch with an exaggerated spring in his step. He believed in his last four words about as much as he believed in the tooth fairy, but that wasn't really the point. The point was: he was acting like a captain. He was making the *team* believe.

A dribble of frozen rainwater fell from Mike's hair onto the side of his nose, and he felt it trickling down to his chin. There wasn't a single part of his body that wasn't sopping wet. Even his eyebrows were saturated. The referee hadn't returned to the pitch, and neither had the opposition. Mike jumped up and down to keep warm, and glanced up at the rows of red seats in the stadium. He watched the umbrellas shift simultaneously to the right as the wind changed direction, and started.

There was somebody sitting alone in the stalls with no umbrella. Some distance away from the other spectators and sheltered from the rain by the overhanging roof, it was someone who hadn't been there before – someone he recognised. Slim figure, dark coat, cream scarf and long, blonde hair that was blowing across her face: Abby Turner.

She was leaning forwards with her arms on the seat in front, staring – as far as he could make out through the lashing rain – right back at him.

What was she doing here? Mike hadn't told her about the match – had he? The two of them weren't even on speaking terms in the office. For reasons known only to Abby, they hadn't exchanged a word since Christmas. She seemed to want nothing to do with him. In fact, she'd taken to being quite unpleasant – giving him horrible

looks, sending haughty emails, slamming doors in his face. And yet…
here she was on a wet, windy Sunday afternoon in Twickenham,
watching him play rugby.

Perhaps she was here to watch someone else, Mike considered,
looking around at the other players. Perhaps it was just a coincidence
Mike was on the team. Or was it not Abby after all, but someone
who looked incredibly like her? Mike shielded his eyes and squinted
again at the figure. The wisps of blonde hair were streaked across her
face, but there was no mistake, Mike decided: that was Abby Turner,
and she was looking straight back at him.

Mike felt confused and slightly excited. Was she here to make
amends? Perhaps she'd decided to quit being moody, and go back to
how things were – how things were that Thursday night. He was
back in her flat, all of a sudden – on top of her, naked. Hot, sweaty,
breathing fast, her fingernails digging into his back…

"OLD BOYS?! YOU READY?" The referee was waving a
hand.

Mike was filled with a gritty determination. Maybe they *could*
win the rugby after all. Yes – he'd show her how good he was. This
would be his best performance yet. They were only losing nineteen-
five, so he only had to score a couple more tries – if the wind
dropped a bit and if Adam kicked well. Yes. They could turn the
score around. Thank goodness she hadn't witnessed the first half, he
thought sheepishly.

"RIGHT!" he yelled. "COME ON OLD BOYS! WE CAN
DO THIS!" And this time he really believed it.

Unfortunately his team mates didn't. The Old Boys were even
more shambolic than before. They trampled about the pitch, making
haphazard attempts at acquiring the ball, while the university team
scored a succession of textbook tries, encountering almost no opposition. Mike watched in dismay as they slipped another one past
Jenkins.

The rain beat hard against the side of his face. Mike had almost
resolved to give up once and for all, when something unexpected
happened. Chris scored a try. And just to confound the onlookers,
Adam proceeded to convert it. The Old Boys roared with delight.

The try was a turning point in the game. Four minutes away

from the end, the Old Boys had managed to bring the score to 33-29. But they still needed one more try to win, and the students looked determined to hold onto their lead.

Both teams started to panic as the end of the match drew near. The ball was batted from player to player, and finally landed in a puddle on the side of the pitch. The line-out was frantic, with everyone desperate for a touch of the ball. BFG, grunting with effort, intercepted and knocked it in Mike's direction. Mike felt the familiar rush of adrenaline as he launched himself forwards.

He tore down the pitch with the ball, deftly swerving as players made grabs at his limbs. He was untouchable. This was it, he thought. This was the try that would win them the match.

The tackle was excruciating. A searing pain shot down the right-hand side of his body from his neck to the base of his spine. His shoulder was bearing the brunt of the impact, and he could feel his grip loosening on the ball. *He had to score this try.* The pressure on his shoulder increased, and his senses began to shut down, eclipsed by the agony. There were voices coming from all around, but he couldn't make out what they were saying – he was too focussed on scoring this try. His shoulder was nearly touching the ground, and his studs were slicing through the mud like knives through warm butter, but there was no way he was giving up. Finally, Mike broke free. Still clutching the ball, he stumbled towards the try-line.

He did it. Lying back on the cold, wet mud, Mike revelled in the glorious moment, enjoying the feel of the frozen raindrops hammering down on his face. He'd scored the winning try. The Old Boys had beaten the uni team, 34–33. And Mike was a hero.

One of the weedy subs trampled past. "Nice try, Captain!" he yelled.

Mike smiled, open-mouthed, and could feel the rain against his teeth.

"Well tried!" cried another sub.

Mike raised his head off the ground.

"So fucking close!" a voice trilled. Minnie stomped past looking less than elated.

Mike staggered to his feet.

Jenkins clomped over. "You didn't hear the whistle, did you mate? Blew when you picked up the ball!"

The realisation hit him, finally. He'd got there too late. His efforts had been in vain. The disappointment was overwhelming; he'd let the whole team down. Mike joined the rest of his team as they traipsed off the pitch, and felt Chris sling an arm round his shoulders.

"Bad luck, Mick. Don't blame yourself, alright?"

Mike looked blankly at Chris' mud-spattered face. How could he not blame himself?

As he pushed open the metal door that led back down to the changing rooms, a figure appeared above their heads. Her hair was cascading in damp, wavy locks over the top of the doorway.

"Good match," Abby said quietly.

Thirty rugby players stopped dead in their tracks and looked up.

"You played well." Abby stepped down to their level and very briefly looked Mike in the eye.

Mike wasn't sure what to say. Everything he thought about saying just seemed wrong, or inappropriate. The last time he'd spoken to Abby had been when they were lying in bed together, and that had been weeks ago. There was so much he wanted to ask her, to say to her, but he didn't know where to begin. And the awkwardness was made worse by the fact that all his team mates were watching.

"Thanks," he said, trying to sound nonchalant. "You only saw the last forty minutes – first half was a bloody *sham*–"

"Actually, no I didn't." Abby was grinning slightly. "I watched the whole game. I was in the shelter for the first half. You're right – it was pretty dire."

Mike heard a couple of team mates snigger, enjoying the sight of their captain being put in his place. Why couldn't they bugger off back to the changing rooms? It was hard enough just talking to Abby, let alone with an audience.

"Look, er…" Mike jerked his head towards the top of the stadium and started to climb. She took the hint and followed.

They skirted round a trickle of rainwater that was splattering onto the concrete. Mike did his best to wipe down some plastic seats with the back of his sleeve. He was stalling for time. She'd caught him unawares turning up like this, and he wasn't sure how to act.

They sat down. Mike looked at her, but her head was turned away. She seemed to be staring at the rain clouds. In the end, the silence became unbearable.

"So, you came?" he said pointlessly.

She looked at him briefly and nodded, then immediately turned away again.

Mike ran a hand through his wet hair. "How did you find out about it?"

"You mentioned it in your email," she said, focusing on the seat in front. "Just after Christmas."

Mike nodded. Of course. He remembered now. He'd asked if she wanted to go for a drink sometime, and she'd declined, in no uncertain terms.

"Took a bit of digging, to find the details," she added.

He looked down at his lap, trying to work things out. Six weeks ago, Abby had been leading him into her flat and practically throwing herself upon him. Then two weeks later, she'd turned all cold. And now, here she was going to impressive lengths to show that she cared after all.

Abby started fiddling with the tassels on the end of her scarf. She wasn't her usual cocky self, he thought.

"I, um, I owe you an apology," she mumbled.

He looked at her expectantly, but her eyelashes were lowered.

"The thing is, after that night–" she paused, and their eyes met momentarily. "I wasn't sure what was going on between us. And then you sent me that card, and I thought, well... anyway..."

Mike thought he knew what she was trying to say, but he let her struggle on.

"But then I heard about your American girlfriend–"

"What?" He whipped round and stared at her. American girlfriend? Who? Miranda? "No! She's not – that was just..." It was Mike's turn to talk gibberish. "That was just back in New York! I haven't–"

"I know," she said, nodding. "Justine told me. Joe got the wrong end of the stick when the lads were talking about it in the canteen."

Mike looked down sheepishly at his muddy hands. So *that* was why Abby had been acting so strangely. That explained the brush-offs, the emails, the snide remarks. She'd assumed he was sleeping around. Well, she'd assumed wrongly. He hadn't been doing anything of the sort. That wasn't his style. It was true that he'd slept with a lot of women, but never more than one at a time. He had morals. He didn't mess girls about.

Mike tried to get angry, but the truth was, he just felt relieved. Abby was talking to him again. He wasn't even cross about the rugby any more. It was only a game, after all.

"Anyway, I'd better go," Abby announced suddenly, letting the plastic seat flip up.

Mike sprung to his feet, trying to think of a way to make her stay. "You don't fancy a drink with the boys? With me? With – I mean–"

"I'd love to," she said, "but I've got an afternoon of pitchbooks ahead of me. Sorry."

They exchanged a fellow-sufferer grimace.

"Thanks for coming." Mike watched as she buttoned up her coat, her fingers working slowly in the cold. She wasn't quite back to her usual self; there was no snappiness, no sarcasm, no animosity.

"See you tomorrow," they said at exactly the same time, and then smiled.

They stood there looking at each other, smiles slowly fading, for what seemed like minutes. Mike had so many questions he wanted to ask. What did this mean? How did this change things? Were they friends now? Lovers? Partners? Colleagues? He toyed with the idea of stepping forwards and kissing her. That would be one way of finding out. He wanted to pull her shivering body towards him, to press his lips up against hers, to hold her... But then he remembered Marcus' advice. He stepped backwards, out of her way.

"Hope you're not in too late."

She glanced over her shoulder with a shy smile, then skipped down the steps to the muddy exit.

36

"NOW ABBY," Jon Hargreaves said gravely, swivelling round to face her and tapping his fingers impatiently on his knees.

Abby squinted harder at her screen, pretending to concentrate on her spreadsheet. She could tell from the sound of his voice what his next words would be. *I've got a little job for you.*

"I've got a little job for you. It's a – Abby?" Jon poked his head into her field of vision, so that she had no option but to respond.

"Oh sorry – what was that?"

"I said, *I've got a little job for you.*"

"Oh," she muttered, turning back to the spreadsheet. Jon's 'little jobs' were a regular occurrence, and generally consisted of all the items at the bottom of his To Do list that he couldn't be bothered to do himself. He usually left these until the very last minute, to add a sense of urgency to the work.

"It shouldn't take you too long," he added, a phrase that usually meant 'it will take you all night.'

Abby grunted, peering furiously at the formula. She couldn't bear to look at the objectionable little man.

"Perhaps if I go through what's required–" Hargreaves pushed a stack of papers onto her desk, knocking her keyboard askew.

Reluctantly, Abby turned to face him. As expected, the 'little job' was an assignment of epic proportions; a forty-page pitchbook he claimed was needed for nine o'clock the next day.

"But I think you should aim to have it done by seven, just to be on the safe side," Hargreaves advised. "Don't want any last-minute panics, do we?!" He stuck out his chin and fixed a daft grin on his face.

Or last-minute homicides, thought Abby.

"Now. I have to be off," Hargreaves told her. "I've got a – a meeting. But I'll be on my BlackBerry if you need me."

Abby nodded almost imperceptibly. She couldn't wait for Hargreaves to leave. Just his presence made her feel irritable. Out of the corner of her eye, she saw him clip shut his briefcase and pick off his jacket from the back of the chair. He clattered about for a little while in the cupboard behind her desk, the noises culminating in an extra-loud bang as he slammed the metal door shut. Then the dwarfish creature sauntered off.

Some 'meeting', Abby thought furiously. She wheeled back her chair and yanked open the cupboard. Hah – sure enough, carefully concealed under the files and papers was Jon Hargreaves' leather briefcase. She seethed. It wasn't the first time he'd pulled this stunt; it happened quite often on a Thursday night. He would shovel his critical assignments onto the nearest analyst – usually Abby – at six o'clock, and head off to the pub. He'd probably composed an email that he'd send to *Corporate_Finance_All* at about 1am from his BlackBerry, as he crawled home to bed – just to prove how hard he was working.

Abby was furious. She hated Jon Hargreaves, and she hated the fact that he and every other associate had every right to shit on her like that. She needed to vent her frustration. With a quick glance over the top of her monitor, Abby logged onto the Cray McKinley instant message system.

Turner, A: Guess what.

Cunningham-Reid, M: Hello. What?

Turner, A: Hargreaves just went off to a 'meeting'.

Cunningham-Reid, M: Oh really? On a Thursday night? Would that be a Project Swan meeting?

Turner, A: Presumably. His commitment on that knows no bounds.

Cunningham-Reid, M: Who else is on the 'deal team'?

Turner, A: Not sure – maybe some of those CRAZY equity traders.

Cunningham-Reid, M: So, have you got a 'little job' to be

getting on with?

Turner, A: Actually, funny you shd say that...

Cunningham-Reid, M: Well don't worry – *shouldn't take you too long, Abby.*

Abby sniggered and logged off. It was good to have Mike Cunningham-Reid on her side. Right now, he was one of the only things keeping her sane in the office. He shared her cynical sense of humour and her loathing for most other members of the department, and he had first-hand experience of Jon Hargreaves' 'little jobs'.

She turned to her new stack of print-offs and made room for them on her desk. She was still thinking about Mike. They only ever saw each other in the office, and occasionally for a Friday night pint after work, but they'd never actually gone out, just them – not since that Thursday night. She wondered if they ever would. Perhaps this was all Mike wanted. Friendship. Perhaps that was the best thing. They were colleagues, after all.

Flipping through the bundle of papers, Abby made a mental list of what had to be done. After a while she ran out of room in her head, and started to scribble things down. It was only when she'd used up two sides of A4 that she realised the extent of her workload. *'Shouldn't take you too long'*, mocked the little voice in her head. *Go fuck yourself, Jon Hargreaves.*

It wasn't as if she'd had nothing on her plate to begin with. Charles Kershaw wanted his offer document completed tonight, and she hadn't even started updating the Rights Issue book. The spreadsheet she'd been working on for Larkham was nowhere near finished, and now there was *this*, overshadowing everything else. There was no way she'd get it all done.

Prioritise, Abby told herself, staring at the daunting list. The other work could wait. For the next twelve hours, she would focus purely on the wretched pitchbook, and come back to the rest tomorrow.

An orange message popped up on her screen.

Cunningham-Reid, M: You coming down to dinner?

As she read it, a tuft of dark hair popped up behind her monitor.

"Or are you having too much fun with your 'little job'?" Mike whispered, looking down at her.

"Hello," she sighed wearily. The situation didn't seem so funny any more.

"What's up?" he asked.

Abby finished aligning her text boxes and growled. "Jon Hargreaves," she said. "*That's* what's up."

"I see. Not coming down to the canteen then?"

"Don't have time. Could you–"

"What d'you want? Sandwich?"

She smiled gratefully. "Yep – ham or cheese or something. And loads of Diet Cokes?"

Abby allowed herself a lingering glance at Mike's broad shoulders as he powered through the doors, then hauled her gaze back to her notes.

By eleven o'clock the office was virtually deserted. The pyramid of empty Coke cans she'd built on Jon's desk was rattling quietly as she typed, and a half-finished cup of brown water was going cold in front of her. The caffeine wasn't helping; it was just making her jittery. What she really needed was sleep.

Abby leafed through the presentation, searching again for the balance sheet figures. The book flipped shut, and Abby stared resentfully at the title. *Cray McKinley as Your Advisors.* She stared for longer than she'd intended, making the mistake of dwelling on her thoughts. She knew what would happen. Sure enough, before long a droplet rolled down her cheek and fell onto the cover page. Another one fell, and another and another until the paper became crinkled with moisture. She wiped her hand across the surface, unable to see through the tears.

She sat for a moment, grinding the heels of her hands into her sore, itchy eyes. Everything just seemed so *pointless*. Here she was on a Thursday night, alone, unhappy, exhausted and trapped, with nothing to look forward to but more work. It was the same feeling of gloom and despair that had descended upon her at Christmas. But at least over Christmas, there'd been a glimmer of hope – an inkling that maybe things would be better in the New Year. But here she was a month later, crying at her desk in the middle of the night. Things weren't any better at all.

Abby forced herself to take three deep breaths, and stumbled to her feet. Crying was not going to help. It never did. A quick trip to the Ladies would sort out her tear-stained cheeks, and then she'd knuckle down.

One of the few good things about being a female investment banker was the fact that you always got the toilets to yourself. Especially at eleven o'clock at night. Abby rested her hands on the porcelain washbasin and inspected her face in the mirror. As usual, the bright white lighting was doing her no favours. Her skin looked sallow, her eyes lifeless. At this rate, she thought, she'd look middle-aged by the time she was an associate. She wondered if that might actually be an advantage. A few wrinkles might earn her some respect from her colleagues, she mused, dabbing the mascara back onto her eyelashes.

The metallic 'clunk' made Abby start. She glanced sideways in the mirror and with horror, saw the lock turn from red to white. There was a flushing sound, and the clip-clop of a high-heeled shoe.

Abby panicked. She was trapped. She'd chosen the washbasin furthest from the exit, which meant that if she tried to make a dash for it, she'd almost certainly collide with the mystery woman. There was no time to dart into a cubicle. Who was it? The secretaries were long gone, and there weren't any other female bankers in Corporate Finance – not junior ones, anyway. It had to be a cleaner, she decided, relaxing a little. None of the cleaners at Cray McKinley spoke any English. But then, they didn't wear high heels, either. Shit!

Abby turned on both taps, hot and cold, full-blast, and bent over the sink. She cupped her hands under the torrent of water – perhaps stupidly – as the jet spurted out like a burst hydrant, surging up the mirror and drenching Abby's trousers.

"I say!" gasped the woman.

Abby pretended not to notice and busied herself with the dubious-looking dark patch that was spreading around her groin. The taps were still gushing ferociously.

"Are you OK?" asked a refined, middle-aged voice, above the noise of the water.

"Mmm, bit wet," Abby mumbled, dabbing fervently at her trousers and refusing to look up. She was damned if this stranger was going to catch her crying.

"You know there are showers downstairs in the gym, if you want one? Ahahahahahaha!"

Abby turned off the taps and pushed the wad of damp paper towels into the bin. This was going to be the tricky part: getting past her without making eye contact.

"You are OK, aren't you?" the woman asked officiously. Her voice sounded vaguely familiar.

Mainly out of curiosity, Abby lifted her head to take in the woman's reflection. It was a peculiar sight that greeted her. Small and dumpy, dressed in a bright blue power suit, the lady looked like a cross between an American footballer and an airhostess: chunky shoulder pads and heavily made-up face. Yes, Abby had definitely met her before, but she couldn't remember where or when.

"I'm fine, yeah." Abby bowed her head to keep her red eyes hidden, but snatched a quick glance at the woman's swipe-card. The name, unfortunately, was lodged somewhere in the folds of blue fabric.

"Oh – I say! That's a pretty necklace," the prim little lady exclaimed, clearly not in any hurry to leave. "I have one *just* like that – it's a Princess Cut, isn't it?"

"I – I'm not sure," Abby stammered, examining the small cube of fake crystal that hung on a silver chain round her neck. She'd bought it in Claire's Accessories for a fiver.

"Yes – it's a Princess Cut, I'm *sure!*" the woman went on. "I remember I once took mine to the jewellers to have it re-set, and I asked him, 'How can I be sure that the diamond I'm handing you now is the same as the one you give back in a week?', and he told me, 'You can't'! Can you believe that? So of course, I never had it re-set. I mean, when something's worth *that* much money…"

Abby nodded, wearing her most sympathetic expression. She didn't have the faintest idea what the woman was on about, or why she had started this conversation, but she was grateful for the distraction from her streaky face.

"Oh, sorry–" the little woman went on. "How rude of me! I'm Jennifer. Jennifer Armstrong."

She held out her hand. Abby couldn't help but stare at the enormous, twinkling orange rock that dwarfed her already dwarf-like fingers. *Jennifer Armstrong*. Abby definitely knew the name.

"Abigail Turner," she sniffed. "Nice to meet you." With a false smile, she stepped forwards to leave, but the small blue lady was blocking her way.

Jennifer Armstrong. Jennifer Armstrong. Abby suddenly remembered where she'd seen her before. Her interview. This was the woman who'd quizzed her on astrophysics and discounted cash flow. The woman who'd warned her about the long hours. She was the only female Managing Director at the firm. Great. So Abby was crying in front of an MD. Still, at least the woman didn't seem to recognise her from eighteen months ago. Perhaps in a few weeks she'd forget all about this encounter, too.

"I – I'd better go," Abby mumbled, unsure about what to do next. The MD was studying her carefully, head cocked to one side.

"Don't you want to tell me why you were crying?" she asked.

Abby blinked. "Oh – I'm fine."

"No you're not."

"Oh – it's just… work. Y'know." She shrugged as casually as she could.

"Oh dear. Now listen to me, Abigail. You're an analyst, yes?"

Abby nodded.

"A first-year?"

She nodded again.

"In Corporate Finance?"

Yes, yes, yes, thought Abby, nodding away. She didn't have time for this right now – there was a forty-page pitchbook that didn't exist yet on her desk.

"So you're an intelligent girl." She looked Abby in the eye. "But it's not all about brains, I'm afraid. It's about *balls*."

Abby frowned, still nodding. It was all rather surreal, standing in the ladies toilets in the middle of the night, listening to a Managing Director talk about balls.

"You've got to stand up to people in this place, Abby. Don't let them push you–"

263

"I don't!" Abby couldn't help interrupting. She *didn't* let people push her around!

"Good. Glad to hear it. So why were you crying just now?"

"Oh," Abby sighed. Why had she been crying? "I've just got loads of work at the moment, and... and... I'm just tired, I guess."

"And how many other analysts are sitting in your part of the office right now?"

"Um, well – none."

"Well if you've got so much work on, why couldn't you get some of the other analysts to do it?"

"Mike was around," she said defensively. "He only just left. But... we're first-years. That's why – well, I can't exactly delegate *upwards*, can I? I guess I just have to... do the work..." She trailed off under Jennifer Armstrong's withering gaze.

"This is what I *mean*, Abigail." The MD clasped her hands together then opened them as if she were revealing a small, rare butterfly. "You've got to stop thinking of yourself as being at the bottom of the pile."

"But I am!" cried Abby. "I'm a first-"

"No!" The MD glared up at her. "You may be a first-year, but that *doesn't* mean you're a slave to all the other analysts. You shouldn't be sitting in the office on your own, struggling through the night just because you were too timid to say no."

"But it was an associate–"

"So what?" She stared expectantly at Abby. Then she sighed and tutted. "I do understand what it's like, you know. As a first-year, you don't have much say in things – I know this because I was a first-year once myself – but there are things that you *can* change, Abigail. You can speak out when people are being unreasonable, and you can let them know them when they're asking the impossible. Believe me, they'll respect you more if you do."

"I do–"

"Good! I can see you're no shrinking violet. Keep it that way, OK? Just because someone's more senior than you, it doesn't mean they can boss you around. They may *try* to, of course – especially the men – but you have to stand your ground. They only do it because they're intimidated, anyway."

Abby tried not to scowl at the woman. *Intimidated?* What was that supposed to mean? How could any of those bankers be intimidated of her? She was a first-year analyst! The associates, the VPs, the Managing Directors – they barely noticed her existence! Abby began to wonder whether this Jennifer Armstrong was one of those feminist bankers she'd read about in the press – the ball-breaker type. Or maybe she was just a crackpot.

"You don't believe me, do you?" she asked, smiling.

Abby hesitated, not quite have the guts to say no.

"I know it sounds silly," she said, "but you'll see – they're intimidated. Most of them have never worked with a woman before – let alone a tall, attractive, intelligent woman–" she waved a hand in the direction of Abby's long legs– "so they'll probably react by trying to put you down. It didn't happen so often with me, of course–" she looked down at her stumpy little figure – "but I've seen this before. Just don't let it get to you, OK?"

Abby nodded earnestly, concealing her doubts about this woman's sanity. Intimidated? Of her? She tried to picture Stuart Mackins, quaking behind his desk as he plucked up the courage to ask her to work on a pitchbook. No way.

The woman glanced at her watch and pulled a face. "Oh dear. It's late. I'd better be going. Now, remember what I said, won't you? And if you *ever* need to talk about anything – *anything* – then I'm here."

She pressed a business card into Abby's palm, and looked up into her eyes, which, to Abby's relief, felt as though they were almost back to their normal state.

"I mean it," Jennifer said. "It's not an easy life here for a woman. You must call me if you need to talk."

With a flash of bright blue and a waft of expensive-smelling perfume, Jennifer Armstrong bustled through the door.

37

"WHAT DID SHE SAY to that?" Mike asked, heaping a mound of brown sugar onto his porridge.

"She said I should stick up for myself," Abby replied, "and stop acting like I'm at the bottom of the pile."

Mike threw down the sugar spoon and let it clatter across the table. The small, Puerto-Rican carpet scrubber in the corner of the canteen looked up in alarm. "We *are* at the bottom of the pile! We're first-year analysts, for God's sake."

Abby nodded. "That's what I said. But she claimed we should answer back, and refuse to do what they tell us to do!"

Mike snorted at the absurdity of the notion. "Answer back?! Yeah – I can see how that'd go down. *No, sorry Jon, I don't want to do your 'little job'*. Huh! He'd just laugh in your face."

"Exactly!" Abby slammed her coffee cup onto the table, making a bit of a mess.

"It's all very well for *her* to preach about the importance of speaking out," he said, "but she's a Managing Director – she's *paid* to speak out. Analysts just have to do as they're told."

"She was an analyst once, y'know," Abby pointed out, reaching for a wad of napkins to mop up the puddle of coffee.

"What, here? At Cray?" he asked doubtfully. It was very rare for an analyst to climb all the way to the top of the firm. And a *woman*, too. That was even less common.

"That's what she said."

"Hmm," Mike grunted. "Unlikely. Most women leave after a couple of years."

Abby glared at him. "Not most women, Mike – most *people*.

266

Anyone with an ounce of common sense would leave this hell-hole after two years."

Oh dear. Now he was really in trouble. "No," he said quickly, "I just meant… lots of women go off and have babies, and settle – oh, Abby!"

The soggy cornflake slithered into his porridge, leaving a wet mark on his blue silk tie.

"Ooh, sorry!" she cried gaily. "How clumsy of me! I was busy thinking about this cute little baby-grow I saw in Next the other day! I *must* pay more attention!"

Mike fought back the smile as he dabbed at the expanding splodge on his tie.

"Well anyway," Abby went on, "I looked Jennifer Armstrong up. She's done very well – she's a Managing Director, and she's only thirty-six."

Mike snorted. "Aren't most MDs about thirty-six?"

"Yeah, but she's–"

"–a *woman*?" Mike finished. He couldn't resist. "That's a bit sexist, isn't it Abby?"

She crossed her arms and pouted. Mike grinned, watching and waiting for the sulk to end. He knew how much she hated being proved wrong.

The sulk was lasting for longer than usual, and Mike began to wonder if he'd overdone the sarcasm. "Abby," he said tentatively.

She lifted her head and squinted suspiciously at Mike. "What?"

This would make her forget about her sulk. "I've got a confession to make."

Abby lifted an eyebrow, her interest grudgingly aroused.

"You know when I got put on Project Coral, just after I arrived in the department?"

"Yes," Abby growled, rolling her eyes.

"Well… you know they asked me to replace you, and start from scratch with the financial model?"

Abby nodded crossly. "Course I remember."

"Well, that's the thing…" he waited for her to look up. "I – I didn't. I copied yours, and changed it a bit. That time you came back to your desk after lunch and found me at your computer?"

267

Another nod, this one more hesitant. She was squinting into his eyes.

"Well, that's what I was doing. I was copying your model. I didn't know where to start, so I... well, I copied yours. It was practically right as well – I didn't even change much," he said, slightly embarrassed.

Abby looked at him for a moment, then screwed up her nose and laughed. "Have you been worrying about that, all this time?!"

"Well, yes," Mike admitted, suddenly feeling a bit foolish. Perhaps it was no big deal after all. "I thought you got in trouble for messing up Project Coral?"

"I *did!*" cried Abby. "I was branded the Dunce of the Department, while you were Mike the Conquering Hero! But d'you think I didn't know what you'd done?"

He dropped his spoon. She *knew?*

"Doesn't take a genius, Mike. I looked at the files you'd opened on my computer."

Mike grimaced, feeling even sillier. Of course she knew. Abby wasn't stupid.

"But thanks for telling me," she said, looking serious for a second and then sniggering.

Mike knew she was laughing at him, but actually, he didn't mind. It was just a relief to have finally come clean. He'd waited six months to make that admission, and now, having plucked up the courage to do so, it transpired that she'd known all along – and didn't even seem to care!

"Sorry," Abby said, still smiling. "Hey. Have you spoken to Joe Cartwright recently?"

It never failed to amaze Mike how quickly and how randomly Abby's mind jumped around. He shrugged. "Saw him yesterday – why?"

"Has he... has he said anything to you?"

Mike frowned and thought back to his chat with Joe, wondering what Abby might be alluding to. It hadn't been a long conversation; more of a passing grumble as they'd overlapped in the canteen. Then Mike remembered. Joe *had* said something, right at the end of the conversation. That might've been what Abby was getting at.

"Well, now you come to mention it, actually, yes. He did say something."

Abby looked at him, her brown eyes full of hope. Mike felt sure he'd guessed correctly.

"He said... oh, let me think. Yes – that was it. He said that his fish tasted like rubber. He'd gone for the mackerel, you see. You know what it's like downstairs..."

Abby's shoulders slumped. "Oh. And he didn't say anything else?"

Mike pretended to think. "Well, yes. He did actually."

Her eyes lit up again.

"He said that he wondered whether the chicken might've been a better option, and that he'd probably get some banoffee pie to take the–"

"Did he say anything *non* food-related?" asked Abby, looking slightly annoyed now. Mike tried not to smile.

"Er, well." He sucked pensively on his lower lip and scratched his head. "Only *one* thing, I guess."

Abby waited.

"He said was I planning to watch the game on Sunday, and if so, did I want to go see it at his."

"Oh." She nodded and started swirling the cornflakes around the bowl. Mike decided to put her out of her misery.

"And he said something about Justine Brown, on his way out."

Abby's head shot up so quickly she nearly gave herself whiplash. "Did he?" she asked, trying to sound casual.

"Yes. He said she's got a great–" *pair of tits*, was the exact phrase he'd used. "Sense of humour. I think they've been out on a couple of dates."

"He said that?" asked Abby, suddenly grinning deviously.

Mike instantly started to worry. He hated gossip. "We shouldn't interfere, Abby."

"Oh, come on, Mike. They'd make a great couple. What else did he say?" she asked keenly.

He looked at her. She was right. They would make a great couple, but that was none of his business, or hers. "Nothing." That wasn't strictly true; Joe had twittered on about Justine Brown all the way from the canteen to the second floor, but Mike didn't think it was wise to relay this to Abby.

"Oh." Abby looked disappointed. "But you can see what I—"

"No," he said, louder than he'd anticipated. He dropped his voice. "It's nothing to do with us, Abby. And anyway, it could be disastrous. I mean, they work in the same—" he stopped himself, but too late.

"Department?" Abby finished, catching his eye for a second. The implications were all too clear. "Yeah," she said coldly. "I guess you're right."

Mike tried to think of something to say. He ran his spoon around the empty bowl, scooping up the last sticky lumps of porridge. He could sense Abby's gaze flicker up to his eyes, and back down to her latte.

Things had been good between Abby and Mike for the last few weeks – good in a platonic, matey way. Neither one of them had brought up the subject of That Night – although Mike couldn't honestly say that it hadn't popped into his mind once or twice. OK, more than once or twice. He found himself thinking about it the whole bloody time. But not intentionally. This was probably the closest they'd ever got to talking about their relationship. He didn't want to rock the boat. The long silence was finally broken by the vibration of Mike's phone on the table. Gratefully, he pulled it towards him and checked the message.

HI MIKE, UPDATE ON MAYDAY
GARDEN PARTY: PARENTS
SAY BRING A MATE.
RECOMMEND U DO, OR WILL
DIE OF BOREDOM. C U THERE,
MEL XX

Mike flipped his phone shut. His sister's text had given him an idea.

Suddenly, Abby started banging her spoon on the table like a four year-old waiting to be fed. Her eyes were wild with excitement. "Oh my God! I can't believe I forgot to tell you!" she cried. Then

270

she lowered her voice a notch. "Apparently, there's a vacancy going in Corporate Broking – you know, Corporate Joking! A vacancy for a *first-year!*"

"Really?" said Mike, raising his eyebrows in astonishment. Not because there was a position opening up in Broking, but because it had taken Abby so long to find out. Surely it was common knowledge among the first-years?

"Yeah – they're planning to advertise the post internally in a few weeks, but Justine heard it on the grapevine through Joe."

"Corporate Broking, eh?" Mike asked, sounding deliberately dubious. He hadn't quite made up his mind about whether to apply for the job, but he knew he wouldn't be the only one, if he did.

"It's supposed to be really easy work, and the pay's the same as ours!" she exclaimed.

Mike screwed up one side of his face. "Yeah, but think about the career prospects... The work's supposed to be really dull in Broking."

"Hmm, I guess," Abby conceded grumpily.

"Apparently they spend all day drawing share price graphs," Mike added, shaking his head scornfully.

"Oh." She looked crestfallen. "Bit of a dead-end job, then."

"Exactly." Mike nodded, feeling a twinge of guilt.

"Might as well stick to our hundred-hour weeks of persecution, huh?"

"Guess so. Speaking of which..."

They pushed themselves to their feet.

38

"NO. IT'S MY TREAT," Abby insisted, aware of the Italian waiter who was poised to strip and re-lay their table.

"Let's go halves," her friend suggested.

"No. I'm paying. I owe you."

"Why?" Beth asked aggressively, clamping her cash card to the saucer.

"Because I've neglected you all day." *And because forty quid meant nothing to a banker earning three thousand pounds every month, but meant two weeks' beer money for a student.*

"I've had a lovely time today, actually," Beth argued.

"What, wandering around Clerkenwell on your own?" Abby managed to prise her friend's fingers off the dish and replace Beth's card with her own.

"I've been flat-hunting," Beth declared, switching the cards back again.

A little laugh escaped from Abby's mouth. "No offence, Beth, but for ninety pounds a week you wouldn't even afford a cardboard box under a cash machine in Clerkenwell."

Beth pouted indignantly. An ex-team mate of Abby's, Beth had stayed up in Cambridge for an extra year to do a Masters in Neurology (play basketball). Talking to Beth was like talking to herself in the mirror, Abby found. She had the same raw obstinacy about her, the same drive, the same impatience. They even looked a bit alike, she thought, watching the brown, hurt-looking eyes slowly melt into a smile.

"OK, you're right. I didn't find much within my price range. But there's some *great* office space around there. I found this funky–"

"*Office* space?" Abby cut in. Her concern mounted as Beth pulled four glossy brochures out of her bag. Surely wasn't planning to live in an office?

"Yeah. For my company."

"I thought you were planning to run a youth hostel?"

Beth shrugged. "Well, yeah. Or a company. I thought maybe a youth hostel in the city, combined with a coffee shop, with sleeping facilities for tired businessmen needing a kip half-way through the day, and a crèche for working mothers." She looked up at Abby and added sheepishly, "or something."

"Right," Abby replied. She couldn't help thinking Beth's business plan needed a bit of work.

"I'm gonna make staff sit on those Swiss Ball thingies they have in the gym," Beth went on, her enthusiasm swelling again. "Apparently they're really good for your back."

"Right," Abby nodded. "Swiss Balls. Well, at least you've got the most important things sorted. What's the wallpaper gonna look like?"

Beth frowned. "Shut up."

Abby smiled and handed the saucer to a passing waiter, subtly replacing Beth's card with hers as he whisked it away. Beth was so ambitious. She'd always wanted to run her own business, and Abby had no doubt that one day, she would. Whether the city hostel/café/motel/crèche enterprise would take off Abby wasn't so sure, but Beth would sort herself out in the end. After a few false starts. It was refreshing to spend time with someone whose aspirations went beyond how to spend next year's bonus. At least Beth had a *vision* – even if it did involve Swiss Balls and bunk beds for businessmen.

"Some of these offices have solar panels on the roof, and this one here – oh no, hang on – you've paid the bill! OK, I'm getting the next round of drinks."

The waiter ripped off the receipt and took a step back, keenly watching their every move. It was when he started jiggling the fresh set of cutlery against his palm like a castanet player that the girls decided it was time to leave. Beth led the way, bounding up the rickety stairs two by two and striding through the ground floor restaurant. Abby felt breathless by the time they spilt onto Frith Street.

"You're so fit," she said accusingly. "*I* want to be fit."

Beth looked at her. "You were always the fittest girl on the squad, weren't you?"

Abby snarled. "*Was*. Not any more. Probably wouldn't even get *onto* the squad now."

"Hmm." Beth cast an eye over Abby's body. "Well, at least you're not fat."

Abby smiled grudgingly. "Thanks."

It was good to know that the all-sandwich diet was keeping her slim, thought Abby as they started to wander through Soho, but she didn't want to be slim. She wanted to be *fit*. To have the energy to leap up stairs two at a time like Beth. To run for a bus and not have to spend the entire journey recuperating. She wanted her limbs to feel light and strong again, the way they used to.

Beth gave Abby's left bicep an affectionate squeeze. "Not *all* flab, yet," she said as Abby tensed it and put on her most menacing expression. "Come on. I owe you some drinks."

It was great to see Beth again. They'd kept in touch over the last nine months, but the emails had become less and less frequent – mainly because Abby never replied to any of them. It wasn't just that she didn't have the time; it was that she never seemed to have anything to say. *Dear Beth,* she'd draft, when another hilarious four-pager popped into her inbox. *Great to hear from you. Swimming the Channel sounds totally idiotic, but good luck, you nutter. I'm editing a PowerPoint presentation this evening, and after that I might fiddle with a spreadsheet for a bit. They've changed the menu in the Cray McKinley canteen, so tonight I had a stilton and chutney baguette which was quite tasty, but a little bit sweet. The Northern Line's been playing up, so everyone's been taking cabs into work...* No, there wasn't a single aspect of Abby's life that was newsworthy.

It had been Beth's decision to visit. She'd forfeited a weekend of basketball – a huge sacrifice, for Beth – and in return, Abby had left her to wander round London while she spent the day in the office. Not intentionally, of course. She'd popped in first thing to finish something off, and collided with a ruddy-faced Charles Kershaw on his way back from the gym. "Ah, Abigail," he'd said casually. "I'm glad you're here. I wonder if you could just take a look at this pitch…" Eleven hours later, she'd left the building.

"So, that's how *I'm* gonna make my first million," Beth concluded, paying for the drinks and grinning at Abby. They were perched on tall, red plastic seats that looked like lifeguard chairs, and Beth had just finished describing her money-spinning venture, right down to the exact shade of metallic blue for the fleet of company cars. "But I guess you must be minted already!"

Abby tried not to cringe as the barman pointedly counted out the change in his palm and dropped it into the cash register, coin by coin. Beth had paid for the drinks in what looked like five and ten pence pieces. "I'm doing OK," she replied. "Not quite a millionaire yet."

'OK' was a bit of an understatement, she reflected, thinking of the thousands of pounds piling up in her current account. Money was not a problem for Abby. If anything, she had too much of the stuff. The problem was that *she didn't have time to spend it.*

"You enjoying Cray McKinley?"

Abby looked at her blankly. "No."

There was no need to bullshit with Beth. No need to pretend to be a go-getting 'bright young thing' with a brilliant job in the city. Beth was one of the few people that Abby felt she could confide in without the risk of being judged. Her mother was deliberately ignorant about Abby's career, content to believe that that her daughter was flying high in the fast-paced world of 'stocks and shares'. Whenever Abby hinted at problems, they were quickly swept away in a torrent of praise about how proud everyone was of Abby, how hard she was working and how much she deserved this job at Cray McKinley. Nicky was too wrapped up in the world of student unions and swimming galas to recognise that there was such a thing as life after university. Her father, well, he'd probably understand, but then he'd tell her mum, and then there'd be a long and pointless phone conversation persuading Abby that everything was fine, totally fine, wasn't it, darling?

Beth looked genuinely perplexed. "What d'you mean, 'no'?"

"I mean, no, I'm not enjoying myself at Cray McKinley. It's awful. I hate it. I wish I'd never taken the job."

"What's so awful about it?"

Abby sipped her wine while she thought about how to explain. This was the problem about being paid so much money; you didn't really have the right to whinge about anything. Beth was looking at her questioningly as she lowered her glass.

Abby sighed. "What d'you think I do every day, Beth? I mean, day to day. What d'you reckon my job entails?"

Beth faltered. "Er, well… you do financial transactions and stuff, don't you? You're like a bank manager, only for companies." She flinched. "Sort of."

"So when I sit down at my desk in the morning, what d'you think I *do* until midnight or God-knows-when?"

Beth puffed out her cheeks, thinking furiously. "Make decisions on what companies should do with their assets?" she guessed. Then, on seeing Abby's expression: "Er, tell *other* people to make decisions on what companies should do with their assets?"

Abby smiled. "You're getting colder. I don't make decisions. And I definitely don't tell *other* people to make decisions. That's the thing. All I do is take orders from the guys above me. I don't have any say in anything. I'm just a little minion at the bottom, same as all the other first-years. The one time I did make a comment in a meeting, the bankers just stopped and looked at each other as if to say, 'did you hear that noise too?' and then went on with what they were saying."

Beth shook her head and looked up to the ceiling. "Cyuh!"

Abby wasn't convinced she'd justified her loathing of Cray McKinley. "I do what I'm told to do. That's all. I'm not allowed to think for myself. And d'you know what sort of work it is that I'm doing?"

Beth shook her head, looking slightly intimidated.

"I'm fiddling with the position of titles on PowerPoint slides, and changing the thickness of lines, and sifting through piles of annual reports looking for a particular number, and creating overly-complicated spreadsheets that are never going to be looked at except by some anally retentive banker who comes back with a comment like, 'Hmm. Shouldn't the totals be right-aligned?'"

Abby reached for her wine and poured a large amount into her mouth. Beth was watching her anxiously. The barman, too, kept shooting suspicious looks in her direction, as though he were worried she might pull out a machete and start waving it at his customers.

"That's not *all* you do, is it?" Beth asked. "Format presentations and stuff?"

Abby raised one eyebrow.

"It can't be!" Beth protested. "I thought you were working on the multi-million pound transactions that you hear about on the news!"

Abby smiled. "That's what they'd have you believe. That's what the Cray McKinley recruiters would tell you at the graduate milkround dinner. 'If you join us, you'll be jetting off around the world to clinch world-changing deals with some of our biggest clients...' It's all bollocks. The truth is, analysts are just slaves to the bankers above them. We don't go 'jetting' anywhere; we don't ever get to leave the office."

"It doesn't sound very..." Beth fought for the right word – "*urgent*. I mean, why d'you need to spend all weekend doing menial stuff like that?"

"Because there are analysts at Morgan Stanley and Merrill Lynch and JP Morgan and all the other banks doing the same menial stuff, and if we don't get it done in record time, then they will, and Cray McKinley won't get the business. It's just the way the industry works."

Beth looked nonplussed. "You should form a union, you analysts."

Abby laughed. "Yeah, except that we've all signed contracts agreeing to opt out of the statutory thirty-seven and a half-hour working week. We have no rights."

"Oh. Well what would happen if you just said, 'sod off, I'm going home' at six o'clock every night?"

Abby shrugged. "You'd be stupid to do that."

"Why?"

"Well, you'd earn yourself a reputation as a slacker, and then nobody would ask you to work on their deals again."

"And the downside of that would be...?"

Abby smiled. She could see how it looked, to an outsider. "The downside would be that you wouldn't get promoted. Then you'd never be able to climb the ladder."

"What ladder?"

Abby sighed. They obviously had some ground to cover. "The hierarchy. That's what it's all about at Cray McKinley. You have to work your way up the ladder, by getting 'in' with the right people. Making a good impression. Sucking up. Telling them they're right when they're wrong. Grassing on other analysts to make you look better. Blaming other people when you've fucked up. Doing plenty of face-time. Putting–"

"Face-time? What's that?"

"Oh, sitting at your desk pretending to be working, when actually you could've left the office hours ago. It's supposed to impress the directors."

Beth opened her mouth to say something, then shut it again. Abby waited for her to speak. She needed to hear that her gripes weren't unfounded – that she wasn't making a fuss over nothing. After a slow, contemplative sip of wine, Beth looked at her.

"Abby, this isn't *you*."

"What d'you mean?" Abby asked, fairly confident she knew what Beth meant.

"This shit about 'climbing the ladder'. And 'face-time'. And sucking up. It isn't you. Why are you doing this? Why don't you quit Cray McKinley and do something you *enjoy*?"

Abby shook her head. "I've got to give it a chance. To make a proper go of it. When I applied for this job, there were so many people telling me I shouldn't go into the city, saying that it wasn't for me, that I wouldn't cope, that I should've stuck with the MoD... I really wanted to prove them wrong. I have to at least *try* and succeed at Cray McKinley. And anyway, there's the golden handcuffs keeping me there until–"

"*Golden handcuffs?*" Beth interrupted. "What the fuck are they?"

"Oh," Abby looked down at her lap. Even *she* was talking crap. Any day now, she'd catch herself saying 'up to speed', or 'on the same page'. "Golden hello. The sign-on bonus they gave us when we joined. Eight thousand pounds. If we leave before bonus day this year, we have to pay it all back."

Beth grimaced. "When's bonus day?"

"End of June."

There was a pause while Beth did some sums on her fingers. "That's only three months away. You can stick it out until then."

Abby nodded half-heartedly. She wanted to stick it out for another year, at least. She hadn't considered doing anything else, really. But speaking to Beth was making her realise that there were options. She *could* leave Cray McKinley after only one year. It would take a bit of explaining to future employers, but then, she was still at the start of her career. Was it worth staying on for an extra twelve months, just for the sake of one digit on her CV?

"We could go into business together!" cried Beth, grabbing her wrist and shaking it. "You could do the financial stuff!"

Abby laughed. Worryingly, Beth seemed to be serious.

"Oh, go on, Abs – it'd be great!" She was practically cutting off the circulation in Abby's arm.

"Um, yeah. Maybe," she replied nervously. Beth's enthusiasm was contagious, though, and for a moment, the idea of becoming a part of her crazy city venture actually seemed tempting – if a little risky.

Abby smiled. "But we'd have to talk about this Swiss Ball idea of yours."

39

Give examples of instances in which you have demonstrated a good under-
standing of financial instruments and transactions.

Mike read the line for a sixth time and chucked the pen across the coffee table.

"Anyone for another game of Rally Fusion?"

Marcus looked up from the copy of Nuts he was 'resting on' to complete his appraisal form. "Maybe a quick one, for inspiration," he said, easing himself out of the sofa. "D'you reckon Jordan's tits are too small now?" He held up the magazine cover.

Mike squinted contemplatively. It was difficult to tell, really, with the eyes and whiskers that Marcus had drawn around Jordan's right nipple.

"Are you done with your appraisal forms already?" Alan asked anxiously.

"Nearly," Marcus replied, draining the last of his Stella and sending the empty can skittering towards his kitchen.

Mike snorted and retrieved Marcus' form from under the sofa. "Section one," he read. "Name: Marcus Mackenzie. Department: M & A." The rest of the form was blank. "Oh yeah, I see you're well on the way."

Marcus sneered at him and started pressing buttons on the games consol. "You playing, or what?"

Mike shuffled over to the XBox. He'd been beaten four times already by Marcus this evening, and he was determined not to let it happen again.

"Has anyone got onto the Personal Effectiveness bit yet?" asked

Joe. "It says, do you willingly accept additional work and embrace new assignments with a positive attitude... I mean, are they just *asking* us to lie?"

Mike untangled the mass of cables and freed his remote control. "Yep. They wanna see who can bullshit. Put: 'I relish the opportunity to take on extra work, especially if it means spending all weekend in the office and *particularly* when I have to cancel an important social engagement for the sake of a just-in-case assignment that I know will go straight in the bin'."

Mike lost himself on the winding, sun-drenched roads of Monte Carlo, where the only distractions were bikini-clad, flag-waving girls and where the sky was a perfect, cobalt blue. He could almost smell the petrol fumes from the car in front as his head was thrown back against the imaginary headrest.

"Huh!" he cried, as Marcus skidded sideways and sent him hurtling into the cliff face. "It's not fucking bumper cars!"

Marcus let out a deep laugh and drove on, leaving Mike's car smouldering at the side of the road. For all his frantic thumb-flicking, the vehicle wasn't going to move. There was thick smoke billowing out from under the crumpled bonnet, and after a couple of seconds, one half of the screen was filled with bright orange flames. "*Loser,*" said Marcus smugly as he dropped his controls on the floor.

"An example of taking the initiative," read Joe, pencil in mouth, frowning.

"Are we *supposed* to take the initiative at Cray McKinley?" asked Alan.

Mike laughed cynically. "Only when someone tells you to." He plodded into the kitchen for another beer, cross with himself for losing again. Still, Marcus was the Rally Fusion champion. He probably practised on his own every night, the sad git.

As Mike cracked open his third can of lager and wandered back into the lounge, it occurred to him that Marcus wasn't the only sad git. This was their weekend: a few beers on a Sunday night, after a full day in the office. And they were spending it *filling out their analyst review forms.* What sort of a life was that?

If only they knew, those people who gasped when Mike told them where he worked, if only they knew what he *really* did. How he lived. What being an analyst at Cray McKinley really meant. Mike threw himself down in an armchair and released the lever on the side. With slightly more force than he'd anticipated, the footrest jerked Mike into the horizontal position, sending the coffee table reeling across the room on its coasters.

"Did anyone reply to that email from HR?" asked Joe, guiding the table back into place. "The one about the milkround dinner thing?"

"No point," muttered Mike, staring vacantly at the ceiling. The email had been asking for volunteers to help with graduate recruitment. The idea was for first-year analysts to go back to their university towns and tell keen banker wannabes how fulfilling life was as an analyst at Cray McKinley. Quite apart from the fact that Mike's acting skills were rather rusty, he knew there was no way Stuart Mackins would allow any analyst on Project Wildfire to fly up to Edinburgh for a student piss-up in a plush hotel.

"Yeah, too much on at the moment," Marcus agreed. He was sprawled on the full-length sofa, his massive calves dangling over the end. The article on How to Make Them Scream had obviously won over the appraisal form in the tussle for his attention.

"Oh." Joe sounded worried. "I volunteered."

"Me too," said Alan. "A free meal at Browns and a night out on Cray McKinley sounded pretty good to me."

"No such thing as a free meal," Mike pointed out, extending an arm and feeling his way around the table for his beer. "You'll pay for it the next day when you have to come in at five a.m. to get your work done." His fingertip skimmed something that wasn't his can. It was his review form. Reluctantly, he pulled it towards him.

"It'll be weird, going back to Warwick," Joe said quietly. "I haven't been up there since we graduated. Not sure what it'll be like, without everyone else."

Mike couldn't help wondering whether by 'everyone else', he meant Zoë. It couldn't have been easy for Joe, splitting up with a girlfriend of nearly nine years.

"Not really sure I wanna go, actually," said Joe, reinforcing Mike's theory.

Mike rolled onto his side and looked at Joe. His eyes were glazed over in thought as he fiddled with the ring-pull on his beer.

"Hey, how are things going with Justine Brown?" asked Mike, hoping to distract him.

Joe looked up, as if surprised to see that there were other people in the room. "Fine." Then he registered the question, and brightened up. "Good. Really good. When I get to see her, that is. Doesn't happen very often."

Marcus looked up from the magazine and snorted. "That's a blessing in disguise, mate."

Joe looked at him. "Why?"

"You're in the *same fucking department*. You're an idiot, going for someone you work with. He glanced at Mike. "You both are."

Joe's head jerked up. "*Both?*"

Mike glared at Marcus, who was gawping back at him, hand over mouth. "Oops. Sorry mate."

"Who…" Joe frowned, then smiled a knowing smile. "Oh, of course. Might've known – you sly bastard. You mean Abby Turner, don't you?"

"Are you going out with Abby Turner?" squeaked Alan.

Mike hesitated. "No," he said, truthfully. Poor Alan was besotted with Abby.

"So why –"

"Oh, we just had a bit of a thing, before Christmas. That's all."

"A 'thing'?"

"Um, yeah. We got sort of close," he said tactfully. It was true, after all. "But we're just mates now."

"Oh, right." Alan didn't sound convinced.

There was an awkward pause. *You dopey fucker,* thought Mike, staring at the side of Marcus' brutish face and wondering what other little gems he might have accidentally let slip. Working in M&A meant that he was privy to information of a highly sensitive nature; did he go around leaking the terms of the latest merger he was working on?

Alan looked like a kid who'd just been told that Christmas was cancelled this year. He was probably imagining all the sordid things that Abby and Mike hadn't been getting up to in the last few months. Part of Mike wanted to tell him: *they were just mates.* There was nothing between them – not like that, anyway. As Marcus had pointed out in one of his more helpful moments, they'd be asking for trouble if they tried to mix business with pleasure. Justine and Joe could give it a go if they liked, but frankly, it was unlikely to work. Mike said nothing, however. There was another part of him that quite enjoyed people thinking that Abby and he were an item. It was perverse, but he got a kick out of people assuming that she was his girlfriend.

Finally, Joe broke the silence. "It says, do you take responsibility for your own mistakes. That's one of those trick questions. You can't say 'yes', because then you're admitting you make mistakes, you can't say 'no', because then you look like an arrogant twat who never owns up when he's wrong."

Mike looked down at his blank form. Joe seemed to be on the final section already. "Just put, 'not applicable'," he joked.

"Good idea," Joe nodded keenly, scribbling 'N/A' in the box. "Awesome. I'm done."

Five minutes later, the words were still swimming around in front of Mike's tired eyes. *Give examples of instances in which you have demonstrated a good understanding of financial instruments and transactions...* He couldn't be bothered.

"Joe," he said, kicking the coffee table gently into the little guy's shoulder.

"Mmm?"

"What would it cost me to get you to fill out my appraisal form?"

Joe looked at him. When he realised that Mike was being serious, a smile spread across his face. "A re-match for that game of pool we played in New York," he said. "If you win, you owe me nothing. If you lose, you owe me one percent of your bonus this year."

Mike did some quick sums and slid the sheets across the table. "OK," he said. "You're on."

40

THE SENSE OF ELATION was growing with every mile that the train put between Abby and London. She watched as the fields flashed past, each one of them separating her a little further from the twenty-storey glass empire she'd come to loathe.

The evening sky was streaked with orange and pink, and across it, thunder clouds were rolling, buffeted by the strong March wind. It occurred to Abby that this was the first time in months that she'd seen the outside world in its true colours, without the tinting effect of the Cray McKinley windows.

It felt so good to be out of the office. Even if she did have a week's work piling up on her desk, it was worth it for this feeling of liberation. Hell, it was worth it just for the look on Geoff Dodds' face when she'd announced that she was leaving at four o'clock. *Four o'clock!* That was halfway through the working day in Corporate Finance. The director had practically given himself an aneurism trying to contain his rage.

The landscape flattened off as they entered Cambridgeshire, the only protruding features being grain silos and the occasional pea-processing plant. Abby let her head fall against the window and closed her eyes. There were supposed to be four of them going up this evening, but Alan had been detained by a last-minute page-numbering crisis, so he'd had to bail. A second-year called Ivan whom she didn't know was probably on the train with her somewhere, but Abby wasn't feeling sociable enough to track him down. George was catching a later train and meeting her there – something Abby was quite happy about. George gave her a headache.

The huge concrete block that was Cambridge University Press rolled past, and passengers started clicking shut laptops and smoothing down coats. The small group of people who felt compelled to wait by the door pressing 'Open' while they drew into the station got up and took their positions. Abby sat back and watched the familiar landmarks slot into place.

It felt strange coming back to Cambridge. In some ways, it seemed ages ago that she'd been living here as a student; it almost felt as though she hadn't been here at all. But at the same time, it was difficult to believe that she'd left. Coming out of the station, she found herself veering towards the spot where her trusty white racer would have been D-locked to the railing. She'd never taken a taxi from Cambridge station. Taxis were for tourists and businessmen, not for students. And despite the free-flowing expenses budget for the evening, Abby didn't feel right queuing up with the suits. It was a mild, spring-like evening, and she had ten minutes to spare. She decided to walk.

The route to Browns took her straight past the house where Ben had lived in second-year, the year they'd met. She turned onto the road, making a conscious effort to think about something else. Like what she was going to say at this dinner. There would be twenty undergraduates attending, all of them in their penultimate year and all of them ready to 'make it big' in the city. They'd been hand-picked by HR on the basis of teams they captained, societies they ran and achievements they'd made – all entirely the wrong criteria for being a successful analyst at Cray McKinley – and they'd all accepted their personal invitations to the dinner just as Abby had done two years before.

She crossed the road at the spot where Ben had once nearly knocked Steven Hawkins out of his wheelchair with his hockey kit. Abby stared straight ahead. Twenty high achievers. What was she going to say? She'd been prepped by HR, and they'd advised her to 'answer their questions honestly,' although the rubber-lipped Barbie had winked at her conspiratorially and added, 'but not too honestly, ahahahahaha!' as if this was all some hilarious practical joke they were playing on the undergrads.

Cray McKinley is a great place to work, Abby rehearsed. Her mind wandered. She was coming up to number fifty. *I've been an analyst for nine months.* She found herself slowing down. The house looked exactly the same, but there was a battered Ford Fiesta in the driveway, and the old water butt where that poor Coi Carp had spent a week (before being returned to the college pond) had been replaced with a high-tech drainage system. She glanced up at the second-floor window. There was a light on in Ben's old room, but the curtains were drawn. Someone else lived there now. Abby felt a sudden pang of – what? Regret? No, not regret. She didn't regret splitting up with Ben. She didn't miss him at all. She just missed her old life.

The doorman at Browns smiled warmly in a way that doormen never usually smiled at Abby. It dawned on her that this was how women in starched black suits and pointy shoes got treated. She looked like someone with money to spend. An adult. Abby wasn't sure she liked it. She didn't need a personal escort to take her through the restaurant or to relieve her of her coat.

The function room was exactly as she remembered it. The tables had been pushed into the same U-shape, again with only enough room for two rows of anorexics to sit back-to-back along the middle. Abby recalled the difficulties she'd had two years ago, arriving late, wearing basketball kit beneath her full-length coat and being trapped between table and chair for twenty minutes while the analysts regaled them with stories from 'the best firm in town'.

She'd thought of herself as so worldly wise, back then. The silver-edged invitation had appeared in her pigeon-hole with the magic words 'dinner' and 'drinks', and she'd accepted without hesitation. She'd had no intention of joining the bank – of being sucked in by any graduate recruiters in flashy suits. Not initially, at least. But then they'd started talking about talent and ambition and success, and Abby's curiosity had been aroused. Through an alcoholic haze, she'd heard the words 'driven' and 'competitive' and 'hard work'. Abby had always loved a challenge. The way they'd described their work – not to mention the harsh application process – had made Abby realise that *here was a challenge just waiting to be met.* Their comments about the 'other banks' and – with even more scorn – the 'other industries' had made Abby wonder why she was even considering a career at the MoD. Clearly, Cray McKinley was the place to be.

"Oh, er, hi," said the gangly man from behind the table of name badges. His limbs were so long that they seemed to have extra joints in them, like a giraffe's legs. "You must be Abby. I'm Ivan." He gave an awkward grin and reached out all the way across the room to shake her hand. "Unless you're George," he added with a little chuckle.

Oh good, thought Abby. Another stand-up comedian. Between them, Ivan and George would bring the house down tonight.

"I've arranged them alphabetically by college," he explained, pointing at the badges. "Bit of an IQ test to start them off." He laughed again.

Abby smiled at the lanky man. "What time are they due to arrive?"

"Six-thirty. But you know what students are like!" He rolled his eyes and threw one of his arms in the air – an action that reminded Abby of a whip being cracked.

She returned his gesture with a long-suffering look of her own, and reached for the nearest bottle of wine. Some anaesthetic was needed for the night ahead.

Abby busied herself ordering extra glasses and jugs of water, enjoying her newfound sense of authority at Browns. It transpired that Ivan wasn't capable of small-talk, so they worked to the muted clatter of the main restaurant next door, interrupted occasionally by little grunts of jubilation as Ivan thought of new and ingenious ways to arrange the badges. Shortly before six o'clock, he came up with the inspirational concept of alphabetical-by-surname, and scooped them all up to start again.

The first student to arrive was a very 'anti-establishment' Kings College scholar, complete with dreadlocks, scruffy shirt, ripped jeans and a double-barrelled surname. Abby wondered how long Christopher Wingford-Digby would keep up the crazy tramp look when he started applying for jobs in the city.

"They'd better do Fair Trade food here," he commented, sneering briefly at the nearest menu on the table.

"It's Browns; of course they do," Abby assured him. "Not sure about the wine though," she added quietly, as he confidently poured himself a large glass of red. He didn't seem to hear.

Next came a small Asian girl who looked utterly petrified. When Abby noticed what was coming in behind her, she realised why.

"Evening!" chirped George as he bounded into the room, looking every bit the city wanker. His shoes were so shiny he could have squeezed his spots in them, and the pinstripes looked as though they'd been painted on in Tipp-Ex. "Hi Abby. You came up earlier, did you? No point in hanging around the office doing nothing, I suppose…" He swaggered over to the table and plucked his name badge off the table.

Abby nodded tolerantly. *Doing nothing*. Ouch. George never stopped playing the game. Even when the only people around to impress were two clueless students and a second-year analyst, he just couldn't help trying to get one up on her.

The arrival of Scotty, a red-faced rugby jock, made the room feel significantly more crowded, and the group broke into twos and threes. Abby found herself talking to a spindly student called Paul who seemed determined to insert the entire contents of his CV into conversation.

"It was only *then* that the conductor informed me that I was the only one on tour who spoke fluent French," he said. "I mean, for a *county* orchestra, that's pretty unusual, isn't it?"

"Mmm, very." Abby nodded and took a large sip of wine as Paul Bartlett went on to describe the trials of being a company director whilst still at university.

When the area by the door became so cramped that elbows started knocking into glasses, Abby decided it was probably time to sit down. She tried to catch Ivan's attention, but he was busy aligning the three remaining badges on the table. George was boasting about his car to some poor, intimidated mathematician who probably thought that an SLK was a chemical compound. She picked up a teaspoon and banged it against her glass.

From her vantage point at the head of the U-shaped table, Abby surveyed the roomful of students. They looked so much younger than whatever they were – twenty? Twenty-one? Their smiles were so fresh, so genuine. And they had reason to be excited. They had a million achievements under their belts, and a whole load more they were ready to make – it was just a question of fitting them in. *The world was their oyster*, they'd been told. And it was, in a way. It was just that the oyster was slightly less colourful, less interesting and less perfect than they all imagined it to be.

It came as a surprise when Ivan suddenly cleared his throat and rose to his feet. Abby wondered what he was going to say.

"Um, hi," he began, addressing a spot half-way up the back wall. The room went quiet. Abby watched as he shakily tipped the jug of water over his glass and sloshed most of it onto the table. "I just wanted to say, thanks to everyone for coming along this evening."

Oh Christ, thought Abby. *He thinks it's the Oscars*. There was a pile of little cards propped up against the wine glass in front of him, and she noticed his eyes flitting between them and the spot on the wall. He'd prepared a full speech. She hoped he'd remembered to thank his mother.

"As you know, we're from Cray McKinley." The water incident had obviously unnerved him, and all of a sudden, he was speaking incredibly quickly. "So that means we're investment bankers so we work on all the mergers and deals that you read about in the FT and me personally I'm a second-year and I've got some big ones that I can talk about later if you're interested—"

He broke off, aware of the quiet ripple of laughter that was travelling around the room.

"Er, big *transactions*, that is," he clarified, flipping over one of his cards and somehow sending the whole lot into the puddle of water. Abby smiled at the students, trying to create an aura of calm and at the same time disassociate herself from her colleague.

"So what is it that investment bankers do?" Ivan asked the spot on the wall, now somewhat short of breath. "Well essentially we make lots of money."

He paused and waited for people to laugh. Nobody did.

"Um, yes. So we make that money in lots of ways for example on the trading floor the traders make money by buying and selling shares and bonds and other more complicated things such as 'plain vanilla swaps' which don't sound very plain at all if you ask me—" he waited for the reaction from the crowd, which never came. Abby thought about helping him out with a little chuckle, but she couldn't bring herself to do it.

Ivan knocked over all but the last of his little cards, clearly desperate to get to the end. "Anyway that's on the 'markets' side of the bank and I think I'm right in saying that all three of us here tonight are from the 'banking' side so I'm going to let my colleagues describe exactly what that entails thanks and erm yes I'm sure we can answer your questions throughout the deal – din – minner – meal."

Ivan was so keen to sit down that he forgot to check the location of his chair, and ended up landing half-on, half-off it, beneath the critical gaze of twenty students.

George took it upon himself to go next, and to his credit, made a much better job of it than his senior colleague. Admittedly, the joke about female bankers and dildos didn't go down as well as he'd probably hoped, and the comments about his 'fuck-off big pay cheques' and being able to afford 'seriously cool clothes' might have come across as arrogant (and largely inaccurate), but at least he didn't flood the table or fall off his chair.

Suddenly it was Abby's turn, and she was standing up in front of a roomful of expectant undergraduates without having the faintest idea what she was going to say. George, in his own special way, had explained what investment banking was all about, but the description of *what an analyst actually did* had been left to her.

"Hi. I'm Abby," she announced, slowly and confidently, smiling at anyone who'd meet her eye. She could see the relief in their faces. "Hello Ed," she said to the latecomer who was trying to slip in unnoticed. She grinned at the blonde hockey player. Ed Granger had been a first-year when Abby had known him. He'd been the youngest, cheekiest and arguably most talented player on Ben's team. "Nice of you to pop in. There's a seat for you right here." She pointed to the least accessible chair in the room, which was bang in the middle of the U and exactly where Abby had been squeezed two years previously. Ed gave her a look that said *I'll get you back later,* and manoeuvred as effortlessly as was possible into the middle of the room.

"So, I'm a first-year analyst, like George," she told them, still undecided as to what she'd say next. Of course, they all expected her to wave the corporate flag and describe how wonderful and rewarding it was to be an investment banker at Cray McKinley. But what if she didn't? What if she told them what she really did in the office? What if she told them how many hours every week she and George spent formatting PowerPoint slides and waiting for the print room to call?

She'd look like a lunatic, that's what. Or maybe a failed 'female banker', which would only provide ammunition for George's punchlines. "I'm in Corporate Finance," she told them, "which means I get to work on those massive transactions that Ivan was talking about." And then all sorts of crap started spouting out. "It's a great place to work," she found herself saying. "There's some brilliant opportunities at Cray McKinley, if you're prepared to work for them." It was all flowing too easily. Maybe a career in politics would've been more up her street, she thought. "It's demanding, and there are days when you wonder why the hell you're still in the office at three in the morning, but then you get to the end of the deal, and you see the headlines in the paper and think, 'I made that happen!'" She was out of control now. The crap was just pouring out of her mouth – and the audience was lapping it up. She could tell by their faces. If she'd been given a wad of contracts to hand out tonight, she would have had twenty recruits, just like that.

Abby brought her rousing speech to an end as she noticed the head waiter hovering in the doorway, trying to gauge whether it was time to bring in the starters. "Let's eat!" she cried, nodding at the man and watching a line of waitresses file in with plates all the way up their skinny little arms. "If you want to know more, come and talk to us during the meal," she said. "That's what we're here for."

It soon became apparent that Abby wasn't going to get much eating or drinking done – not for the first two courses, at least.

"How late do you work?"

"Do you travel a lot?"

"What did you get in your degree?"

"Would I get to use my numerical skills alongside my French at Cray McKinley?" asked the linguistic, artistic, entrepreneurial, clarinet-playing, three times Under-15 Kent chess champion. Some people name-dropped; Paul Bartlett talent-dropped.

Abby dispatched them as quickly as was polite and looked down to see that her half-eaten pot of prawns had been whisked away. She tore off a piece of bread, stuffed it into her mouth and washed it down with a large swig of wine. It was gratifying to see that no one was directing their questions at Ivan or George, she thought, although it would have been rather handy if they could have fielded a couple, just to give her a break.

"How much d'you get paid?"

"Is it true they have vending machines with toothbrushes and razors and stuff, for when you work through the night?"

"Yep, it's true," Abby nodded and held out her glass for a top-up as Ed Granger waved the bottle in her direction.

"How's things?" he asked quietly.

"Not bad." Abby smiled, grateful for Ed's intervention. The other students took the hint and soon the questions petered out.

"And how's Ben?"

Abby hesitated. "Er, he's fine, I think. We split up."

"Oh. God, I'm sorry," he said, looking genuinely apologetic but at the same time, she thought, slightly flirtatious the cheeky bugger.

"No – it's OK. It was for the best," she said. "It just didn't work in the real world."

"Oh, right." He nodded. Yes, the cute blue eyes were definitely lingering on hers for longer than was strictly necessary. "Well, thanks for telling us about the 'real world', Abby. It was useful."

"Yeah, but Ed—" Abby suddenly felt compelled to tell him the truth. "About what I said." She dropped her voice so that nobody else could hear. "It was mainly bullshit, you know that, don't you?"

He shrugged coolly. "Yeah, of course," he said, looking a little less sure of himself.

"I mean, it really *isn't* that glamorous, working for Cray McKinley. It's pretty crap, to be honest."

Ed laughed nervously. "Yeah, but the salary's not crap, is it?"

"No…" Abby thought about how to dissuade him. Clearly he'd fallen for the money = success argument. She really didn't want him to go for a job there. Cray McKinley wasn't for nice people like Ed Granger. "It's the work. It takes over your life. And it's totally menial and pointless. You'd hate it." She looked him in the eye. "I do."

Ed nodded slowly, holding her gaze. The message had clearly got through. "Oh, right."

"The money's good – that's true, but –"

"No, yeah, you're right. Thanks for the warning."

Abby smiled.

"It's good to hear it from someone on the inside," he said.

"Well, yeah. I wish *I'd* had someone on the inside."

Abby took a sip of wine, hoping she'd done the right thing by putting Ed off.

"But I think I'll still apply, anyway," he said, after a thoughtful pause. "It seems silly not to. Everyone says I'd be good enough. And they love sporty people, apparently."

Abby said nothing. She should have realised. There was only one way to learn. She just hoped it wouldn't take Ed too long. "OK. Well good luck."

Ed grinned, chinked his glass against hers, and downed his wine in one.

41

"SUPER CHAP THOUGH. *Rolling* in money. Doesn't know what to do with the stuff. Oh, I say! Splendid shot, Michael – splendid!"

Mike smiled modestly as the ball headed straight for the flat, then landed only centimetres away from the flag. It rolled on and came to a gentle halt on the edge of the circle, making a hole-in-two look like a distinct possibility.

He was playing well, especially considering he hadn't touched a club in over six months. Mike could tell that the other men were impressed. His father kept giving him that affectionate *I-don't-know-how-you-do-it* look (which was actually rather embarrassing), and Hugo and Rod kept breaking off their conversation to congratulate him on his shots.

"Jeez, that's a hard act to follow!" Rod chuckled, yanking a club out of his bag and manoeuvring himself into position.

Rod looked ridiculous. He always did. It was as though he'd ordered every item in the back pages of Golfers' Weekly, then donned the whole lot at once. The Pringle tank-top stretched over his sturdy, American frame to meet a pair of heavily-tapered Rupert Bear trousers, which failed to conceal the horrendous, white-tipped golfing shoes. There was no need for a sun visor on a day like this, and as far as Mike was concerned, there was never any need for a poncy left-hand glove – not when you played like Rod did, anyway – but he was wearing them all the same.

Mike watched as the large man waddled on the spot above the ball, shifting his considerable weight from foot to foot like a penguin. He was a 'golfing friend' of Mike's father, which meant that the two men played golf together, but they weren't really friends. Rod was the sort of person one might describe as 'larger than life'. He was loud, he laughed a lot – mainly at his own jokes – and he was inclined to slap other men on the back. He was a stockbroker for a handful of wealthy Americans in London, and judging by the size of his paunch, he seemed to do very well out of it.

The other three men took a synchronised step backwards as Rod performed his trademark practice-swing routine, which involved at least ten high-speed swipes of the air before the club made contact with the ball. Finally, the small white missile was launched into orbit, and after what seemed like a very long time, came plummeting down about two hundred metres beyond the hole, just inside the lip of a bunker.

"Ah, bad luck, old thing!" Hugo commiserated, with a hint of glee in his voice. He'd hit an uncharacteristically good shot minutes earlier, which now put him just ahead of the burly American – something that didn't happen very often.

Hugo Besterman was a tall, upright chap with a grey moustache and a surprising amount of hair for his fifty-something years. Like Mike's father, Hugo was ex-RAF, but unlike Mike's father, he'd opted to spend his retirement in the city, making more money by – as far as Mike could tell – putting chums in touch with other chums. He seemed to spend most of his time in expensive restaurants and private members' clubs, with regular trips to Ascot, Twickenham and the Oval.

Years ago, it had always been Mike who'd held them up, trailing along behind them, making dents in the well-kempt lawn with one of his father's clubs, or swinging from the back of the golf caddy like a chimp as it purred round the course. Now, ironically, it was Mike's father who kept them waiting, mainly due to his atrocious shots. Today was especially bad, thought Mike, cringing as the wild, left-handed swing came into play.

"Ah, yes. Sorry," he mumbled, as the ball rolled off its tee and stopped about two metres from where they stood. "Having a bit of bother with my um, my elbow."

"Take it again," offered Hugo magnanimously, bending down to retrieve the ball. There was a subtle exchange of looks between Hugo and Rod, and Mike felt a rush of compassion for his old man.

"Bloody hell!" remarked Hugo, as the ball was hit cleanly off its tee and followed almost the same trajectory as Mike's. It was actually a slightly better shot than Mike's – more due to luck, he suspected, than to skill – but it wiped the smirk off the other men's faces.

"Runs in the family," Mr Cunningham-Reid remarked, with another proud glance at his son. For a second, it looked worryingly as though he might reach across and give Mike's hair an affectionate tousle, but thankfully the moment passed, and the men busied themselves shoving golf clubs into bags and lugging them into the caddy.

Mike hung back a little as they meandered through the flawlessly landscaped terrain, Rod taking the driving seat (and most of the passenger seat) while the others strolled nonchalantly alongside. It was a crisp, spring-like morning, and the sun was just about strong enough to warm the dark material on Mike's back. His thoughts migrated from the overly green countryside to the place where his thoughts always seemed to migrate these days: the office.

Review day was coming up. He wasn't sure what to expect. There were rumours flying around that the bank had deliberately over-hired on the analyst front this year, with the intention of cutting out the 'dead wood' after appraisals. Of course, Mike knew that his job was safe. He wasn't 'dead wood'. They loved him in Corporate Finance. But then again, they'd loved Patrick Gilligan, too. He'd been the star associate. Maybe nobody's job was safe?

Abby was worried about it too – she'd confided in him the other day. Mike was slowly coming to realise that Abby Turner wasn't the cocky little madam that everybody took her for. She came across as feisty and rude, but that was an act. The real Abby Turner spent her time feeling either useless or out of her depth – although you'd never know it by looking at her. Of course, she'd be OK though, if the cuts came. They'd never dare sack a female analyst. Cray McKinley was as paranoid as the next city firm about the threat of a lawsuit, and women bankers weren't known for leaving their jobs quietly. Mike had tried to remind Abby of this, but she hadn't seemed convinced.

"Smashing fellow," Hugo was saying, prompting Mike's father to nod even harder. Everyone Hugo knew was either 'smashing' or 'super' or 'splendid'. "Sails a lot down in Cowes. It's either Cazenove or Cray McKinley he works for – can't remember off the top of my head."

Mike caught up with them, his interest sparked by the mention of his firm – although he was fairly sure that he wouldn't know anyone who mixed in Hugo Besterman's circles.

"Simon Marchant. Stocky little fellow. Round, wire-rimmed specs. Know the one?" He made a pair of glasses with his fingers and stared at Mike through them. "Only man in London who still wears braces. Huh!"

Mike laughed politely. Neither the name nor the impersonation triggered any bells, but that was hardly surprising. The only senior bankers Mike knew by name were the ones in his department and the ones he read about in the FT. "Probably Cazenove," he replied, hauling the first set of clubs out onto the grass.

"Hmm. D'you have a Corporate Broking department at Cray?"

Suddenly, the spark became a full-blown flame of interest. "Corporate Broking? Is that where he works? Er, yes. Yes, we do."

"Ah – fairly sure that's where he works. Thought it was Cray McKinley. Have to get him along for a round of golf sometime. Hits a good game, does Simon. Handicap of five, you know."

"Really?" Mike enquired, genuinely excited. Corporate Broking was a who-you-know business. If Mike could secure himself a game with this Simon Marchant bloke… hmm. This could be the foot in the door he'd been after. Perhaps today wouldn't be such a waste of time after all. "Let's set something up. Sounds like a great idea."

42

"HOW WAS IT?" Abby hissed.

"Pointless," Mike whispered back, rolling his eyes as he brushed past her.

Abby breathed deeply and gave two confident knocks.

"Come in!" called the voice.

Rupert Larkham was sitting rigidly behind his desk, hands clasped tightly in front of him as though in prayer.

"Sit down," he muttered, briefly breaking the symmetry of his profile to wave at the leather chair.

Abby tentatively perched on the seat, trying to mirror Larkham's impeccable posture. He was a peculiar looking man: wiry and thin with an unhealthily pallid complexion. His tuft of remaining hair sat like a garnish on top of his head.

"As you know, I'm in charge of analysts' wellbeing in Corporate Finance," he began.

Abby nodded sagely. Was he? She hadn't noticed much attention being paid to *her* wellbeing in the past eight months. Larkham had barely spoken to her.

"So it's up to me to conduct your self-appraisal meeting today," he explained, glancing down at his watch. "Hmm. We'll have to be relatively quick; I've got four analysts to get through before lunch. Now…" he peered at the neat stack papers in front of him. "Annabel Turner."

"Abigail," she corrected.

Larkham glanced at her irritably as if this wasn't the slightest bit relevant. "You're a first-year analyst."

Abby nodded.

"Hmm, yes," he mused. "It shows from the way you've filled out your form."

Abby looked at his pasty face. She'd expected comments like this; Larkham probably had her down as one of those clueless first-years who didn't understand about bullshitting. How wrong he was. She watched him frown at the sheet in his spindly hands.

"You haven't really grasped the concept of self-appraisal, have you?"

Abby didn't flinch; she just stared, waiting for the patronising comments to start.

"Hmm, yes. I see what you've done." He scanned the page and then focussed on the top section. "You've taken this a bit too literally, haven't you? Yes... 'opportunity to assess your progress and achievements'... 'identify areas for improvement'... 'note your main strengths and weaknesses'... Yes, I can see where you've gone wrong."

"I'm sorry?" Abby maintained her stony expression. She wanted to hear what she'd done 'wrong' before she started arguing her case. Perhaps Rupert Larkham had never seen an appraisal form filled out like this before – filled out with the truth – but that was his problem. Abby wasn't going to sit here and be told it was 'wrong'.

"You do realise what this piece of paper *is*, don't you?" He picked up the form and jiggled it in the air.

Abby raised an eyebrow. It was exactly that: a piece of paper. A piece of paper filled with questions that were constructed entirely from jargon.

"This piece of paper," he said, stabbing it with a finger, "in conjunction with the cross-evaluation that your colleagues will complete over the course of the next three months," he paused to give Abby a meaningful look, "*will determine the size of your bonus*."

Abby looked at him, nonplussed.

Larkham leaned forwards, like a primary school teacher trying to explain multiplication to a very stupid child.

"In twelve weeks' time," he said slowly, "you will be sitting in this office, receiving your end-of-year bonus, and hearing what your colleagues have to say about you."

Whoopee, thought Abby. Another meeting with Rupert Larkham!

"Between now and the end of June, your performance will be reviewed by your contemporaries and your superiors. This evaluation will be coupled with your self-appraisal–" he nodded at the piece of paper – "and sent to HR, to be placed alongside all the other analysts' reviews."

Rupert Larkham looked solemnly at Abby, checking she understood. She nodded sulkily.

"Then *all* the junior bankers will be ranked – one to three hundred – and divided into four groups: Top, middle, bottom and… now, how shall I put it? *Crap.*"

Abby flinched. She wondered if he was trying to tell her she was 'crap'. It sounded so wrong, that word, coming out of Rupert Larkham's mouth.

"The top group will receive good bonuses, the middle group reasonable ones, and the bottom group just a token few grand. The rest will be made redundant." He raised his willowy eyebrows.

"So you see, this form is key to your success. It has to show that you're *good*." Larkham gave Abby a lingering look. She stared back, holding her tongue. She'd have her turn in a minute. The fact was, Abby *was* good at her job, and she didn't need a silly self-appraisal form to prove it.

Suddenly, a change came over the man. It was as though someone had changed his batteries. He picked up the sheaf of papers, re-aligned them by bashing them noisily against the desk and then slammed the bundle back down, muttering to himself.

This was it, thought Abby. This was the bit where he started ripping her answers to shreds, and she got a chance to defend herself. She wanted him to think about what she'd written.

"Of course, we can't change what you've put; unfortunately it's too late for that. But at least you'll know for next time."

Know *what* for next time, Abby thought furiously. She didn't need to be told what to write.

"Ah. See – here. The very first question. *List five major transactions you've worked on.* You've only listed *four*! I mean, really. In an investment bank, one is expected to be able to *count!*"

"There were only–"

"If it says 'list five', then you've got to list five!" Larkham cried.

"Attention to detail! Isn't that what they taught you in New York?"

There were only four transactions worth mentioning, Abby wanted to say. It wasn't *her* fault she'd been assigned to a succession of trivial pitchbooks. "I only got to—"

"And here!" he interrupted, poking at the page as if Abby could read through the back of it. "This one! *Describe a situation in which you have overcome a problem using ingenuity and original thought.* You've written less than three lines! And what's this nonsense about 'very little scope for an analyst to use ingenuity'? What are you trying to say?"

Larkham looked furious. His cheeks were actually flushed – something she'd never seen before. Maybe he thought she'd written those things for a joke, that she wasn't taking her appraisal form seriously. In fact, the opposite was true. She was taking it *perfectly* seriously. A good deal of time and effort had gone into her responses; she wanted her views to be heard. She *wanted* people to know what she'd been doing for the past nine months. She *wanted* them to understand how worthless she was feeling. And her appraisal form seemed like the perfect way to make her views heard.

"I just meant," Abby paused to consider her words. She didn't want to antagonise the man unnecessarily. "So far, in my job, I haven't had to use my ingenuity."

Larkham sighed. "I will reiterate what I said at the beginning of this meeting. Your self-assessment is one of the key indicators of your performance as an analyst. I would advise you to remember that."

But there really isn't any scope for ingenuity! Abby wanted to scream. *It's all about following instructions!* It was hard to see why Cray McKinley bothered recruiting bright university graduates, when a well-trained chimpanzee could do just as good a job. The only time she'd felt *vaguely* ingenious since starting at the firm was when she'd helped Lara fix the colour printer.

Larkham ran a finger down the page, searching for the next audacity.

"And here!" Another random jab. "Why have you left this blank?!"

Abby knew what he was referring to: the Communication with Clients section.

"Because I don't *have* any comm—"

Larkham growled despairingly. "That's not the point!"

"So, what... Am I supposed to... make something up?" she asked – firmly but politely.

"No! Yes! Oh—" he sighed furiously. "I don't care! Just write something to show that you're good at your job!"

Abby glared at the VP. This wasn't going according to plan. He didn't seem the least bit interested in what she had to say.

"And why have you given yourself a 'Reasonable' for your financial modelling ability?"

"Well," Abby said, "I've only really done one proper financial model, and it took me quite a long time, because it was all new to me, and—"

Larkham groaned loudly. "This is a multiple choice question, OK? You have the option of picking Excellent, Good, Reasonable and Poor. Might I suggest you opt for Excellent next time?"

Abby nodded silently, biting her bottom lip. She wondered if Larkham was trying to be funny.

"Look," he placed his palms face down on the desk. "We're running out of time. Perhaps if I quickly show you an example of one of the other analysts' appraisal forms, that might help?"

He leafed through the bundle of identical forms, skimming the first few lines of each.

"Here. This is a good one. I'm afraid I can't show you whose it is—" he covered the top left corner with his hand – "but take a look at some of his responses."

Abby glanced sullenly at the sheet. The list of 'major transactions' told her it was Mike's self-appraisal form. She peered closer, and studied some of his answers.

'...consider myself to be a highly competent analyst'... 'have been instrumental in a number of deals'... 'often find myself taking the initiative'... 'make full use of my teamwork abilities'... 'am efficient and accurate in every aspect of my work'... *What a load of shit*, thought Abby. Even Mike was playing the game.

"See what I mean?" Larkham said slowly. "Does that clarify things a little?"

Abby was still reeling from what she'd just read. Highly competent. Instrumental. Efficient and accurate. How could anyone use those words to describe someone who fiddled with PowerPoint slides for a living?

"This is what you should be aiming for. These answers tell me that the analyst is confident and competent, that he's enthusiastic about his work, that he's keen, he's bright, and most importantly, that he's *good at his job*. Now that's what I want to hear. That's what will earn you a good bonus. There's no point in being self-deprecating, is there?"

Abby looked at him, her blood boiling. "I just—"

"Think of it like a CV," he went on. "Exaggerate the positives, leave out the negatives... Twist the truth a little."

She gawped at the man, nodding dumbly. She'd just wanted to be honest. She'd wanted to tell them how it was. But he wasn't listening to a word. In fact, he hadn't given her a chance to *say* the words. All he wanted was another identical appraisal form filled with the usual corporate waffle.

Larkham was still looking at Abby when she finished nodding, staring intently into her eyes as if he was trying to communicate some sort of subliminal message. She held his gaze, having one last go at transmitting her own message: *I know how to fill out a self-appraisal form. I wrote that stuff because I wanted you to sit up and listen.*

As they sat there trying to out-stare each other, Abby gradually felt herself weaken. Hers was a lost cause. There was no point in trying to fight the system. She should have just played along like a good little analyst. There was no room for mavericks at Cray McKinley – particularly not down at the bottom. The whole self-appraisal thing was a sham. Those lines about 'analysing your capabilities and achievements' and 'identifying areas for improvement' were just put in for show; nobody *really* cared about her career progression. And as for her 'wellbeing' – what a joke! She nearly laughed out loud, then saw the look on Larkham's face.

This form was all about the bonus. It was an opportunity for bankers to brag about accomplishments they hadn't made and deals they hadn't worked on, in order to boost their end-of-year bonus. Even Mike had understood that much. How could she have been so dense?

"I mean, look at your responses," said Larkham disdainfully. "Look at the great long list you've given for 'Skills to work on in the forthcoming year'... You've practically written a book! People are going to wonder if you *had* any skills to begin with!" He threw a hand in the air.

Abby didn't try to protest any more. What was the point? Rupert Larkham didn't want to hear her whinging, and neither did anybody else, for that matter. As if they'd care what a first-year had to say. They didn't even want to know her name! She sat in silence, letting her gaze rest on the stack of appraisal forms. How naïve she'd been. Abby marvelled at her own stupidity. To think she'd answered those questions truthfully! To think she'd believed she could change how things were!

Larkham must have noticed the crumpled look on Abby's face, and sensed that his message had got through. He glanced down at his watch and started muttering about time slots. "D'you have any questions for me," he stated, yanking his office door open. "Now, don't forget what I told you about the cross-evaluation. I suggest you use the next few weeks wisely, Annab – Abigail. It's important you receive favourable reports from the other members of Corporate Finance – particularly the senior ones."

The raised eyebrow and condescending stare were becoming permanent fixtures on Larkham's face, and Abby was beginning to despise them. She gave a wide smile that extended no further than her mouth, and marched out of his office.

★ ★ ★

Use the next few weeks wisely. She pondered these words as she sat, slumped at her desk, pretending to study an annual report. He meant, of course, *use the next few weeks to suck up to your colleagues.* The concept was not an appealing one. Abby never sucked up to people. She wasn't a creep. Why couldn't she just be judged on her abilities?

The back of her chair started wobbling from side to side. Abby whirled round to confront her neighbour, wanting more than ever to spit in his face and get rid of that stupid, self-satisfied grin. This was not the time to provoke her – especially if he had one of his 'little jobs' up his sleeve.

"*What?*" she hissed venomously.

Abby found herself glaring at someone's belt.

"Ooh – easy!" Mike exclaimed, taking a large step backwards and smiling. "Just wondered how it went."

Abby grunted. She didn't want to talk about it. Not to *him*, anyway. Not to Mr Highly Competent Analyst. He was probably just coming over to gloat.

"All go OK?" he asked.

"Complete waste of time, like you said," she replied curtly. And then, in a moment of paranoia, she wondered if Larkham had showed Mike *her* appraisal form, as an example of what *not* to do. She cringed as she envisaged the pair of them, pointing and scoffing at her foolish responses. *Look what she's written for this one! Oh – and this one! She's lucky to be still in a job!* Mike nodded, then stepped closer and bent down. "*I think he's had a hair transplant,*" he whispered.

Abby grunted again without turning her head. OK, so they hadn't been laughing at her. But those warnings he'd given her – *they* weren't part of her paranoia.

Mike straightened up. "You OK?"

"Mmm – just busy," she told him, just as the screensaver obliterated her long-abandoned spreadsheet.

"So I see!" Mike reached for the back of Abby's chair and gave it a sharp tug, sending her spinning round uncontrollably until her flailing hands grabbed hold of the desk. When she regained her balance, he was gone.

Arrogant git, she thought viciously, thinking back to the words on his form. How could he write such blatant crap? She watched as he got back to work, staring resentfully at the back of his head. He'd be OK in his cross-evaluation. He was playing the game like a pro. Trust Mike.

Abby jiggled her mouse, waiting for her monitor to come back to life. Deep down, she knew that she wasn't cross with Mike. She was cross with herself. Somehow, in trying to make things better, she'd managed to aggravate a VP, demonstrate her ignorance, demolish her chances of a decent bonus, and maybe even jeopardise her career. *The rest will be made redundant.* The worrying truth was: Abby was in danger of losing her job.

She couldn't concentrate. It was an overwhelming realisation. She might only have a couple of months left at Cray McKinley. Or maybe not. She just didn't know. Would they sack a first-year analyst? Was it true what George had said about them filtering out 'the duds'? She needed to find out. There was only one person Abby could think of who would know about these things – although the idea of making the call filled her with dread.

"Angela speaking," sung a bird-like voice. "How can I help?"

"Oh, er, hi." Abby was thrown. For some reason, she hadn't considered the possibility that Jennifer Armstrong might have a PA.

"Ms Armstrong is in a meeting right now," the voice chirped. "Perhaps I can take a message?"

Abby hesitated. She *couldn't* ask Jennifer to call her back; the woman was a *Managing Director.* But if she didn't, what else could she do?

"I can note down your name if you like?" the woman prompted. "She'll call you back right away."

"Yes – could you? Thanks." Abby replaced the receiver, with no hope that her call would be returned. She understood secretary-language; 'in a meeting' meant 'not wanting to talk to you', and 'right away' meant 'in several hours or possibly never'.

"That was a cryptic phone call," Jon Hargreaves commented.

Abby shot him a sidelong glance that told him it was none of his business, and focussed intently on her screen. She scrolled down the spreadsheet, then up to the top again. Down, up. Down, up. She just couldn't concentrate. She thought about composing her resignation letter – that idea cheered her up temporarily – but she knew that wasn't the solution. She needed to find out where she stood.

"Abby?" Lara shouted across the office. "Aren't you picking up your phone? I've got Jennifer Armstrong on the line!"

★ ★ ★

It felt strange to be walking into a pub in the middle of a work day, particularly one where the clientele were dressed – almost without

307

exception – in jeans, sweatshirts and steel toe-capped boots, and carrying yellow workmen's hats. Abby followed the little lady – who was sporting a flecked brown two-piece suit that looked a bit like a toilet-roll tube – through the hoards of riotous workmen.

"I like to come here," Jennifer Armstrong explained as she nestled between two chop-like elbows at the bar. "It's a guaranteed Cray McKinley–free zone."

Abby looked around at the young men, their greasy, hat-flattened hair reflecting the shafts of coloured sunlight that poured through the stained glass windows. They appeared to be inside a converted church – a converted church full of builders, most of whom were gawping in her direction. *It's alright for you,* she thought, looking down at the dumpy MD.

"And they do great sausage sandwiches," the woman added with a wink.

Abby's annoyance receded a little.

"What are you drinking?" she demanded.

"Lemonade, please."

Jennifer looked at her disapprovingly. "Don't you want a proper drink? A pint? A gin-and-tonic? Wine? Spritzer? Vodka? Cinz–"

"OK then–" Abby said, when it became apparent the MD was planning to reel off the entire drinks menu. "Half a pint of lager please." She didn't really like drinking at lunchtime – particularly not when there was twelve hours' work waiting for her back at the office – but Jennifer Armstrong was clearly not going to take lemonade for an answer.

"Half? Don't be ridiculous."

The woman stepped onto the ledge at the base of the bar, which put her almost on a level with her neighbouring lumberjack's shoulder, and thrust a twenty-pound note in the air. "A pint of lager, a large white wine and two rounds of pork sausage sandwiches please Lenny!" She sounded like the Queen trying to rap.

"Thanks for agreeing to meet me," Abby said meekly as she squeezed in between the low-hanging beam and the rickety chair.

"Not a problem!" Jennifer replied dismissively. "Actually I'm flying out to the States in a couple of hours, so you're lucky you caught me!" She knocked back a slug of wine. "So, what made you call? Oh – wait. Mid-April. Let me guess. Self-appraisal. You've just had your self-appraisal meeting, and you think you've messed everything up. Am I right?"

Abby smiled and nodded, grudgingly impressed at her intuition. Jennifer Armstrong didn't seem the perceptive type. She was far too high up the career ladder to have time for other people.

"Thought so. It's not so uncommon, you know. First-years are at a distinct disadvantage. 'Self-appraisal' is a misleading term, don't you think? I always say 'self-praise' would be more appropriate. Ahahahahaha!"

Abby took her first sip of beer, relaxing a little in the realisation that Jennifer planned to do most of the talking.

"I remember *my* first self-appraisal meeting. I thought I was going to lose my *job!* I was a bit of a fool, you see; I tried to be *honest* on my form. Didn't work, obviously. I ended up with the bottom-tier bonus, and a huge black mark against my name. They thought I was completely inept after all the self-criticism I'd crammed onto my form…"

Relief flooded Abby's mind. So she wasn't the only one. And Jennifer Armstrong had obviously done alright for herself. Abby wanted to reach across and hug the little woman.

"Ooh! Tuck in," she instructed, as a plate of little brown triangles was set down in front of them. They were hot, greasy and oozing with ketchup – exactly what Abby felt like.

Washing the salty sandwiches down with gulps of cold lager, Abby let the woman prattle on, fitting at least a hundred words in between mouthfuls and still managing to throw back large quantities of wine. Abby desperately wanted to say something to her – to tell her how happy she was to hear that somebody else had made that mistake – but she didn't quite have the nerve.

Suddenly the woman stopped talking, licked her lips and looked up. "So. Tell me about *your* appraisal. What was so bad about it?"

Abby hesitated. "Well, it was just like yours. I'd filled out my form all wrong. Written the truth about my work and my performance and stuff – I thought I could shock them into seeing how it really was–"

Jennifer nodded vaguely, as if this was entirely predictable.

"And – well, I got told about the ranking system they use – the way they grade the analysts and divide them into groups. Top, middle, bottom and the one that–"

"Gets the sack?" Jennifer finished, her eyes twinkling. "Dear me, Abigail," she chuckled. "You'd have to try jolly hard to get kicked out of the firm in your *first* year! First-years are cheap labour! You only cost the firm about forty grand a year! They won't get rid of you now – not unless you're *really bad* at your job!"

"But I–"

"No you're not, I can assure you. What time did you get into the office today?"

"About eight o'clock," Abby replied, unnerved by the irrele-vance of the question.

"And when d'you think you'll be leaving?"

"Well, I've got quite a bit of–"

"What time?"

"Maybe midnight, or one, I suppose."

"Exactly. That's a sixteen hour day. That makes you a perfectly good analyst. Now, whether you're a *brilliant* analyst depends on a number of other factors – like who you know, which deals you get put on, how well you suck up to the management… luck, I suppose, to some extent… but the point is, you *won't* be losing your job this June."

Abby wasn't so sure. Rupert Larkham's words were still fresh in her mind. *The rest will be made redundant. Use the next few weeks wisely.*

"These appraisals really aren't as important as people like to make out," Jennifer said, shaking her head and looking up to the ceiling. "Yes, they go some way to determining your bonus at the end of the year, and to some extent, they're used as a filtering mecha-nism, but… really, they're not that important. What matters is how you behave in the office." The woman glanced at Abby and bit into another sandwich. "Elp ushelf!"

"Your attitude," she continued as soon as she'd swallowed. "That's what'll make the difference in the long-run. Analysts – and female analysts in particular – have a complex about being at the bottom of the ladder. You, Abigail, you seem to think that you're inferior to your colleagues,"

"But I am!" Abby interrupted. "I really am! I mess—"

"No you're *not*. You are exactly the same as the other first-year analysts. You are a graduate from – which one did you go to?"

"Cambridge," Abby replied sheepishly.

"WELL THERE YOU GO!" she cried triumphantly. "You're a graduate from Cambridge University, with a string of achievements to your name no doubt, and two months' intensive financial training behind you – just like all your colleagues. You've got to *believe* in yourself!"

"But—"

"No buts! You've got to act like a man, I'm afraid. Be gutsy. Confident. Tell people you're good. Swagger about a bit!"

"I am confident on the outside," Abby said in her defence. It was true. Nobody would guess that the cocky blonde analyst who strutted about the office with a snappy response to every remark had an ego the size of a pea.

"I'm glad to hear it. But you can't just *act* like a man – you've got to *think* like one, too." She leaned forwards across the table. "Know that you're good. You must shake off this silly idea that you're not as capable as the rest."

Abby looked sceptically at Jennifer. *Act like a man. Think like a man.* Did she have to?

"It's not easy, adapting," the MD admitted, obviously seeing the doubt in Abby's eyes. "But it'll make things easier in the long-run. D'you want another drink?"

Abby shook her head, and watched the determined little figure hurry back to the bar. She certainly led by example; the woman was brimming with confidence.

"So yes – act like a man," Jennifer reiterated, settling back down with a fresh glass of wine. "Talk the talk – that's what this industry's all about. One percent banking, ninety-nine percent bullshitting. You're focussing on the first one percent, which is where you're going wrong. You'll never get anywhere if you do that."

Abby pursed her lips, thinking about some of the men she'd worked for. Stuart Mackins, Charles Kershaw, Geoff Dodds... yes, they all 'talked the talk'. In fact, in Dodds' case, he talked so much talk that nobody understood what he was on about most of the time.

"And I suppose you've been told about your cross-evaluation?" Jennifer asked.

Something started fluttering in Abby's stomach. It was those horrible words again. "Yes – I'm slightly worried about that," she confessed. "I don't think I'll be getting very good reports from my superiors."

"And what makes you think that?" quizzed Jennifer, knocking back half her wine.

"Well, they just don't like me. I'm not very good at–"

"Will you STOP THAT?!" Jennifer Armstrong slammed her glass down on the table. "If you tell people that, they'll believe you! There is no point in saying you're 'not very good' at anything. No point." She glared at Abby. "Now. You may think that your colleagues don't like you, but I can say with absolute certainty that that's not the case. Like I said, they're probably just intimidated. They're men. They don't know how to handle you. They'd rather be seen treating you harshly than pampering you because you're a girl. If they criticise your work – or criticise *you* – you've got to let it wash over you like water off a duck's back. Don't take it personally. Their comments don't mean a thing. Do you really care what they think, anyway?"

"But sometimes they're right," Abby argued. "I *do* get things wrong, and–"

"Everybody gets things wrong. *I* got plenty wrong in my first year. So did – who's your Head of Department – Daniel Greening!"

Abby smiled at the notion of a younger version of the almighty man, with fewer wrinkles and a lot more hair, sitting helplessly in the middle of the open-plan office as a torrent of abuse tumbled out of a senior banker's mouth.

"You've got to get tough, Abigail," the woman went on. "Look at me. I did. Who'd have guessed I was brought up at a convent in Bath?"

Abby looked across at the bossy young woman. Her pencilled eyebrows were arched questioningly, and her bright red lips – not even smudged by lunch – were pressed very tightly together. Convent in Bath? She had to be joking.

"Don't worry about your cross-evaluation," Jennifer advised.

"Your colleagues will write good reports on you – if you're as good as you say you are."

"But I'm not–"

"Hah! There you go again!" Armstrong exclaimed defiantly. Abby's shoulders slumped. It was a trick. "Putting yourself down! You've got to stop doing that!"

"Mmm yeah – sorry," Abby mumbled, realising how pathetic she sounded. She wanted to show Jennifer she was strong, that she wasn't just a puny little first-year with no self-esteem, but it was difficult to know how to do it.

"I'm afraid I'll have to whiz off now–" The MD quickly drained her wine. "Plane leaves at three."

"Thanks so much for meeting me," Abby said earnestly, with fresh enthusiasm. "And for lunch."

Jennifer batted her thanks aside. "Don't be silly. Any time. And I mean that. I think you can go far at Cray McKinley, Abigail – just as long as you remember you're *good*."

"Oh, I will – I do – I am," she stammered, and then, with a sudden burst of self-confidence, she looked Jennifer in the eye. "I'm actually very good."

The stout woman broke into a smile, nodded, and bustled towards the door.

43

"PLEASE ENSURE your safety belt is tightly fastened by pulling on the end like so," chirped the botoxed Barbie doll into the microphone, with extra emphasis on the pointless words such as 'is' and 'by' and 'like'. Mike reached forward for his in-flight magazine and started to flip through.

He was finding it hard to concentrate. The peroxide-blonde air steward in the gangway was yanking on the ends of his truncated seatbelt, flexing his biceps in Mike's direction as though the belt was some sort of sex toy. Mike glanced up at the man with his most heterosexual-looking snarl. The air steward pouted back provocatively.

Mike didn't care. He was in a good mood. It wasn't every day he came into work to find a plane ticket on his desk. He was flying to Germany. He'd been hand-picked to represent Cray McKinley on official business abroad. Hah. Well, OK. It wasn't quite like that. He was going over to the Cray McKinley office just outside Frankfurt known as the 'Data Center'. And he hadn't exactly been hand-picked; there'd been some wrangling over which analyst they were going to send. Frederick Jensen had been the obvious choice, with his unrivalled data-processing skills and his German roots, but he'd been working for Stuart Mackins, and short of cloning the guy – something they'd probably looked into for previous projects – they'd had no option but to send another analyst. Still, thought Mike. It was flattering they'd chosen him.

Demonstration complete, the crew strutted and minced their ways to the ends of the aircraft and strapped themselves into their flip-down seats. The hum of the engine ramped up, and the panels above Mike's head started to rattle and shake. The noise continued to rise in pitch until the vibrations were lost beneath an almighty roar, and suddenly they were hurtling along the tarmac at a hundred miles an hour inside a metal tube on wheels.

Mike strained to look out of the porthole window without catching the eye of his neighbour – a plump, middle-aged woman doused in intoxicating perfume who'd seemed rather keen to engage in conversation ever since they sat down. The buildings dropped away beneath them, and then suddenly everything went white. This was the best bit. It always amazed Mike that a lump of aluminium could lift itself up into the clouds like that. It just seemed wrong. Wrong, but fucking brilliant.

The rise in altitude seemed fitting, Mike thought, with his elevated status. This trip represented a huge opportunity for him. It was his chance to shine. If things went well over the next couple of days, Mike would be seen in a totally different light, back in the office. He'd be the star of Corporate Finance. Another Frederick Jensen – only with social skills and a full head of hair. Everyone would want him on their deals, and he'd get to do real work – not just the dregs that got passed down. He'd earn himself a reputation, maybe even get promoted next year, get a top-tier bonus... OK, enough. There was no need to get carried away.

The over-fragrant woman was waving a packet of fruit pastilles in front of Mike's face. "Go on," she said, nudging him gently and sending a fresh blast of whatever it was towards his nose. "Helps to equalise the pressure."

Mike declined politely, and pretended to study the specifications of a small, furry polar bear key ring (washable) in the in-flight magazine.

"She's right, you know," said a soft, low-pitched voice on Mike's left. He turned, reluctantly, to find the blonde air steward leaning against his drinks trolley and smiling down at him in a very disconcerting way. "It's the *swallowing*," he explained. And then, looking along the row: "Drinks, anybody?"

Mike waited 'til last, then ordered a sparkling mineral water. It was too early in the day to start drinking – and besides, he needed to keep a clear head. Data analysis wasn't the sort of thing you could do half-pissed.

The young man looked disappointed. "Nothing stronger for you, Sir? A *stiff* gin and tonic?" He tilted his head and raised an eyebrow.

"Just a *straight* water, please." Mike smiled civilly and ignored the muffled giggle coming from the woman on his right. The air steward finally took the hint, thrusting a miniscule can of mineral water at Mike before noisily releasing the brake of his drinks trolley and flouncing down the aisle.

Mike clamped a set of headphones onto his ears and pretended not to hear the woman's lame joke about the air steward's backside. He flicked through the in-flight entertainment channels until he realised there was nothing entertaining on any of them, and gently pulled the jack out of its socket in the armrest. His eyes fell shut, and he let his head fall backwards, leaving the unopened can in his lap.

It was a bit disappointing that he wasn't flying First Class, but apparently it was firm policy that analysts travelled as cheaply as possible – and as rarely as possible, it would seem. Mike had almost blagged himself an upgrade from the girl on the check-in desk, but she'd got all flustered when she'd realised her boss had been standing right behind her throughout the conversation about her skirt, and dispatched him with a Standard Class ticket and an embarrassed smile.

It was just as well Cray McKinley had sent him away on this business trip, he thought. Lately, Mike had begun to have serious doubts about his choice of career. Investment banking was losing its appeal. It was still wildly interesting *in theory*; he could still boast to his friends and his family about the action-packed life he led, and the money was still ludicrously good, for someone of his age, but… although he didn't like to admit it, Mike just couldn't get excited about his job. He didn't enjoy it. He couldn't understand why *anyone* would enjoy moving lines around on documents at two o'clock in the morning, or staying late in the office to look up figures in quarterly reports. But now, hopefully, things would change. They were sending him abroad. Nobody went on business trips in their first-year at Cray McKinley. Maybe this would be the beginning of the end of all those pointless, menial tasks.

Through the ineffective headphones, Mike heard a metallic

clattering sound, and opened his eyes to see that the trolley was back by his side, this time – thankfully – being steered by a tall, leggy brunette with scraped-back hair and an orange tan. Small, plastic trays, each containing an arrangement of smaller, tessellating plastic trays, were being passed along the row. Half-heartedly helping them along, Mike tried to ascertain whether the contents were edible. As he deliberated, the air hostess reached across him, undid the catch on his flip-up table and yanked it towards him as though he were physically incapable of doing so himself, then plonked a meal down in front of him and disappeared inside the food trolley.

For several minutes, Mike focussed on penetrating layers of plastic and trying to find places to put the excess cellophane that seemed to spring up from nowhere, smeared with sauerkraut and sausage meat. The food tasted as artificial as the air hostess' face looked, and in the end Mike settled for stuffing the slab of rubber chicken inside the sugary brown bread roll and picking at some of the more recognisable vegetables.

He wondered what he'd be doing in Frankfurt. Geoff Dodds had briefed him this morning – 'brief' being the operative word – and explained that the Frankfurt office was home to a large database associated with one of Cray McKinley's clients – a database too large to email across, hence the need for Mike's visit. The task was to sort through the entries and come up with some sort of 'summary', which could then be presented to the client company's board of directors by Geoff Dodds on Friday. That was all Mike knew. He wasn't sure what was *in* the database – Dodds had referred to 'key institutional insight' and, when pressed, 'a goldmine of info' and 'a research analyst's wet dream', which had indicated that he didn't actually know himself – but Mike wasn't phased. Well, not *that* phased. He'd manage.

Just as the last spherical carrot been speared with the plastic fork – washed down with a swig of groin-warmed sparkling water – the 'Fasten Seatbelt' sign pinged on and the ransacked trays were whisked away.

"Ladies and gentlemen," crooned the captain over the intercom, "We are about to begin our descent into Frankfurt. On behalf of the crew, I'd like to thank you for flying with us today…"

The drop in altitude did nothing to lower Mike's spirits. This was it. This was the turning point in his career. No more fucking around with mindless pitchbooks. No more following instructions for the sake of it. After this trip, they'd see him for the banker he really was.

"Goodbye, have a nice day, goodbye, have a nice day, goodbye, have a nice day," the air steward sung, giving Mike a little wave and a cheeky smile as he stepped off the plane.

Walking up the wobbly gangway that linked the plane to the airport, Mike reached into his pocket and switched on his BlackBerry. Seven emails, it declared when it had finally finished bleeping. He scrolled through them. One was from Stuart Mackins, demanding to know where he was. Three were from Geoff Dodds, all of them failed attempts to attach a document containing instructions for his trip. One was from Michelle, Geoff Dodds' secretary, attaching the document. One was from Facilities, announcing that the showers downstairs would now be made available to all analysts, including non-gym members, for the benefit of those working through the night (there was no mention of hammocks being put up in changing rooms, but no doubt they were working on that). The last was from Abby Turner, and read simply, *Good luck, you 'high flier'*.

Mike instinctively clicked on *Reply*, then thought better of it. What was that supposed to mean? Was she bitter? Pissed-off? Joking? Teasing? He couldn't tell. He dropped the device back in his pocket and pulled out his passport for the unsmiling man in the little glass booth.

44

"IT'S GONNA BE another ten minutes, innit," informed Shaz from the print room.

"That's fine – I'll go away and come back for it." Abby smiled as if she'd enjoy nothing more than to waste another ten minutes of her Thursday night.

The secret, she'd learnt, was to make friends with the support staff. Or at least, if you couldn't make friends with them, be nice to them. As an analyst at Cray McKinley, you needed all the support you could get. And indirectly, they held a lot of power. Marcus Mackenzie had once made the mistake of referring to an IT support guy as a 'geeky knob-head' after being advised to reboot one too many times, and now couldn't work out why technical assistance was so hard to come by. Mike was another one. He still hadn't grasped the concept that his work would get done quicker if he was a bit nicer to the Graphics girls.

Abby wandered down the fluorescent white corridor and mindlessly pressed the button for the lift. She had nothing to do. That was the frustrating thing about her job. One minute she was working flat-out to meet some ultra-critical deadline, the next she was twiddling her thumbs.

It was a quarter past ten. Her corner of the office was virtually empty. Frederick Jensen was there, as usual, squinting at numbers and stroking his flaky scalp. A third-year analyst whose name Abby couldn't remember was hunched over a thick report, turning pages with one hand, picking his nose with the other. She sighed, and threw herself into her chair.

Mike wasn't here. That was what really bugged her. At this

moment, he was probably drinking Martinis in some swanky five-star hotel, schmoozing with important German businessmen and discussing the size of the cocktail waitress' arse. Well, maybe. She didn't actually know what he was doing. The idea of emailing him flitted across Abby's mind, but she'd already sent him one that morning and he hadn't replied, which meant that either (a) his email wasn't working, (b) he'd lost his BlackBerry or (c) he was too busy being important and successful to have time to reply. Of all the options, she had to admit that (c) seemed the most likely. Abby deleted his address from the *To* line of the message and replaced it with Beth's.

Ever since Beth had come down to London, she'd developed a full-blown obsession with this start-up idea of hers. She was planning to open some sort of youth hostel-cum-café for tired businessmen who fancied a kip or a coffee half-way through the working day. It was going to be called City Slippers, and the first branch (there would be a nation-wide rollout within four years) would be located in Cannon Street, not far from Cray McKinley. It was a hare-brained scheme destined for failure, and Abby felt it was her duty to point out some of the more obvious flaws – such as Beth's unfounded belief that young professionals were able to slope off for a couple of hours in the afternoon without anyone noticing.

Hi Beth, she wrote, then looked up. Her phone was ringing.

"Hey, Justine. How's things?"

"Hi babe!" cried Justine in a stilted, high-pitched voice.

Abby hesitated. "Er, Justine, did you just call me 'babe'?"

"Yes, I'm fine thanks," Justine said tersely. "You?"

"I'm… well, I'm fine too," Abby replied, perplexed. Justine had just called her 'babe'. Was she drunk? "Is this some new housemately ritual we've got going? Checking up on each oth-"

"No no," Justine interrupted sweetly. "I just wanted to let you know, I might not be back tonight."

"So why are you telling…" Abby frowned. "Justine, am I right in thinking you have someone else up there with you?"

"Yes, that's right," she said enthusiastically.

"Who?"

"Oh, I've just a lot on at the moment. Got to get it *over* to the client this evening."

"Justine… are you alright?"

"Yes, yes!" she replied. She sounded slightly hysterical.

There was an awkward pause while Abby tried to work things out. Justine had company up on the fifth floor – most likely, Philip Oversby, she thought. But why the cryptic call? And why was he rearing his ugly, bald head again? There'd been nothing from the man for three months – Justine had assumed the whole fiasco to be over. "Right, well, thanks for letting me know," Abby said brusquely.

"Love you too, babe!" sung Justine weakly.

The line went dead.

Abby grabbed her swipe-card and charged towards the glass double doors, hammering on the button for the lift. She gave up waiting and flung herself into the fire escape, charging up the stairs, three at a time. Panting, she emerged on the fifth floor and headed straight for Justine's desk. It was empty. Her computer was on, but locked, and her jacket was gone from the back of her chair – assuming she'd been wearing one today.

A quick rummage through Justine's top drawer revealed a neat array of Cray McKinley stationery, a stash of Cray McKinley canteen food and Philip the Voodoo Doll that Abby had made for her out of crisp packets, thoroughly punctured with paper clips. No clues as to her whereabouts. Abby marched over to the corner of the fifth floor and pressed her face up to the frosted glass. Oversby's office was deserted.

"Excuse me," said Abby to a dopey-looking analyst nearby that she vaguely remembered from lectures in New York. "D'you know if Justine Brown's around?"

The analyst looked at her, then back at his spreadsheet, then back at her. "Sorry?" he asked, slowly removing an earphone.

"Do you know if Justine Brown's around?" she repeated.

"Justine who?"

"Justine Brown. The analyst that sits there."

He screwed up his nose. "The short one?"

"Yes," Abby nodded encouragingly.

"First-year?"

"Yes–"

"With dark, frizzy hair?"

"Yes – that's her!"

"Nope, sorry. No idea," he replied, popping the earphone back in.

Abby scanned the open-plan office for someone who might have seen Justine leave, but the place was uncharacteristically empty. She dialled Justine's mobile number and hung up at the sound of her voicemail. She tried again, with the same result. And again. She was beginning to wonder whether Justine *wanted* her help after all. Abby headed back to the stairwell.

She was half-way through a detailed description of her friend with the night security guards on reception when Abby heard a patter of feet on the tiles behind her. She turned. Tiptoeing out of the Ladies, very slowly, head bowed, was Justine Brown. She was heading for the main door, oblivious to the assembled search party.

"Justine!"

Justine stopped in her tracks and looked at Abby. "Ooh! Hello!" she managed, although her eyes conveyed relief, not surprise.

That was when Abby saw him. It was just a blurry silhouette, but she instantly recognised the long, stooping body standing in front of the floodlit Cray McKinley statue outside. He probably thought he couldn't be seen.

"*What are you doing?*" Abby hissed, moving away from the security guards with a grateful smile and a wave.

Justine shrugged nervously and glanced in the direction of the exit.

"Come on," said Abby. "He can see you from there, but he can't hear you. He'll assume that I'm dragging you upstairs for work or something."

Justine nodded. "OK."

"So!" Abby sighed, once they'd reached the safety of the lift. "What was *that* all about?"

Justine groaned. "Thanks, Abby. I'm sorry."

"Don't be sorry. Explain."

"Well, basically, it's started all over again. He sidled up to my desk this evening – oh, we just missed my floor, didn't we?"

"Yep. You're coming with me. We're collecting some stuff from the print room, then we're going home."

"Oh, right. Well, yeah – he perched on my desk and started chatting about…"

Abby swiped her card and guided Justine into Graphics. "About what?"

"About his conversation with Paul Tucker, and the-"

"Who's Paul Tucker?"

"The VP that does all the appraisals for analysts in Leveraged Finance."

Abby nodded. They were entering the hub of the Cray McKinley gossip machine: the Print Room. Conversation was suspended while Abby picked up her work.

"That's great – thanks Shaz. Perfect. Ooh – nice nails." Abby picked up the pitchbooks and flashed a smile at the girl, who looked slightly taken aback, then started gazing adoringly at her hands. "Flattery will get you everywhere," Abby said under her breath as the door swung shut behind them. "So, what, Philip Oversby was implying that he could influence the results of your appraisal by talking to Paul Tucker?"

"Er, yeah." Justine nodded, skipping along to keep up with Abby. "Basically. And then he asked if I wanted to go for a drink."

"Some might call that blackmail," Abby remarked, stabbing at the lift button with her knuckle.

"Well, yeah," Justine agreed contemplatively. "But I didn't know what else to do. He *does* have the power to sway people like Paul Tucker, and he probably would, if it came to it. And anyway, he was really pushy."

Abby shook her head, angry but mystified. "Does he just proposition you, in the middle of the office, just like that?"

Justine nodded. "He picks his moments – when no one's around. Apart from Elliot White, obviously, but Elliot's so wrapped up in his work he wouldn't notice if Philip stripped off and did cartwheels around his desk."

Abby smiled. Elliot White. The zombie with the headphones.

"I just don't know how to get rid of him," Justine went on, sounding desperate. "I mean, I've *tried* telling HR, and they won't listen. I've tried ignoring him, and he just comes back. He even knows I have a boyfriend – sorry about that 'babe' thing, by the way,

I couldn't get hold of Joe – but it doesn't seem to make any difference."

They stepped into the lift. "I guess it wouldn't, if a wife and child aren't enough to hold you back," Abby remarked.

Justine looked at her searchingly. "What am I going to do?"

Abby stared back at her unhappy face. As the anonymous voice announced their arrival on the fourth floor, inspiration struck.

"OK, I might have a solution."

45

IF THIS IS A research analyst's wet dream, thought Mike, *then research analysts are fucking twisted*. He pressed Save and leaned back on the uncomfortable office chair, doing a couple of rugby warm-up exercises on his neck as he waited for the egg timer to disappear.

A business trip. That's what they'd told him. A business trip abroad. Well, here he was: in a concrete bunker just outside Frankfurt, filled with row upon row of high-spec machines and row upon row of identical Cray McKinley analysts, each tapping away on their German keyboards, faces devoid of all expression. It was like a modern-day concentration camp, thought Mike. The white strip lights had clearly been carefully chosen for their headache-inducing humming/flickering properties, the flat screens set centrally to maximum brightness.

It really should have been Frederick Jensen here, thought Mike. He would have fitted in perfectly. His type thrived in environments like this – no colleagues to distract him, no Starbucks down the corridor, no on-site gym, no windows, no women… Mmm. Bliss. Mike tipped himself forwards and looked at the column he'd highlighted. *Subsidiaries*.

At least today there was a sense of urgency about his work. He was catching an eight-thirty plane home, which meant that he had to be out of this hole by six, data sorted, processed and sent back to London. That gave him eight hours. *Eight hours*. Mike was reminded of the time he'd run through Brooklyn during the New York Marathon. Sweaty and knackered, he'd looked up to take in some of the support from the crowds, and been confronted with a huge yellow banner that said, KEEP IT UP! ONLY 20 MILES TO

GO! He could still see it now. *Keep it up*, he thought. *Only eight hours to go.*

The analyst at the next desk along started humming a little tune. Mike turned round, slowly and deliberately, and glared at him. The analyst stopped humming and after a moment of blissful quiet, started to tap out a rhythm with his foot. Mike groaned and swivelled back to his hundred-watt screen, wondering why Germany seemed to lag behind the rest of the developed world in fashion by approximately fifteen years. High-waist, flannel trousers and turtle-neck sweaters had surely died out with mullets and drainpipes?

The Frankfurt Cray McKinley canteen was a half-size replica of the London one, only dotted with fluffy grey rabbits and plastic baskets filled with over-sized, colourful plastic eggs. Along the top of the serving hatch was a row of jolly-looking yellow chicks, each bearing the slogan, *gluckliches Ostern!* across its breast. The place was like a European motorway service station – only without the prospect of a holiday at the end of it.

God Bless the BlackBerry, thought Mike, as he chewed his way through a plate of frittered lard. The little gadget that he'd nearly thrown into the Thames so many times had turned out to be his saviour on this trip. Even if it did just inform him of improvements being made to the office car park and updates on the refurbishment of the nineteenth floor – at least he felt connected.

Abby's email was still there, opened but not replied to. Mike scrolled down to it, thumb hovering over *Reply* as he re-read the message. He wondered what she was doing now. It was nearly four o'clock over there. She was probably adopting brace position, ahead of the afternoon dump – surrounding herself in paperwork and opening complex-looking spreadsheets in an attempt to look as busy as possible for when the directors came round asking which analysts had 'spare capacity'. His thumb went down on the button, then instantly moved up to *Escape*. No. He was trying to keep thoughts about Abby to a minimum, and embarking on flirty, cross-channel e-banter was clearly not the way to achieve this.

As he stared at the BlackBerry, thinking about how not think about Abby, it beeped and vibrated in his hand. A message.

MAYDAY. NEED NUMBERS.
PLEASE ADVISE ASAP OR
WILL ASSUME JUST ONE.
CONWAYS COMING -
ME THE RACECOURSE!
JUST MOVED IN!
MUMMY X

A couple of weeks ago, a momentous event had occurred in the Cunningham-Reid household: Mike's mother had sent her first SMS. Since that day, she'd taken to corresponding with her children by means of what looked like encrypted World War I telegrams. Mike had tried several times to explain that you no longer had to pay *per character*, but he knew it would take a while.

Despite its tone, the message was not actually a plea for help; it was a reference to the May Day garden party that the Cunningham-Reids were holding on bank holiday weekend. Mike gleaned from the first three lines that his mother wanted to know if he was bringing a guest. As for the second half of the message, he was baffled. Who or what were the Conways? Had his mother turned into a racecourse? Had his parents moved house again?

Mike didn't reply straight away. Instead, he flicked back to the email from Abby, and clicked on *Reply*. He tapped out a quick response – as quick as the little toy keyboard would allow – and pressed *Send*. Then he shovelled his excess batter and limp lettuce leaves into the nearest bin and banged the tray down next to a plastic chicken. *Come on. Only three hours to go.*

46

THE SCREEN WAS flashing '*Home*'. Abby took deep breath, and mustered a smile. "Hi mum!" she hissed, grabbing her swipe card and rushing towards the double doors.

"Ooh!" cried her mother. "How did you know it was me?"

"*Mum,*" Abby groaned, reversing through the doors and freeing herself from the hush of the office. "You ask me that *every time*. I've got your number programmed into my phone. It says 'home' when you call. As would yours, if you ever turned it on."

"Oh yes – you did say. You'll have to teach me how to do that sometime, if it's not too complicated. Where are you, by the way? You sound like you're in the bath!"

"Oh, I'm in the lobby-thing next to the lifts – it's a bit echoey, I know. Can–"

"You're still at work?!" she exploded. "It's nearly eleven o'clock! Why–"

"No no – I'm just..." Oh dear. "I just popped in to finish something off. I'm on my way out," she lied.

"You're not being over-worked, are you?" her mother asked suspiciously. "We don't want you turning into one of those workaholics who burns out by the time they're twenty-three. You remember Joan, from number thirty? Her daughter's a merchant banker, and she's just had to take eight weeks off to recover from a nervous breakdown, poor thing. Goldmans Axe, I think it is. She can't even make a cup of tea without crying–"

"*Mum,*" Abby growled, jaw clenched. "I'm *fine*. I'm not over-worked and I'm not planning to have a nervous breakdown." This was the thing; Abby's mum wanted it both ways.

She wanted to boast to all her friends that her daughter had a brilliant, highly-paid graduate job, but she also wanted to know that Abby was a happy, rounded individual with a healthy work-life balance and lots of friends. Abby had given up trying to persuade her that the two were incompatible. "And by the way, it's *investment* banking now."

"Well, Joan said *merchant* banking. So what are you working on at the moment? Is it something I might have heard about?"

Abby snorted and rolled her eyes in the mirrored wall. "I don't think so." It was unlikely that her four-megabyte spreadsheet would make headline news.

"Oh, I'm sorry. I shouldn't have asked. I'm sure it's all highly confidential, whatever it is. Don't go saying anything you're not supposed to," she said, with a hint of pride in her voice.

"It's not that I'm not supposed to—"

"No, it's fine!" she trilled. "I know you have to keep these things under wraps. Don't tell me anything at all."

Abby sighed and studied her reflection. Her skin was the palest it had ever been. "How's Dad?"

"Oh, he's fine, he's fine. Mending the lawnmower as we speak – oh, have you spoken to Nicky recently?"

"Er, no – not recently," Abby replied guiltily. The last time she'd called her sister had been nearly a month ago.

"It seems she's doing ever so well with her 'mooting'."

"Her what?"

"Her 'mooting'."

"And what is 'mooting', exactly?"

"Er, well," Abby's mother hesitated. "I'm not entirely sure, but she's doing very well at it, anyway. I think it's something to do with arguing against other trainees. She said something about a mock-up court."

Abby smiled. "Well, if it's arguing then I'm sure she's doing brilliantly."

"Yes – well, I suppose she's got you to thank for that." There was a pause. "Has she talked to you at all about what she wants to do after Oxford?"

"What d'you mean?"

"Well… She seems to have got it into her head that she wants to be one of those lawyers who works for the state – you know–"

"What, legal aid?"

"Yes – that's it," she replied dubiously.

"What's wrong with that?"

"Well… It's not very *impressive*, is it?"

"I think it's very impressive – representing wrongly-convicted citizens who can't afford their own legal representation?"

"Not always *wrongly*-convicted, dear," she pointed out.

"Well neither are the rich convicts who hire the expensive lawyers," Abby argued.

"Mmm, yes I know," her mother admitted reluctantly, "but there are different *types* of lawyer, aren't there?"

"What d'you mean?" asked Abby, wondering what her mother was getting at.

"Well, I was speaking with Diana – you know, who used to live at the end of the road? Had a little boy called Thomas, who used to wee onto the street through the bathroom window? Well, it turns out Thomas has just qualified with Linklaters, as a *solicitor*."

Ah. So that was what this was all about. Her mother wasn't concerned about the morality of Nicky's preferred career path; it was the status and salary that were in question. "Right, so Thomas is helping companies make money by exploiting loop-holes in tax laws and helping them fiddle their books – how commendable!" she cried.

"Oh, don't get all crotchety with me, Abby. I just think it's an avenue worth pursuing, that's all."

"Well, maybe Nicky doesn't want to pursue it," Abby said irritably. It was late, and she was tired. She didn't want her sister following her into the city trap.

"He's obviously very good, anyway," her mother went on peevishly. "They paid for all his legal training, and then gave him a six thousand-pound bonus when he qualified!"

Abby groaned, long and loud. "That's what they *do*, Mum. That's how city firms work. They're all the same! They suck in their 'bright young things' by chucking money at them. Thomas is no different from anyone else!"

330

"But you got *eight* thousand, didn't you, when you joined?"

Abby sighed. Her mother wasn't listening. "Look, Mum, did you call for anything in particular? Because I've got to—" she looked around for inspiration – "go for a drink with Justine."

There was a disapproving tut and a sigh. "Always drinking, Abby! I read an article about binge-drinkers the other day. D'you know, some girls get through a whole bottle of wine in one night, when they go on a 'binge'?"

"*Shocking,*" muttered Abby. "So, why did—"

"They deliberately starve themselves before a 'binge', so that they don't put on weight from the alcohol. And of course, drinking on an empty stomach makes them even *more* drunk! We saw some the other night, Daddy and I – they were lurching around outside the Rubberspoon pub on the high street. One nearly lurched into our car!"

"Wetherspoon," Abby corrected, mildly amused at her mother's portrayal of the binge drinking species. "Were you calling to—"

"I blame the late licensing laws," she went on.

"Mum, did you call for—"

"Alright, alright! I just called to tell you about Uncle Pete – you know, the one who moved to Australia. He's just bought a house in Peckham. Says it's for when he needs to come back to the UK, but he only does that once or twice a year. I think it's more of an invest-ment, really. He's asked me to keep an eye out for anyone who'd be able to look after it while he's away."

"What, live in it?"

"Yes."

"Full-time?"

"Yes."

"For free?"

"Well, yes."

Abby frowned. "He's looking for someone who'd be 'willing' to live in his house in London, without paying rent. Right?"

"That's right," she said brightly. "I told him you'd keep your ears out, as I know you have lots of friends moving to London. So have a think, won't you?"

Abby didn't need to think. She already had someone in mind. "I'll get back to you this week. Thanks Mum."

"Jolly good. Now off you go – have fun. And don't drink too much!"

"I'll try not to *lurch*," she said, smiling as she swiped herself back into the office.

"Cheerio!"

47

THE MIDDAY SUN was shining down on Mike's tanned, muscular forearm, and heat was shimmering off the red paintwork. Dance music pumped from the stereo across the gravel car park.

He smiled as he spotted her in his wing mirror, and readjusted his sunglasses. She was wearing a red summer dress that flared out at her tiny waist, and looked like a flamenco dancer – only blonde. Just inside the station, a ticket inspector could be seen lurching from side to side as the door flapped open and shut, trying to catch a glimpse of the girl's backside. The high heels were unnecessary, Mike thought, with legs as long as hers, but he wasn't going to complain. Abby looked stunning.

His was the only vehicle in the car park, and Abby seemed to be making straight for it, but Mike tooted the horn all the same. What was the point in driving your dad's Aston Martin if nobody noticed you doing it?

"You're such a poser, Mike," Abby accused, slinging her bag in the back and sliding elegantly into the passenger seat.

Mike grinned. He turned the key in the ignition and revved the engine so hard that it drowned out the beat of the music. "Nice dress," he commented. "Matches the car."

"Nice car," she replied, glancing around at the beige leather upholstery, letting her eyes rest on Mike's new Paul Smith shirt. "Matches the image."

He smiled and pulled away. They didn't speak for the ten-minute journey; it was impossible to compete with the juddering wind in their ears and the rumbling engine. Once or twice he glanced over at Abby, who was leaning awkwardly out of the side of the car, wrestling with her wild blonde mane. He'd forgotten to warn her about this part of the day. Mike let out a laugh that was carried away in the wind, and pressed a little harder on the accelerator.

Pulling off the winding country lane, Mike slowed the car to a crawl and let it purr its way up the stretch of gravel that led to Brimsmead House.

"You OK?" he asked, just about managing to hold a straight face. Abby looked windswept and furious.

"Just about." She released the bundle of hair from the nape of her neck and shook her head like a wet dog. The result was pretty good. In fact, Mike thought he preferred it to the sleek, immaculate city-girl look he was used to. The rosy cheeks and tousled hair made her look... well, cute.

As usual, Mike's parents had gone way overboard. The house looked like a wedding cake. Its vast, whitewashed exterior had been draped in streamers and bunting, and the French-style shuttered windows were adorned with huge, colourful silk bows. There were ribbons in pink, white and yellow dangling from the eaves, matching the newly-planted roses around the front door. Abby looked baffled.

"It's an annual event now," Mike explained. He yanked on the handbrake and silenced the engine, then paused for a moment to listen. The sounds of squealing babies, chattering old ladies, bickering children and chuckling middle-aged men travelled across the warm air. The party was in full swing.

As they stepped onto the doormat, Mike tapped Abby on the shoulder and put his mouth to her ear. "I should warn you," he whispered, "most of these people are awful!"

The hallway was jammed full of bodies. "Hello, hello," called Mike, squeezing between two well-dressed ladies he felt he probably ought to have recognised. "Can we push on through?"

There was a general shuffling of feet, but no overall progress in breaking the gridlock.

"COULD EVERYONE MOVE INTO THE DINING ROOM, PLEASE?" he shouted, herding people along. "Oh, hello Mrs Salmon – THE ROOM AT THE BACK OF THE HOUSE?! Yes, I'm very well thanks. THAT'S RIGHT! Hello John, great to see you!" Mike edged through the crowd, urging Abby to stay close, and steered them towards the kitchen.

A figure emerged from a cloud of flour.

"Michael!" she cried loudly. "How *are* you? I won't hug you as I'm *covered* in pastry – but come here and give me a kiss!"

Mike did so, avoiding the white smears on her face. He was amazed at how young his mother looked. Her hair had been touched up for the occasion, he noted, but it looked almost natural against her Mediterranean skin. She could have passed for thirty-five.

"And Aunt Clover's here too – look!" she added, flinging an arm out wildly and sending a shower of half-made pastry across the floor.

"Oh! Aunt Clover!" Mike cried, as if it was the best piece of news he'd heard all year. He looked into the corner of the room, where a frail-looking lady with shimmering purple hair was perched in a wicker chair. He'd never seen her before in his life.

"Michael!" she said shakily, breaking into a smile. "You've grown!"

Mike stooped down to kiss her on the cheek. He could never understand why old people seemed to find growth such an incredible phenomenon.

"You do remember Aunt Clover, don't you Michael? Well, Great Aunt I suppose, really – your father's aunt... Oh you must introduce us to–" She threw out her hand in Abby's direction, sprinkling more floury crumbs on the floor.

"This is Abby," he said. "She's a–" he hesitated. He hadn't actually planned this introduction. "She's from work."

"Oh, how *lovely!*" Mrs Cunningham-Reid exclaimed. "And what a beautiful dress – such a vivid red! Mustn't let me get flour on it!"

Mike cringed, desperate to whisk Abby away. His mother was so embarrassing. "Mum, we've–"

"Oh, now darling." She turned to her son, serious all of a sudden. "You *must* meet the Conways – they're here. They've literally *just* arrived – I saw their car pull up."

Mike looked at her blankly.

"The *Conways,* Michael – our new next-door neighbours!"

"Next-door neighbours?" he frowned. "The nearest house is about two miles away."

"Well, yes, I know that." She rolled her eyes. "But they're still *neighbours*, aren't they? I told you about them in that text-mail I sent you!"

"Text message," Mike muttered under his breath. "Who are the Conways, anyway?"

"Oh, Michael! You know the Conways! *Harry* Conway – the one that owns the racecourse – you know!" She flapped a floury hand in his face.

Mike squinted up at the corner of the room, pretending to think through a long list of racecourse-owning acquaintances.

"Well anyway," she went on impatiently, "they've moved in next door. And their son, Hugh–" she paused for dramatic effect– "is an investment banker!"

Mike tried to match her enthusiasm. "Ooh, great! We can all talk about work together!"

He stole a quick glance at Abby, who was clearly trying not to laugh. Mike suddenly felt guilty, taking the piss out of his mother. He was showing off. "Sorry. D'you know where Dad and Mel are?"

"Well, your father's supervising the bouncy castle out the back, and your sister's rigging up one of her fancy obstacle courses in the yard."

Mike made a move towards the door, and indicated for Abby to follow. They hurried through a series of passageways littered with scooters, Lego and children.

"Urgh! *Sorry* about mum," he said, when they finally hit fresh air.

Abby laughed. "Actually, she's just like mine! They'd probably get on really well."

Mike smiled, trying not to dwell on her words. *They'd probably get on really well.* That implied that the two women would meet one another, which implied that Abby and Mike... no. He looked out at the garden and cleared his mind. "Let's go find my dad – that shouldn't be quite as painful."

They meandered across the patio, stopping frequently for Mike to kiss people he vaguely recognised and exchange how-are-you-yes-fine-must-dash-see-you-laters.

He leapt down the flight of steps that led to the paddock and realised that Abby was no longer with him. She was standing at the top of the steps, her hand lightly touching the stone lion's head.

"Is this all... all yours?" she asked, looking confused.

"Yeah," he replied, wandering backwards on the springy grass.

Abby raised her eyebrows briefly, then trotted down the steps after him.

The piercing yelp made him stop and spin round. Abby was hopping around, barefoot, at the top of the paddock. "My shoes!" She pointed to a spot at the base of the steps, where the dainty red sandals were positioned a footstep apart, heels driven deep into the earth.

Mike laughed, wandered back and wrenched them free, then strolled nonchalantly away, dangling the shoes from a strap.

"Hey – give them back!" Abby yelled, leaping angrily from foot to foot.

"Why? You don't need them, do you?" Mike teased, breaking into a trot.

"Give me my shoes, Mike!" She started to run after him.

"What? *These* shoes?" He waved them tauntingly above his head and proceeded to sprint down the lawn.

Abby was remarkably fast, for a girl. In fact, no, she was just remarkably fast. Looking over his shoulder, Mike realised that the gap between them was narrowing. He picked up speed, until something made him stamp to an abrupt halt.

"Now then, children," said the voice, which was low-pitched and familiar. "Let's not get over-excited."

Less than six feet away was an enormous, yellow inflatable castle, filled with bouncing, screaming kids. Next to the castle, Mike's father was reclined in a deckchair under the sun, wearing chinos and an open-necked shirt. On his lap was an unopened Sunday Times, held down by a panama hat.

"Come on now, don't be silly, children," mumbled Mike's father, without opening his eyes.

Mike could hear Abby panting softly next to his ear. He shot her a guilty smile, holding out her shoes as a peace offering. Her face was flushed, like a little girl's after playtime. She was grinning back at him.

Mr Cunningham-Reid rolled his head to one side, and squinted blindly into the sun. It took some time for him to recognise the silhouette of his son.

"Michael!" he cried finally, struggling to his feet and shedding Sunday supplements all over the lawn. Then, after the usual manly, backslapping, shoulder-shaking hug, they both turned their attention to Abby.

"And you must be—"

"This is Abby, a colleague of mine," Mike said hastily.

"Pleasure!" he exclaimed, shaking her firmly by the hand. "You work with my son in the city, do you?" he smiled. "You keeping him out of mischief, eh?"

Mike and Abby exchanged a quick glance that was lost on the older man.

"Come along now children," chided Mike's dad as a riot broke out among the children. "This is going to end in tears," he warned ineffectively.

Mike looked despairingly at his father. Eighteen years in the RAF had clearly done wonders for his powers of authority. "Doesn't this belong in the pool?" Mike asked, picking up a large inflatable frog as it landed in front of them with a splat.

Abby looked at him. "Pool?"

"Yeah."

"What... *your* pool?"

"Yes – I told you to bring your swimming stuff, didn't I?"

"Um, yeah." She looked at him uncertainly. "I thought you were joking."

Mike rolled his eyes. "Nope. You'll have to borrow some stuff from my sister. Can't miss out, on a day like this. In fact, let's head there now."

Mike's father sunk back into his deckchair, and attempted to balance the panama on his face. "You go and enjoy the party," he mumbled from inside the hat. "Tell Mummy I'll join you later."

Mike took the long route round to the pool, delaying the moment he'd have to switch to hob-nobbing mode and savouring Abby's company. It felt weird, in a way, introducing Abby to his family, showing her the place he'd grown up. It was a bit like letting her read his diary or something. Not that he kept a diary. But that was how it felt. None of his London friends had been to Brimsmead House. Or his uni mates. Or even his Wellington mates, come to think of it – apart from Chris. The family home was just for village friends, and for family, obviously. It represented his childhood. But with Abby, Mike wanted to let her in. He *wanted* to point out the gap in the hedge that he'd made by releasing the handbrake on the tractor when he was five. He *wanted* to show her the spot where his sister had buried the Aston Martin keys, forcing his dad to break the car window.

"And this is the pool, where my sister and I used to –"

"Mikey, daaarling!" trilled a voice that he recognised with a sinking heart. "How *lovely* to see you!"

Mike turned round, instantly becoming engulfed in a swirl of turquoise fabric and a plume of sickly perfume, deafened by a noise that sounded like a school percussion box being knocked over. The young red-head was wearing so many gold bangles it was a wonder she still had full use of her right arm.

"I can't *remember* the last time – oh yes, it was Amanda and Jeremy's engagement do – that was it. I was thinking of you the other day – mummy gave me some photos of us when we were little. Amanda's getting in such a flap over the shoes for her bridesmaids. Stark naked in the pool, we were – d'you remember? I've told her that satin's a silly idea; they'll be ruined the minute we leave the church, but you know what Amanda's like. They're all the same in that family. I put them in a cupboard, but they're easily accessible. I'll get them out again when you come round – there's a great one of you playing with your little-"

"Ahahahha!" Mike chuckled strategically.

"So, when are you coming to dinner? Did I tell you I've bought another house? In South Ken. Fancied something north of the river, for a change. Well I say house, but it's more of a flat. Two up from Max Parker-Bowles, you know. Do Fridays work for you? He stopped me the other day – he's having problems with his drains. I gave him the number of a little Polish chap who sorted me out. He's not a bit like his great-aunt. You'd never know he was related to that dreadful Camilla woman."

Mike tried to extract himself. He could only assume that she was doing that circular breathing thing that clarinettists do – inhaling through her nose while she spoke so that she didn't need to stop for breath.

"Doesn't understand a word I say, poor chap, but he seems to get the job done. Oh, of course. Yoga. Sorry, Friday's no good after all. Maybe Saturday? Got two little dogs – Chihuahuas or something. The heaters should be working on the roof garden by then. We'll get Amanda and Jeremy along too – make it a nice round number. They yap their little heads off most of the time, but you get used to it. Saturday looking good then, great. I'll have a think. Lovely. I must dash – Leticia's been stuck with some frightful old BORE for the last half hour, and I feel it's my duty to rescue her! I'll be in touch. Toodlepip!"

The cerulean sensation whirled away, bracelets ajangle.

"Woah!" breathed Mike, dramatically wiping his brow.

Abby stealthily plucked the card from his fingers. "Harriet Ingleby," she read. "'Beautician, Colour-me-Beautiful'. Is she one of those people who charges eighty pounds to tell you that you shouldn't wear orange eyeshadow in winter? God, you'd think with dress-sense like hers, she'd choose a more appropriate career."

"Yeah," Mike nodded, sighing with relief and exhaustion. "I'm not sure I'd call it a 'career', exactly; she seems to spend most of her time buying houses with her Daddy's money. She's–"

Suddenly, Mike felt himself buckling at the knees. His plastic champagne glass leapt out of his hand and landed with a crack and a splosh on the patio. Someone in army combat gear and thick black boots had pounced on him from behind and was holding him in an arm-lock, with a knee in the small of his back. Mike's arm was twisted behind his back while the aggressor pummelled him in the stomach.

Mike knew who it was, of course. After a couple of painful twists, he started to regain control, and eventually flipped the assailant onto the ground. Sure enough, squirming on the patio beneath him was a girl with thick, brown hair and angular cheekbones that were smeared with camouflage paint.

"Sorry about that," he gasped, turning to Abby and straightening his collar. "Meet my big sister, Mel."

Swilling the whisky round in his glass and sinking down further into the velvet armchair, Mike let his eyes drop shut. He felt mildly drunk from the steady consumption of champagne, and tired from the strain of small talk. A sense of contented exhaustion washed over him.

It had been Mel's idea for Abby to stay; there'd been nobody sober enough to drive her to the station, and the main guest room was already made up. Mel and Abby got on well, and – slightly to Mike's annoyance – had spent much of the afternoon together messing about on Mel's assault course. They were remarkably similar, Mike reflected, in personality if not in looks. They both had a Tomboy, rebellious streak, and neither would stand for any nonsense – especially not from men. Abby had started an argument with his father; he could hear her boldly defending her cause as he bulldozed through her reasoning.

"That's not the *point*, though–"

"Of *course* it is–"

"They wouldn't have the funding–"

A smile crept across Mike's face. They were as stubborn as each other.

He was nudged awake by a gentle pawing at his arm. Mike opened his eyes to find Mel squatting down next to him, her chin resting on the velvet arm of the chair.

"Hello," he mumbled sleepily.

"Hello," she whispered. "How's life? Haven't really talked to you today."

He grunted. He didn't have the energy for a proper conversation.

"What're you up to?" she pressed, her voice still muted.

Mike's spirits instantly dampened. Cray McKinley. He'd managed to put it out of his mind for the whole weekend, but now it was back, haunting him like a tumour.

"Look, I don't wanna talk about work, Mel, I–"

"No!" Mel shook her head. "Not work – I mean *life!*"

Mike frowned. He never normally discussed the meaning of life with his sister.

"Or, if you want me to spell it out, *you and Abby*," she whispered, mouthing the last three words.

"Oh God – not you as well," Mike groaned, lowering his voice to match hers – although he probably needn't have bothered; the argument between Abby and his father would have drowned out a marching band. "I've already had this from the guys at work. We're just *friends*, OK?"

"Why?"

"Because–"

"I think she's great," said Mel. "She's smart. And witty. And she's got a personality – not like your usual bimbos. You'd make an awesome couple."

They both glanced across at Abby, who was shaking her head violently as their father blustered on.

"We're colleagues."

"So?"

"So we can't be a 'couple', can we?"

"Why not?"

"It just wouldn't work – you can't do that at Cray McKinley." Mike shook his head as if to say *you wouldn't understand*. Mel was still frowning at him. Mike shrugged. "You just can't."

"What…" she looked at him sceptically. "So what if you *weren't* colleagues?"

"I – I dunno," Mike replied hesitantly. He didn't like where this was leading. His sister was asking questions he hadn't dared ask himself – and she didn't even know the history between Abby and him.

"Well," she said quietly, "you obviously like each other."

"Eh?" Mike tried to look baffled, but he knew it wasn't convincing.

"Don't bother trying to argue, Mike. What are you gonna do about it?"

Mike looked stormily at his older sister. He wanted to put a stop to this conversation, but his sister's placid, open face was drawing him in.

"I don't know," he said. "I don't think there's anything I *can* do."

It was true. There was nothing he *could* do. Maybe things would be different if they didn't work together at Cray McKinley, but he wasn't planning to quit his job, and neither was she, presumably, so there was no point in speculating.

Mel was tugging at a loose thread on the arm of the chair, deep in thought. Mike let his gaze wander over her shoulder to where the light was shining off Abby's hair. It was matted and slightly wavy from the sun and the chlorine, and her cheeks were dotted with a fresh smattering of freckles. Her expression told Mike that she was winning the argument.

Yes, he liked her. That's why he couldn't stop staring at her. That's why he couldn't concentrate when she was around. Mike felt unsettled, as though there was something he needed to resolve, but couldn't quite get his hands around. His sister's words had stirred something in his subconscious that he'd wanted to leave untouched. It was unnerving, this feeling.

"Hmm, OK," Mike's father conceded, "I suppose you've got a point."

Abby grinned at Mel, then at Mike, her eyes dancing with victory. It wasn't often Mr Cunningham-Reid backed down.

"Anyone for more whisky?" the old man asked, sounding a little bit peeved.

"No Dad – time for bed," Mel replied pointedly, looking from Abby to Mike then back at her father.

Mike cringed. His sister was about as subtle as a hippopotamus.

"So," he muttered, when his father had been clumsily led away. "I'll, um, show you to your room."

They crept up the stairs in silence and padded to the end of the landing. Mike felt a curious sense of anticipation and he showed Abby into the master guest bedroom.

He pressed the door shut behind him, and glanced at Abby's face, which had a slightly nervous expression, he thought, so he re-opened the door, in case she felt threatened. He suddenly became worried that their voices would wake his mother, and shut it again.

Abby looked at him quizzically. "What are you doing?"

He opened the door again. It was creating quite a draught around their feet.

"Uh, um, sorry," he mumbled, deciding it was better off closed after all, and pushing it shut for the last time. "I think Mel's lent you some night-clothes, and um... there's towels..." he pointed to the pile on the bed.

"Oh – is *that* what they are?" she said, smiling, then instantly looked away, embarrassed.

Mike stared at the floor. At the back of his mind, he knew that he had to show her the bathroom, ask what time she wanted to be woken and check she had everything she needed. But he couldn't. Something else was occupying his mind, blotting out common sense. It was happening all over again. Just like that night in Farringdon. The feeling was overwhelming.

Abby looked up. "I think I've got everything I need," she said quietly. Her eyes flitted uneasily around the room as she took a small step forwards. She picked up the bundle of towels from the bed, and hugged them against her chest.

Mike nodded awkwardly, distracted by the thin, red strap of her dress, which had slipped off her shoulder. The towels were pressed against her breasts, pushing them up, and – *oh God*. He knew he'd have to leave the room, or he'd be standing in the middle of it with an erection.

"Goodnight, Mike," she said quietly, starting to move towards the en suite.

Mike reached out impulsively as she passed, and stopped her gently with a hand. "Goodnight then." He kissed her lightly on the cheek, and turned to go. "My room's the second on the–"

She pulled him back, and kissed him.

He froze for a second while Abby wrapped her arms around his neck, and ran a hand up into his hair. The towels fell away between them, and he felt her kick them across the floor. This was it. The thing that he'd spent so much time imagining – it was actually happening. He was kissing Abby again.

Mike abandoned the arguments he'd been using on his sister only minutes earlier – the reasons why Abby and he should just be friends, why letting anything happen between them was a bad idea. He pulled her close, pressing himself against her and slowly edging them both towards the bed.

He remembered it all from the last time: the feel of her soft, wet lips on his, the smell of her hair, the feel of her tits pushing against his chest, the touch of her fingers in the small of his back... Suddenly, Abby broke away.

Mike looked at her anxiously. Was that it? Was she planning to shut the door on him now, and say good night? No. She smiled, then peeled off the flimsy red dress and stood there, a couple of feet away, just looking at him. Her breathing was fast and shallow – he could see by the rise and fall of her tits in their semi-transparent red lace. They were just *asking* to be set free, he thought. Mike held off for a second – just for long enough to undo a few buttons on his shirt and to lift it over his head. He was hard. He unzipped quickly and moved towards her, running one hand up into her hair, and the other – he couldn't resist – to the catch on her bra, and kissing her again.

He pushed her backwards onto the bed. Mike wanted to touch her all over at once: her long legs, her arse, her tiny waist, her tits, her smooth, tanned shoulders... They were naked, Abby on her back, Mike hovering just millimetres above her. He ran a fingertip lightly up the side of her stomach, tracing patterns around her tits and watching her nipples turn hard. He could feel the heat of her breath on his face, and lowered himself to kiss her again. She had a look in her eyes that he'd only seen once before.

Abby hooked one leg round his body and slowly pulled him down on top of her. Then Mike was inside her – hot, breathless and out of control.

"Mike," she said finally, as she rested her head on his hot, heaving chest ten minutes later, her legs still entwined in his.

He looked down, combing his fingers through her knotted hair.

"Wow," she breathed, letting out an exhausted sigh.

48

JUSTINE PAUSED BEFORE answering the question and glanced nervously around the bar. It was a Thursday evening, and they were virtually the only three customers in there.

"I replied to one," she said, looking at Abby for support. "I told him I didn't want to see him. Politely, of course. We didn't want to offend him–" She looked again at Abby, who nodded encouragingly. Justine was obviously hating every second.

"I didn't hear anything for a couple of days, so I thought he might've taken the hint. But that's when I realised, the whole bank was laughing at me." Justine looked up at her listeners and took an anxious gulp of wine.

"He's been showing people text messages," she said. "Texts that are supposed to be from me, making out we're having an affair or something. *Dirty* messages, like–" Justine grimaced and shrugged. Her hands were shaking. She looked fragile, as though she might break down any minute.

"They're fake," Abby pointed out, buying Justine some time to compose herself. "She hasn't sent him any dirty texts, obviously. He must've sent them to himself."

Justine nodded and took a deep breath. "I went to HR, but they say there's nothing they can do. They need 'evidence' apparently, and text messages aren't enough. The thing is, he's a Managing Director. Cray McKinley doesn't want to hear about this. They'd rather let a first-year analyst suffer than lose one of their MDs."

The women sat there in silence. Justine was right. She had little chance of getting this resolved.

"He's heading up the deal I'm working on at the moment," she went on. "He's in charge of project allocation, so he can put me on *all* his deals if he wants to. He comes up to me when the office is empty, and perches on the side of my desk, saying all this stuff–" Justine was getting herself in a state again. Her face was blotchy and Abby noticed her jaw was starting to tremble. She inhaled and went on.

"Then, a few weeks ago, I was the last one left in my part of the office – or at least, I thought I was. It was about one in the morning, and I suddenly heard a noise behind me. I looked round, and before I could see who it was, I felt his hands around my–"

"Enough!" cried Jennifer Armstrong, glaring at Justine. "This is sexual harassment!"

Poor Justine just gawped at the woman. She'd never met the MD before, and Abby had forgotten to warn her of what to expect.

"I cannot *believe* you have let this go on." Armstrong looked fiercely at Justine.

Abby stared in disbelief. *This wasn't Justine's fault.* Suddenly Abby felt wracked with guilt. It had been her idea to involve the MD; she'd thought that the woman could pull some strings from the top. But now she wasn't so sure. Perhaps Jennifer Armstrong would just toe the party line and side with her fellow MD. Abby began to wonder if she'd made things a whole lot worse for Justine by getting her involved.

"I tried to say something," Justine protested, "but HR didn't wanna hear."

Jennifer Armstrong remained silent. Abby watched her anxiously, dying to know what was going on behind those beady eyes as they darted around the empty bar.

"I – I wondered about switching departments," Justine said tentatively, after a long, painful pause which happened to coincide with the barman's decision to change CDs.

Armstrong looked at her sternly. "You will do *no such thing.* Don't be daft."

Justine bravely argued her case. "I'd rather do that than lose my job altogether. I mean–"

"No. You will *not* be switching departments because of this. And you will *not* be losing your job."

Justine slumped back in her chair. Abby watched as the MD gulped down the rest of her wine and banged the glass heavily on the table. She was waiting for Jennifer Armstrong to say something miraculous, something that might instil a little hope in poor Justine. She needed to know that the woman was on their side.

The Managing Director looked from Justine to Abby, then back again. "Now," she said brusquely. "Am I to know *which* Managing Director you are referring to here?"

The girls looked at each other. Abby wasn't going to say anything. It was up to Justine to spill the beans.

After a second's hesitation, she did.

They both watched the woman's face as she absorbed the information. Disappointingly, there wasn't much of a reaction – just a slight lift of the well-plucked eyebrows and a draw-string action on the shiny lips.

"OK," Jennifer Armstrong said. "Leave it to me. I'll see what I can do."

49

"SO I THINK THAT just about covers everything. You've obviously had a successful first year," Rupert Larkham concluded, no doubt for the umpteenth time that day.

Mike nodded mutely, trying to contain the stupid grin that was threatening to spread across his face. Sixteen thousand pounds. He'd never imagined his bonus would be anything *like* as much as that.

"Do you have any questions for me?" Larkham asked wearily, turning back to his monitor and squinting irritably at something in the corner of it. Clearly the meeting had come to an end.

"Good – and send in the next analyst on your way out, would you?"

Mike rose assertively to his feet. The stupid grin broke out as soon as the door clicked shut behind him. *Sixteen thousand pounds!* Never mind the fact that he'd only achieved a mid-tier ranking – they probably only gave out the top-level bonuses to the real arse-lickers anyway – he'd just been awarded a lump sum of *sixteen thousand pounds!* That was more than the size of some graduates' salaries! The things he could do with sixteen thousand pounds... He started to run through the possibilities.

"Looking pleased with yourself," Jon Hargreaves commented, clocking the smirk.

Mike gave him a knowing look and bent down at the next desk along, stifling the silly grin. "Your turn!" he whispered in Abby's ear.

Her head flicked round and she glanced anxiously at Mike. He knew how worried she was about this.

"Hey, chill!" he said softly, touching her on the forearm. They were still in that stage where they didn't want anyone knowing about their relationship, which made it all the more exhilarating, but at the same time slightly frustrating. Still, that wouldn't be for long. In a few weeks, they wouldn't need to worry about being the gossip of Corporate Finance. Mike couldn't wait to tell her his news.

Abby made a lame attempt at smiling. Taking a deep breath, she clasped her hands together and strode deliberately towards Larkham's office.

50

ABBY CRACKED each of her knuckles in turn and shifted her weight onto the other foot. Her heart was somewhere in the back of her throat, and there was a horrible, edgy feeling that she couldn't shake off. She'd been too nervous to eat anything for breakfast. It reminded her of A-level results day. Of course, there was no point in getting worked up, she told herself. There was nothing she could do about the size of her bonus, just as there'd been nothing she could have done about her exam grades. But the logic did nothing to calm her nerves.

The silhouette behind the opaque grey glass moved sideways, and she heard a muffled bark that sounded like 'Come in!' from inside.

Rupert Larkham was scowling. Not at Abby, but at his computer screen. His long, bony fingers were splayed over his mouth while his thumb idly tickled his jawbone. He grunted at his monitor.

Abby glanced around her uncomfortably. Clearly the man was busy. Perhaps he hadn't said 'Come in' after all, she thought, panicking. Perhaps he'd said 'Coming!' and was in the middle of something. Abby tried to make herself blend into the wall.

He tutted, and started shaking his head. "Dear me," he muttered. "Dear me."

There was something in his tone of voice that set alarm bells ringing in Abby's head. He was looking at her cross-evaluation, she thought, feeling her stomach lurch again. That was why he looked so disappointed. She slowly leaned forwards, and took a peek at his screen.

TEST MATCH TODAY! UP-TO-THE-MINUTE REPORTS ON–

Abby was overwhelmed with a mixture of relief and outrage. He was checking the cricket scores! Thank God he wasn't looking at her cross-evaluation. There was hope for her yet. But how *dare* he waste her time like this? How inconsiderate! How rude! She crossed her arms and stood there sullenly, waiting for the man to look up.

The VP made a discontented growling noise and continued to squint at the screen. Abby stared at the ugly man, feeling angrier by the second. What did he think he was doing? She had better things to do with her day than wait for a score page to update. Her eyes bore down on the VP, but still he refused to look up.

Abby's irritation turned to fury. She flung herself down in the leather chair, and cleared her throat very loudly.

"One moment," ordered Larkham, without looking up.

Abby let out an impatient sigh. She knew she was behaving disrespectfully, but frankly, she thought, so was he. And besides, the sucking-up season was over for the year. They'd already determined her bonus. It was written down somewhere, in that neat pile of papers, she presumed. Nobody could change that now.

"Right," he said finally, just as Abby finished counting the ceiling tiles.

"Annab – Abigail. Hello again."

She smiled falsely. "Hello."

"How have you been since we last spoke? Have you had a successful three months?"

If you mean, have I grovelled to plenty of senior bankers, then the answer is no, she thought, nodding politely.

"Good. Now, as you know," he said, suddenly putting on a grave tone of voice, "the main purpose of today's meeting is to look at your progress in the department so far. To discuss your strengths, your weaknesses, areas for improvement, and to see what your colleagues have said about you." He patted the wad of paper on his desk.

The panicky feeling returned. Abby thought back to her last encounter with the gangly VP, and remembered his meaningful words. *All the junior bankers will be ranked... top, middle, bottom... The rest will be made redundant...* There was a possibility that Abby would lose her job today. It wasn't likely – if Jennifer Armstrong was to be believed – but it was possible.

"And of course," he went on, "to inform you of the value of your bonus." He glanced idly at his screen.

Abby sat, expressionless and rigid, suppressing the urge to jump up and snatch the bundle, shouting 'TELL ME MY BONUS, YOU PO-FACED FREAK!'

"The first thing I'd say, on seeing your reports, is that you seem to be a popular girl." He wrapped his lips around his gums in a strange, toothless pout – presumably his idea of a smile. "You had nearly twenty evaluations submitted. Most people only get eight or nine."

Abby nodded. At least that was something. But quantity wasn't really the point. She wished he'd just spit it out. If Larkham didn't tell her in the next five minutes, she'd hold the staple-gun up to his head and force the figure out of him.

"Some of them are reasonably complimentary, too."

Reasonably complimentary, Abby mused, wishing her intestines would sort themselves out. Was that supposed to be encouraging?

"The second thing I'd say, An- Abigail, is that while you've worked on a good number of deals this year, unfortunately, you don't seem to have *achieved* very much."

Abby opened her mouth to object, then clamped it shut again. There was no point in whinging to Larkham. She'd learnt that lesson last time.

"Now. You probably want to hear about your bonus, don't you?"

Abby nodded casually while her stomach made a noise like a spaceship taking off.

"Well, I've explained the ranking process, haven't I? So you know how the analysts get divided into four groups? Top, middle, bottom and... er, well, the rest, which get *let go of,* shall we say?"

Abby tried to swallow, but her throat was like a tube of cardboard.

"I'm pleased to say, you're not in that category."

Abby relaxed a little. So she still had a job.

"You've been awarded a third-tier bonus."

Third? As in, bottom? Abby made a half-hearted attempt at nodding, but her mind was on other things. All that work. All those hours spent sitting at her desk. All those miserable weekends in the office. And she'd been awarded a third-tier bonus? OK, so it was better than getting the sack. But the truth was, she'd never really expected that. She'd seen it as a remote possibility, but not a serious risk. She hadn't performed *that* badly this year, had she? OK, there had been a few glitches. A couple of little mistakes. A couple of not-so-little mistakes. But hell, she was a first-year! She was allowed to go wrong in the first few months!

"… sum of eleven thousand pounds."

Abby's head jerked up. She stared at the man's gaunt face.

"That's not bad, for a third-tier bonus," he commented, glancing at his monitor and pressing a button on his keyboard.

Eleven thousand pounds? Questions flooded Abby's mind. Why so much? Was that really the smallest bonus? If so, then how large was the largest? Why was she in the bottom third? Who was in the top tier? What did Mike get?

"As I said," he went on, wrenching his attention from the screen back to Abby. "The main problem for you is that you haven't really *achieved* much this year."

Abby was only half listening. Her head was swimming with a cocktail of emotions: irritation, frustration, indignation, relief, confusion and disbelief.

"I'm looking at your reports, here—" he thumbed through the pages in front of him. "Shadowing, shadowing, assisting, modelling – ah, here! See? You worked on Project Coral, didn't you?"

Abby nodded crossly. Trust him to pick out the worst example of her work.

"Says here, you were 'removed from project due to complications'. Replaced by another first-year, by the looks of things…"

'It was my first project!' Abby nearly yelped. 'I didn't even get it wrong! Mike took over from me and ended up using *my* model!' But she sat there in silence. Abby knew when something was a waste of time, and trying to argue her case to a haughty VP who didn't even know her name was most definitely a waste of time.

"Doesn't reflect too well on you," he sneered.

She said nothing. The man flicked over the page.

"Oh yes," he said, not quite keeping the satisfaction out of his voice. "The reports from the M&A bankers. *Very* disheartening. You worked with Tim Sanders and his associate didn't you, on Project... Project..." he squinted at the text.

"Buffalo." Abby offered grudgingly. "Project Buffalo."

"Yes. That's right. It seems that you let them down," he commented.

She thought back to that horrible night. The memory was still fresh in her mind: the cab ride, the tiredness, the waiting around – and then that phone call from the project MD, blaming her for Anthony Dawson's mistake. The injustice of it stung even now.

Rupert Larkham was rifling through the stack of white forms, tutting and shaking his head.

"Now what was the other thing I noticed? Ah yes – here. An evaluation from a colleague in this department. You worked on the Pharmacolt deal?"

"Yes – I helped Mi–"

"Hmm. Disappointing outcome, that. Very unsatisfactory, losing that deal – a letdown for the whole bank, I'd say. Although I'm sure you weren't entirely to blame, were you?" he snorted. "Huh!"

Entirely to blame? Abby stared incredulously. She couldn't tell whether this was Larkham's idea of a joke. Was he really holding her responsible for the collapse of the Pharmacolt deal? If anyone had been at fault on that it had been Mike – he'd admitted as much himself – but surely neither was actually to blame? They were *analysts*, for God's sake. Number-crunchers!

Larkham was talking again, but Abby was barely listening.

"...can't just go drifting through your career..."

Her hackles were up.

"...people think they can get away with it..."

It just wasn't fair, this unwarranted criticism.

"...bottom tier, just not pulling their weight..."

She had to say *something* – to stick up for herself.

"...of course, you'll have to try *extra* hard next year..."

It wouldn't do any good, she knew that. But at least she'd feel better inside.

"…you'll be the only second-year analyst when Michael Cunningham-Reid's gone…"

She couldn't just sit here and listen to his insults.

"…probably won't bother getting anyone to replace him…"

She took a deep breath, and waited for a pause in Larkham's tirade.

"Euh?" was all that came out.

"Well, I don't see any need to replace him *immediately,*" he said. "Of course, if the workload were to become excessive, then we'd have to think about recruiting from inside the firm, but for the moment, we'll just see how it goes without him."

Abby spluttered something unintelligible. All her questions were coming out at once.

Larkham looked at her pityingly. "I beg your pardon?"

"I – er – what… Did you say Michael was… *leaving?*"

"Well, he's joining Corporate Broking, isn't he?"

Abby started nodding like a puppet. "Oh yeah," she mumbled. "Of course."

"So there'll be more of a burden on the remaining analysts…" The man was off again. Abby continued to nod, although her thoughts had long-since left the room.

Mike had gone for the Corporate Broking job? After telling her it wasn't worth going for? That couldn't be true. It couldn't. He would have told her. They'd talked about the vacancy lots of times – he saw it as not worth going for. It was a 'dead-end job' – he'd said so himself! There was no way he'd have interviewed for the position. There *had* to be some other explanation. Larkham had got it wrong. Mike wouldn't have gone behind her back like that.

"…really start making an effort…"

He was off again. The words floated into Abby's mind then floated out again, without making any impression.

"…might struggle to absorb the extra work, as Michael is a very competent analyst…"

She swallowed, gradually coming to terms with what Larkham was saying. There was no mistake. Mike was leaving the department. He was taking the job in Broking.

Abby felt numb. It was as if someone had injected her head with a local anaesthetic. She couldn't feel or think anything. In fact, the only thing she was capable of thinking about was the fact that she wasn't able to think. It was very odd. She could see that Larkham was moving his lips, but it was just a noise spewing out of his mouth.

The anaesthetic wore off abruptly, and the thoughts flooded back into her mind. The anger kicked in. Mike had lied to her. He'd gone behind her back. He'd gone behind *everyone's* back, in fact – all the other first-year analysts, not just Abby. The rage tore through her like fire. How could he have done this? How? And why?

Strangely enough, after all that had happened between Abby and Mike, good and bad, the one thing she'd never expected was this. Whatever he was to Abby – a friend, a boyfriend, a colleague, whatever – she'd never imagined he'd be callous enough to do something like this. She wanted to fling herself at Mike – shake him, beat him, scratch him, scream at him... Clearly their friendship – or whatever it was – had never meant anything to him. Why had she believed that it had?

To think that she'd persuaded herself that she might actually *love* Mike Cunnningham-Reid. She suddenly saw him for what he really was. Mike was no better than any of the other bankers. He was just a greedy, selfish, conniving bastard. Her original impression had been right, and she should've stuck with it. He was an arrogant, heartless backstabber who was only after one thing: money. Just like all the rest.

"Oh dear," said Larkham, piercing her bubble of contemplation. "We seem to be out of time. D'you have any questions for me? Anything you'd like to say?" He glanced absent-mindedly at Abby before turning back to his screen.

Abby stared silently at the side of his abhorrent face, willing him to turn towards her so that he could see the look in her eyes. Did she have anything to say? Yes, plenty.

I've had enough of your insults and your belittling remarks. I'm sick of being blamed for things I didn't do, and sick of seeing other people take credit for my work. So you think I haven't achieved much. Well how about judging me by the quality of my work, instead of the quality of my bullshit and backslapping and sucking up? And you're supposed to be in charge of Analysts' Wellbeing? Well try switching roles for a day, Rupert. See what it's like down here at the bottom, following orders from self-satisfied bigots on power trips, sacrificing your health – your whole life – to meet impossible deadlines and getting no thanks. See how you like being treated as a disposable asset, to be chucked away when you get worn out. "No, I think that just about covers everything."

Larkham continued to squint at his monitor, and started drumming his fingers on the desk.

"Oh – there is one more thing actually," Abby added quietly, still waiting for him to look round.

"Hmmm?" he said absent-mindedly to his screen.

Abby couldn't be bothered to wait any longer. She took a deep breath. "I'm leaving."

"Mmm. Could you send in the next analyst as you go?"

"No – I mean, I'm *leaving*," she explained. "I'm leaving Cray McKinley."

Larkham's ugly profile was swiftly replaced with a front-on, goggle-eyed stare.

A rush of adrenaline hit Abby's bloodstream. She'd only just realised the implications of what she'd just said.

"*Leaving?!*" he spluttered, banging his palms on the desk. "Why?"

Abby looked up at the man, determined to hold his furious gaze. It was incredible, the change that had come over him in a matter of seconds. The pasty skeleton that had been sitting there, nodding, muttering, vaguely aware of her presence had been transformed into a furious, snarling animal.

"Because, evidently, I'm not very good at my job."

The corner of Larkham's right eye started twitching. He opened his mouth then closed it again, and exhaled noisily through his nose. It was both petrifying and fascinating to watch. He actually seemed to be lost for words, thought Abby, with a hint of satisfaction. She'd had no idea her announcement would provoke such a reaction.

"Now – now hang on," he stammered. He was obviously having difficulty finding a flaw in her argument.

Abby didn't hang on. She'd made up her mind. Springing to her feet, Abby turned her back on the man while he sat there making guttural noises behind his desk.

The glass nearly shattered as the door slammed shut. Abby cut a straight line towards her desk, sending chairs reeling into filing cabinets along the way. She was aware of a number of eyes following her through the office, but for the first time in nearly a year, she didn't care. She didn't give a shit what they thought. They weren't her colleagues any more.

Secretaries stopped typing. Someone drew a sharp intake of breath. Jon Hargreaves made a stupid comment. Archie Dickinson fell into a coat-stand as he tried to leap out of her way. Abby stooped down by her desk and whisked her bag out from under it.

For the last time in her life, Abby stepped into the lift and pressed the silver '0'. She waited impatiently for the doors to close, and glanced around her. She nearly yelped with shock when she saw her reflection. The girl in the mirror beamed back at Abby. Her eyes glistened. Her cheeks were flushed. It was a face that Abby recognised, but one she hadn't seen for months. The excitement ran through her like a drug. Finally, she thought, she was doing something right. She was leaving Cray McKinley. She was the Abby she used to be.

There was a scuffling noise in the lobby, just as the lift doors started to close. Abby spun round in time to see a hand reach out towards the metal jaws.

"I'm sorry Ab—"

The doors slid shut. *Too late,* she thought, feeling herself plummeting downwards. She had no time for people like Mike.

With a mounting sense of liberation, Abby marched through the atrium. Lots of important-looking men were swarming around the turnstiles, shaking hands with each other and chuckling. Abby took pleasure in elbowing them aside. She charged at the revolving door, and with excruciating slowness, it began to rotate.

Finally, Abby was ejected into the hot, polluted air. The June sunshine beat down on her face and she could feel a light breeze in her hair. At last, she was free. She was free to be herself again. Abby stood at the top of the granite steps, looking down, still struggling to take it all in. The street was lined with identical black cabs, dropping off identical pinstriped passengers outside identical glass-fronted offices. Two sweaty businessmen were poring over documents on a bench outside Café Nero. A pretty young blonde in a cheap trouser suit was venturing nervously up the steps clasping a bundle of papers and a map. Abby gave her an encouraging smile. She'd learn soon enough, she thought.

Abby leapt down the steps, two at a time and darted across the road. Unable to resist a final backward glance, she turned on the spot and looked up. The sunlight was glistening on the ugly bronze Cray McKinley statue, and she could just make out the words inscribed beneath – the five principles of the firm:

UNITY – INTEGRITY – CREATIVITY – HONESTY – LOYALTY

She actually laughed out loud.

51

THE LATE SUMMER heat-wave was one of the longest in living memory, and was showing no sign of letting up. Even at nine o'clock in the morning, the air felt warm and the sky was a deep, monotone blue. It was going to be another glorious day. Another glorious day that Justine would miss. She slammed the front door behind her and hurried across the street.

"Morning!" cried Helen, the temp who was covering for their secretary.

Justine tried her best to look cheerful. She wasn't even sure which morning it was. They were all the same to her – even weekends. Except that temps didn't work weekends, so it couldn't be one of them.

She chucked her bag under the desk and stabbed at the on button. Riaz, the slimy associate who sat opposite her, leaned sideways and gave her a disapproving look. She checked her watch. Nearly twenty past. She was getting later and later each day. Justine hastily logged on and sat down, pretending to start work immediately. Riaz wouldn't have known it, but her poor punctuality wasn't accidental. For one thing, Justine needed her sleep. She'd been working into the early hours on this wretched deal for the past fifteen days, and hadn't had a proper break in weeks. But also – and this was the main reason for her lateness – she wanted to make sure she wasn't the first one in. She didn't want to risk running into Philip when there was nobody else around.

The Philip Oversby situation hadn't improved. He was still visiting her desk on a regular basis at night. He was still asking her out for drinks at 'his club', and making openly suggestive remarks when no one was around. She was still declining his every advance, perpetually scared of what he might try next. It seemed that there was nothing she could do. Jennifer Armstrong had been no help at all. Justine hadn't heard back from her since that night they'd met in the bar. Her only option seemed to be to avoid him, and hope that he'd give up eventually.

As it happened, Philip Oversby didn't seem to be in this morning. Perhaps he'd gone to the States, she thought hopefully. Justine was a different person when he went away. Her life seemed a whole lot more bearable. She pushed back her chair and headed to the nearest water machine.

This was getting silly, Justine thought. She couldn't go on like this, living every moment in fear. She'd give herself a nervous breakdown. She had to speak to HR about a departmental transfer. It was that or quitting, and Justine didn't want to do that. She was planning to stay at Cray McKinley for two more years – if she could stomach it. Maybe she'd go up to HR today, she thought, wishing that another solution would magically materialise. HR was not in the habit of letting analysts move around the bank.

"Ooh! Your phone's ringing!" cried Helen, as though this was something that had never happened before. She started frantically pressing buttons on her switchboard, getting more and more flustered as the ringing went on.

Justine sped back to her desk and slammed the cup of water down. She didn't get a chance to look at the display.

"Justine Brown speaking?"

"Ah, hello there Justine." A woman's voice. It sounded frightfully posh. "I presume you've received the email; hope this helps you out a little—" She was talking very fast, and didn't pause for Justine to reply. "Oh, and I'd take the wording with a pinch of salt if I were you. Read 'decided to' as 'been made to', if you know what I mean! Ha!"

Justine didn't know what she meant, but she hastily opened up Outlook in an attempt to find out. It was Jennifer Armstrong, she realised.

"Not so hard to get someone fired when they've been in and out of rehab. for the past three and a half years!" The woman chuckled.

"I'm sure you're familiar with the firm's zero tolerance policy on drugs!"

Justine's mind was racing – unlike her Outlook, which was being infuriatingly slow. *Get someone fired? Rehab? Zero tolerance?* Was somebody losing their job because of drugs? It was possible; Abby had told her about some guy in her department who'd supposedly been sacked for snorting cocaine at work. But what did this have to do with her? Had the MD dialled the wrong number by mistake? Oh, why was Outlook being so *slow?*

"Turns out, he did actually get caught a few months ago, but they decided to get rid of the associate who reported him, instead of sacking him! Anyway, must dash. Philip Oversby isn't the only one with places to go!"

"Phil–"

"Good luck!"

Justine mumbled something into the receiver, but the line was already dead.

Philip Oversby had been fired? Is that what she'd said? This was just too good to be true! Justine forced herself to stay calm. She had to see the proof before she got too excited.

Finally, the computer finished doing whatever it was doing, and the emails dropped into her inbox. There were only two from this morning, one from IT Support and one – ooh yes! – from Philip Oversby.

From: Oversby, Philip (London)
To: All (London)
Subject: Pastures new

Dear all,

It is with great sadness that I bring you news of my departure from Cray McKinley. After eight enjoyable years at the firm, I have decided to move on and explore pastures new.

I'd like to thank everyone with whom I have had the pleasure of working in my time at Cray McKinley. I will look back on these years with great fondness.

May I wish all my colleagues every success for the future.

Kind Regards,

Philip

Philip Oversby

Managing Director

Leveraged Finance

Cray McKinley International

Justine could hardly keep herself from whooping with delight. She was *free!* He was *gone!* She could get on with her life again! Oh, the thought of working alone without Philip Oversby creeping up on her! She wanted to run up to Jennifer Armstrong's office and kiss her little feet. Instead, she kicked back her chair, grabbed her mobile phone and headed for the lifts. She had some calls to make. Hurrying past the empty office in the corner of the fifth floor, she couldn't help smiling. Her life had just got better.

52

MIKE SURGED FORWARDS with two hundred other passengers and found himself a space between a pinstriped, dandruff-speckled shoulder and a Rastafarian's hair. He held his breath while people shuffled about, and while the smell – an intoxicating mix of sweat, dirt and perfume – was at its strongest.

This was one of his least favourite parts of the day. This and the journey home. And, if he was being honest, the interim twelve hours he spent sitting at his desk. He tested the air, inhaling very gingerly. It was bearable, so he filled his lungs, angling his face away from the dreadlocks.

The doors closed, trapping a woman's handbag between them, and promptly opened again. Mike watched irritably as the woman pushed further into the carriage, using the bag as a battering ram. The Rastafarian moved sideways, and Mike could feel the mat of hair rubbing against his collar. He tried not to think about the number of species that were crawling and hopping their way onto his suit.

Today's explanation for the ten-minute delay was 'signal failure in the Wimbledon area'. The fact that this train had started in Richmond and hadn't gone anywhere near Wimbledon had obviously not occurred to the person in charge of inventing excuses. Mike loosened his tie and undid his top button. The temperature must have been verging on ninety degrees.

As they pulled away, he wondered, not for the first time, why he was putting himself through this. He knew it wasn't a very original thing to wonder, but he pondered it all the same, and remained deep in thought for the next two stops. Surely life didn't have to be like this, he thought, as he was buffeted from elbow to armpit, reaching out unsuccessfully for something to hold. There had to be alternatives, for someone like him. As usual, Mike came to the conclusion that no, there weren't alternatives – not ones that provided fifty thousand pounds a year. Not ones that provoked an awe-struck look every time you told someone what you did.

The Rastafarian got off at Victoria, and was replaced by a teenaged Goth with a dagger going through his left earlobe. A stretch of handrail became available, and Mike fought his way towards it. Somebody got there first. He resigned himself to stumbling around, supported by the mass of sweaty bodies.

At least he was out of Corporate Finance, he thought, trying to cheer himself up. In Broking, he was averaging a mere twelve hours a day. OK, so the work was mundane, his colleagues were dull and his chances of promotion slim, but so what? Compared to the torture of Corporate Finance, Broking was a walk in the park; he hadn't worked a weekend in nearly three weeks.

As passengers rearranged themselves around him, Mike thought about this new life of his, and convinced himself that switching to Broking had been a good move. He had so much more spare time now. He was no longer constantly exhausted. He was playing rugby again, and seeing his mates – occasionally even on weeknights.

But the problem was, something had changed in the last few months. Back in Corporate Finance, despite the hours, despite the atmosphere, despite the soul-destroying nature of the work, there had been something keeping him going. Something that helped him get through the days. Back in the spring, there were times when life had actually seemed quite fun. OK, maybe 'fun' was too strong a word. But things had been tolerable in the office. He wasn't sure exactly what had changed, but something definitely had. This new life was dreary as hell.

The carriage jerked sideways and Mike was thrown into a young Asian woman. He staggered back wearing his most apologetic expression, which evidently wasn't apologetic enough. She glowered up at him through dark eyelashes, then pointedly readjusted her headscarf. The brakes made an unpleasant squealing noise as they pulled into St James' Park.

His aspirations were shifting. When he'd first joined the firm,

Mike's plan had been to work his way up. Shoot up from the bottom, like the star that they'd told him he was at the milkround dinner. He was a 'high flier'. He was going all the way to the top, making VP before he was thirty. That had been his intention, anyway.

Things had changed, though. High flying wasn't as easy as he'd envisaged. It was nearly impossible to prove yourself as a first-year, because nobody noticed what you did. All the first-years were the same. And there were so many *other* people, too, fighting for the next rung of the ladder. Now he was in Corporate Broking, the problem was exacerbated. The work was so routine that he'd never get the chance to impress – and Mike was beginning to feel that his superiors didn't *want* to be impressed; they just wanted the work done.

There was a mass exodus at Westminster, and Mike eased sideways towards the door and away from the Goth with the severed ear. A seat became free and he went for it. He got there just ahead of a large, purple-faced businessman who huffed loudly and proceeded to stand on Mike's foot. He probably wouldn't have fitted between the armrests anyway, thought Mike.

Mike was slowly coming round to the view that working his way up through the ranks of Cray McKinley would be a long, painful climb, and one which frankly wasn't worth the effort. His new plan involved sticking around for a bit, and keeping his ear to the ground. He wouldn't be actively *looking* for a new job, but if something came along, he'd think about taking it. He reached behind him to grab a discarded magazine that was fluttering on top of the air vent. Perhaps there was a job section inside.

The magazine fell open on a full-page advertisement which started, 'Will you remember today forever?' *No,* thought Mike, whipping over the page with a stab of guilt. No, he wasn't doing anything worthwhile with his life. And no, he wasn't particularly proud. But no, he wasn't going to work for VSO building pit-latrines in Botswana for 21p per day.

It was some sort of high-brow girly magazine, Mike realised, flicking through with waning interest. The pages were filled with the same shitty columns and the same blurry photographs that appeared inside every glossy mag. Why did women pay money for this stuff?

Suddenly, Mike stopped flicking and turned back two pages.

The headline read 'GYM'LL FIX IT? APPARENTLY NOT', and beneath it was a colour picture of two leggy blondes in T-shirts and tight black shorts, leaning against a tennis net, laughing. The one on the right was Abby Turner.

Mike was torn between the image and the article that went with it. She was even more stunning than he remembered. Her hair had grown long over summer, and she'd obviously spent some time in the sun. What was she doing in this magazine? He took one last look at her smile, then started to read.

GYM'LL FIX IT? APPARENTLY NOT.

Fit blonde babes? Or simply blonde babes trying to help other people get fit?

Abigail Turner and Beth Dawes are founder members of Sporticity, a city-based company which, they hope, will transform the way we work out.

The firm was set up with people like Derek Barnes in mind. A thirty-year old management consultant, Derek is the first to admit he's got 'a bit of a one-pack' (that's a belly to you and me). With gold membership of his office gym costing £900 a year, Derek hasn't been down there in over six months. "It's the beers after work," he explains. "And the sitting at my desk all day. I don't get a chance to keep fit."

We've all been there. We've all started new jobs with good intentions, only to find that three weeks later we've lost our gym membership card and can't find our trainers. And as Beth Dawes, Head of Marketing at Sporticity points out, "Who actually *likes* going to the gym?"

"Most people have this bizarre notion that being a member of an expensive city gym will help keep you fit. Well, that's only true if you go, and 40% of us don't."

Keeping in shape is made harder for those of us in demanding, high-stress jobs where 80-hour weeks are the norm. One investment banker (26) said, "I used to play football for a West Hampstead team, but I couldn't make weeknight training. Or weekends, for that matter. I quit, as I just kept letting them down."

The solution? Team games with no commitment, according to Sporticity. Just find out what's on offer, and take your pick. No membership, no registration, no hassle. Abigail Turner, CEO of Sporticity, claims "Most people loathe the office gym. Team games are different; they're enjoyable."

But that's not to say the girls are anti-gym. In fact they've joined forces with most of the large city gyms including Holmes Place, Fitness First, Cannons and LA Fitness to take advantage of under-used facilities.

In the last two months, the company has grown to eight people, and now receives over twelve hundred enquiries per week.

The sports on offer range from rugby to rounders to table tennis, and are played at over fifty-five locations around London (see www.sporticity.com). "We provide pretty much any sport involving more than one person – you name it," says Dawes. The company has already built up such a following that nearly a third of their games are over-subscribed (but don't let that put you off!).

After graduating from Cambridge University last year, Turner and Dawes spent just twelve months in the rat race before pulling out – to enter what might end up being an even more competitive pursuit. But they're aware of the challenges that lie ahead. Beyond their astute knowledge of the marketplace and an obvious passion for winning, the girls appear to have a very clear vision of the company's future.

We're off to the basketball courts for a workout now – surely better than a trip to the gym?

For more information on Sporticity, see www.sporticity.com or call 0800 467 8181.

Mike looked at the picture again. The girls had obviously been told to look as though something hilarious was happening on the next court along.

She'd set up a *company?*

Mike skimmed through the article for a second time, and was overwhelmed with – what? He didn't actually know. It reminded him of the time she'd walked onto the Pharmacolt deal team – onto *his* project. Was it jealousy? Resentment? She'd escaped from Cray McKinley. She'd taken a risk. She was *doing* something with her life. She wasn't a slave to her salary – come to think of it, she probably wasn't even drawing a salary – but she was out there, succeeding, getting recognition. Why didn't he have the balls to do something like that?

No, it wasn't resentment he was feeling. Jealousy maybe, but not resentment. Building up a company in the space of two months was one hell of an achievement, but thinking about it, that was exactly the sort of thing Abby Turner would do. He felt no malice. He just wished they were still in contact, so he could congratulate her – or just talk to her. He wondered if she'd changed, since leaving the bank. She certainly looked happier, if the photo was anything to go by. Being CEO probably suited Abby. She'd always hated being told what to do. *CEO, aged twenty-three.* OK, it was only a tiny company, but still, that was better than being an analyst.

The fat businessman removed himself from Mike's foot, and Mike realised they'd arrived at his stop. He leapt up and barged towards the bleeping doors, managing to wedge them sufficiently to squeeze himself out. It was only as he hurried along the platform, brushing the dirty marks off his shoulder that Mike realised he'd left the magazine on the tube; he must've dropped it as he got up. It didn't matter. He hadn't intended to keep it anyway. He was pleased that Abby seemed to be doing so well, and it was a shame that they weren't still in touch, but the fact was, they weren't. He had to move on, to forget. He stepped onto the escalator and began to think about his share price graphs.

53

Peckham, London, early September

THERE WAS A GENTLE knock on the office door.

"Mmm?" Abby grunted, without looking round. A slim figure crept into her field of vision.

"You nearly done in here?" Beth asked quietly.

Abby nodded, her eyes still fixed on the cash flow statement. She glanced down the column one last time, then turned back to the Profit and Loss. It had been a record month for the company, with top-line sales up eighteen percent. Sales were still in the tens of thousands, not hundreds, but it was early days. They'd only been going three months. Abby checked the figures again. She wanted to get this finished tonight so that she and Beth could spend the weekend on marketing.

Beth padded across the room behind her, blocking out what little light there was coming through the window. There wasn't much of a view from here at the best of times – slate roofs, chimneys and telegraph poles – but now the sun had slipped behind a tower block, rendering it even dingier. The ugliness didn't bother them, though. They didn't have time for gazing out of the window. Abby finally unglued her eyes from the spreadsheet and swivelled round. The chair made an ominous clonking noise.

Beth whipped round. "Oh my God – don't move!" she cried, rushing forwards and diving to the floor.

Abby leaned forwards gingerly and watched as she rammed a metal pin into the shaft of the chair. Uncle Pete's two-storey townhouse in Peckham, which served – temporarily, they hoped – as the company headquarters, was filled with a selection of rickety, second-hand furniture that the girls had acquired from various sources.

"Am I safe?"

"Think so." Beth sprung to her feet and began to suck on her bleeding finger.

Abby couldn't help grinning. "Don't worry; we'll be out of here in a bit. When sales reach a million, we'll move to a ten-storey serviced office, with a proper reception and a team of cleaners and security guards, and… and chairs that work!"

"Mmm," she mumbled, smiling through a mouthful of flesh.

"Sorry – did you want to talk to me?"

Beth removed the finger. "Just wanted to remind you, we've got two interviews tonight."

"Shit – you're right." Abby leaned forwards and clicked on her calendar. "Six-thirty and seven. D'you wanna do them or shall I? No point in us both hanging around – it's only for office assistant."

Beth hesitated. "Well, I thought…" She squirmed. "Given that they're gonna help with the book-keeping…"

Abby smiled. "That's fine. I'll do them. You wanna play netball, right?"

Beth nodded sheepishly.

"That's cool – makes sense." Abby checked her watch. "Shit – it's six-thirty already! Who are these people?"

"It's all in your calendar – I sent you their details."

"Oh yeah." Abby hastily opened up the attached CVs. "David Hunter, and… Sahan Amarasakara," she read out carefully.

"The conference room's all ready – I've just checked it. By the way, we're gonna need to meet with our web guys again next week – the site's struggling to keep up with demand. I think we'll have to upgrade our server."

Abby nodded, pressing Print on the first CV. There was so much to think about; her brain felt swamped. They sure as hell needed this assistant.

"And I just negotiated a bigger discount with Fitness First. I've got a bit of a bidding war going on between them and Cannons – it's great. Right, I'm off. See ya! Oh – I've got my BlackBerry if you need me." She turned and skipped out the room.

Abby smiled to herself. *I've got my BlackBerry if you need me.* The words sounded so familiar, yet they'd almost lost their meaning. Abby had never considered acting on those words. The thought of Stuart Mackins leaning over her, waving another night's work in her face as he swaggered off to the opera seemed almost funny to Abby now. Those days were over. Long gone. She wasn't an analyst any more.

Cray McKinley was just a distant memory – like something she'd watched in a film, years ago. Her life had changed so dramatically in the last three months it was hard to believe that the character in the film had been her. Never again would she feel that plummeting sensation as a new assignment landed on her desk. Never again would she need to slip away to the Ladies, afraid that a tear might trickle out in public. And never, *ever* again would she find herself filling out forms, spouting bullshit or licking arses in order to advance her career.

She picked up the CV from the printer. Name: David Hunter. Age: 22. Abby rubbed her eyes, and allowed them to stay closed for a moment. They ached. She was probably working longer hours now than she'd ever worked at Cray McKinley. But she didn't mind. This was different. It didn't feel like work. In the mornings, she actually looked forward to coming in – however little sleep she'd had. She opened her eyes again, and realised that the only light in the room was the bluish glow of her laptop screen.

The buzzer went, and Abby heard a light patter of footsteps on the stairs, followed by the sound of Beth's kindly-but-firm voice. She grabbed a pen and the applicant's CV, and hastened towards the door. Her phone started ringing. She darted back to her desk.

"Hello?"

"Hello, is that Abby?" said the sing-song voice of Beth in receptionist mode. "I have a Mr David Hunter downstairs to see you."

Abby laughed down the phone. "I know that, you silly cow!" she yelled. "Now go and play netball – you're gonna be late!"

"Excellent. I'll do that right now," she said brightly.

"Oh and Beth? Drop the secretary act, will you? There's no

point in pretending we're something we're not – this guy's applying for a job here!"

"Quite right," came the clipped reply. "He'll be waiting in the conference room." The line went dead.

Abby smiled. The 'conference room' was Beth's lounge. Situated at the front of the house on the ground floor, the room was sparsely but stylishly decorated, everything white, black or silver – the corporate colours of Sporticity. On top of the chrome coffee table – which Abby had acquired for free from her dad's office move – sat a matching pot of branded pens and a discreet array of company leaflets – courtesy of Gary from the Cray McKinley print room. The 42-inch plasma screen (a reject from Beth's mate Lloyd) was set against the back wall, displaying their latest promotional video, a professional-looking job from some media guys Abby had met through basketball.

You'd never know that the room had been done on the cheap. They never went short on headed notepaper. They never waited long for IT support. They never ran out of desk stationery, and they had an endless supply of small, magnetic Sporticity pyramids covered in miniature paperclips – an offer from Beth's ex-boyfriend that had been difficult to refuse.

Abby burst through the conference room door, knowing nothing about the applicant other than his name and age – which was probably more than most Cray McKinley interviewers knew about their candidates, she reflected.

"Hi there!" she gushed, all smiles, pressing the door shut behind her.

David Hunter was sitting with his back to Abby, reading one of the Sporticity leaflets. He turned to face her.

Abby stopped dead in her tracks.

"Hi Abby," said Mike Cunningham-Reid.

She got over the shock and composed herself – remarkably quickly, she thought, considering. "What the hell are you doing here?" she asked coldly.

Mike shrugged, and made an attempt at smiling; something which Abby imagined would be quite difficult from under her crushing gaze. "Well, I just came by to see where the nearest game of rugby–"

"Don't take the piss," she said nastily.

For a moment, Mike looked upset. Perhaps he'd been expecting some sort of warm welcome, she thought. Too bad. He wouldn't be getting one from her.

"How did you find our address?" she demanded. The Sporticity 'head office' wasn't listed anywhere other than Companies House; they'd been very careful about that.

"You gave it to me. Over the phone."

"No I–" Abby faltered. "Oh, right," she said, nodding slowly as she made the connection. "David Hunter."

Mike looked guiltily at the floor. "And Sahan what's-his-name," he mumbled.

"I see." Abby tried to think of something horrible to say. But her mind was preoccupied. Mike looked more gorgeous than ever, damn him. His skin was darker, and she'd missed that sharp jawline and the cute little dent in his nose.

"Why did you bother?" she snapped.

"What – invent applicants and fabricate CVs, you mean?"

Why did you bother coming to see me at all, was what she really meant, but she nodded.

Mike looked at her. "I wanted to be sure you'd make time for me." He rose to his feet, still looking at her, and took a step forwards. "I thought you'd probably be really busy, what with–"

"You're right," she cut in. "I *am* really busy, and I *don't* really have time for you."

This was it, she thought, composing her next line. She'd been through this speech a thousand times, never believing she'd actually get the chance to say it out loud. Yet here he was. On her territory. At her mercy. The conditions were perfect. Abby narrowed her eyes and prepared to let rip.

Nothing happened. She couldn't think of what to say. After all those rehearsals inside her head, all that ranting, screaming and shrieking, Abby had forgotten her lines. It was like the recurring nightmare she used to get – the one where she got pushed onto the stage in front of the whole school, only to realise she'd never been shown the script. She tried again. Nope. The words just weren't flowing. Nor was the anger she was supposed to be feeling.

"Look Mike," she started, trying to summon some fresh hatred for the guy. "I thought you – I thought we–" Abby cast her eyes around the room in frustration. This wasn't coming out right at all.

"I thought there was–" *Christ!* Abby glanced up to see the patronising, false frown she remembered so well on Mike's nauseatingly handsome face. It wasn't there. He was looking straight at her, questioningly but not patronisingly. Abby broke his gaze and wandered over to the coffee table, putting some stray pens back in their pot. She wanted to get her thoughts straight before she tried to speak again. Why couldn't she tell him how she felt? How furious she was with him for tricking her and for going behind her back? For leading her on – making her think there was something special between them. For turning out to be an arrogant, self-centred git, just like everyone else at Cray McKinley.

"So," Mike said quietly. He hadn't moved a muscle, except to follow her around the room with his eyes. "You heard about Philip Oversby?"

Abby snorted in his direction. "I do keep in touch with *some* people, Mike. My *friends*. Yeah, of course I heard."

Mike nodded solemnly and started chewing on his lower lip.

"So you know about your pal Jennifer Armstrong, then?" he asked, after another awkward pause.

Abby looked at him suspiciously. "What about her?"

Their eyes locked. She couldn't tell whether this was a trick. Justine hadn't mentioned anything about Jennifer Armstrong. Then again, she probably would have overlooked Armageddon, so overjoyed had she been with the news of Oversby's departure.

"You don't know, do you?" he said, looking more surprised than smug.

Abby glared at him, cross with Justine for neglecting to share what was obviously very important news. "What?"

"She quit. And she's taking Cray McKinley to court – filing for sexual discrimination. Eight million pounds, she's asking for. Surprised you haven't heard."

Abby stared blankly at Mike, trying to absorb this without appearing too gob-smacked. *Eight million pounds?* After all that hang-on-in-there advice that Armstrong had been dishing out? How could

Justine have forgotten to tell her this?

"Haven't you seen the headlines today?" Mike asked, glancing around for a newspaper.

Abby shook her head guiltily. She hadn't read the news in nearly two weeks. "I didn't have time," she explained. "I was – well, I've got a company to run."

He nodded. "I know. And congratulations, by the way. It's pretty impressive."

Was that genuine? Abby wanted so badly to believe that it was. But she knew that she'd fallen for this before: the earnest expression, the sincere-sounding voice. She wasn't going to make that mistake again.

"Abby, I'm really sorry," he said quietly. "About everything."

He certainly looked as though he meant it, she thought, watching Mike through slitted eyes.

"I know what you must be thinking," he went on. "And I know how you must've felt when you realised I'd applied for the job in Broking. You probably hate me – and I don't blame you. I know *I'd* hate me, if *I* were you. I didn't think about how it might look, from your point of view." Mike glanced awkwardly around the room. "But the point is, I went for that job because–" he ran his fingers through his hair – a gesture that Abby remembered. "I went for that job because I wanted us to be working in different departments," he said.

"What, so that you could swan around in Corporate Joking, while I – and everyone else – sweated blood in Corporate Finance?"

"No!" Mike looked mortified. "I meant, *us*." He looked at her pleadingly. "I meant… It was difficult, us working in the same office. I didn't…"

If this was part of a ploy to regain Abby's trust, she thought, it was liable to work. He seemed to be telling her exactly what she'd spent the last three months longing to hear.

"So anyway," he went on in a more confident, Mike-like tone. "I just wanted to explain. I know you hate me, and that's fine. I'll go now; you've obviously got loads to do. Good luck with the new business and everything." He looked at her one last time, and reached for the door.

"No, wait! I don't hate you!" Abby heard herself blurting out. She went for his outstretched arm. "The opposite, in fact," she admitted quietly.

The serious expression Mike had been wearing since he'd entered the room finally cracked into a smile. "Oh."

Abby grinned and grabbed his hand. "Come on – let's go for a drink. Hey – what's this?"

Nestled in Mike's palm was something small and scratchy.

"Ah, yes." All of a sudden, he looked embarrassed. "Well... you left in a bit of a rush when you quit your job. I thought I'd just check you hadn't left anything behind. And – well, I found this in your top drawer." He dangled the small gold chain from finger and thumb.

Abby looked at it, and laughed. Abby♥Mike, said the inscription on the cheap metal pendant. Her Christmas present from Secret Santa. She fastened it round her neck, grinning, and pulled Mike through the door.